# Girl on the gallows

ISBN-978-1720372684
ISBN-1720372683

Printed in the United States of America

Book designed by Jean Boles
jean.bolesbooks@gmail.com

# Girl on the gallows

## JOHN DEVLIN

John Devlin lives with his family in the High Desert above Southern California. This is his first, but not his last, novel.

# PROLOGUE

Police lights stream red in a hypnotic dance across a building facade. Yellow tape, festooned about like leftovers of opened gifts from a child's Christmas morning, surrounds the area.

Inside the building, knots of men scurry about as electronic voices rumble through the aisles.

Toward the back of the pharmacy is the murder scene.

Suited men, whose jacketed backs appear to be attempting to teach children their ABCs, ring others on cell phones.

Voices tangle, but remain calm.

A funereal hush that even the squawk of the walkie-talkies' can't seem to penetrate blankets the gruesome scene.

Cinematic red blood is stuck to the ticky-tacky white floor tile, forming a splattered rug.

The path of the crimson flow snakes back down the aisle of the pharmacy where it has congregated near the dead; traceries of blood meander back and forth between the two corpses, like they're playing a game of tag.

Men holding devices swoop down near the dead, interface with their machines and zoom back up like deep-sea divers making for the surface.

Both victims are old. The female is seated in a chair, her hands tied behind her back. Hematomas appear around her neck, a necklace of angry fingers. Both eyes are blotched red from the bursting of capillaries as the blood tried to escape the pressure. One half-closed orb appears to be giving the side-eye to her many examiners.

The detectives who see her wish someone would lid her eyes, but no one asks because these men don't want to seem weak and unprofessional.

The male victim is bound similarly, but his death was of a different variety. A head wound is the proximate cause, but the slashes on his arms and many suppurations speak to pre-mortem infliction.

His arms carry deep, gouged slashes. Tracks through the skin and meat look like a deranged and near-sided person's attempt at suicide.

Over these wounds, like a child's science volcano project gone amok, are burning rivulets of acid. Like slug trails through flesh, they ooze and stipple.

Someone's observant and points to what looks to be an old bruise. Blue, embedded in a swirl under the right bicep.

"Tattoo," one says. "Military, I think."

Disbelief from the cohort. "No way. Probably a bruise."

"Remembering my grandfather; he was in Nam. Looks similar."

Out of respect, the skepticism becomes muted.

Moving from the tragedy of his arms, the old man's gunshot wound to the head appears ordinary. The bullet entered just over the sub-orbital ridge and carved out a trough of skull and grey matter that ended up back splashing a display of aspirin.

There's a third chair, but this one is empty. The cast-off packaging of emergency medical supplies decorates the chair's skirt, as if someone gave a very localized ticker-tape parade.

"This one was alive; they bagged her and boogied."

"Is she gonna make it?"

"If it's your wife with the garbage man, I'd say yeah."

"You're a fucking asshole, Hollins."

"Well, so I'm a fucking asshole. At least I'm getting laid."

**Several days later...**

A dilapidated motel that rents rooms by the hour.

An angry immigrant owner who's got a new tenant who hasn't paid since yesterday.

Local community outreach and a foot patrol is flagged down.

Two officers.

A door bangs as it's struck with the butt of a flashlight; the loud knock gets no results.

Keys jingle in counterpoint.

Police voices offer a loud and sharp chorus. Door is unlocked and opened.

The owner squawks at the chaos.

The bed has been moved to the middle of the room.

In the farthest corner, the sheet, the blanket, and the pillow have been commandeered by the room's one occupant.

Like a vulture amidst a nest of bedding, the girl sits, wedged and propped up by the two walls' meeting point.

Pill bottles, like the cast-off bones of carrion, litter the floor at her feet.

An officer picks up a bottle and sees the pharmacy's name stamped on its side.

Like taking a cattle prod to an animal, the scene electrifies. Shoulders become mics, and the angry motel owner is deposited on the other side of the door.

The woman sits in near stupor. Young, but sculpted by the ravages of drug addiction.

Her face is ashen; sores of red swell her features. So skinny that without clothes one wonders if she might just disappear altogether. Seated and propped in the corner like a corpse at an old-school Irish wake, the girl mumbles an incoherent incantation and sways her arms like she's performing some spell to raise the dead—or herself. She seems unable to recognize that police are in the room.

Questions become shouted, and finally, because one officer grabs her angrily by the wrist, her spell breaks and she shrieks, "It was him. Don't you see him? It's always been him!"

Asked about who rented the room and who stayed with the woman, the motel owner can't recall.

"I get a lot of customers," he says. "Some come and some go. Some check in with friends; some make new friends on street. Maybe she have a man. I no remember. I stay in office, watch *Wheel of Fortune.* That Vanna White still a beautiful woman. Why she stay with that Sajak, I can't understand. America make no sense sometimes."

# ONE

My law office sits above a strip mall, the lower half housing a Madame Yang Nail Parlor. Madame Yang actually pulled up roots and moved to Fresno, but she sold it to another Korean lady and the lockstep of the chitinously challenged has not faltered. There's also a donut shop and an Italian pizzeria run by two Arab fellows going by the names of Jimmy and Achmed. On the upper floors, the only other working establishment is a travel agency run by Janis, a woman who has the longest nails you've ever seen, and who likes to tell everyone she does not patronize Madam Yang's.

Needless to say, the new Mrs. Yang and Janis do not get along. Janis does a fairly good business, something that I'm grateful for, as it brings foot traffic by my place.

My office is two rooms with a small adjoining bath. The outer room has a sofa made of something called leatherette, and it has those great big buttons shot through the upholstery, which at one time was supposed to look stately and now looks old and uninviting. Stella, my secretary, stands five feet tall and weighs two hundred pounds. She's a member of my church, and I put up with her missing whole days because she comes cheap and I pay her in cash. Stella may be a pious woman, but that doesn't stop her from not paying taxes. I'm reminded of Jesus saying something about giving unto Caesar what is Caesar's, but she outweighs me, so I keep my mouth shut.

My office houses a factory-produced desk that took me an entire working day to put together because I lacked a power screwdriver. After I finished, my wrist was so sore I was afraid I'd be stuck in my office, unable to turn the doorknob to get out. I've got an In and Out box decorated with scripture—a gift from Sarah, my wife—a computer, and several low shelves housing various books on the penal code. These are a must for every lawyer, though they might as well be cardboard for the amount they're used.

I'm just settling in after saying hello to Stella and finding I have no messages when the phone rings in the reception area and I'm trying to hook an ear in and listen. Before I can hear more than an uh-huh, my phone's buzzing and a man's on the line. He's got a reedy voice and what sounds like a deviated septum, and he starts telling me about how he needs legal representation for a drug arrest. The man, a Mr. Bedell, says the police found half a pound of marijuana in his house. A real case, so I cut him off, tell him to make an appointment with my secretary for later today, and ask him, "Oh, by the way, how'd you hear about me?"

I get the man explaining how he saw my picture in the *Gazette* for my work with animals, and I'm thinking the notion *any publicity is good publicity* is finally paying off.

It's later in the day and I'm pulling out the Costco-size jug of Pepto I keep in my desk for the heartburn that Achmed and Jimmy's pizza always causes. The fact that I've also been drinking more Scotch than usual is a notion that passes me by, like a strand of cobwebs getting run through by a New York Giant's linebacker.

Stella escorts in Bedell and he's not exactly what I'm expecting in a drug dealer. Somewhere near sixty, he appears bookish. His hair remains only as a fading line atop his head, and his face is dominated by a long nose and loose jowls that, with his spectacles, give him the sad look of Droopy, the cartoon dog. Well, I think, all those baby boomers gotta end up looking like something.

"Nice to meet you, Mr. Bedell. I'm Joe Heyerdahl. So the police found a half-pound of marijuana in your house. Were you growing it? Was it in plant form?"

"Oh no, it was in a big baggy, like the kind you get in the supermarket."

"Excuse me; you got the drug from where?"

"I mean like the baggies containing that pre-made salad. You know— American, European, radicchio. It looked about the same," he finishes lamely.

"Well, sir, I don't think the local supermarket is gonna be selling marijuana leaves anytime soon. What we're going to try to show is that you had no intent to distribute. Did you bring that file I asked for?"

He hands it over and I start leafing through it. "You've got no record, and you spend time volunteering twice a week at the animal shelter. We'll try to paint this as an impulsive act, try to use the large quantity you purchased as evidence of your ignorance. You just bought too much to really use and..."

"Oh, I didn't use any…"

"But your intent was to, so simply because the police stopped you..."

Now, Bedell talks like he thinks he's the only one who knows Nicky Minaj's boobs aren't real. "No, I mean, you're my attorney, so I guess I can tell you. I really had about three times that much to begin with."

"Quite the habit, ayy, Mr. Bedell?"

"Uhh no, the marijuana wasn't for me. It's for Wally, my dog."

Bedell gets comfortable in my leatherette chair and begins unspooling his story. As I listen, I sink lower and lower into my own chair. Throughout

Bedell's tale, in my head I'm hearing Al Pacino, in *Godfather III*, complaining about being forced back into the mafia with, "Then they pulled me back in."

I get to the right place, check in at the reception desk, and find an empty velvet-covered chair that's a lot nicer than my leatherette ones.

"Joe, what brings you down here? I thought you'd be cruising the animal shelters looking for clients."

Thomas Dean was one of the few people I knew in the D.A.'s office.

This is not a good thing. Dean is a highly successful A.D.A. who spends as much time putting bad guys away as he does pimping for anybody with a mic or a television camera. Several years ago, I had the good fortune to beat him in a trial over an old lady who kept a lot of dogs (the best count I could ever get was seventy-five) on her big piece of property. The neighbors complained and it looked like a no-win situation, but I gave the lady the idea that she should buy some sheep and use the dogs to herd them. There was no ordinance against sheep farming, and the dogs could be seen as a reasonable investment in the maintenance of her business. I won, and though Tom went on to put rapists and murderers away, I was stuck defending the same lady three years later, when her sheep population threatened to overrun the area. He still held a grudge, something along the lines of losing a shit-poor case to a shoestring attorney who came from a third-rate law school.

"Tom, how's the golf game? Still sculling the hell out of the ball?" Tom was one of those golfers where, if you gave him a nine iron, he'd still hit line drives no more than a few feet off the ground.

"Naw, now that I've got the titanium Big Bertha, I'm driving the ball 350 easy. I've been playing at Riverside once a week with the Big Boss. You know, Warren Metcalfe, the District Attorney?"

Tom was enough of a dope that he might believe I didn't know who the D.A. was, so I simply stared blankly back at him. I noticed this unnerved him when we lawyered against one another.

Tom got that old bothered look, like he couldn't decide how stupid I really was. "Who you here to see?"

"Ms. Stanhope."

More to get away from me, I suspect, than to help me, Tom says, "Ah, she's new. I'll pop in and see if I can grab her."

I look at the other waiting defense attorneys, with their three-year-old suits and eyes that betray their precarious perch as attorneys of last resource and of the resourceless, and I know that, like a fun house, there's a mirror of myself everywhere I look. Unfortunately, the distortion isn't much, and it's not much fun either.

Several A.D.As come out from behind the doors. One is a woman, and I'm just getting up to shake Ms. Stanhope's hand when a well-heeled man with Anderson Cooper hair comes striding by me with a greeting for those A.D.A.s. Quickly, he's ushered into the back. Caught rising, I continue upward to get the just-decided-upon paper cup of water. I take two steps and lose my seat to a blockheaded fellow with a similarly sized briefcase. Luckily, Tom appears.

"She'll be out in a sec, Joe. Got a rape case to try. Guy's got an additional four assaults and two B and E's."

"Just don't kill any gophers with that driver there, Tom."

"If I did, you'd be the one to defend me. Oh, and here's one you'll like. What does PETA stand for?"

Something told me Tommy wasn't going for the correct answer, People for the Ethical Treatment of Animals. "Why, I don't know, Tom."

"People who are *extreme and total assholes.*" Tom laughs as he sails out the door.

Then why aren't you a member, I'm thinking, as my A.D.A strides forward.

"Mr. Heyerdahl? I'm Claire Stanhope, assistant district attorney on the case. Let's go back to my office and see if we can stop this from going to court."

I nod and follow behind. And I do mean *behind.* Stanhope's a rather Plain Jane who heightens this look by wearing glasses instead of contacts and makes boring choices in blouses and office suits. She has black hair, cut medium length that flourishes at the bottom. Her face is V-shaped, and the darkness of her eyes gives her a cowled appearance. However, as I follow her to her office, I find it difficult to pull my eyes away from her large and protruding ass. I mean it sticks out. Even through her rather demure skirt there's a bulge. Well, two bulges that look like she's auditioning to be a Kardashian butt double.

We get to her office and I'm shaking my head at how unprofessional I'm being.

"I hope that head shaking isn't a product of the deal I'm about to offer, Mr. Heyerdahl."

I stammer, "No," and try to clear my head, while reminding myself that I'm here to get Bedell free of any jail time.

Stanhope zings me from the outset. "You're the animal guy, like the Ace Ventura of litigators."

She's new and she's trying to show me how *tied in* she already is, and how she feels free to needle me.

"Who's Ace Ventura?" I offer, mystified.

"You know, the detective played by Jim Carrey...the actor."

"Oh, the actor." My eyes alight with recognition.

"The movie where he has to find the dolphin..."

"Oh, I haven't seen any of his movies."

She thinks I'm lying, and she's right, but what's she going to do? Start explaining the plot of a goofy comedy about a revenge-minded transsexual field goal kicker who kidnaps dolphins, when we should be discussing the case?

She abruptly shifts gears. "One year in and two years suspended."

"No coffee, no friendly lawyer banter, Ms. Stanhope? You know what I'm gonna argue to the jury? There's no way they're gonna want him to do time."

"I don't know. I don't buy this 'everybody loves a dog' thing."

"Well, who doesn't?"

"I don't, for one. Okay, halfway house, drug program, three years' probation."

"No way. My client is not going to jail for being a compassionate human being."

"He wouldn't be the first. C'mon, he had half a pound; we got intent to distribute, the police found a scale..."

"Which wasn't a drug dealer's triple beam, but some old food scale the police found in the back of a cabinet."

"That's something for a jury to decide."

"Yeah, you're right, it is. See ya in court, Stanhope."


Driving back to the office, I was hoping I hadn't just gotten my client into worse trouble. A Class-A felony would have him out in a little over two years, and most likely he would've gotten that reduced with good behavior.

Something told me he wasn't going to be a troublesome prisoner.

What did I have on my side? For one thing, emotion: people love animals, sometimes more than humans do. When the first *Godfather* came out, Coppola got in more trouble over the beheading of that horse (in the scene with the movie mogul) than for those forty killings where actual people got eighty-sixed. The fact that it was a real horse that they'd got from a rendering plant (that uses all the extra animal parts, like hooves, and bones, and heads to make glue and such) didn't seem to matter.

In front of me, the driver of the Ford Aspire continues traveling at 25 in a 35 zone. It's bad enough when people actually travel the speed limit, but this borders on sacrilege. I can't pass him on the left because he's going so slowly that the cars in the other lane are flying past us, like we're the pace car at the Indy 500 and they just dropped the white flag. A few swerves, a few dives back into my lane as cars honk their horns at my brashness, and I'm wishing the guy in the Aspire would aspire to get the hell out of my way.

The Aspire slows further, but it's to make a right, and I'm back up to speed, wondering for the fifth time if I should've taken the deal. But Tom did say Stanhope's new, and I do know juries' reactions when I'm dealing with the animal kingdom. Maybe I could get my own TV show out of this— the *Trial Lawyers of America's Wild Kingdom.* I could take cases where dangerous animals are involved, then sit back at the studio drinking margaritas while my trusty sidekick, Jim, wrestles the litigious anaconda.

Can't believe she had the nerve to call me the Ace Ventura of animal litigation. I am a lot better looking than Jim Carrey, though he is a helluva lot funnier. It's when I'm lost in my Jim Carrey daydream that an idea hits me that just might tip the scales in my favor. If only I can get Stanhope to open a certain door, I might save Bedell a prison term.

I'm turning into my office parking lot. Getting out of the car, I notice the auto's sheen of dirt and I hear Sarah reminding me that my car is a projection of my persona. Before my marriage, I thought a dirty car was the reason God invented rain. Anyway, how much personal respectability could a guy get out of a Saturn?

I walk by Madame Yang's and the door opens to a quick burst of singsong Korean. I'm taking the steps two by two, a quick hello and raise of the hand, and I'm hunkering down in front of a turkey sandwich. Surprisingly hungry, I hope in some twisted universe way this bodes well for my wife getting pregnant.

Stella bustles in, sliding her hand along the door in some faint imitation of a knock. She shoves a milk shake in my face that looks like either vanilla or milk of magnesia.

"Here, drink this."

Now I've got a concoction in my hand that's got the consistency of Ponds Cold Cream. "What is it?"

"It's got herbal extracts to increase sperm motility."

"Stella, my sperm is not the problem. It's Sarah's..."

"Tut, tut, tut. My sister, Carnie, swears by this, and she's got four little ones, though the youngest looks like she's gonna be a tramp. God bless'm all."

"Does your sister Carnie ever swear while she's drinking this paste?" I've begun poking at the meniscus that has formed on the shake's top. Several finger prods and the cream at the top is not breaking.

"I mentioned it to Sarah and she said for you to give it a whirl."

Trying to delay the inevitable, "Speaking of whirl, where'd you get the blender to make it?"

"The pizzeria."

"Did you tell Achmed what it was for?"

"Actually it was Jimmy; Achmed's home with a bad cold."

"Did you happen to mention what it was for?"

"Of course, my Momma and Jesus didn't raise no fibbers."

"But they did raise someone who whips up sperm energizer."

"I ain't no fundamentalist, Joseph. The Good Lord gave man a mind that could send him to the moon. No reason that that mind can't help couples receive God's bounty through having children. Oh, Jimmy says that if that don't work he'll fix you up one of his Arabian pizzas with the special ingredients that'll get you nothing but boys."

I'm still trying to break the hardened shell that formed at the shake's top. I finally do, and I'm less than heartened at the milky, yellow glop resting below. But what are you going to do? I can't question Sarah's devotion, so I close my eyes and take a gulp. I never ate paste as a child, but I imagine this would be the taste. I have to run into the bathroom for some water; the shake has made my throat as dry as one of Jimmy and Achmed's deserts. I poke my head back in my office and Stella's still sitting there, and I realize I'm not going to get out of drinking the whole thing.

# TWO

Checked the Internet and I'm off driving through East Hampstead. This is the part of lawyering I love. I get paid to do research. The law is such a big, complex place, no one thinks you have the answers, and everyone knows you're going to have to look things up and do some detective work.

The place I'm looking for is down the next block on the right. I graduated law school before I realized that even-numbered businesses, houses, go on one side of the street, odd on the other. I'd like to say I never needed to know this piece of info, but as a kid, I was a paperboy delivering some advertiser rag. Then again, I remember taking a lot of those papers up to the dirt-gray train tracks behind my house and dropping them in a gully. No one subscribed; you were just supposed to give them to every house and ask people to gift you a monthly subscription fee. No surprise, I only made it as a news deliverer for about three months.

I get lucky and there's a parking spot not two doors down from the office. I walk by the few rundown businesses selling carpet remnants or doing shoe repairs, and I get the greatest idea for a business, or maybe just the best place to put one. I'll get a Krispy Kreme, or a White Castle burger franchise and set it down right smack next to my destination—the Kannabis Club, one of the few outlets for the legal distribution of medicinal marijuana in Virginia.

The headquarters of the Kannabis Club is what you might imagine. It looks like a warehouse that's been converted into some kind of ragtag Starbuck's, with posters of the latest Brazilian espresso deluxe replaced by information on AIDS, cancer, glaucoma and marijuana. The carpets are all ratty, and I remember the place a few doors down and I think, *it figures*. There's a long counter that looks like it's a hundred years old stretching across the room. Over in one corner, there's a waiting area with a few chairs, a bench, and even two beanbags. Right next to the bench is a coffee machine and an empty plate of what used to be muffins.

My "Munchie" food store idea's looking better and better.

I walk up to the counter and talk to a black guy with butt-hanging dreadlocks. He directs me to the waiting area and says it'll only be a minute. I walk into the waiting room expecting to see people toking up, getting high. Instead, it's just two old ladies who obviously know one another, and one white guy, spider-like in his thinness, who's sitting in such a posed way that I think for a second that someone I can't see is painting him.

So no contact high for me.

The two women have the bench, and the beanbag chairs are pretty undignified for a lawyer. (When I was a kid we had one of those, and the cat kept pissing and crapping in it. That wasn't as bad as the fact that I kept forgetting, sitting down, and coming back up with cat poo on my pants.)

I sit down next to the guy who's probably not long for this earth. I think of Tom Hanks in the movie, *Philadelphia*, and that scene where he leaves Denzel Washington's office, and he's got nothing, no hope, and he walks outside, and there are people of all sorts going by, living their lives, oblivious to the depth of his pain, and he's just this island, and his face fills with such anguish, and the real kicker is, we're all that guy, or we will be. Sure, some of us will get hit by a bus, have a massive coronary while spooning our wife of 52 years, but for most of us, we're going to be front and center for our final act. We'll be leaving some doctor's office and maybe we won't have AIDS, instead it'll be metastasized colon or liver cancer, or a heart that's ready to give up the ghost, and us too old for a transplant.

I break off from such morbid thoughts. Well, almost. I think about Tom Hanks' shaved head, and the guy next to me's similar appearance, and the guy at the counter and his dreadlocks, and how cool dreads look on black men (like Bob Marley and Lennie Kravits—yeah, I know Kravitz cut'm off) and how good black guys look bald (Michael Jordan and almost anybody in sports). The only white guy who looks good without hair is Patrick Stewart, captain of one of the Star Treks. Not that this black advantage somehow makes up for several hundred years of oppression, but if I was some black guy, I'd sure feel good seeing all these bald, stupid-looking white guys, and notice all the brothers looking cool and dapper, even though they were similarly follically challenged.

The guy next to me looks like his skin has been Saran wrapped to his body—that's how close it lies on his bones. I'm thinking about how Ms. Stanhope seems arrogant and over confident, and how I might be able to use that to my advantage, when I notice the guy next to me is humming. I only listen closer because I think I recognize the tune, and I'm usually the one in the car everyone tells to stop singing because I'm so tone deaf.

I start to mumble the words to the song I think the man's humming:

> *I smoke two joints in the morning, I smoke two joints at night,*
> *I smoke two joints in the afternoon, it makes me feel all right.*

Now the hummer's smiling and joins in.

*I smoke two joints in time of peace, and two in time of war*

*I smoke two joints, and then I smoke two joints—and then I smoke*

*two more.*

*Smooooooke two joints.*

One of the old ladies looks a little horrified, but the sick one adds, "Ain't it the truth, ain't it the truth."

"I know that's not Marley," I offer questioningly.

"Peter Tosh," my singing counterpart replies.

I remember he's right and offer him my hand. "I'm Joe."

"Well, it's good your an honest Joe, cuz' you can't sing worth a damn." He grins, and even in his merriment he looks a little like a death's head. "I'm Daniel."

"I got to tell you, I'm pretty pleased I even knew the song. I have a tin ear that's rusted shut."

"Well, it must've been the skill of the hummer."

"Most definitely," I nod.

"You're not a patient."

There's no question on the end of his statement. "No, I'm a lawyer."

"So you're sick, but it's more of a mental health issue."

For looking so corpse-like, this guy's still full of the good banter. Or maybe I'm having a bad couple of days. "Just doing a little research for a client."

"Yeah, I figured something like that. You lack the *look*."

"The *look*? What's the look?"

"The sheen on the eyes that says 'I'm fine' just a bit too frantically. The look that up close says, 'I feel hollow and afraid, and boy do I wish I could be someone else.'"

He says this in a relaxed fashion, like he's a scientist of this particular phenomenon and not one of its sufferers. "Do you have the look?"

"Most definitely." He smiles and I realize he's stealing my line.

"The protease inhibitor not working?" I'm feeling a bit adventurous. After all, it's not every day I sing reggae about smoking bud with a man dying of AIDS.

He holds out his scarecrow arms. "Asked and answered, counselor. It did for a while, but I have a resistant strain that's taking over now."

"So you've been before where you are now?"

"I wasn't always the picture of health you see today," he responds deadpan. "The last time, I was coming around the final turn. Now it's the last straightaway. So, your case have to do with AIDS?"

"Uh, no." I'm a little embarrassed now for the seeming silliness of what's to come. "My client was caught with over a pound of marijuana..."

"And he says he needed it to manage his pain."

"Actually, his dog's nausea."

Daniel laughs and the sound comes out loud and clear, running over the warehouse, banking off the postered walls, striking the few office-goers, before pulling back, going throaty and harsh like the laugh was caught off-guard and forgot whose throat it was coming from. Daniel's hacking now, having trouble getting his breath. I run over to the coffee machine to grab him a cup of water. I'm probably the same guy in pioneer days the women would've sent out to boil clean sheets when the baby was coming. I grab a couple of napkins. In the few seconds I'm gone, the healthy old lady is over offering her assistance. I give Daniel the water, which he takes with a bowed head.

It seems to work.

He's about to thank me, when he holds up his index finger like a conductor pausing the orchestra. I see his eyes go red and can almost visualize the cough that goes rolling up his thin, starved body. Somehow from this chest-filled tidal wave, the barest hiccup of a cough issues forth. There's a pause and his chest relaxes.

"Sorry, didn't mean to start that," I offer meekly.

"It's okay. I get a certain amount every day no matter if I sit in a bed or venture out. At least I got a laugh out of that one." The clerk's calling him over for his prescription and he's shaking my hand again, asking for my card. "Every time I survive this thing and come back around the last bend I need to amend my will. You do that sort of thing, Joe?"

I nod and hand him my card. "Only if it's pretty minor, Daniel."

"Minor's all I need, Joe."

He gathers up his magazine and walks over to collect his prescription.

Next thing, a Mr. Scrowden, who runs the place, is calling me in. Scrowden's got a head that's too big for his body and a long ponytail that trumpets the hair he's got down his back while highlighting all that's missing from the top of his dome. Scrowden is adamant he wouldn't have sent Bedell home with any marijuana unless he had the proper forms. He says that since that Supreme Court case, the law has really been on its toes, watching them for any violation. Of course, Bedell never went here, but at least I can use this to rebut the A.D.A. if she tries to counter my Good Samaritan argument.

I'm parking in the strip mall's back lot and hurrying to grab some food from the pizzeria. Achmed's there, and I tell him it's good to see him up and around. He nods and informs me Jimmy now has the sickness and is cursing him as the son of a whore.

"Achmed, don't you guys have the same mother?"

Achmed just shrugs. "Jimmy can be a real sissy when he gets a cold."

I'm ordering a garlic roll and Achmed gives me a smile and a wink, and I think he's going a little fruity, but then he offers to make that special Arab concoction known only to the ancient kings, guaranteed to bring male children. I tell him I'll just buy the garlic rolls and leave the magic potions to Aladdin.

I'm talking to Ms. Stanhope in a side chamber next to the courtroom. This is the last minute legal posturing that everyone likes to do. I think we've all watched too many *L.A. Laws* and *The Practice* episodes, and though almost no deals are ever made, too much has been said and both sides have a head of steam for the case. We walk through the ritual, preening like peacocks. Stanhope's opening play is a revisitation of her last. "Halfway house, drug program, three years' probation."

She gives me this like she's doing me a great favor, as if she had to pull this bequest from her bosses upstairs. Why does she bother? It's like the car salesman saying he can't give you the deal he'd like to because his boss would have him for lunch, but he'll go back and take a stab at the old man because of your relationship. Does Stanhope think I'm that green? Now, I'm on the soapbox a bit, even though a little voice inside me is saying, "Take it; don't let your ego get in the way with a glass that's three quarters full." I don't listen. "No way, straight probation."

"See ya in court, Ace," Stanhope says, as she exits stage left.

# THREE

The courtroom is one of those new-style schizoid versions that keep cropping up on Court TV. You expect something magisterial, and you do get the state's insignia set in some deep expensive wood, and a judge's bench that looks as if Solomon or Thomas Jefferson might have stood there and delivered edicts out across the land, but the rest of the room is 1970s school building, with plainly functioning tables for the attorney and the defendant, and a jury's sitting room that is one step above plastic folding chairs.

Judge Westin enters. He's a stout, white-haired man with a cane that I think he uses more for show than any weakness in his legs. He's known for being a rather fair judge who despises wasted time (might be a problem there), but who also has become a little eccentric—or at least willing to let lawyers be that way if he finds the whole deal interesting.

I've often wondered what makes judges get more and more quirky as time goes on, and I guess I've got it down to the God Principle. If you act like God long enough, you're either going to be a first class asshole—who's going to tell that to God's face—or you're going to develop one serious love of comedy. It's like in physics. Here's Newton, and he comes up with all these laws that basically explain everything except light. When you get to light, all the rules we know change. It's as if God got to light and said,

"Whoops, this doesn't fit," so in a joking sort of way He says, "Hey, why don't I make up special rules just for light."

Ms. Stanhope's talking to me. "Still time to deal. We'll go felony, three year probation, no time served."

"Misdemeanor possession, $500 fine." The voice in my head is like the crowd of crazies who scream on the *Price is Right* for the contestant to bid just one dollar over the last contestant on that new Frigidaire.

"Now who's high?" Stanhope says with a shake of her head.

The Judge enters and is formally introduced.

"Eva Stanhope for the District Attorney's office."

"Joe Heyerdahl for the defense."

The morning concerns itself with opening statements and the A.D.A. setting up her probable cause. I know she's got it, so instead of looking weak, I object only twice. This is more an attempt to remind the jury there's another side to this story than it is having anything concrete to argue against in Ms. Stanhope's narrative.

It's later in the day and I'm cross-examining an older, black beat cop. He's a practiced hand at all this and manages to come off as earnest, honest, and interested in the truth.

"We got a tip from some of Mr. Bedell's neighbors about a lot of smoke and a distinctive odor coming from the defendant's apartment. We investigated and found over a half a pound of marijuana, with numerous smoked-down marijuana cigarettes."

"Thank you, Officer Marbury. When you searched Mr. Bedell's residence, where did you find the bulk of the marijuana residue?"

"Well, like I said there was the ashtray..."

"Didn't you find the bulk of the residue in this?" I lift from under the table a large cat litter box, the kind with a snap-on plastic hood.

The officer takes several moments to examine it, like this is some defense attorney trick and I'm planning to show he misidentified the cat box. "Yes, that's correct."

"There was no cat litter in here, was there?"

"No, thankfully it was empty, 'cept for a lot of marijuana ashes."

I carry the box closer to the officer. I see the jury lean in like some butts might still be there. I always remind myself that jurors are paid essentially nothing and what they want is drama, some story to take back home when the day is through. Well, it's not a murder weapon I'm bringing forward, but it'll have to do. "Were the ashes directly below the hole that was drilled in the side of the box?"

Again the officer pauses, earnestly examining both the box and the hole. "Yes, I believe they were."

"Would a marijuana cigarette, like the kind you found in the ashtray, fit comfortably through this hole?"

"Yes, yes, it would, Counselor."

"Thank you, Officer Marbury. No further questions."


The prosecution's resting their case, and like every time at this point in the trial, I have the impulse to rest our case as well, demonstrating to the jury the confidence I have that the prosecution has not met its burden. But of course they have, so I don't. What I do is call our first witness—the veterinarian. A nice looking man with glasses and thinning blonde hair takes the stand. "Doctor Hand, do you remember saying to Mr. Bedell that he should give marijuana to Wally, his dog, to stop him from dying?"

"I see Dave a couple a times a week on account of the volunteer work he does for the shelter. Of course, we'd talk about Wally. The poor li'l guy was wasting away. Wally had been in a clutch of puppies someone had brought in. Usually they die when they're that small; his four brothers and sisters did, but not Wally. He hung in there—because of Dave."

Ms. Stanhope knows a tearjerker and tries to cut it off at the pass. "I object! Your Honor, the witness is giving a speech that is completely outside this case."

"His testimony goes to my client's state of mind, Your Honor."

"I'll allow it, Mr. Heyerdahl, but let's move it along."

"What did Mr. Bedell do, Doctor Hand, that saved the puppy's life?"

"Well, most puppies that young die because they haven't been weaned from their mother, so they can't take milk any other way. But, Dave, Dave hand-fed Wally milk from a bottle every day, several times a day, for a couple weeks. Naturally, when Wally got healthy, Dave adopted the li'l mutt. Then later, more bad luck—Wally's diagnosed with cancer."

"Doctor, in your medical opinion, did Mr. Bedell's administering of the drug save his dog's life?"

"I object, Your Honor. Dr. Hand is a veterinarian, not an oncologist."

The stick that Ms. Stanhope has up her ass is starting to show. Now, if I can make things a little worse, maybe she won't be able to pull it out. After all, I'm sure this is not the kind of case she imagined herself taking part in when she studied law. "Exactly. He's a veterinarian, so he's qualified to discuss a dog's illness."

"Your Honor, there are no studies on the medicinal effects of marijuana on dogs—supposedly, sick dogs."

Just a little further, Ms. Stanhope, I think. "He can at least testify to what he's directly observed Wally's condition to be."

"I further object to defense counsel constantly referring to the dog as Wally."

Okay, even I don't expect that bit of dog hating, and I respond in a way that others have said I do best: I state the obvious. "That's his name."

"The first objection is overruled, Ms. Stanhope. The doctor is certainly capable of appraising the health of a sick animal. As for the second objection, I'll pretend you were kidding. Let's move on."

We're in a court conference room and Mr. Bedell is fidgeting and brushing imaginary lint off his neatly creased slacks. I'm sure his palms are slick with sweat, and right now I'm glad that's the case. I'm going to need Bedell's help, and I know he couldn't lie convincingly to save himself, much less his dog, so I'm going to have to get what I need with a trick.

"Now, Dave, let's go over this one more time. Are you sure you never tried to legitimately purchase the drug from the..."

"I told you, I didn't."

"I'm just saying it wouldn't hurt our case for the jury to know you had tried to go the legit route."

"Mr. Heyerdahl, I told you in your office that it never occurred to me. We had Mr. Scrowden from the cannabis place testify it wouldn't have done me any good anyway."

"The problem, Dave, is that you couldn't have known that."

"I'm not lying if that's what you're asking."

I'm not, I think, smiling behind shocked eyes, but that's what I want you to think.

"I don't know why you'd want me to. You can see I'd be bad at it. I'm sweating just thinking about testifying, and I'm planning to tell the truth."

He's even more agitated, so it's a good time to let the other shoe fall. "Dave, I'm just trying to give the A.D.A. something to chew on. I want her distracted on cross. If we can bring up some secondary issues, maybe we can keep her from quarantining Wally."

He's incredulous now; he goes wide-eyed, like a kid who's just been told Santa's a fake.

"Why...how...why would she do that?"

"Dave, the basis of our case is that Wally's a sick li'l pup." He's about to assure me the dog really is, but I cut him off. "If you're the D.A., wouldn't it strike you as an effective ploy to cast doubt on your motivation? Prove the dog's not that sick and there goes your Good Samaritan image."

He's fumbling with the keys in his pocket now, eyes dancing over the bare piss-yellow walls of the conference room. That was my bad cop, now for the good cop. "Don't worry, Dave, I'll keep the case pointed in the right direction. You just tell the truth. You've got nothing to hide."

"Yeah, but Wally, if he..."

"Just stick to the truth. I'll take care of the rest." I check my watch and tell him it's time to go in.

Bedell nearly rushes into the courtroom. I really didn't like doing that, but Stanhope's no dope. A nervous Dave Bedell might just get her lawyering antenna up, and surprisingly, that's just what I want.

We're back in the courtroom and Mr. Bedell's on the stand. I've got him in a light blue suit and wire rim glasses that make him even more inoffensive than the regular contacts he wears. I think the whole package has definitely accentuated his cartoon Droopy the Dog look.

I'm up to question him. "Mr. Bedell, you live on 211 Chestnut Street?"

"Yes."

"You live alone?"

"Uhh, yes. My wife passed away about seven years ago. It's just been me, well, and now, Wally, since then...I'm not too outgoing."

"Mr. Bedell, why did you buy the marijuana?"

"I was desperate, I guess. Wally was losing too much weight, and then I remembered what Jack, I mean, Dr. Hand, said about medical marijuana."

"You've never had anything to do with drugs before, have you Mr. Bedell?"

"No, never. Even in college, I guess I was kind of a square. That's what Tricia, my wife, used to say at least."

I notice a few of the jurors nodding, and I think of course you didn't do drugs, Droopy the cartoon dog would never have sparked up a fattie. Bugs, maybe, he was always a rebel. As for Wile E. Coyote, I mean, how do you deal with the frustration of that skinny-ass bird that can't even fly getting away day after day? "So, how did you use the sample you acquired?"

"I bought that litter box and made a small hole in the top. I then put Wally inside and blew into the box."

"Was that the first way you tried to give Wally the drug?"

"Well no, I first looked into getting some cannibal—marijuana in a pill—but you need a doctor's prescription, and the medical reports seem to indicate that an aerosol delivery is more effective."

"Aerosol, meaning smoked."

"Yes, I first tried just lighting some of it in an ashtray and letting it burn while it and Wally were locked in the bathroom. But the marijuana wouldn't stay lit, and my bathroom is pretty big. I even tried blowing it in his face."

"You really researched this," I say humorously.

"I didn't want Wally to die." His seriousness is a nice contrast to my levity. And then he sums it all up with, "I don't, I mean, well, he's...he's my one real friend."

"Nothing further at this time, Your Honor."

I slide back to my table, trying to make eye contact with Stanhope in the hope I can get in her head and irritate her a little more. The small smirk I give her in passing seems to do the trick.

"So, Mr. Bedell, is it your testimony to the court that you've smoked marijuana but never inhaled?"

"Objection!"

"Sustained, no theatrics, Ms. Stanhope."

"I apologize, Your Honor. Mr. Bedell, I'm curious. How, if you supposedly knew so little about marijuana, were you able to obtain such a large amount?"

"I might be square, Ms. Stanhope, but I do notice what's going on around me. The animal shelter's parking lot is about a block away from the building. A block that's not in the nicest part of town."

"As you testified earlier, you don't get out much, do you, Mr. Bedell?"

"No, not much."

"So, no one sees much of you or your dog. Isn't that right, Mr. Bedell?"

"Uhh, I guess not." Suddenly, Bedell can't meet Stanhope's eyes. He looks my way for some kind of support, but I'm busy grabbing a pen from my briefcase.

"So, no one is aware of, or can vouch for, your dog's present condition?"

Bedell stops and takes a gulp of water. Even from my seat, I swear his hand shakes. I can't see Stanhope, but I bet her eyes hone in on this because she's taking a few strong steps toward Mr. Bedell. "Really, you could just be concocting your dog's side effects so you can sit at home and toke away."

The door's opening, "I object, Your Honor, and I move the court to allow us to bring Wally in so that the jury can see what his condition really is."

The Judge starts doing that kingly come-hither thing with his hands. "Approach, Counselors."

Up to the bench, Ms. Stanhope is having trouble containing her displeasure at all this. "This is ridiculous; the court is not a kennel. We can see a picture of..."

"Your Honor, Ms. Stanhope questioned my client on Wally's present condition. I simply want to bring in evidence to refute her allegation."

The Judge appears undecided. "One comment coming as it does in the body of another question does not constitute a significant act. Ms. Stanhope will be admonished for..."

I can see where he's going. "Oh, but Your Honor, she did earlier as well, when she said 'supposed' sick animal. This impugning of my client has been a pattern."

The Judge motions the transcriber front and center. After a few back and forths about where the earlier comment was, we find it. The Judge looks thoughtful. "He's right, Ms. Stanhope, you opened the door. Let's bring in Wally."

Stanhope shoots the Judge a look and he emends his previous statement. "The dog, I mean."

From the witness chair, Mr. Bedell has been listening to this legal chatter and almost shouts, "No! I mean, Your Honor, Jack...Dr. Hand, said that Wally needs to rest and not move much. The stress of the drive down here, and all the people and..."

The Judge trying to calm Bedell. "Point taken, Mr. Bedell. Is that vet still here? Ten minute recess 'til I can get the doctor on the phone."

We're in the Judge's chambers and he's just off the phone with the vet. "Mr. Heyerdahl, Dr. Hand says the dog shouldn't be moved."

"Let's bring the jury to Wally," I counter.

Now the Judge is the one surprised. "Excuse me, Mr. Heyerdahl."

Like all attorneys, Stanhope knows when it's her turn to object for the good of the system and the honor of the court. "With all due respect, Your Honor, that is absurd. It's an egregious waste of the court and jurors' time. Also, I move that the defendant's earlier utterances to your order be stricken."

"An utterance is admissible..." I barely get out when the Judge cuts me off.

"You want what Mr. Bedell said about protecting his dog redacted? Let me think about that." The Judge pauses for a second. "Uhh, no, Ms. Stanhope."

Stanhope's silly objection has given me a few moments to get my argument together. "Your Honor, on point, already ruled that the jurors needed to see Wally. A short bus trip shouldn't get in the way of the court's mandate or the people's mandate for a fair and just trial."

The Judge is shaking his head patronizingly. "First, I've got Ms. Stanhope reminding me of the court's mission, and now you, Mr. Heyerdahl." Abruptly, he shifts gears—this judge is quirkier than I thought. "But, he's right, Ms. Stanhope. I ruled that the jury needed to see the dog. Do you have any more questions for Mr. Bedell?"

Stanhope manages to squeeze through clenched teeth, "Ahh, no, Your Honor, not at this time."

Back in the courtroom, the Judge is laying down the law. "Mr. Bedell, you can step down. This court is in recess." Then to the jurors, "Wear some comfortable clothes tomorrow because we're going to Mr. Bedell's house to check on"—the Judge glances toward the frustrated A.D.A.—"the dog in question."

# FOUR

A real dog show: A small German shepherd mutt, connected to an I.V., looking thin but not emaciated, thumps his tail, perks his droopy ears, and stares soulfully at the Judge, myself, the A.D.A. and, most importantly, the twelve jurors, who almost audibly sigh at the sight of this lovable pooch. The dog struggles to his feet in an attempt to greet his guests. Bedell sits next to Wally, trying to keep him from getting too excited. Several jurors and the Judge hurry over to forestall the little dog's valiant efforts to stand. The jurors are over to the dog, petting the now happy canine. Only the Judge stops after a look from Stanhope seems to say, "Oh, how impartial." The Judge looks chastened, but then, from a distance, is quickly back to making happy faces at Wally.

I can tell Stanhope's getting this little-crappy-case-man-buys-dope-for-dog-is-slipping-away-from-her look. The Judge moves over to say something to me. "Uhh, this wouldn't be ex-parte communication, would it, Your Honor?"

He ignores my wit and points at the dog. "Counselor, enjoy this."

I look a little confused.

The Judge elaborates. "No matter what cases you try after this, you'll never get a better witness than Wally."

It's the next day. I've wrapped up my case and I'm sitting patiently, trying not to fidget as Ms. Stanhope goes through her closing. As a defense attorney, I'm trying to scan the jury, see who's nodding at her arguments, who's nodding off, and who's sitting stone-faced. The stone-faced ones are the ones I want, and that's where being good at sports comes in. I don't actually stare at the jurors; I've got to get them in my peripheral vision—just like LeBron seeing Kevin Love out of the corner of his eye, though I wonder how difficult it is to see a man that size. Those jurors on the fence are my prime targets. All I need to do is keep one of them on my side to deny Ms. Stanhope a conviction.

She starts addressing the court, and I'm hoping her slip is showing. I've seen jurors distracted by less. "First, let me apologize for my crankiness during this trial. Truthfully, I'm one of those people who doesn't like animals. Well, cats I never cared one way about, but dogs? Dogs shed, they slobber and they fart...Well, I've just never quite smelled anything as awful. When I was five, I saw what I thought was a cute puppy. I went over to pet it. I was lucky because the pit bull's owner was nearby and the dog only dragged me around the yard for a few moments, but it seemed like hours. I know Mr. Bedell's dog is no pit bull, but what about those pit bulls? Or Dobermans, or Rottweilers? Or, hey, what if Mr. Bedell had a cat? People are gonna want to have their kitties doped up, too. I know, what about mice? Or tree frogs? Somebody out there must love tree frogs. What animal is not worth saving? Or what if Mr. Bedell had decided to end Wally's pain by stealing morphine or heroin? What you do, as a jury here today, will legitimize future cases, allow drug dealers to use their pets as a defense for possessing large amounts of drugs. Under the law, even if you have no problem with Mr. Bedell's decision, he needs to be held accountable for that decision. Accountability—that's the key. These days, it seems like no one wants to be accountable for what they believe or do. They just want it to be okay. Mr. Bedell knew the penalty for his actions, and knowing the penalty, he risked it anyway. Now the penalty's upon him, and Mr. Bedell is suddenly quite hesitant about accepting the consequences of his actions. You hold him accountable. Thank you."

My turn, and like always I'm a little nervous, but less here because I think I've got the jury on my side. All I have to do is give a few of the jurors enough to hold onto when they go back in the jury room and start bearing the brunt of the majority's inquisition. "The Assistant District Attorney tells you that if you decide against her, that people will be going out and buying crack for their goldfish."

I get at least a smile from every member of the jury. I loosen up.

"She thinks I'm going to tell you to use your heart to make your decision, but I'm not. I want you to use your head. Simply, honestly, ask yourself what you would have done in Mr. Bedell's shoes. Or ask yourself what you would have done had you my client's courage. Mr. Bedell simply wanted to save his friend's life. Yes, his friend in this case is a dog. But how many of you, or people you know and love, feel the same way about their Wallys? Are all these folks under some mass delusion about the importance of these 'friends'? I don't think so. God set us apart from the rest of the animal kingdom so we could exercise our brain. We have a noble obligation to exercise that brain in the best way we can. Ladies and gentlemen, when you go back into that jury room, you think with that brain, and you find my client *not guilty*. Thank you."

In the conference room, I'm trying to calm a worried Mr. Bedell.

"It has been four hours. Do you think that's a good sign?" he asks.

"The longer they stay out, the better our chances. A dry recitation of the facts doesn't give us much of a leg to stand on, but time most likely means the jury's split on the felony or the misdemeanor." Mr. Bedell looks reassured, but I'm just hoping I'm not giving him a false sense of security.

One of the clerks comes to the door and gestures for me. I'm over in a second, and he's talking in my ear. As I listen to him telling me the jury's going to need the next day, I'm staring at Mr. Bedell. The man's quivering, hunched, his hands knitted together. For about the tenth time in the last hour, I'm wondering if I should have taken Stanhope's last offer and whether I should try to get it back.

Driving home, I call Sarah and tell her I'm on my way. She reminds me we have to make love at least two more times before her window closes this month. Something in her tone makes me think of an Air Force general urgently telephoning the President, telling him the deadline to launch the nuclear weapons is closing fast.

She also tells me that having sex three times in 24 hours in the time it takes her to boil an egg is sure to create some bad habits in me. I tell her we could try it a little differently, say, in the kitchen or on the living room carpet. Sarah nixes the idea, reminding me that I'm not the one who's going to have to lie face down for twenty minutes after the deed (face down because Sarah's gyno told her she has a tilted cervix). This is the closest Sarah comes to talking about sex in a free and easy way, so I go with it and promise to light some candles, oil up my body, and do a striptease. This gets a huff of embarrassment from her.

I've gone too far, it seems.

Attempts at having a baby have loosened Sarah up in this regard, but it would seem years of religious instruction depicting sex as original sin have done more than left a small rug burn on her psyche. Sometimes, I think our inability to get pregnant is a direct result of my wife's brittleness over sex. I also think the fact that she knows about some of my storied past doesn't help. Of course, all this is nonsense, but I can't stop these thoughts from flitting through my head, and I'm afraid Sarah has picked up my vibe through the universal power of female intuition.

Pulling into the driveway, I notice the plants that line the fence need cutting back, and I remind myself to tell Jose the next time he's here. The bushes are the kind I hated as a kid: long slender blade-like leaves that give you wicked paper cuts if you barely touch them. I briefly consider hacking the sons of bitches down, but I'd have to get the landlord's approval. And since I don't want to pay to replace them, I'm pretty sure the landlord wouldn't be happy with four or five holes in his lawn.

I'm in the house and Sarah's left a trail for me leading to the bedroom. Not rose petals—she's far too practical at this point—but a teddy bear, a book of Sesame Street characters, a rattle, a diaper, and a small blue blanket. If I didn't know better, I'd think my Christian wife was trying to cast some sort of pagan spell.

In the bedroom, I'm dropping my briefcases and then my briefs and making my hundredth prayer, and honestly, the only heartfelt one I can muster these days is that this time we'll hit the motherlode, or babylode, as the case may be.

Afterwards, I run into the kitchen to get us a glass of water. I'm reeling in the afterglow and doing a little naked prancing through the house. I'm thinking if they could bottle this feeling, they could make a fortune. Then again, maybe they have, and I just didn't take the right drugs back in high school and college.

The water comes out in a thin stream from the fridge's container—Sarah never pokes a big enough hole in the top—and the afterglow starts to inevitably slip away.

I'm there naked, sweaty, bent over, and it occurs to me this would be the perfect time for the Con Edison man to knock on my sliding glass door. I check, but he's not there. It's like when you live alone, watch some scary movie, get paranoid, and go through the house checking in every closet and under every bed. (I once checked in the fridge after a particularly gruesome stalker movie.) As if you actually found the ax murderer in the guest room closet, he'd just say, "Ah, you found me," and poutingly take his cleaver and hockey mask and go home.

Because of Sarah's reluctance to make a big enough air hole in the water dispenser it has taken me quite some time to fill one glass, so I decide we'll share. Away I go, water in hand, naked, my wife waiting, her face pushed into the pillow, her ass in the air—who said married life wasn't exciting.

It's the next day. The verdict's in. The Judge is querying the jury foreman. "Foreman, you say you've come to only a partial verdict?"

"We have, Your Honor."

"What say you all?"

"On the charge of felony possession and possible distribution of an illegal substance, we find the defendant, David Arthur Bedell, not guilty. On the lesser charge of misdemeanor possession, we are deadlocked, Your Honor."

"What is the vote on the lesser charge, Foreman?"

"Seven to five in favor of acquittal, Your Honor."

"Since there seems no hope of resolution, the jury is dismissed with the Court's thanks." The Judge motions Ms. Stanhope and me over. I'm hoping

I'm not about to lose the game on a ninth inning homer, but the Judge quickly allays those fears when he says to Ms. Stanhope, "Counselors, let's make this last charge go away." I'm just smart enough to stay out of this.

"Your Honor, Mr. Bedell had distribution level weight, and my office...

"That's gone, Ms. Stanhope. How about no fine on the misdemeanor and one hundred hours of community service."

"He already does that, Your Honor."

"So, you want to punish Mr. Bedell for previous good acts, Ms. Stanhope?"

"No. Fine, whatever."

"Is the court's finding agreeable to your client, Mr. Heyerdahl?"

"Yes, Your Honor."

"Then, case dismissed."

The gavel bangs and we return to our seats. I get to tell Mr. Bedell the good news. In his excitement he shakes my hand like he's milking it.

Like two pro athletes we start our post-contest walk to the locker room.

These are the times I'm glad I'm a lawyer, and I think maybe all my ambitions to cover some big cases like assault or murder are full of it. If I stay small, at least I can get a clear read on who's the good guy and who's the bad guy.

Bedell's already scurrying out, passing the few reporters who smell a good human-interest story. I grab my briefcase and notice where the table is still wet from my client's palms.

One of the local reporters, Stan Shane—an Irishman like myself, whose only real link to his Gaelic heritage is his love of a pint of Black and Tan— catches my eye as he tries to hustle up to me with his tape recorder, hoping he'll get a quote that he'll take wide over AP. The other two reporters are a portly man, whom I noticed taking notes during the case on his iPad, and a woman who's collegiate pretty and probably working the local court scene to pay her dues and gain some legitimacy so she can move on to TV, where neither of those things matter nearly as much as her God-given face.

The lady's up to me first, meaning one of the court officers is sweet on her. She asks me if I'm pleased with the verdict and, for a wild moment, just to see her expression, I want to say no, I'm not, and start yelling about the injustice of the U.S. government and the spies they've put in my microwave. Instead, I say the usual blather about how pleased I am about how the trial went, give a nod to the Judge, and mention how responsibly the jury deliberated, which is my nod to any schmo who might one day sit in the paneled box while I'm arguing a case.

Stan, swearing about violations of his First Amendment rights, pushes past the smitten court officer, and in an awful Irish brogue says, "Joey, me lad, give me an exclusive and the pints of Black and Tan are on me." The magic words and I'm out into the hall, promising the fat man who barely got into the mix that he can call me later for a quote.

Later, while Stan and I trade drinks, he asks me if I think this case'll win me this year's legal award for the protection of animals. I'm about to talk long and longer about that and everything else, as only a drinker of ale can who's a little full of himself after winning his case, when Stan adds, "Maybe this year you'll get the satisfaction of beating someone for the award. Weren't you the only nominee last time around?" He's laughing now, and I tell myself I'm going to have at least three more of these concoctions just to run up his tab.

# FIVE

A month later, I'm sitting alone in a bar on the Northside of town known for its Irish heritage and its fast growing population of transvestite hookers. I'm barely affiliated with the former. I'm Irish, with a little Scot (like to play up the Scot, since it seems kind of exotic), but really, overall, I'm about as Irish as the Boston Celtics. If by chance you haven't been keeping up, Larry Bird and Kevin McHale do not ride the pine at Boston's parquet floor anymore.

I've got a friend who believes everyone's got a superpower. Unfortunately, we've all got powers that are so small, so inconsequential, most people don't even know they've got'm. For example, this friend, the discoverer of the phenomenon, believes he has the power to find pens, no matter where he's at—inside or outside, day or night. Ask him to find a pen and within a few minutes he'll notice one stuck in the cracks of the sidewalk or down in the cushions of the sofa.

The only reason I'm mentioning this is because of the guy who just walked past me. He's got hair, the remnants of which make like an angel's halo, a nose that looks like it has walked into a few walls, and he's probably 350 pounds, wearing a belt that makes a lopsided circle on account of the huge mountain that's his belly. But even through the distortion of more than a decade, a few thousand burger joints, a comb that owns more of his hair than his head, I recognize him. He's Stan Baker, a guy I just barely knew from high school.

See, recognizing people is my superpower.

He sits down at the stool next to me, oblivious to our connection. Having this superpower, this situation has come up more than you'd think. Usually, I do nothing, but for lack of a good reason I decide to remind Stan, former hoopster, about Mills High School, the Quad and our mascot, the Viking.


We've now had a few drinks, catching up on old times. What happened to this guy or girl, who's pregnant, who's married (they're not always the same), who's dead (a handful), and who's now using a different bathroom than they did back in high school (just one).

Right now the sound on the TV's muted, but the words are scrolling across the bottom detailing how one Cheryl Preninger is set to be put to death in six months, making her only the fifth woman, and the first in twenty years, to be killed by the State. The guy on TV, with the perma-plaqued hair, goes into Cheryl's heinous deeds as a young woman and, while incarcerated, her subsequent discovery of Jesus.

"Yeah, now if she'd only found Jesus before she started killing people," Stan adds.

My friend's got a point.

The bartender, a grunge-scene reject, slaps our glasses down like he's some gangbanger playing dominoes, gives us the long pour (when you're ordering Black Label Johnny Walker you want to see the bottle), and starts telling me about the history of the place.

He must have noticed my glances. The guy goes on about the bar's relationship to some ancient whaling boat, and I'm looking for a way out.

My old friend, Stan, gives me a hand. "It's like the Queequeg, in *Moby Dick*, and we're in the belly of the whale."

He's mixing in the Bible, but I don't care cuz' our shipwright barkeep appears scared of this new info and looks ready to bolt. So I help him go. "Call me Ishmael, some time ago, never mind how precisely, having little or no money and a desire to see the sea."

They're both nodding their heads at my smarts. After all, it takes quite a guy to memorize the opening to *Moby Dick*. Actually, I got it from a *Love Boat* episode where Doc and Gopher try to fool Julie, the cruise director, by making her memorize Melville so she can get into a fictional Seamen's Club. Don't worry, it all comes out okay and everybody stays friends.

Our drink bearer is called over to tell his spiel at the far side of the bar and I'm figuring I just wasted a good literary allusion.

"So how'd you get that, hmm?" My friend's gesturing at the award that's standing on the bar, the one I've got decorated with those tiny cocktail straws you can never suck anything out of.

I remove the straws like I'm unbuilding a Lincoln log house. The award says, 'For his inestimable efforts in making life better for animal companions everywhere,' and the award's kicker is the little golden alloy guy on the top, crowded by a dog, a cat, and a bird on his shoulder. It reminds me of the trophies I won in Little League. You know, with the ballplayer hitting, running, or fielding. Well, now it's St. Francis of Assisi and his companion creatures.

My law career has come to this, but then my baseball career never got out of tenth grade, so I should have had it figured.

"So you, like, help animals, legally?"

"I've worked all kinds of cases, some B and E's, some wife beater assaults..."

"Yeah, but your specialty is animals."

"You get a rep for doing a certain kind of case. Bailey did murders, Shapiro is known for his plea bargains..."

"And you?"

"Let me give you an example. A lady comes in the other day and tells me how she and her son are busy watching *Touched By An Angel* when she hears a thump-a-thump coming from the dryer down the hall. She says to her kid, 'I don't remember putting your tennis shoes in the dryer,' and like that the big giant light bulb, you know, like they got on the Monopoly board, goes off over her head."

"Electric Company, the bulb on the Monopoly board. There's Electric Company and Water Works. I never understand why anyone buys those two. What can you get like ten times a dice throw?"

I wait for him to finish, give him the shrug that says the universe is a wacky place and we all just got to go with it, and continue my story. After all, I bought this round. "The lady jumps up, goes running down the hall, opens the dryer door, and out flops her kitty. Poor thing's breathing like it just completed the triathlon and it's walking crazy eights."

"She put the cat in the dryer?"

"No, it turns out the cat likes to get cozy in there because it's so warm. Woman just stuck her hand in, noticed some damp clothes and turned it on."

"Was the cat okay?"

"One emergency vet visit costing $545 and she was. The vet even threw in a little comedy."

"What'd he say?"

"Said, 'Ms. Lane, next time you put the cat in the dryer make sure you use Bounce fabric softener.'"

My friend gives a good laugh, which is not bad considering neither of us are that drunk, and this is a bar, and we're two guys, so the only jokes that are usually officially sanctioned amount to making fun of gays or women.

"What'd she want from you?"

"She wanted me to sue the dryer manufacturer for her animal's pain and suffering. I told her I couldn't do that. That I could only sue for *her* pain and suffering. She says just imagine it from a human's point of view. You walk in a room, the door slams, and the whole room starts flip-flopping, while this huge wash of heat just starts coming from everywhere."

"She's got a point. That'd be messed up."

"Yes, but she doesn't have a case."

"Well, that's one pussy who won't forget the ride."

Like I said, the usual women and gay-bashing jokes.

"Pussy'll do it every time. I just watched an anniversary show on the O.J. case, and hey, I've got black friends."

I'm nodding, when what he really means is he knows one black guy at work and calls him by his first name.

"O.J. wasn't about black and white; it was about man and woman. O.J. got all lathered up over his wife, ex-wife, doing the deed, and him not in the pilot seat. This stuff is aboriginal."

I don't think he's got the right word, but I let him go. After all, he put up with my cat-in-the-dryer story.

"If you don't believe me, just look at a different part of the same case. Officer Fuhrman gets caught on tape about how he beat this nigger here and another nigger over there..."

The fact that he doesn't even look up when using such un-PC language tells me this is still an Irish bar.

"...baseball bats and blood everywhere. It's a huge media sensation, all this hand wringing. Of course, it comes out months down the line that everything—I mean everything, Fuhrman said—was a lie. Why? Because of the little screenwriter babe he was talking to. Listen to the tape. He's talking up being this mean, macho, SuperFly pulverizer and she's giggling... giggling. And you know he's thinking, hey, I'm getting somewhere here. And let me tell you, that screenwriter chick, I mean, do you remember the udders on that mammal?"

This is all a little too much to digest, so I finish my drink and make to get off my cherry oak podium that weathered the North Sea through winter swells and now needs to only weather the indignity of squeezed out beer farts.

My high school chum, seemingly drunker than I thought (I guess my cat-in-the-dryer story wasn't that funny), stops me, "Don't believe me? What about Marion Berry?"

"The former mayor of Washington D.C.?"

"You bet. Remember, he got busted for crack. You ever see the tape of the arrest? He's got the girl in the room, and he doesn't want to do crack (a big pause and a conspiratorial aside), he wants to get laid. Three times he's like, 'c'mon baby let's lay down here.' Each time she's like, 'Hey, let's do this, the crack'. You can see the wheels turning in ole Marion's head. I'll do the crack so I can get laid. Finally, he agrees. Boom. The cops are there and he's busted, and what does Berry say?"

I just shrug, wondering if this was the way the first Jews felt when Moses, tablets in hand, came down from Mt. Ararat babbling about talking to God.

"'The damn bitch set me up. The damn bitch set me up.' Ain't no truer words ever been said, man."

I'm nodding and tossing a few bucks on the bar for Kurt Cobain's stepchild.

"Where ya going in such a hurry?"

I hold up my phone; 911 can be seen. "It's my wife, I gotta go."

He looks like I just let him down, lost my key to the ole Boys' Club.

"She's ovulating," I say, and that lifts his spirits. 'At least you're gonna get some,' I figure he's thinking. And as I sail out the door, I wish that wasn't the only thing I was sure of.


Even though this guy had to hike to Nepal to get my car, and I hate to have him think I'm a skinflint because of the cheapness of my car, I still only hand him a buck as I take the keys. I mean, how many indignities can one guy suffer for not having a cool car?

I pull out onto the streets and I'm shifting through the gears onto the highway. I've had a few too many and I know from previous experience there's a surefire way to confirm that fact. I look down to adjust the radio, a quick snap back up, and I notice the car swerving a little. If my head was on straight, the car wouldn't have swerved. So I know I'm dangerous, and I'm in a piece of metal weighing several tons, traveling at 65 miles per hour. As a remedy, I roll down the window, flooding the car's cabin with cold air. I turn the radio up a notch and I keep my eyes peeled to the road while sticking to 65.

I'm pulling the car into one of the split-level stucco homes (that looks like almost every other house you've ever seen while driving through suburban America). I've even got the white picket fence. And in the front yard there's what I thought was a stunted orange tree that turned out to be making tangerines, and a decent size yard that Jose, our gardener, cuts every other week.

All this would be a little more kosher if we actually owned this slice of Americana, but we rent, the great stigmata of the lower middle class, the Mason-Dixon line of respectability. Now don't get me wrong, working away your days under the heel of a mortgage is not my idea of Club Med.

I've spent my ten years huffing through a third-rate law school, working lots of jobs that paid my tuition, and several years of private practice that have managed to afford me only the slightest cushion against monthly bills. In this time I've come to the conclusion that *work* is an over-rated phenomenon.

I'm up to the front door. Since I got that first text, I received three more. Before I was married, when I wasn't cramming or working, I spent my time bar hopping and picking up women. Can't say why exactly, just seemed the thing to do. Also, it wasn't hard, and the dividends, at least in the short term, seemed to pay out nicely. I figured short relationships made it easy to walk away with little emotional head-spinning to go through, and when I didn't call them back, I figure that about the same number would have never picked up the phone to ask why. So I figured I was even in the cosmic dating equation.

Then I met Tish. Nothing exceptional: dark hair, brown eyes, long legs that could be used for great effect. Went out a few times, spent some time together, and one night I'm driving her home and she asks if we can stop at one of those all night pharmacy slash grocery store slash home appliance centers that I guess the country is clamoring for.

We go in and she's moving down the aisles looking for Easter bunny stuff for her daughter. No, I did know she had a kid. She goes for her money, and I offer to pay the fourteen dollars and she's instantly grateful, almost gushing.

I take her home, and I haven't noticed before, but she lives in a tired neighborhood bordering some real dangerous ones, and I can see her and her daughter waking up tomorrow and her kid getting all excited at the wicker basket with the measly amounts of chocolate hidden in all that fake grass that will show up under the sofa seats in six months, and I realize that it's all just sorta sad. Her life, my life, and even the fact that I didn't know the next day was Easter, or if her kid was a boy or a girl.

A few weeks later I'm joining a church group. Trying to get back to some real values, something that has heft to it, like a good Louisville Slugger and the crack it makes when you hit the sweet spot.

I avoid the whole Catholic thing.

Officially, I've received First Communion but I was never confirmed, so that puts me somewhere between purgatory and heaven, and honestly, I shouldn't have even got First Communion. I failed to go to almost all the catechism classes. They were on Wednesday and I always remembered not to remind my mother, who even then was getting on in years. When I did go, I found the whole thing a colossal waste. I spent most of my time in the Catholic School library, coloring pictures of Jesus helping the needy and reading such classics as *Charlie and the Great Glass Elevator*—that's the follow-up to *Charlie and the Chocolate Factory*. The former being a far superior book, though I did still steal the elevator book from the church library. So in retrospect, maybe my position in Purgatory is not halfway to heaven, but halfway to Hell.

Church was where I met Sarah, sweet, sincere, definitely fragile, with long blonde hair that turned in at the ends, like the ole Jennifer Anniston hairstyle on *Friends,* with a cute nose that those caricature artists on the street give everybody because they want a big tip, and a slender little body—kind of like a bird's.

I guess what I liked most about her was how she was certain of her life's path, and how it harkened back to Norman Rockwell and a land devoid of sarcasm and cynicism. So in the language of that day, I wooed her. Really, it was simple. I was the wisdom-seeking lapsed Catholic and she was the shepherd leading me back to the fold. What woman wouldn't find that appealing? I mean, women exult over getting men to pick up their clothes, take out the trash, keep the damn toilet seat down. Sarah had that beat; she was redeeming my soul and guiding me along the path to accepting Jesus as my personal savior. So I did, and I tried not to be sarcastic or cynical as the Reverend intoned over my baptism of renewal, but there was still that little voice on my shoulder. No, I don't think it was the devil; I actually think it might have been Louie C.K.

So we got married, and we made love for the first time on that very night, and it was surprisingly sweet and special, and I'll probably remember it even when I'm old and can't recall if I have to shit or even where the hell the bathroom is. That was three years ago and Sarah's plans—and I guess mine as well—have not proceeded apace. What can you say when you've been trying to have a kid for the last year or so and have come up empty?

Well, not precisely empty.

Sarah has miscarried twice. One showed up on the ultrasound as just a little dark thumbnail in this big uterus, like a little pile of gold sitting in some dragon's cave. But this pile of gold didn't have a heartbeat and after some tears on Sarah's part, we tried again. I felt guilty because I had once paid for a girlfriend to have an abortion and I couldn't help feeling that this squandering of God's most precious gift pissed the Lord off and this was His way of returning the favor. The second miscarriage came four months ago and its repercussions are still being felt. This time, no gold in the dragon's lair, just one big empty cave. Blighted ovum, the Doc called it, and

I couldn't help but think of my Irish ancestors fleeing their Emerald Isle because of the potato blight. And yes, I again thought some Karmic payment was coming due. I might be a New Age touchy, feely Christian, but I was born Catholic, where guilt is hard currency. The doctors told us that this second miscarriage may have a real depressing effect on Sarah's chance of carrying a child to full term.

She's not been real well since. Like I said, she's always been fragile. Religion can be a great thing, but it can also be a crutch—credit Jesse Ventura for that apt truism. In Sarah's case, it seems to me that her carefully orchestrated life has started to tip precariously.

It's about an hour later, and I'm sitting on the couch after a quick session of lovemaking (these days there doesn't seem to be any other kind). I had just walked in the door when I heard Sarah demanding that I get in the bedroom (music to any man's ears). At the same time, she's asking me why I didn't answer my umpteen texts. I tell her it's not wise to text and drive. That seems to satisfy her, though she doesn't think to ask why I didn't text her from the bar.

Immediately, she's tossing back the covers and telling me to get on (an orchestra starts to swell in my ears), then she's telling me she's so tired she doesn't care if the whole thing takes a minute (the entire Boston Pops is now warming up in my head).

Later, back on the couch, I've poured myself a Scotch. Richard Simmons is on the *A&E Biography* and he's spending his adolescence agonizing over his weight. All I can wonder is what kind of dregs will A&E be left to profile five, ten, twenty years from now.

My only companion is the cat who sits on the far armrest, ignoring me in the profound way cats do. I've got a drink and I can't help remembering my father sitting just like I am now, me coming home from some teen party or Dungeons and Dragon get-together (okay, the party part is mostly bullshit). I tell myself the diff would be that he'd be asleep, the drink in his hand balanced serenely on his thigh.

I used to wonder how he slept like that. Late in life, my father became a full-blown alcoholic, or at least as full-blown as a guy can get who's eighty, who's got one lung from smoking (thank you, cancer), and who's just a shadow without his wife. Mostly, he just sat on the couch arguing with the TV over subjects as diverse as "Is Miley Cyrus a slut," or "Should the government be allowed to tell you what size toilet you can buy?" His opinions in a nutshell were that he'd never share his oversized toilet with a tramp like Miley.

A great advantage to my father's alcoholism was that if you didn't like the drunken harangue that night, you could just leave, he being too frail to remove himself from his Barcalounger, which had formed to his torso like one of the special couches they made for the Apollo astronauts. After the sledgehammer stroke that killed my mother, Dad removed himself from his space capsule lounge chair only when he needed to go to the bathroom.

I'm not complaining; I've seen a lot of people go through worse with their families, and sometimes I even liked to hear Dad's grandiose theories on how the universe worked. One I remember—and I'm still dickering with myself—is that he believed pop music's appearance was really the Second Coming of Christ. Now you understand his interest in Miley Cyrus, though I'm still not sure how the oversized toilets fit in.

And that's how I fall asleep.

I wake up the next morning in the chair with cotton in my mouth and a dull ache behind my eyes that's being produced by the several little men who are pounding back there. I startle, and then I relax. No drink in my hand

and no drink dropped nearby. I must've gotten up and dumped it in the sink. With the soothing thoughts that I've yet to become my father, I head for the shower, never aware that Sarah has checked on me early in the A.M., taken the glass from my mummified hand, given me a kiss, and emptied the drink in the sink.

# SIX

Sarah smiled as Joe related for what must have been the fourth time in a month how he had so skillfully saved Mr. Bedell from a prison term, a story that got longer and longer in the retelling, and more and more dangerous.

In some ways her husband, Joe, was a little boy. Talking with the women at church gave Sarah the impression that all men were, so she indulged her man in his fantasies of Perry Mason, or just that he was the king of his castle.

He was up and out the door, grabbing a few brownies from the church plate, tossing them in his jacket pocket when she turned away to grab his lunch.

She was left cleaning the dishes she had used to make his morning breakfast. She was also left with a day, much like all the others, that stretched out before her like some featureless expanse of water.

She feared this ocean.

As a result, she had become like some military man, planning her days with a meticulous tick-tock rigor. One: go to the grocery store, where she never bought more than a day or two of food, allowing her more trips and thus something more to do. She relied on her trips to the grocery store, and even though Joe often mentioned getting a membership to one of those giant warehouse stores, she politely steered him away from that idea. Two: clean the house, which was already spotless, and though she complained about Joe dropping his clothes (like as soon as he decided to take them off they acquired some great weight) and leaving his bowls unwashed, she knew his messiness gave her something to do.

Sarah understood the real problem was the loneliness and boredom, and that the solution was to have a child. She had visited her friends and their houses, amazed that children appeared and disappeared like goblins, making messes, needing food and attention, like pit-stopping race cars.

So she waited like a statue of Mary, arms open, hoping to be called.

The desire for a child was a physical thing for Sarah; as it appeared that God might deny her this boon, she prayed and believed. But she was a practical woman, and regardless of her strait-laced upbringing, she read everything she could on fertility, listened to anyone with homespun sense on the how-to, and she bought an ovulation kit, which would pinpoint her most fertile times.

Now, she had scheduled an appointment with a fertility specialist for later this week. She would just use the charge card, she told herself. Joe had her pay all the bills, so he'd never know. Never know, that is, until she had something good to tell him.

As the months, and now years, had passed, she had become more and more certain that the infertility was her fault. When she and Joe had gotten serious and she had sat as his Witness on his path back to Jesus Christ, he confessed that he'd once fathered a child and paid for the woman to have an abortion. She had been shocked, but she knew that if Jesus could forgive, she should demand the same of herself. After all, having a child would show him to be a good father, erasing his sin in the eyes of God.

With time, her thoughts grew less redemptive and much less wholesome, and she wondered why Joe's one-night stand, and all those women like her, was worthy of the gift of a child and she was not. She knew this was simplistic thinking, but as the Reverend Tolliver said, "God is as simple as He is complex."

Just last week, after yet another inquiry into her state, Paula, one of the women she was friendly with from church, had counseled, and reminded her that God only gave us things we could bear. She had heard this homily many times and had always found solace in it; though interestingly, she now noted it had always been over other people's problems—deaths, separations, betrayals. But now, like a flash, a response filled her and she had to make a conscious effort to still her tongue. Yes, Paula, she thought, if God only gives us what we can bear, then I guess if I were a weaker woman He'd make me pregnant, and He wouldn't have taken my father through liver cancer, poor man wasting away until he was a shell, gripped to this earth only by machines.

And for a moment her mind cracked, and she felt more than saw a blinding light, a light not of God but of a harsher sort. What if her revelation over Paula's comment was just the tip of the iceberg? What if all she believed would fall one by one to this new understanding? She grew frightened, waiting, wondering, what other grim realities or devil's deceptions lay in wait to cast her into the tetherless fog of faithlessness.

She'd been holding a drinking glass, staring into it. I'll see the specialist, she thought, and start getting to the bottom of the whole thing.

She noticed the time and hurried to finish her housecleaning. The small table in the dining room was covered with pies, cakes, cookies and brownies, all headed for the church and its outreach program for the sick and the invalid.

It seemed to her that people at church always assumed she could do the lion's share, perhaps because she had no child to take care of. Even her best friends at church, Paula and Karen, bowed out of some of the harder work, citing obligations with their kids' soccer teams, orange wedge cutting, or school plays. She did her best to exemplify Christian charity, but these women grated on her. She imagined them behind her back, oozing with pity over her childlessness, at the same time giving themselves hearty pats on the back for making it into a club from which Sarah was barred, the one club it seemed most women defined themselves by. She had once overheard Paula use the word *barren* while talking about her, as if she were some unplantable field.

In the garage, Sarah opened the back of the Chevy Tahoe. The car had become another reminder of her failure and her arrogance in assuming the Lord would bless her with many children. She had talked Joe into the gas-guzzler two years ago, using the argument that they would need it for the brood of children she was sure to have. Joe had quickly given in, sold his brilliant red *Oh-I'm-such-a-bachelor* sport's car, and purchased the economy Saturn, making up the difference with the late model SUV.

As time passed, she had felt sillier and sillier tooling around in this black whale of a car, taking what had become an almost masochistic glee in noting the other SUV's that prowled the road, and how many of these held the telltale child car seat, the *Baby on Board* sticker, or the pulldown sun blocker picturing Tigger, Pooh, or some character from Dora the Explorer. Her math was far from perfect, but she put that figure at easily over a half.

She took the desserts two by two, something Noah would've been proud of, she thought with a grim smirk, and loaded them into the car. The back seat made her sad and she remembered a big fight she and Joe had had a month ago, when he had innocently mentioned how they could always use the car for camping or road trips. Surprising even herself, his comments had elicited an angry accusation that he was backing out of having kids.

"We've only been trying a year," he said. "Your doc says we have another year before we should think something might not be working." She had agreed, but underneath her moist eyes she knew it was a lie. She had been trying since the first night of their marriage, while letting Joe believe they'd only been trying for the last year. Sadly, she looked at her marriage night as a bitter memory, what with her naive belief that their first night would beget a child.

Sarah remembered waiting until the end of that month, rehearsing her glee and practicing what she would say to Joe, drinking in her own happiness, the happiness she would see in his eyes, and this confirmation of her real womanhood. Sarah's feelings were like many people's reason for purchasing a lottery ticket—for the win, yes, but also for the joy of bearing the good news to friends and family. This visit to the fertility specialist was carrying the deceit even further, and who knew what other paths she would be willing to follow if God granted her the nerve?

She guided the car from the garage and headed for the Benevolent Christ Church, not five minutes from their home. She had insisted they rent a house close to church, for practical reasons, and because she secretly feared that any distance between Joe and religion might let him revert back to his lapsed Catholic self.

She turned into the church parking lot, had a fading, fleeting thrill from parking in the area reserved for church business. Sarah put the car in park and set the emergency brake, even though the lot was as flat as a cookie sheet. Through the church doors she made a left, following several adjoining corridors into the room next to the rectory's kitchen.

As she approached, she could hear the voices of Paula and Karen filtering through the hustle and bustle of their food preparation. She paused a minute before entering. In her mind, she could hear her mother. "Never eavesdrop. You might actually hear something. And most likely if you do, it won't be anything nice about you, cuz, after all, who likes a snoop?"

Paula and Karen were actually directing all their chatty horror at Marge Schembleck and her tendency to wear too much makeup, tight skirts, and be overly friendly with many of the many married men of the church. The ladies were sure Marge was a fake, from the tips of her colored hair to the size of her cleavage. Like candy-coated mobsters, they related what would happen to Marge if she ever got too friendly with their husbands.

Sarah walked in holding two plates of brownies. To her annoyance, she discovered that Joe had pilfered several more after the ones he had insisted on eating as an after-breakfast snack.

The two women greeted her warmly and made room for the desserts on a foldout table. Paula wore no make-up, but used her cute and perky exterior to hide a keen dissatisfaction with life. Sarah had never been able to figure out the cause of Paula's discontent. She had three children, a husband—who if not doting, was ready to go most any which way Paula's mood blew—and a house that was one of the nicest in their Evanston suburb.

On the other hand, Karen was the kind of woman who attached herself to a dominant friend and went about making herself indispensable, simply by her universal agreement with everything the friend said, be it Marge Schembleck, the sermon of Reverend Tolliver, or which fast food restaurant had the best drive-thru.

More irritating still was in the case of Paula and her butt-kisser friend Karen—Paula took Karen's various agreements on her opinion as if they came down from the Lord on high, but then again, Sarah thought, the easiest person to agree with is yourself.

There are the hellos and the clucks over how good her sweets look. Of course, Paula has to notice the missing brownies. "Joe, right? That's okay, if

I had to make cakes and brownies I'd be showing up with a plate of crumbs. The kids absolutely love my baked goods. I can make one of those big brownie boxes—you know, the one's you buy at Costco—and a day later there's nothing left."

Karen, the agreeing sidekick, has to add, "That is so true, both James and Luc eat anything sweet. You know I caught Luc just the other day eating the cake icing right outta the plastic tub—straight, just icing and a big spoon. He didn't know I was there and just swooped out a huge tablespoon of the stuff and started licking it like a lollipop."

Paula and Karen finish with, "Boys."

"Let's unpack your car. I've got a turkey in the oven that should be checked in about five," Paula directed.

Out at the car, the women unpack the boxes. As the Tahoe emptied, Paula zings with, "I forgot how big these SUV's are without the back seat up, and without the kids' skates and the car seats. This just seems huge."

Sarah almost winces, but strengthens herself with a reminder of her visit to the specialist.

Paula becomes a Road & Track reviewer. "These older Tahoes are maybe two-thirds the size of my Navigator. You know, I think the last time I saw my car this empty was that camping trip Phil and I took through the Appalachians, the same trip where we made Phil Jr."

Almost unbearably, Paula is lifting an eyebrow in Sarah's direction, giving her the eye, hinting that maybe she and Joe should give the back of their car a go. Sarah is not going to play Karen's part and continues stacking boxes of desserts into Karen's arms. Karen's face is about to disappear behind the last apple pie when Sarah finally notices and stops.

Paula, with a box-laden Karen in her wake, is moving inside. "Careful, Sarah, you don't want to give Karen too much."

No, Paula, *you* are too much, Sarah thinks.

It's late afternoon and Sarah is driving home, exhausted from the cooking that added to her already large number of pies, cakes and brownies. After putting up with hours of Paula's petty sniping, all she wants is to take a hot bath, relax, and remove the grime of sugar and flour from her hands.

She has decided to ask for van duty. Visiting the sick and the old seemed too depressing, but that latest round of Paula's girl talk convinced her that some things could be worse than talking to the nearly dead, such as talking to those who were better off dead.

For the tenth time today, she reminded herself that on Friday she'd talk to the specialist, she'd be back on track, and then the Paulas of the world be damned.

The fertility clinic was an indistinct office space inhabited by four floors of dentists, dermatologists, aestheticians, doctors, and one orthopedic shoe store that made a killing giving kickbacks to those doctors who directed their patients to 'the store right below.'

Sarah walked nervously to the elevator, glanced at the office number written on the Post-it just this morning because she was hiding evidence from Joe in case he found any clue and deduced her intentions. She had gone as far as to leave her cell phone at home on the table so she couldn't be contacted. Regardless, she had a ready-made alibi if he did ask. Several pillow shams and a bed skirt were tossed in the back of the car as proof she had been visiting the mall. Sarah suspected all this deviousness was unnecessary, but she prided herself on being quite the little plotter if necessary. Welling up from some lost place inside her, a darker voice reminded, "Just pray this is all you have to plot."

She checked the office number for the second time, headed up to the third floor, sharing the elevator with an elderly couple. The woman used a walker and seemed as fragile as thin crystal. The exception was her liver-spotted, blue-veined hands that gripped the walker's handles strongly enough to bring a pinch of color to the otherwise pallid skin. Her husband was one of those men who gradually disappear. His suit hung starchly from his shoulders, and as if having drunk the wrong teacup at Alice's party, he was now shrinking to nothingness.

The man smiled at Sarah as she held the door for them. Very nervous, she saw the Eyes of God everywhere and took the old gentleman's smile as an omen of good things to come.

Navigating the third floor corridors, Sarah reached Dr. Mecklenburg's office. Fake oak double doors that opened on one side greeted her. With a racing but hopeful heart, she walked into the office. It closely resembled her gynecologist's, with a few plants, ferns and palms growing in the recesses. Sarah wondered if these pollen-rich plants were some kind of subconscious message of fertility to the desperate women who came here. There were sketches of women's torsos, hips, and arms, along with pictures of budding plants that had scientific labels.

Sarah noted that there were no baby magazines on the table. Instead, she found the regular dose of women's mental and physical fitness mags that trumpeted the power of being yourself and knowing yourself, while their photos and ads rang out to change yourself, change yourself, change yourself!

Sarah reported to the little opaque window that resembled a shower door. Thirty minutes early, she would have to read Women's Fitness or Oprah's 'O' Magazine. She dumped herself onto the pastel covered couch with cushions that felt like cardboard. She bounced a few times to assure herself of the discomfort and stopped when she noticed a turbaned woman glancing her way. To cover her silliness she grabbed a fitness magazine and began leafing through.

Sarah glanced at the woman and her turban. The headdress was a bright purple affair with small yellow designs like cookies interspersed throughout. The woman's left ear held a large, silver hoop from which hung several silver chains, like a sun radiating or a cloud raining, while the other ear held a simple diamond stud. That the woman had cancer seemed obvious to Sarah; the turban was a screeching alarm. The woman's eyes were a brilliant blue and were accentuated by her lack of eyebrows.

Mouthing a short prayer for the woman, Sarah wondered what brought her to this clinic. The lady had a more serious problem than whether she could have a baby, and chemo often made fertility procedures impossible. Perhaps she was banking her eggs in case the chemo makes her infertile, Sarah surmised. Satisfied by this line of reasoning, she went back to perusing the different ways to tone her abs.

Sarah felt as if she wore a scarlet letter. There was no red A emblazoned on her chest nor were there wide-eyed children on her hip. Hester Prynne had been guilty of adultery, yet God had allowed her the comfort of her angelic daughter. Sarah was willing to make a similar deal, face similar punishment. Mark me with a grave sin, Oh Lord, but give me a child. And that child needn't be a cherub straight from heaven, Sarah added. I'll wear whatever disgraceful badge you deem, Lord, just to see my baby's eyes stare back at me.

Sarah's mind was so full of this religious frenzy that she nearly missed hearing her name being called. That it was her maiden name, used for added secrecy, no doubt played a role.

Sarah hurried forward, suddenly afraid that someone in the office would hear this name and it would get back to Joe. She apologized her way past the door.

Another long hallway, more plants, and small rooms jutting off from the main.

"Right in here, Mrs. McClure. Dr. Mecklenburg will be here in a moment. Take off your clothes and jump into our paper party dress," the rotund, Afro'd receptionist delivered with a slight smile. "Oh, and on the forms you filled out, you only listed a cell phone."

"Oh, yes, well, our wiring is all messed up and the phone company is coming out and, well, you know how late they can be. Anyway, that's the only phone I have right now," Sarah finished with a practiced ease. An odd look from the receptionist might have made her think the woman knew she was lying, but the moment passed and her carefully thought out plan seemed to be working.

She felt her heartbeat increase, knew she was on the final approach to discovering if she could or could not bear children. It would be there, undeniable, with her throughout her time on Earth. If someone had asked Sarah, "If a tree falls in the forest and no one's there to hear it, does it make a noise?" Sarah would have answered a resounding, "No." She had long felt this almost superstitious certainty about the reality of life, especially since that fateful day she went looking for her baby sister. A voice pulled her back into the room.

"Mrs. McClure, I'm Dr. Mecklenburg. I want to give you a quick run through of what we're trying to accomplish today."

Dr. Mecklenburg was a woman, which was something Sarah had insisted on, calling three clinics before finding this one. The doctor was in her early forties, short of stature, a little slouchy, wearing a light green blouse under the white lab coat that everyone who takes the Hippocratic Oath seems to agree to wear at all times. Her hair was black, except for islands of white that dotted her head, and she wore bifocals attached to an antique chain. All of this gave her a funky charm and made her seem older than her forty-some years. Sarah welcomed the doctor's 'young' granny look as a much-needed sedative.

The doctor's down-home manner contributed as well. "First, we're going to stick you to take some blood, then I'm going to perform an ultrasound to get a picture of your uterus. Just looking to see if anything seems drastically out of the ordinary. Then we're going to scan your belly. Right now I'm going to do a pelvic exam, but it might hurt a bit more than usual because I have to feel your tubes. I'm also going to insert a little camera to get a better look-see. Ever thought you'd see the insides of your body on TV?"

Sarah offered a weak "No."

"Relax, Sarah. Chances are we aren't going to discover anything today that's definitive. When the tests start coming back, then you can get nervous."

Sarah's up in the stirrups and staring down at the top of the doctor's head. Stirrups, she thought, like no horse she had ever ridden. The doctor was inserting the speculum, which always made Sarah grimace. Couldn't they make it out of plastic? That way you wouldn't feel like somebody was putting a can opener inside you. A strong stab of pain and Sarah winced.

"Sorry" came the doctor's measured response, although Sarah doubted the apology's authenticity, since the doctor continued doing whatever caused the discomfort in the first place. She tried to concentrate on the top of the doctor's head, count the hairs, note dandruff, dye jobs, and bald spots, anything to keep her mind off what potentially bad thing might be revealed.

Dr. Mecklenburg's head proved difficult to focus on. Her black hair gave no context or texture, her simple style of feathering it gave little for Sarah to note. The one distinguishing feature, the white swatches, left Sarah with the puzzle of whether they were dyed or was the rest of the hair dyed black.

A TV monitor Sarah hadn't noticed was switched on and the doctor took her head away from one view to examine another.

"Here's the mouth of the uterus."

Sarah was startled to see a lot fleshy pink skin, ridged but smoothed. "Is that what it's supposed to look like?"

"Yes, Sarah. Let's see now, moving through the uterus, looking for the entrance to the fallopian tubes. There's one, where's the other?" The doctor manipulates the camera back and forth. The small video device moves like a hungry rat, nosing itself about trying to find the cheese in this internal human maze.

Sarah was starting to grow frightened.

"Ahh, there it is, little more off center than usual, but that's fine. I can't nose the probe up there, but I can take a look at the preeminent fallopian aperture."

The probe poked its way to the foot of one of her fallopian tubes. From this vantage point, the tube looked like a small hole sheathed in bright red filaments. The doctor was talking quickly, having caught on to Sarah's alarm at almost anything that looked foreign, which in this situation was just about everything. "Looks fine, opening looks good, and see that red color? That means blood's getting in there, so no sign of necrosis, that the tubes are dead or dying. That pain you felt earlier was me just giving them a little squeeze, rebounding felt good—normal."

The doctor pulled another machine closer, one arrayed with another screen and a display that looked like a computer with a mouse ball. "One second," she said, and Sarah could feel something thin and hard move up inside her. "Let's check the ultrasound." The small screen was lit and Sarah almost aahhed with twisted nostalgia. Her previous times, she had been so full of dashed hope and weakness, needing Joe's comfort, being ashamed to ask for his caresses because she had failed him. But this time would be the province of television, and she had watched her share of movies. The doctor humming, clicking here and there, the picture resolving into a hazy gray mesh of lines that looked like a charcoal sketch of a somber day.

"Doctor, why don't I have the jelly on my stomach?"

"That Sarah," she answered with a very doctorial pause, "is because this is a vaginal ultrasound. Abdominal ultrasounds are not as precise."

Sarah imagined the day with Joe by her side, the two of them gazing at the baby, so perfect inside her, sharing the moment of joy and awe that comes from taking part in God's greatest plan.

"The ultrasound's not showing any abnormalities," Mecklenburg says. "Sometimes it does a better job at catching irregularities just below the uterine lining because, unlike the camera, the sound waves it bounces can show a little depth. Kind of like a topographic map showing ridges and valleys. Everything here looks smooth. I'm going to get a few swabs of the uterine lining and we'll be done."

Sarah heard few words of the play-by-play because she was immersed in the dreamscape unfolding in her mind, on the ultrasound, all filtering through the numerous television shows she had seen depicting this special moment.

Once again her eyes alighted on her womb and this time she stared, enjoying the emptiness, the healthy emptiness, not having to deal with the rising fear that there would be nothing there. Or worse, that something small would be attached but there would be no blinking light denoting her baby was alive. There was a new barrenness of sorts, but it seemed to be a barrenness filled with possibilities.

The doctor removed the probe and Sarah was sad to see it go. Before the machine was turned off it hiccuped out a picture of her insides.

"Whoops, darn thing does that automatically if you don't tell it not to. I don't suppose you want a picture for the photo album just yet."

Sarah laughed a bit while shaking her head.

"There's nothing outstanding to make me think anything is wrong, Sarah. Nothing major—no occlusions, blockages, tumors that would impair reproduction. But like I said, this would be all rather rare. So go home, try not to worry, and I'll call you in a few weeks when I get the lab workup, okay?"

Sarah nodded and began pulling her gown over her with one hand, while trying to grab her clothes from the door's hook. The doctor reached over to help, handing Sarah her skirt and blouse.

"Now, promise me you won't worry."

"I won't worry, Doctor, I promise."

"Ahh, Sarah, you're going to need to lie better than that if you're going to have kids. I mean, unless you want them to know exactly what you got them for Christmas and exactly what you did as a teenager. You mentioned on the phone that your husband is a lawyer trying a murder case?"

"Yes, he wanted to come, but he's right in the middle of it."

"Okay, well as soon as he's able, I'd like to meet with you both. No reason for just the woman to bear the whole load in this, right?"

"I'll get him in here as soon as I can."

The doctor nodded and Sarah couldn't help suppressing a little glee, while thinking, "Am I lying better now, Doctor?"

"Okay, when you're done getting dressed, go back to the receptionist. She'll make an appointment for a month from now and she'll give you directions for the lab upstairs. They'll draw your blood. Everything looks good so far, so keep a positive attitude and let's take this thing one day at a time."

The doctor gave her a firm handshake and left the room. Sarah left soon after, taking her purse, her car keys, and one small black and white photo of an emptiness that, ironically, represented her hope.

# SEVEN

I'm in the car battling the traffic that seems to stack up as people leave Arlington. The jam is caused, as near as I can figure, because there's a little hill that cars crest, giving people a look at all the cars for a mile or so in front of them. The view just makes people think there's no way all these cars are moving through there quickly and, in a self-fulfilling way, everybody slows down. As proof of this, two miles later, the road bends and you lose the long front perspective; the traffic goes from twenty to fifty miles an hour. Same number of cars, but people can't see far ahead so they step on the accelerator, which is a little frightening when you think about it.

My brain's buzzing over a *slip and fall* I've got that looks like the insurance is going to settle easy. To get my mind off work, I turn on the radio. The afternoon drive time guys, Frank and Ken are actually pretty entertaining. Right now they're talking up that death penalty case that's got that woman—I forget her name—on death row, sentenced to die. I'm vaguely more familiar with this case, though obviously not well enough to know the death row inmate's name. Seems since she knocked over a pharmacy twelve years ago and tortured and killed the mom and pop proprietors, she's found Jesus (that's my vague connection) and lots of folk here in Virginia think she shouldn't get the needle.

Sarah and my church meetings have both talked about the case, and most seem to be in favor of letting the woman waste away in prison for eternity. Our church has even teamed up doing outreach for prisoners of all kinds, trying to counsel them into accepting the ways of Christ.

Probably a good place to get converts. After all, the audience is captive and they've got a lot of guilt (at least some probably do, which is why the place is called a penitentiary). The first part, about going soft on them because they've begun to walk in the path of Christ, I'm pretty dubious about. I mean, how many hardened black thugs find Islam and begin treading the path of Mohammed while in prison? I haven't checked the statistics, but I can't believe it has stopped even one of them from getting that final I.V. stuck in his arm.

Overall, I don't buy the whole pro-death penalty platform saying it deters anybody from killing someone else. Only first-degree murderers can get executed, and the definition of first degree is that you premeditated—planned—the killing. Well, who plans to get caught? If anything, I'd plan harder, so I wouldn't get the chair, but I do think that some people do things that are so horrendous—killing kids, eating people, committing mass murder—they just need to be expunged.

It's like we as a society are saying, "This isn't personal; we are not killing you to satisfy revenge or get closure." I know that if someone killed Sarah or a child we had, killing the asshole wouldn't bring them back. "We're killing you because we find your deed so vile, so reprehensible, that we've decided to simply remove you from the planet. Nothing personal, you understand, just think of your execution as the ultimate earthly eviction."

A commercial for a Jiffy Lube reminds me that my car needs an oil change every 3,000 miles. Mine's at about 10k, so I figure it's about time.

Frank and Ken are back and now they're talking about two shark attacks in the last week off the Northern California coast. This was what I was really waiting to hear. One guy was just floating, snorkeling, and a Great

White came up from below and bit him nearly in half. Guy bled out and died before they could even get him to the beach. The latest one was a young surfer who got clipped in the hand when the—same shark? nobody knows—took a chunk of his surfboard as an appetizer.

The attacks have taken place off the same beach, and Frank and Ken are asking people if they'd go into that water. A surprising number of people, at least to me, are blithely answering yes. I hear about these deaths. These horrors—shark attacks, plane crashes, getting pulled into a wood chipper—and am I the only one who wonders if these people kinda knew they were doomed? Like they kinda always had a dark cloud hanging over them, premonitions that they would leave this planet early and horribly.

I guess I want to believe I'm not special. That these people are bigger than life; they're our real movie stars. They exist as object lessons to us all, but I know that's just a smokescreen to hide my fear that one day they'll be talking about me on the news. "Yesterday a shark attack took the life of Joe Heyerdahl. He left a family of four blah, blah, blah." Or maybe my death'll be as mundane as another traffic fatality.

I'm leaving the turnpike onto the surface streets where it's just a few quick turns until I'm pulling up to my house. I'm opening the garage door and grabbing my tattered briefcase (I've had it since my last year at Laverne) and the clicker, the latter so nobody can break into my car and use it to get into the house.

In the bedroom I find Sarah in a happy mood, taking off her clothes. I know we're not in a fertile time and I'm thinking this is unexpected fun, and then she tells me that we've got a date with the Anderson's for dinner and bowling.

First off, I don't know why Sarah knocks herself out being friendly with a woman like Paula. She doesn't even like Paula. She's just too afraid to admit it, and I've always figured God hates liars more than opinionated folk. In that vein, I should say, I don't like Phil, Paula's husband. Phil tires me. He insists on bringing Jesus into almost any conversation. I tell Sarah this, but she's unmoved.

"We've made this date weeks ago, don't you remember?"

No, I don't, probably because it was weeks ago. "Hon, why do you try so hard with Paula? You don't even like her." She gives me a look that says my statement is totally absurd, but the severity of the expression tells me I'm right. "Listen, they'll still let us go to church, even if you don't bake one thousand brownies and make nice with the ladies of the Benevolent Christ Congregation." I think I've got her, but she throws me a change-up.

"Oh, and thanks for taking those extra brownies after I asked you not to—and you made me look stupid in front of Paula and Karen when I got to church."

I throw the change-up back. "See, what kind of person is Paula if you have to worry about what she thinks about some missing brownies? Hell, Sarah, you make more food than Paula and Karen combined. Let's call in sick. I've got the flu, I'm puking, head's over the toilet, head's in the toilet. You've gotta get off the phone because I'm in danger of being flushed down the toilet."

"We backed out of the last date. Don't you not remember anything? I said I had a terrible cold, even did some pathetic faking on the phone, talking all nasally and sneezing."

All this time, she, like any woman, hasn't stopped getting ready. In fact, she's managed to try on three blouses, a skirt, jeans, and a cute pearl-buttoned sweater. She stops for just a moment and gives me the look I figure parents give their kids right before the little squirts launch into a tantrum about not getting the $1.49 plastic Army Man at the grocery store. Like why are you bothering, you know I'm not changing my mind.

So I open the closet door, remove my tie, and grab some slacks and a polo shirt.

"Oh, Joe, your clothes are right here. I laid them out for you."

A glance from behind the closet door to the bed shows slacks and a shirt, ironed and ready to go. I give my wife a 'you're so thoughtful' peck and tell myself that at least the food'll be good.


The restaurant is housed in a unique building. A huge A-frame ceiling allows a large juniper tree to wend its mossy leaves to the skylight some forty feet above. Massive oak beams crisscross the interior's heights, but the restaurant's spaciousness makes the tables, the food, even the people an afterthought to the immensity of the available indoor sky.

The tables are as mundane as the schmaltzy triangular drink advertisements, the plastic football pennants reminding everyone of dollar drink Monday Night Football, and the waiters and waitresses wearing uniforms that remind me to ask about the Sizzlin' Steak Tar-Tar, or the new Cruisin' Calamari. It's like TGI Fridays was an infection that came, went, and left a scar across the American landscape.

Thankfully, we're at a booth and not in one of the middle tables, where everyone can see when Phil takes out his Bible and starts turning our dinner into a Sunday school class. I've told myself I'm not going to drink much tonight, and even before dinner I'm already putting that promise to the test.

"So, Jesus wasn't saying that man should aspire to be as God. Even the Old Testament," Phil's distrust of the 'Jewish Book' showing through, "has the Tower of Babel, which vividly displays what can happen when men start acting like God."

I nod. "I see your point, Phil." The trace of sarcasm is something only I can hear. A long time ago, I gave up trying to speak rationally to Phil about almost anything other than sports. Phil believes with a rock-hard certainty that his and the church's interpretation of Christ's words explain it all. I have my doubts, but I really can't complain. After all, I bought into this world—its simplicity, its respect for tradition—because for a long time I had drunk from the cup of decadence, and while I often experienced highs of all kinds physical, at the end of the day I felt no closer, and sometimes further from, understanding my true reason for being here. I guess in retrospect it's not that I thought a revival of my religious interest would supply the answers, but that at least I'd have some quiet in which to reflect.

Phil's talk continues, veering into the more practical issues of the media, homosexuality, and the ACLU, all of which Phil has less than Christian love for. Paula, Phil's best student, chirps in with words of agreement and illumination.

Sarah listens intently, nodding her head, offering her agreement, though less judgmentally. The irony here is that Christ, this religion, is what brought us together, and now is something we never speak of. Sure, I go to church on Sunday, and I make it out for the occasional charity event, but more often than not our comments about religion are confined to a few perfunctory pieces of chitchat when we're in the car after Services.

The guacamole arrives, and it's the sweet kind I like. So now I'm torn between hoping Phil shuts up and hoping he keeps talking, allowing me to eat more guac. Phil continues to chew my ear while, unfortunately, scooping great gobs of guacamole onto his chips. I realize that if my wife fell in love with me because of my fallen past, just as surely I fell in love with her because of her lofty past. The naive angel come to save the botched devil.

During my introspection and failed attempts to keep up with Phil in the guac-scooping competition, the conversation has come around to the death penalty, and Phil has just laid down 'The Law' that says killing is wrong, whatever the reason. However, he doesn't seem too happy about it as he goes on to mention the perverts, the rapists, and the murderers he hopes will receive eternal damnation for their transgressions.

Paula, in a break from the Canon of Phil, takes up the position that some people don't deserve to grace God's good Earth. I'm startled to actually agree with something Paula has to say; however, I don't let this newfound agreement get in the way of wolfing down the last guacamole or ordering another beer from the fifty-year-old waitress with the silly suspenders and buttons.

Sarah, always the sappier, agrees with Phil, but stresses rather passionately forgiveness and rehabilitation of sinners. Phil snorts at this like he's a pig in a trough, which, looking at the way he's eating, isn't that much of a metaphor. Never one to miss a chance to jab, Paula cracks wise, mentioning how Sarah's work with the ill, the homeless, and the incarcerated has made her too soft, and that if she had kids she'd know what true loss could be, and then you bet she wouldn't be arguing for clemency for every bum who's scheduled to die.

As if on cue, everyone looks at me. I can see with my husband radar that my wife's hurt expression would make agreeing with Paula, something Sarah usually is for, not the wisest course of action. I'm saved by the arrival of the food, and by the time it's all settled, and everyone's dug in and has eaten enough to where they decide to take a breath before stuffing another piece of steak, chicken, or fish down their throats, I mention sports, and Phil and I are off into the religious and political discussion free zone of sports. Which, in my opinion, are two of the great things sports has going for it. Is conservation better than meeting energy demands? Is it Pro-Choice or Pro-Life? How about Guns vs. Anti-Guns? Or maybe the Death Penalty versus Life Imprisonment? Hey, let's all just put them out on the field and see who scores the most touchdowns.

The dessert tray rolls up nice and easy, like a cop cruiser knowing it's gonna have to make some arrests. Phil's ordering for all of us, even though I try to tell him I don't like restaurant cake. My mother used to make me store-bought Duncan Hines, with the plastic tubbed white icing. Ever since, other cakes have paled in comparison.

Phil hears me out and says, "Nonsense," and orders for me anyway.

That's Phil in a nutshell. State a fact—*I don't like this cake*—and he tells you, *nonsense*. He is so used to overriding people's opinions in church that he's lost the ability to discern between the Gospels and someone's desire not to have dessert. Since I'm going to be having a piece of chocolate cake that will be too rich in the cake and too sour in the frosting, I order a Bailey's coffee to smooth them both out. I remind myself about my drinking promise, only half a night to go, and how bad can bowling be?

One giant meal of steak and prawns and potatoes and, of course, the guacamole appetizer, and I'm feeling my pants cut into my waistline, reminding me I've got to stop eating like this.

At the bowling alley, I'm wearing the two-tone clown shoes and listening to Phil rhapsodize about all things Christian. I feel overripe, and every time I see Phil's butt in his light blue leisure slacks I feel a little nauseous.

I want to be reclining in front of the TV, and gawd, I admit it, I want to undo the top button of my pants.

Phil's busy detailing his kids' 'Bowling for Jesus' program and their slogan: Can you SPARE the money for a STRIKE against Satan? He's pleased with himself, so I smile and toss my head to the side a bit, like it's really very funny.

Phil's up to bowl—another wide view of his butt. I tried taking over the scorer's job to avoid such a view, but the damn scoring is automated now. As if bowling was a real jeopardy-like challenge before. Now you can drink all you want and don't even have to worry about keeping score or losing that little pencil that seemed to exist only for bowling—though I guess that's gone now—and mini-golf.

Phil's backside shakes as he makes his approach. Really, I'm not staring at Phil's butt. I'm not gay, and if I was, Phil's fifty pounds overweight, and got a thin blonde mustache with a puffy face that gives his eyes that beady untrustworthy look. But Phil's winning by a bunch, so maybe my description is tainted and I'm just a sore loser.

Phil strikes, finishing in that famous Earl Anthony pose that looks stupid everywhere but in the bowling alley, or in the pool if you're a synchronized swimmer.

"I love this sport," Phil croons.

"Phil, buddy, I'm not sure bowling's a sport. I mean, I believe anything you can do while drinking beer is not a sport. They're games. Bowling, croquet, even softball." I once played in a college softball league where a beer cooler was situated at second base. Anyone making it that far was required to drink a whole beer before proceeding. It actually evened things out. A team would get ahead, get drunk and allow the other team to catch up. The dean canceled the games after about the sixth fight and one naked base runner. "Hockey, football, boxing, and basketball are sports."

"Well, I don't drink beer, Joe. If it wasn't on the Lord's Table, then it's not right for me." I'm saved from responding because it's my turn, and what d'ya say to that? Maybe God's a picky eater, or I'm pretty sure the Lord didn't eat ice cream sundaes, Phil, but that didn't stop you from wolfing one down for dessert. But then again, Phil's almost doubled my score, so maybe I'm just bitter.

I'm up to the ball carousel just as Phil's ball comes out, knocking into Paula's pink neon monstrosity. Phil's ball, on the other hand, is imprinted with the shining face of Jesus, who's motioning to go forth and spread his Word, but in this place the Jesus logo's giving me the impression He just wants me to knock the crap out of the pins.

Sarah and I, on the other hand, are using house balls and borrowed shoes. Sarah's yelling encouragement, because that's what Paula does for Phil.

Honestly, I'd love to beat Phil for just the reason that it would make Sarah feel good. I get the idea that she feels inferior to Paula in just about every aspect of our lives, and obviously a husband who can't bowl is a small thing, but it's bigger when everything seems to be a positive on the other person's ledger.

I'm moving, and I fire the ball hard, no spin, though a little off center. I'm awarded with the removal of the three pins on the far left. I'm definitely not good, but at least I throw a hard ball.

Thankfully, Phil doesn't get up this time and start instructing me right out on the lane, trying to hold my hand, showing me the right wrist flip, it's all too latently homosexual for me. Not that any self-respecting gay man would be seen wearing these shoes or the multi-colored block letter shirts that are in evidence just a few lanes down on the crew of Morty's Bait and Tackle Emporium. Is it actually possible to make money selling bait these days?

My ball comes spinning back up and I hurry to catch it before it slams into the Jesus face logo on Phil's ball. There seems to be a limit to my heresies, after all.

I throw another ball, and while this attempt is well centered, I get no pin action; after the crash, two pins are left standing. I slouch back to my seat, trying to ignore Phil and the rolling wrist motion he's making. Besides, he's got one of those stupid guards on his wrist that makes me think he's got carpal tunnel syndrome or that he thinks he's Michael Jackson.

I'm cheered by the fact that the night is nearly over and I haven't done anything to embarrass Sarah. The fact that I'm sitting here sipping what is only my fourth beer of the night probably has something to do with it.

Paula's up now, using her chance to bowl as one more opportunity to put herself in the limelight. She walks down the lane like she thinks she's a model on the catwalk. That's also probably why she delivers the ball nearly directly into the gutter. (I'm sure none of those Victoria Secret girls can bowl as well.) "I told you we should've played with the bumpers," I shout encouragingly. "I mean, wouldn't it make it a lot more interesting? Say you had one pin up and called a two-bank shot, like in pool, you could get extra points if you made it."

Sarah's smiling. Paula's looking like she does when I say almost anything—puzzled—and Phil's glowering at me like I just said that the designated hitter and Astroturf were good things for baseball.

I move over to my wife and give her a kiss and a hug. She's the only one who's real in this waxed wood wonderland and I suddenly want her to know it.

Paula throws her second ball and Phil takes two tosses to knock all his pins down. It's my turn again, but I'm still snuggling with my wife (before I finish a six-pack I usually go through this overly amorous phase). When

Sarah quizzes me on it later, I always say I'm a man, and since I'm uncomfortable displaying intimacy, the alcohol allows me to get in touch and display those feeling without my machismo getting in the way. Like a lot of what I say, it's bullshit with the smell of truth, or it's the truth with the smell of bullshit.

Noises from Paula get me over to the ball merry-go-round and I look back at Sarah and she's glowing, really happy, and it reminds me of how I haven't seen her happy lately, and how precious that smile is to me. For a moment, I wonder if her sadness lately comes from me—my tiredness, my inattention—or maybe I'm just imagining the whole thing.

Phil's telling me to throw the ball and Paula's glancing at Sarah with something that seems like muted alcohol derived envy. "This one's for my beautiful bride," I shout loud enough for the guys from Morty's to hear.

I turn about, try to summon my kai, or the spirit of Obi Wan Kenobi, and stride purposefully toward the line. The ball sails free, running down the lane, smashing into the head pin just off center. Like God parting the Red Sea, the pins dissolve into the pitch black of the tarp backing.

Like they say on ESPN, "Ninety percent of life is being clutch," and as I see my wife's eyes, shining at me, for me, I just wish she'd remember that being happy is the best revenge of all.

# EIGHT

The phone in Sarah's purse starts playing 'Oklahoma' right in the middle of her attempts to pour the superheated jello into the molds. She sets the pitcher down and runs over, grabbing her purse, digging for a phone that, despite its cheery tune, is small enough to get lost in someone's pocket.

"Hello, hello," Sarah's trying to get the phone's earpiece directly opposite her ear.

"Mrs. McClure?"

"Yes?"

"This is Mindy from Dr. Mecklenburg's office. The doctor needs you to come in to go over some of the results with her."

A huge anvil seems to drop into Sarah's insides, and its passage leaves a shaky, empty hole that immediately begins to fill with a thick, runny type of despair, carrying Sarah's thought speeding, almost screaming ahead. Why would she be calling unless there was bad news? "Uhh, why? I mean sure."

"Can your husband come with you?"

"No," she says, remembering her previous lie, "that murder case is still going on."

"Okay. Do you have time tomorrow?"

"Umm, what time?" Sarah's trying to stay cool, but her voice comes out cracked and strained. *Why do I care if some receptionist hears me start to*

82

*break down? She's probably heard this kind of thing dozens of times.* "Morning, after ten," she adds hurriedly. Sometimes Joe has too many drinks on the couch and doesn't get off to work until late.

"Ten-thirty okay?"

"Sure, ten-thirty. What is this about, exactly?"—Sarah, trying to sound nonchalant, like the woman's going to start discussing her choice of HMOs.

"I really don't know, Mrs. McClure. Dr. Mecklenburg told me to call you for an appointment. So then we'll see you tomorrow morning at ten-thirty."

Sarah barely forces out a yes when the phone clicks off.

She tries to push the disconnect, but the button's so small, and her hand has begun to shake. Finally, she crashes her thumb onto the entire key pad. There's a medley of beeps and tones and the phone shuts down.

Sarah's breathing is coming quicker and quicker, getting ahead of her. She's beginning to hyperventilate. She starts walking about the house, not straightening things, which is one of the drawbacks of having a nearly spotless house in the first place. Her mind, too, is moving—moving fast.

*Why does she need to see me? Why change my next appointment? Maybe she's got to go out of town.* Sarah quickly sees the problem with that line of reasoning. *But surely the receptionist would've known that when I asked. She might not have told the receptionist she was traveling, but she'd have to have said something because then all the appointments would have to be changed.* Sarah remembered that her own ob/gyn had canceled appointments before and the receptionist had always been forthcoming in telling Sarah that the doctor had been called away for a delivery. A simple "the doctor decided to go to that convention" would be enough.

Sarah walks through the bedroom, stops to straighten a picture that didn't need straightening, paces the room off three times and heads for the kitchen.

One of the chairs at the table is pulled out, and Sarah briefly considers sitting down, but something about the notion of not moving frightens her. Sarah opens the sliding glass doors and heads for the backyard and her garden.

The call kept replaying itself in Sarah's mind, and no matter how fast she walks, or how busy she tries to prune and pick at her plants, she can't stop her memory's tape of the conversation from spooling out in her head, her mind offering more and more implausible interpretations in avoidance of the single, more obvious conclusion. A part of her witnesses all this, sees herself being wound tighter and tighter, caught in a frantic loop, whimpering like a little girl or a trapped animal. This endless series of fright was all that life could offer her; so overwhelming was her fear that Sarah seemed unable to see past this moment.

Sports stars often talk about being in the *zone,* where the world seems to stop, the crowd, even the opponent, seems scarcely to exist. Sarah was in a similar place, the world shut out, completely in the moment, but her zone was one of nightmare.

Sarah began to berate herself for not telling—no demanding—that the doctor call her immediately. She still could, she realized. She could call back and say she'd forgotten all about the appointment she had tomorrow. That made sense. After all, the receptionist had called her out of the blue. How was she to remember exactly what her plans were going to be?

No wait, it'd have to be some kind of trip. Otherwise, the office would just want to schedule it later or the next day. But if it was a trip, Sarah could demand that the doctor talk to her now, because how was she supposed to go off to Hawaii and enjoy herself with this thing hanging over her head? She remembered the doctor saying not to worry until the tests came back. Well, at least she was doing what the doctor ordered, Sarah thought grimly.

The rhododendrons needed pruning. This was the first breakthrough thought Sarah had that was not centered on her cascading anxiety. Sarah made it to the small shed where she kept the gardening equipment when she found her legs weak and her mind like iron pulled by an impossibly strong magnet, back, clamped against the phone call and its implication—she was infertile.

Sarah knew it wasn't the end of the world. She could adopt, maybe even using her eggs and Joe's sperm, but she knew in some profound way it wouldn't be the same. It'd be a universe away from being the same, her inner voice rising, shouting at and to the little voices, to herself, and most of all to God. And how would they afford adoption, or the outlandish fertility measures people had to pay for, and in the end she might have a child, but she'd be like some rich woman who goes into one of those expensive shops that sells only one of a kind clothing, ordering what she wanted, walking about the mall, spending her time shopping, only to return with her dress neatly folded and packaged, delivered to her with the minimum of mess, fuss, hard work or love.

You are overreacting, Sarah McClure, another voiced warned (even after hundreds of doodles of her married name, Sarah had not internalized it). All you know is the doctor wants to see you. Her schedule might have changed; she might want to hurry the process along because things look surprisingly okay.

Sarah didn't buy this last thought, and the sour taste it left in her mouth only made her feel worse. Regardless of how strong the negatives were, a weak positive possibility just made the negative that much more plausible.

Perhaps someone else might have greater needs than me, Sarah thought, and in the spirit of confidentiality the doctor can't just up and shout them out to every neurotic housewife who thinks she needs to know.

What could she do? The thought of calling and lying seemed ineffective, and she honestly doubted she'd have the presence of mind to remove the shaking from her voice or improvise answers to the receptionist's questions.

How stupid she'd look, Sarah thought. A poor, infertile women calling back, trying to fork over some lame excuse while her voice trembled. She was like some cancer patient who dodged the doctor's call, thinking that if she never knew she was dying, she wouldn't die. The ultimate engagement of out of sight out of mind, Sarah thought darkly.

Her thinking was becoming exhausted by the frantic pitch it had been running. She tried to slow it down, but like a tongue that can't stop poking and prodding a trapped piece of food caught between its teeth, Sarah continued to return to the conversation. The reality of which was rapidly dwindling under the onslaught of Sarah's pressured analysis of every word, inflection, and pause.

She left the garden, went inside and walked back into the living room, talking to herself, making point and counterpoint. All the while, the cat looked on, studying Sarah and her atypical behavior, wondering if this might affect its feeding schedule.

Sarah grabbed the cat and tossed it into her lap. Only after she had petted it for five minutes did the cat begin to purr and forgive her for the rough handling. The cat stared, and for a moment Sarah felt as if its eyes were the eyes of the world: cold, uncaring, utterly indifferent to the mental anguish she endured. While everyone ate, and loved, and watched TV, Sarah was locked in her head, unable to free herself from this cycle of runaway fear.

Sarah considered going back outside, into the tool shed, and doing something unthinkable; however, though still wholly lost in dismay, she had gained enough perspective to know that she had to find out, and not do anything drastic, until the doctor's visit. In what, a day? No twelve hours, actually closer to fifteen, Sarah quickly figured, as the darkness of the approaching night stretched out before her. She felt deathly tired, but she knew she wouldn't get more than a few minutes of sleep this night.

She shooed the cat from her lap. It went without a backward glance, and Sarah was up trying to manufacture the manic energy she had had only a half hour ago from what was now a quickly developing depressive stupor.

Back in the kitchen, she remembered her jello mold. She saw the now hardened cherry jello sitting in the pitcher, thought of trying to get a knife and sliding the jello out where she could cut it into little shapes, but something inside her didn't like knives. Besides, Sarah knew enough about the fragility of jello to know she'd just end up with a lot of broken pieces.

Oh well, Sarah thought, who cares if the jello's not smooth. Most of the people Sarah visited were old and dying, they had more on their minds than the wholeness of their jello. Sarah carefully gathered up a spoon and went to work, dishing irregular pieces of jello into the ranks of Dixie cups.

# NINE

"Help me with this, guys. I'm making my rating system for the ultimate manly sport index." Me, Stan, and the new guy, who's talking right now, are knocking back some Johnny Walker and a variety of ales at the bar. The new guy's one of those shiny, happy people Michael Stipe was talking about in that REM song. He just wants to be liked. He's fat, he sells something, and he's got a clot of blond-red hair that makes him anywhere between 35 to 45. Right now, he's telling us about his passion—obsession?—which is to be on Charlie Verona's Sports talk show.

"The Ultimate Manly Sport Index. Not the best sport, you understand, just the most manly," he clarifies.

FYI, Charlie Verona's the host of the most popular sport talk show in America. He likes to say things like melon, when he means head; crib, when he means home; smack, when someone's criticizing another. He annoys me. He's one of those little white guys who probably can't make a left-handed lay-up and never played sports past running around outside his house at the age of ten, imagining he was Emmet Smith. But Floyd here can't think past making it live on the air with the Verona. Oh, he says he was named after the rock group, which I think puts him closer to 45 and makes him lucky he wasn't a girl because his name would've been Pink. Oh yeah, and Charlie

Verona's studio is the Jungle. I think Jim wishes he could go to sleep one night and wake up a black man, but that's just my opinion.

Right now, Verona's on the bar TV doing his show on Fire bit (too bad it's not really burning). Andy Warhol said that in the future everyone will be famous for fifteen minutes. He was understating things. I think in the future everyone will have their own TV show.

Verona's talking, "We're here with my guests Bill Walton and Merl, the Bobcat, Jones. First off, gentlemen, let's discuss this story in New Jersey where the second—the second!—professional athlete, my boy Alton James, in as many years, has been ordered to pay child support after this reject from the trailer park, Aneesha Parkins, admitted—admitted mind you—she'd lured Alton back to her crib for a little naked three pointers so that she could get herself pregnant. However, seems at least one guy's keeping his head up outside the free throw lines—Alton wore a Jimmy. So Aneesha up and snatches the used prophylactic and heads for the bathroom, where she turns it inside out and plugs it back in. Somebody needs to tell this mama there is no returnable deposit on rubbers. I mean Return to Sender only applies to Elvis Presley songs. What of it, Bill—the maestro of the hardwood—Walton...?"

The night stretches on a tad, as do the beer and bravado, and I end up getting home a tad too late.


"Get up! You've got to go to work." God that's loud. Sarah's voice cuts cut through my hazy dream of dinner tables and cartoon animals. "It's eight thirty; you need to get up!"

"Give me a break. I just made four months of bills with that case yesterday."

"That doesn't mean you get to miss work today."

I pull into myself like a turtle into its shell, or more honestly, a seriously hungover turtle.

Whip, whip, my pillow's gone, I reach to grab its twin, but Sarah's quicker than me in my sleepy-eyed, cotton-headed state. I'm left in my boxers and an old T-shirt that reads *Don't tell anyone, but I'm Elvis.* I'd like to just fall back into my semi-daze, thereby avoiding the congestion in my head, the pressure behind my eyes, and the roiling of my stomach, but for some reason it's hard to sleep on a bed with no blankets or pillows.

There's a terrifying wail and I'm instantly in the upright position. Sarah's running the vacuum on the hallway right outside the room.

"Oh good, you're up," she says, as if that's her invitation to start vacuuming the bedroom.

Like a kid playing chase with the tide, I run, stumble, into the living room. I plop down on the sofa, curling around the throw pillows, trying to find a calm place in this house of pain and noise.

Sarah and the vacuum enter the living room; like the Terminator, they are relentless. "Go take a shower, Joe. You'll feel better."

Beaten, cowed, and knowing she's right, I trace a path around the screaming dirt sucker into the bathroom. I relieve myself. My piss is white, which is a clear sign that the alcohol's drying me out and I'm pissing straight water. The shower's great and makes me feel like the day is not so bright and everything is not so loud. I spend the better part of ten minutes standing in a position that allows the hot water to run down all four sides of me.

The shower door opens, and Sarah's reaching by me, turning off the water. I'm too surprised, or maybe my reflexes are still drowning in all those Black and Tans. Nevertheless, she turns the hot off first, and I'm greeted with a blast of mind-numbing cold that reminds me why no one took showers a hundred years ago, and why perfume sprang into existence.

"What's with you, for Chrissakes!" Taking God's name in vain is a sure-fire way of showing Sarah how pissed I am at her, but she doesn't even pause to reprimand me.

"I need to do the dishes, and you're using all the hot water. Your clothes are laid out, and I know you only want some toast and juice to get through your hangover."

The dismissive everyday way she says all this takes me up, stopping any smart-ass comment I was about to make. Her tone, her body language, they remind me of something about my father and how I knew with certainty that a thrown ball will fall to Earth that he would not be home Friday until long after I was asleep. I remember walking home, knowing my Mom and I would get to watch movies, and that she'd make me cocoa. The sunniness of that memory almost obliterates the reason I remembered. My Mom had the same look over my father's drinking escapades as I just got from Sarah.

Dressed. I'm in the kitchen drinking my orange juice and eating lightly jellied toast. After a moment or two of mumbling, my stomach decides to accept this offering without offering me something back in return. The orange juice always tastes good. As I chug the glass, I can almost feel the liquid running down into my gut, refreshing as it goes. One of the reasons I never drink screwdrivers is I know that I'd lose this feeling if I got myself drunk on them. The hair of the dog definitely does not work for me.

"What's with you this morning? I just made ten grand, and you're hustling me out of the house like I'm selling vacuums. Which, by the way, was a very nice touch."

"I have things to do today. I've got to be at church at ten to help with Saturday's raffle."

"Well, just go and leave me here—Jeez."

Sarah's way too high strung today. I can tell from her expression that she hadn't even thought of that. As if I don't exist in the house unless Sarah's here to tend and fend for me.

Driving was mildly therapeutic, Sarah thought. She had spent the night agonizing over the upcoming appointment. Unable to sleep, she thought she might go out of her mind with nothing to do but think of the possible bad news she'd have to face.

She realized two things had been lifesavers: one was her insight that the lab results could easily have been tainted, mixed up, or destroyed. After all, results were messed up all the time. Sarah watched *Court TV* and attorneys were always proving the labs had lost things, even switched samples. And why would the doctor feel the need to shout that info to a lowly secretary? A woman who wasn't even a nurse couldn't be expected to understand these kinds of complexities and pass them on to anxious mothers-to-be. The second saving grace had been the television in all its mundane glory and its sedating effect, casting her for a while into the twilight world of semi-consciousness.

She had been completely asleep when Joe arrived home. Awakening from the noise, she had turned off the TV and hurried into the bedroom, not wanting Joe to note the rarity of finding her asleep on the sofa. Not that he'd be sober enough to notice, she thought regretfully.

Unlike other nights, Sarah had been wide-awake when Joe stumbled into the house, made his way to the fridge and pulled a beer from it. All of this Sarah only heard: the whirring of the refrigerator, the knocking around of its contents, Joe's belching, all painting a picture that, Sarah, already weighed down, didn't want to imagine.

As she drove back to the clinic, the small act of remembering the directions detracted from the dark funk she felt upon awakening this morning. Her fears about the visit came rushing back, almost stronger than before, threatening, like the tide, or some angry ant army, to overrun her.

Off the expressway, onto surface roads, Sarah navigated her way across town, happy that her mind wasn't so shot she couldn't remember how to get to the clinic, and slightly disappointed that she could. She could've seen herself unable to find the clinic, going home, calling the doctor's office, regretfully apologizing for getting lost, and then saying how unfortunate it was that she was leaving for Bermuda tomorrow and the appointment would have to wait.

She could still do that, she knew. She could turn around and go home, talk quickly to the doctor's office and simply not answer the cell phone when the doctor's number rang. It wouldn't be hard; the phone showed her what number was calling. Oh, but what if the doctor tried to reach her on a number other than the clinic's. Well, Sarah could simply not answer the phone unless she recognized the number. Or better yet, she could tell Joe the phone was bad, getting a lot of wrong numbers, and insist on getting a new one. Make sure there's no forwarding number, and voila, no way for the clinic to track her down.

Sarah's SUV sat in the clinic's parking lot. The idea had appeared whole in the instant before she was readying to leave the car. She could do it, run away. They wouldn't be able to track her down and she could go back to the ovulation tests, and the monthly lovemaking ritual with Joe, the contortions after sex, and things would go back to normal.

She cursed her stupidity for not thinking of this earlier, when she was safe at home and needed to do nearly nothing to put the plan into effect. Her anxiety had even made her not realize that she didn't need to rush Joe to work, and thus look suspicious, but instead she could've just left him at home on the excuse she had church work to do. Joe was purposefully as ignorant as he could be over her church duties, and he was so hungover, she probably could've let him sleep and been back before he had made it past the couch.

Yes, definitely, Sarah could see her mind was not working well.

The one thing that kept Sarah seated, the car not turned on, the wheel not turning to reverse the car out of the lot, was fear. The fear that this not knowing would hound her, hound her until it had taken over all of her thoughts and dreams. That would be hell on Earth, one that Sarah felt was, if only marginally, worse than facing the truth. At least if she went in, she would be acting bravely, courageously, facing her fear. In her mind she hoped that God was watching and that He looked favorably on her act, as she pulled the keys free, stepped from the car and walked toward the clinic.

She suppressed a sigh when the elevator arrived and it was empty. Superstitiously, Sarah had told herself that the old couple from the previous visit was a good omen, and sneakily she had reasoned if there were children in the elevator that would be the best omen of all. But the empty elevator seemed to foretell a different fate, and with a whiff of, "Well, of course there aren't children here, it's a school day, and people who needed the clinic wouldn't need it if they already had children." "Yes," another voice countered. "But that's what would've made the omen so powerful." By the time Sarah exited the elevator, these thoughts were all but forgotten.

Arriving in the waiting area and checking in, Sarah half expects the receptionist to show some sign of sympathy, an encouraging hand and empathic glance, or at least a downturn of eye. However, she receives nothing but a nod of acknowledgment and "It'll be just a few minutes." This mundane greeting briefly rekindles her hope that she isn't waiting to hear bad news.

Now seated, Sarah notices four women sitting in the waiting room, and with a kind of indignation feels like they're intruding on her private misfortune. None branded as the cancer sufferer from her last visit, which wouldn't have been half-bad, Sarah realized. Might give me some perspective on things, she thought.

One, a frumpy woman in her fifties, sits busily digging through her purse, displaying its contents on the coffee table for anyone to see. Finding her lipstick and pocket mirror, the woman begins the task of repacking the bag before applying her cosmetics. The second women is young, wears hip-hugger jeans, a thick leather belt out of the seventies, and has her upper half buried behind an out-of-date *Ladies Home Journal.*

Much to Sarah's annoyance, the other two women obviously know one another and keep up a running commentary on their lives, the soap opera *The Young and the Restless* (or as Sarah likes to call the show, The Young and the Senseless) and Kelly and Michael, even getting into a heated discussion over whether Michael Strahan is superior to Kathy Lee. The two women were never able to reach a consensus on more than that Kathie Lee was a better singer, since Michael didn't sing at all. Being an MVP defensive end doesn't count for much with these ladies. The younger blonde, whom Sarah noticed at the last minute sports braces on her teeth, is summoned, disappearing behind the salmon-colored office door.

Through this weighty discourse, Sarah remains locked in a state of numbing agitation, her thoughts flying pell-mell about her head. Her mood fluctuates—one minute full of hope, the next veering into despair. She had been unable to eat, and her stomach protested, as it had since she'd received the phone call, which seemed like a hundred years ago.

The glass partition slides open and Sarah's name is called. Sarah makes a great fuss of gathering her purse and returning the *McCall's* magazine she had pretended to read to its place on the coffee table. Her deliberations as serious as someone who, after sitting aboard a plane flight for fourteen hours, carefully unbends and begins to dismantle the nest they've built.

Inside the white-painted, plant-decorated hall, Sarah follows the receptionist, but not to the examination rooms, but farther into the office's belly toward the doctor's suite. As Sarah walks forward, each step increases her fear and makes her legs feel like rubber.

Dr. Mecklenburg's office is a clutter. Piles of books stand in ranks along the floor and a corkboard sits behind her chair with photos of a happy family. For a moment, a zany thought has Sarah thinking of the hair weave guy. 'I'm not just the Hair Club president, I'm also a client.'

The doctor looks up from a sheaf of papers. She's wearing reading glasses that make her look older, and when she removes them, gesturing for Sarah to take the seat opposite her chair, the glasses leave the telltale red marks on opposite sides of her nose. For some reason, Sarah's mind zeros in on these little slashes of chicken feet.

"Mrs. McClure, I still haven't got all of your results, but there are two readings that are not good news. Definitely not good news." She says the last with a bouncing bobbing head that stops its up and down motion on the last word "news."

"The smears we took from your uterus reveal you have some spermicidal toxicity. But more seriously, very rare actually, an excessive mucusoid base. Essentially, your uterine lining is over lubricated, slippery. It would make it nearly impossible for a fertilized egg to implant successfully."

"Can I take something to change it?" Sarah thought she had been prepared for the reality of infertility. For the last day, and really for months, she had imagined little else. The merry-go-round of fear had lulled itself into the background from sheer mental exhaustion.

She'd expected bad eggs, a lazy ovary, a collapsed fallopian tube; not her body chemistry. It was a worse rebellion. It wasn't that a piece of her body was broken. It was that—what was the word the doctor used?—she was toxic. With the first strong flash of guilt, Sarah understood that she was, had been, poisoning her babies.

Sarah's mouth is pursed, her eyes are open, she's listening to what comes next about her condition, but it's like she's in an empty train car. Light shimmering through the slats in odd random ways, moving fast, making it hard to stand, the train roaring, clattering, her mind on rails to nowhere.

The doctor is still speaking, had been speaking, talking about options—possible dietary changes, adoption, in-vitro, surrogate mothers—but for Sarah, who firmly believes life begins at conception, the news is a hammer blow aimed directly at an already crumbling mind. How many infants had her body killed, she wondered, quivering.

Had she broken down, been unable to function in those next few moments, Joe would have had to have been called, and all of Sarah's secrets would have come out, averting what was to follow. But Sarah didn't cry.

The enormity of her 'crime,' the killing of the absolute innocent—for that was how Sarah's over-revved mind saw the biochemical poison of her uterus—precluded an emotional response. It was too big, just too big. She felt not so much hollow, but that she existed only on the surface of herself. Like if you looked at the Earth from space, and you noticed that life existed on only the thinnest cream of the planet. So it was with Sarah and her empty core, a buzzing mind bouncing off her insides, with her weakening physical sensations the only reminder she still lived.

On automatic, Sarah listened to the doctor's prognosis and tried to nod in the right places and look significantly hopeful and sad when the doctor's tone rose or fell.

Sarah was not the best actress, and most doctors might have noticed Sarah's glassy-eyed demeanor as something similar to long-term battle fatigue and directed her to a psychiatrist, Dr. Mecklenburg among them. But the doctor's newer glasses had been broken a day ago, and she was now using a two-year-old pair that hadn't kept up with the doctor's deteriorating eyesight. Doctor Mecklenburg was encouraged by Sarah's bittersweet, but hopeful, response to investigating other avenues and made an appointment to see her in a week. Sarah eagerly agreed and left with a shake of Doctor Mecklenburg's hand.

Sarah drove home without incident, owing more to luck and the emptiness of the midday roads. She fell onto the bed, pulled the covers around her still-clothed form and began to weep huge, body-shaking tears. Tears that lasted while thoughts rolled, engulfing her, a tide that seemed that it would never go out, never leave her dry. She should know what to do, Sarah thought. After all, she had known this would happen.

A hundred thoughts, plans, curses and prayers bounced ceaselessly through Sarah's mind, until the thankfulness of mental oblivion cast its net around her. As sleep took her for a time, she could only think that she'd been right about her infertility, and that she should be right about what course she should plot next.

By the next morning, Sarah, with a courage born of utter fear over telling Joe about her string of lies, put on her mask and went about her household duties with a strained air of normalcy. She did this while her insides felt like a thousand shards of glass screaming against one another, following her everywhere she went.

# TEN

The light on the answering machine's pulsing and it's making that damn blink, blink sound. One day I spent two hours reading the manual, trying to disengage that sound because it kept ruining my midday naps. Every thirty seconds it was like some gawd awful giant water droplet hitting a tin roof. Obviously, I wasn't successful. On top of that, I don't know how to erase my messages, so the machine tells me that I now have two new messages and 112 saved ones. I'm ready with a black felt-tip because if I don't get them right away, I'd have to wade through the other 112.

I hit the message button. There's one from an old client wondering if she received her entire check. No, Mrs. Stipple, Allstate Insurance is going to show up at your door and start handing you cash out of a Brinks truck after you've already settled. When I hit the skip button, she's still chronicling her new aches and pains that she's sure will re-open the case.

The second message gets interesting right away.

"Hello, Mr. Heyerdahl. This is the District Attorney's office on Tuesday the 17th. We need to hear from you immediately, today. It's a matter of some urgency. You can reach D.A. Metcalfe's office at…"

The black felt tip is scrawling down the number while part of me wants to ignore the message. I've never appreciated the D.A.'s office's arrogance and condescension toward P.D.s or me personally, and my less than stellar education, but I'm just too curious.

"Joe Heyerdahl, returning a call from D.A. Metcalfe's office."

A gravelly-voiced secretary tells me to wait a moment. For once, someone isn't exaggerating about that 'moment' and comes right back. "Mr. Heyerdahl, it's urgent that the D.A.'s office sees you. Can you come in later today?"

"Today? What's this about?"

"I really don't know, Sir. It's just been passed through to me that this office needs to see you today, at whatever time is convenient for you."

I could be contrary and say I'm too busy, but I'm wondering what I've done to rate such quick action. The case against Bedell couldn't have stirred them up this much. Maybe some problem with the trial judge. Judge Westin is old, but letting the jury visit the dog wasn't that unusual. They aren't going to appeal the thing after we made a deal, are they? Maybe public pressure from all those anti-drug goofballs is making the D.A. change his tune.

"Mr. Heyerdahl is three-thirty a good time for you?"

"Sure," I say, readying to go to war. "I'll be there at three-thirty."

I'm in the gleaming office center that houses the D.A, but in a different waiting area with chintzy furniture and defense attorneys who sit tabulating their billable hours, looking like they could use the money to buy new suits.

The front desk fellow with a Mickey Mouse tie (and grin to match) greets me and takes my name. Before I can find a seat and nestle down with a copy of Virginia Law Review, he's calling me back.

"Mr. Heyerdahl, you're supposed to be upstairs, meeting with Deputy-Chief Shriner. "

I turn back with faked nonchalance, like a gunfighter who has just been called out by a particularly well known and feared gunslinger. "That would be where?"

"Tenth floor."

"Where on the tenth?"

The man who loves the Magic Kingdom smiles at my naiveté. "It's hard to miss, pretty much the whole tenth floor."

I nod, do an about face and head for ten. I notice several of the waiting attorneys giving me the once over, no doubt wondering why the guy in the second-hand Brooks Brother's suit rates a meeting with the Deputy-Chief.

I'm about to puff out my chest and look self-important when I realize they may be right—who the hell am I to be meeting with the city's top brass?

I board the elevator, trying to remember as much as I can about the guy I'm about to meet. A. Malcolm Shriner is the hard-nosed, hard-driving deputy shark for the D.A., and some say future Governor, Warren Metcalfe. Shriner is short, fortyish, with a bullet head and Pat Riley hair. A. Malcolm—the A stands for Arthur, but many of the attorneys he's bested think Asshole is a more accurate tag—made his reputation, oddly enough, in the Department of Justice, busting organized crime outfits along the Eastern seaboard. It was there that Malcolm took his parents "old money" and began primping and preening himself toward much greater things.

Finally, after several high profile arrests, he came to the attention of a similar hard-charging young up-comer in the Virginia D.A.'s office, Warren Metcalfe.

Quitting the D.O.J., Shriner signed on for a string of major stings involving government corruption in contract awards, jury tampering, and one celebrated case of hospital malfeasance that resulted in four deaths.

Known as Superman and Batman because Metcalfe, like the Man of Steel, could fly above the fray, while Shriner, like the Caped Crusader favored the down and dirty streets. Together, they made an excellent team.

Last year their stock rose even further when Metcalfe won the conviction of John Martin, professed lover of the symphony, the ballet, and haute cuisine; a man who also took pleasure in the wholesale slaughter of the young women he killed after using his cousin's policeman's uniform and badge to infiltrate their homes.

Martin carried on his impersonations and desecrations for eight years, a precise man who never killed more than two women a year and who seemingly never took trophies of his victims. With no physical evidence linking Martin to the crime, the prosecution's case was tenuous. That is, until A. Malcolm Shriner figured out that dainty Mr. Martin actually *had* taken trophies, but trophies so mundane they had slipped by the police. From Gloria Deluxia, whom he sodomized and beheaded, he took a toaster; from Sheila Bride, asphyxiated and burned, a breadmaker; Delores Washington, a blender. Dubbed the Appliance Killer by the media, Martin broke down and confessed on the stand, but not until D.A. Metcalfe placed each appliance, one by one on the railing of the witness box in front of the sweaty-eyed Martin.

So why did the famous, or infamous, A. Malcolm Shriner want to see me?

The elevator beeped and opened onto the tenth floor. Across the small hall sat a polished set of mahogany doors girded by a metal detector, in case anyone planned to carry a grudge farther than the courthouse steps.

Could they be that pissed about losing the marijuana-smoking dog case? Did they want to offer me a job? The latter was doubtful, what with the budget squeeze and Governor Sumner's right wing reactionary politics of law and order. I could be a card carrying N.R.A. member; defense attorneys were still seen as tainted the minute they stepped across the aisle to fight against the government. It was the equivalent of being labeled a pinko back in the fifties and sixties, at least in regards to your legal prospects.

A black woman with elaborately curved hair, long dragon-like nails, and a gun at her side motions me over.

"Mr. Heyerdahl?"

"Yes."

"Could I see some ID? It's just standard security procedure." I flash her my driver's license. "Do you have a renewal, or one that's not expired?"

Like a boy caught out late for class, I shrug and grin. "The DMV kept giving me renewals, so the picture I showed you is, like, twelve years old. I finally got a new one." I produced my updated license, hidden away in one of the folds of my wallet. "Don't I look heavier?"

The lady's playing along, giving both IDs a once over. "I don't know, but you do look older."

"I guess it's better to look older than heavier."

She changes to a matter-of-fact tone. "So the DMV didn't make you turn in your old license?"

I nod.

"And do people often notice your old one's expired?"

"No, you're the first."

"Honey, I'm with you, I gotta get a new one in a couple of months. No reason I shouldn't be staring at myself a little bit younger." Before I can respond, she's grabbing her wallet from her purse beneath her desk. "Lookee, here."

It's her ID, and she's looking, well, a lot thinner. I'm not sure what to say, but she helps me out.

"Oh, you can say it. I've gained some weight. It's my husband's fault. He likes me to make all this rich food and, well, I never trusted a chef who wouldn't sample what she cooked."

As a consolation, I say, "You sure don't look like you've aged."

"Ah, sugar, you know what they say about black people and wrinkles, don't ya?"

I feel like the Eddie Murphy impersonation of every witless white person, looking quizzically, with the strong nasal voice, mystified by the strange wackiness of the Negroes. "Umm, no."

"Honey, black don't crack."

We both laugh; she taps something under her desk. The door clicks open. I'm taking my license back, smiling, and I'm wondering how they got the door to open without the annoying buzz, and thinking maybe the same guy would know how to stop my answering machine's beeping.

Inside, there's a large octagonal greeting area replete with oak bookcases holding magisterial tomes on various aspects of jurisprudence, plush green carpet, and three desks for the secretaries of Shriner, Stanley, and Metcalfe. Stanley's probably not here, since he's trying to get elected to Virginia's state house as a junior congressman. Odds are he'll win, too.

The office in the middle is D.A. Metcalfe's, but I'm steered to the right by the well-modulated voice of a warm-eyed, older woman who has probably been shepherding D.A.s through their paces for the past thirty years and knows way more about the law than yours truly. (A fact that will be proven out after all this craziness, when I'm trying to put the full story together, and this lady, looking to pad her retirement, acts as my 'Deep Throat').

"Mr. Heyerdahl, Deputy Chief Shriner wants to thank you for coming at the spur of the moment. You can go right in. He's waiting."

The silly good humor I'd cultivated with the driver license lady evaporates. Suddenly, this seems serious.

The secretary is up, getting the door for me, and I'm inside a richly appointed office that's probably as big as Achmed and Jimmy's entire pizza place. More bookcases, awards, objects d'art stand around the room; however, the most noticeable feature is the steel blue rug and the chrome that seems to cover most every surface. For a moment I feel like I'm swimming in a metal fish bowl. There's a view of the city behind Shriner's desk, which I'd really like to see, but glancing that way takes my vision across Shriner himself.

He's rising, coming my way with a smile he wears surprisingly well for a man with a first initial that stands for Asshole. As he greets me with a handshake, I promise myself I won't stare out the window at the great view, like some hayseed attorney just into the big city.

"Mr. Heyerdahl."

"Joe."

"Malcolm Shriner, nice to meet you. Have a seat, have a seat."

I see Shriner's just like his pictures: a barrel with legs, and just a little less greased back hair that moves him from Pat Riley to Dr. Lecter-land. His suit probably ran him two grand, but even its expensive tailoring can't make it drape itself to this man's proportions. The suit's a cobalt blue, giving me the uncomfortable feeling that, like a chameleon, he's walking right out of the office's background.

Now, I'm sitting in a deep leather chair that I wish I could steal for my very own. My seat seems higher than his, which reverses the age-old wisdom that height gives someone a leg up if they're trying to intimidate.

As it is, Shriner reverses course and is back behind his desk, his head low, giving me the impression of a bull shark or torpedo just waiting to take off.

The torpedo speaks. "I know you're wondering why I called you."

I'm smart enough not to offer up a number of scenarios that'll just make me look foolish when I'm wrong. Besides, I really don't know the answer.

"There's a case coming up that the Public Defender's office will be calling you about." The thought of fulfilling my noble pro bono obligation does not fill me with gladness. Even though I've got a bit of savings, money's still a little tight. And do I really want to be involved in something that has attracted attention this far up the prosecutorial food chain?

"I'll cut to the chase. Do you know who Cheryl Preninger is?"

He could just come out and tell me the case, but instead he's testing me on my current events, maybe making sure I haven't been living in a hole in my driveway. I get the thought that this might be a murder case and I get a thrill that's two parts excitement, one part fear. "She's on death row for torture and murder." The thrill courses through me again. "An old married couple ran the pharmacy and she killed them and tried to kill someone else while stealing drugs. She's scheduled to die in about six months and there's been a lot of who-ha over the fact that she's a woman. No woman's been executed in Virginia since before World War II, and she's been a model prisoner for, like, eight years, ever since she found Christ."

Shriner's nodding like a teacher pleased with what he's hearing. I find the manner vaguely annoying and I glance around the room, noting for the first time an interior door that must go to D.A. Metcalfe's office. There's a sculpture of a blood red crystal standing on a small podium somewhat behind his desk, kitty-corner to the wall. The vermilion contrasts vividly with the rest of the room's decor. "Nice sculpture." Shriner looks at it with enthusiasm, which surprises me, since I assume it's not a new addition to his office.

Shriner rises from his chair takes the few steps, and flips a switch on the sculpture's base. It appears to be two people melding together, contoured with some harsh spiral lines and it begins to twist, eternally, screwing itself skyward.

"An old girlfriend made it for me," Shriner says with too much pride for a man who's no stranger to being the welcoming arm to any number of very pretty east coast models.

The sculpture's color, its subject and action tell me Shriner isn't the most abstract thinker and doesn't get the blatant sexual message. Then again, he simply might not give a damn.

He's back in his seat, while the sculpture moves at the corner of my eye, distracting enough that I almost miss what he says next.

"She needs an attorney and she wants you."

I'm trying to catch up. "She, Cheryl Preninger, needs an attorney." Shriner nods. Thanks to Frank and Ken's radio show, I'm looking a little more informed then I normally would on death row cases. "Frank Bradshaw's her appeals attorney."

Frank Bradshaw is one of those old school, Southern attorneys that usually get manufactured in movies but don't really exist. Charming, urbane, with a shock of white hair, he'd taken on dozens of civil rights cases in the sixties, only to switch gears in his later years to defend the wealthy when they got too wild, did too much coke and someone ended up dead at the bottom of the pool, or strangled after some questionable sexual practices. This kind of fence jumping earned him the enmity of those who want their legal heroes either wrapped in the Bill of Rights or the Bible, and the respect of the few, who either enjoyed a genuine American personality or simply knew enough to give proper respect to a consummate trial attorney.

"He's got a client list of some of the wealthiest people, he's got the highest respect from anybody who knows the legal history of Virginia, he's got..."

"A recurring case of acute myelogenous leukemia." Shriner finishes. "The cancer went into remission a couple of years ago, but it's back and the doctors tell him he's got maybe six months. Unless." Shriner pauses. "Unless he undergoes a new kind of chemo for the next eight weeks. Problem is, this chemo's more virulent than your run-of-the-mill chronic vomiting, diarrhea, hair loss, no-energy chemo."

"Medicine is able to do such wonderful things," I respond sarcastically.

"He can't stay on as Preninger's attorney, so..."

"Why me?"

"I know this isn't quite your league." It's a slight dig, and considering I just beat his office in the courtroom, not a very good one. "She saw your name in the paper for some case you won." I know he's got an ego under that polished exterior. Am I supposed to believe he doesn't know the dog-smoking marijuana case, I won? He doesn't want to throw me even that small bone of praise? Oh, that's a bad pun.

Anyway, I'm caught reflecting on this, so I almost miss what comes next.

"... had a dream, and an Angel of the Lord, or something, told her you were the one to take her toward her ultimate fate."

"Say that again."

"Ms. Preninger's incarceration has made her a bit of a mystic, given her that deep, somewhat loopy, look that people get when they hold the Bible in their hands and start thinking that it's the answer to everything, from faith to family to what TV shows they should watch." There's barely a pause, and he says the next with open-eyed disinterest. "Oh, no offense."

He's done his research on me.

"Anyway, you've both got a similar background. She's exhausted her appeals, and she's made it clear she wants nothing more to do with the legal process. Again, the angels," he says, with a fluttering of his fingers and a big-eyed silly look. "Six months and she's toast or in Virginia—Hamlet's mom." I appear not to understand. "Poisoned," Shriner finishes.

I've always felt there was an advantage to people thinking you were a bit dim. Maybe I should have shut up and not played the good little student reciting the pledge to Shriner's Preninger questions. I take my own advice and ask a stupid question, "No chance of the governor commuting her sentence to life in prison." Acting now, with an earnestness I wished I felt, "I mean, she's accepted the Gospel of the Lord." Shriner looks like he might be buying what I'm selling.

Regardless, he leans back, smooths his two hundred dollar tie and smiles like the Cheshire Cat. "Not much of a political animal, huh, Joe? Governor Sumner hammers away at a get-tough on crime agenda and wins the election after four years of, let's say, a rather liberal sensitivity in matters of jurisprudence.

"Sure, Bible thumpers and bleeding hearts will whimper and whine, stage candlelight vigils, write their congressman and the governor. Pat Robertson'll probably even feature her on his 700 Club so he can wring more dollars from his faithful. And after all of this, Sumner'll get up at a well-covered press conference," he stresses the press conference with a pointed index finger. "...and he'll state the length of time he spent on this case, thinking and praying, and express his sensitivity to the seriousness of the responsibility the people of Virginia have invested him with. And then he'll go on to remind the TV viewers that Cheryl Preninger brutally tortured and murdered a husband and wife—a husband and wife who'd been married just shy of their fiftieth anniversary. Joe, she's getting the needle, you can count on it."

This is all coming too fast—Shriner's candor, his digs at my life, and the case. I'm getting caught up in the details on the one hand and its huge scope on the other. I need to focus on what this will do for my practice. Do I have the logistics and the time to handle this? Why do I want this? "The exposure" is the thought that comes to mind.

"It's a no-brainer, Joe." I'm starting to regret offering him my first name. "Just hold her hand as she takes her walk to be with God...or the devil."

I'm nodding, honestly trying to figure if there's a way I can get out of this. Not to be mercenary, but I'm really not into escorting somebody to their heavenly reward, via a lethal injection.

Shriner slides forward now, hands steepled. He's giving me what must be his earnest look, but all I'm getting is a shark's view of me as a wallowing seal.

"We in the D.A.'s office just want to make sure that you can run the last ten yards with this one, take it into the end zone." A bizarre picture comes to mind of myself at Preninger's execution, football held high, the ball coming down SPIKE, just as the executioner's brew jumps across the plastic tubing into the woman's veins. "She's had twelve years. We don't want the will of the People, and their money, thwarted by another stay, all because she needs to switch attorneys because hers spends too many nights at the local tavern drinking Guinness."

Shriner's still looks like a fireplug, but now he's looking at me like I'm a dog that might piss on him. He's trying to show me he holds all the cards, and how easily he can get the skinny on some street lawyer like myself, but I don't like it, and my anger gets the best of me.

"I don't drink Guinness; that's just a rumor. Kind of like the one about your boss and his habit of frequenting the End Up and the Stud." I've never heard of Warren Metcalfe being anything other than the happily married family man that his publicist claims he is, but what the hell. If Shriner wants to be rude, I can tear at his boss. After all, he's got a much longer way to fall than me. I remember the inner door to Metcalfe's office and wonder if he could be listening. Then I think, screw it, which is easy to do on account of that stupid sculpture twisting away.

Shriner looks a little caught out. He must view my crude remarks against his friend—in his office of all places—beyond rude. No reason to start on the right foot, I tell myself. He starts leafing through the papers on his desk and I stifle the impulse to look over at what he's reading. In a moment, it doesn't matter.

"I see you graduated from Laverne. Then you know that joke, right?"

What can a guy say in defense of an alma mater named Laverne? Like, oh boy, it's good we didn't have a football team because they'd have been called the DeFazios.

"No," I say, like the pitcher who has just hung a curveball to Barry Bonds and has the dazed look of one about to watch the ball leave the yard in a big hurry.

"It's only called Laverne because they couldn't afford to pay Hollywood the licensing for its full name, *Laverne and Shirley*." He's chuckling like that was supposed to be funny.

"I hadn't heard that one, but I did hear the one that had Laverne moving to Richmond after California..."

"I thought she lived in Milwaukee."

"Her and Shirley moved to California, later in the show's run."

"That I didn't know. There are gaps in a Harvard education after all."

"Of that, Mr. Shriner, I'm quite sure of. Anyway, Laverne wanted the university to be called DeFazio, but DeFazio College sounded too much like a school for beauticians." He's chuckling now, letting my cut about his prestigious law school slide right off his $2,000 suit.

Something has been bothering me, and between the verbal jousting and the bombshell that I'm supposed to nursemaid a death row inmate, I haven't been able to put my finger on it. "Aren't we skirting some kind of exparte communication?"

"Remember your ethics class, Joe." At this point I'm really regretting letting him call me Joe. "You are not the attorney of record in this case. As such, nothing can be attached to our discussion."

"How is it that the D.A.'s office knows which attorney she's requesting?"

"We have ears in lots of holes, Joe."

"I'm sure that's not the only thing you've got in a lot of holes. Since, I have no real business here, I'll be leaving." I get up, not bothering to shake hands.

"So the D.A. can rest easy that you'll take this trial all the way? No last minute crisis of Christian conscience or detours to the wee ole tavern?"

"Goodbye, Mr. Shriner. See you in court."

"I certainly hope not, Joe. I certainly hope not."


I'm back outside the office and the Stepford wife of a secretary is offering to validate my parking slip.

"Here's your stub. Goodbye, Mr. Heyerdahl. I'm sure we'll be speaking again." With that statement, I realize I've just been made a chump.

Ironically, a little of my anger recedes and I know that, while this lady probably does know more law than yours truly, she's not very quick when it comes to psychological game playing. I was supposed to get mad back there. Shriner, with all his rude references to my school and my personal habits, was setting me up to be angry. The answer to the question of why is obvious.

The D.A.'s office, through whatever back channel they've got into Sussex Prison, gets wind of Preninger's selection. They think, great, the guy she wants practices law on animals more than people. Her case is already stirring up media attention and it'll get worse as the execution date approaches. What they don't need is some high profile lawyer like Frank Bradshaw mucking things up with last minute appeals and polished sound bites. The problem is how do we ensure that this nobody takes the case. After all, it's pro bono, essentially over and done with, and damn depressing when you stop and think about it. What we do is we piss him off. Get him mad, so he's indignant enough to take on this thankless task.

My black lady friend who doesn't crack is absent from her desk. As I hustle onto the elevator, I realize I fell for Shriner's bait hook, line, sinker, tackle box, and row boat.

By the time Joe's parking pass was getting punched, Warren Metcalfe had already entered Shriner's office through the intervening office door they shared. The much-touted Warren Metcalfe resembled the comic book Superman. His blue-black hair, that just now into his mid-forties was taking on the salt and pepper look, made him even more striking. Where Shriner was short, Metcalfe stood six three. Where Shriner was barrel chested, Metcalfe, through a strict running regimen, managed to say svelte, even slim, and in a profession filled with men who quickly acquire the belt-sagging gut of those who work long hours, eat crappy fast food, and exercise only at the mandatory company picnics. Why Metcalfe retained his college frame was simple: he knew he was handsome and he planned to stay that way as long as ambition pushed him to greater positions of authority and there was TV to chronicle his appearance to would-be voters.

During long cases, where work would stretch on night after night, someone would invariably ask Warren Metcalfe if he felt okay. His stock response was, "Do I look okay? Then let's assume I feel okay." And the scary thing was that he did. Twenty-hour days managed to place small bags under his eyes, but couldn't crease his tailored Armani shirts.

Now, as he stood in Shriner's office wearing a solid white example of the Italian designer's work, District Attorney Metcalfe was all smiles.

The two men began talking in that friendly, casual way of long-soldiered veterans of military campaigns.

"Well, Mal," said Metcalfe, "I think that went well. You certainly chummed the waters for our Mr. Heyerdahl."

"He's a real charmer, that one."

"That's hardly fair; you insulted the man's school."

"That school is an insult," said Shriner.

"And you implied he's got a drinking problem."

"I'm just worried he won't finish the case. There'll be more delays and suddenly, this execution's running over toward your election."

"I understand we want a powder puff so there are no waves."

"Yeah, but we need a powder puff who'll finish the fight, go the distance, and take the loser's seat. You heard this guy; he's volatile."

"Oh, and you're not, Mal?"

"I'm just a little earnest," said Shriner.

"Yeah, I'm sure that's how Joan of Arc would've described herself."

"For Chrissakes, Warren! The guy's a Laverne grad. He defends dog-bites-man cases. The media alone will eat him up; they'll say he doesn't have the qualifications to defend her."

"Which is no concern of ours. We have no say in who Ms. Preninger chooses to represent her. If we had, we certainly wouldn't have chosen Frank Bradshaw to defend her on appeal."

"Will that be our press statement?" asked Shriner.

"Something to that effect, and that Mr. Heyerdahl passed the bar." Metcalfe sits on Shriner's desk and starts leafing through the papers. Pressing his finger on the page for Shriner to see. "The first time, just like you and me."

Shriner grudgingly, "He did do a nice bit of lawyering with that last drug case of his."

"Yeah, he did, but just watch Lady Counselor Stanhope. If she gets sandbagged again, shitcan her ass. I can't stand losers, especially losers who play on my team."

Malcolm responds with mock seriousness "By your command, Lord Vader."

Metcalfe goes to leave the way he came, pausing at the door, "Is there really a rumor that I frequent gay leather bars?"

"I wouldn't be the first to be told, would I?" Now in lisping gay speak, "But you would look quite fetching in a pair of bottomless leather chaps, Mr. District Attorney." Now all business, "Do you want me to check it out?"

Metcalfe, after a moment's thought, "Naww, who cares. I hope there is a rumor. Maybe it'll help me up in Valley Circle and Crossley."

Shriner's lisp is back. "That's very coy of you, playing like you don't know, Warren."

Metcalfe gives him the finger. "Hey, wasn't there talk a few years ago about us being gay for each other?"

More lisp, "Yes, but you ruined it by getting married to that hussy."

"And your model of the month had nothing to do with ending our romance?"

Now flouncy hands are added to Shriner's lisp. "There's still time, Warren. You could be my bottom."

"I'd be wasted as a bottom. I'm too good looking. Remember, Mal, I'd fuck you; you wouldn't fuck me, you'd get fucked."

Back to his normal gritty monotone, "You know, I think you've just hit on something. I'd fuck you, you wouldn't fuck me, you'd get fucked. Why that's the lawyer's creed. I think we should emblazon it on our stationary, make it our motto so to speak. Oh, mind if I use that with Cynthia; she likes that kind of who's-your-daddy tough talk."

"The six foot blonde, the one that dwarfs your—well, dwarf-like status?"

Shriner smiling, all teeth, "Yeah, the one who was in Vogue last year."

"Just *in* Vogue, Mal, not on the cover. You've really got to set your sights a little higher. You know every man needs to have goals."

"Would you two cut it out; I feel like I got two Rich Little's back here." Susan, secretary extraordinaire, shakes her head at them. "How two grown men with such positions can act this way."

The men shake their heads, and doors open and close as work jumpstarts itself.

# ELEVEN

$I$'m getting ready to run over to Sussex for the first time when Sarah pops into the bedroom. There's a shiny glee in her eyes.

"I got you something for your first big murder case."

I think it's not as much a case as it is a job to bear witness, but she's been excited by all this and I don't want to curb her enthusiasm when it comes to thinking highly of me. "What'd you get me? A laptop?" I've wanted one, but Sarah, like an old lover of LP's, stubbornly stays away from computers that don't have to be planted on a desk.

"No, here," she says, handing me a wrapped box covered in red and white ribbon and pictures of Santa.

"I see they were all out of 'congratulations, your client's a murderer' wrapping paper."

"Well, whoever sees Ms. Claus, anymore, huh, Joe?"

This is rare banter from a girl who's been outstandingly out of character since she heard I was getting this 'big case.' She can't be that excited about a murder case, I think, so she might be sitting on some good baby news, but I figure I'll wait for her to tell me.

The wrapping and the box are opened and inside is a lovely, soft-leather briefcase. Sarah's clapping her hands softly and directing me to notice the thick metal pen affixed to the briefcase's handle. It's one of those big steel tube jobs with several buttons and a silicon grip.

"See, it's a pen," Sarah states obviously.

"Yes, I see" I'm checking the pen up and down, noticing several colored buttons. One of which, the red, changes the LED display on the pen's side from time of day, to date, to temperature, to... is that the altitude?

"There was one that also had a global positioning indicator built in, but I thought that was a bit much."

I only nod. Now James Bond and I have two things in common: we both like our martinis shaken, not stirred, and we both have a nifty cool secret agent pen.

The green button doesn't seem to work until Sarah shows me how it turns the pen's ink from blue to black and back again. I try the black button, but it doesn't seem to do anything, even after Q—I mean Sarah—gives it her best shot.

"Oh, well. I set the time for you, see?" She's right, though my Q seems a little less technically gifted than Bond's. "I'm not sure what I did with the directions, but I'll find them and figure it out for you."

"Maybe the black button arms the nuclear weapons."

"No, that's if you push the red and black together," Sarah deadpans. All this humor from my lovely wife. I can't help thinking she must have a happy secret. I'm about to ask what's up and press her on when her period's due, when the veteran married man inside of me says to shut up and enjoy my wife's good humor. Asking a woman about her mood, the voice counsels, is inviting some kind of discussion, where I'll no doubt end up catching heat.

Instead, I give her a hug and a kiss, then reset and do it again because it's a little silly, and thus sort of romantic, and most of all because I really do love kissing my wife.

It's a beautiful late spring day and I'm finally on the road to the Maximum Security Prison at Sussex. I count myself lucky. Preninger could be housed at Corcoran, which is more than a two-hour drive. She was there until the authorities decided that, since the lethal injection set-up was here, why should the mountain go to Mohammed. A kind of one-stop shopping for executions, I guess.

Growing up, I lived in California, and while I certainly miss the five-lane freeways with their high cement walls protecting homeowners from the noise and fumes of the thousands of cars flying by, while making a driver feel like he was at Le Mans swooshing through partitioned streets, it did little for a guy who needed a relaxed drive as the antidote to a stressed-out day. Virginia's two-by-two lanes, separated by a huge strip of green planted with sycamore, oak, and pine, and the real woodlands you travel through, all make driving here a much more enjoyable experience. Of course, I'm on my way to visit someone on death row, so the forest kind of loses its knotty charm.

Allowing prisons in any area is about as popular as nuclear reactors, or giving returning sex crime offenders the okay to camp next door. As a result, prisons are located pretty far from high-density population clusters. Having an escaped murderer showing up at your four-year-old's birthday party pretty much covers the why and wherefore of that.

I pass through a lot of rolling countryside before making a turn onto Sussex Prison Road. (Not very imaginative, but neither is the prison.) I'm looking for the Death Row Cul-de-Sac, when the prison comes into view.

Built in the early eighties to house the increasing number of drug offenders, Sussex consists of four squat buildings that form an X. Standing on the perimeter of this X are four towers with sinister black reflective glass, no doubt so prisoners don't know who or how many guards are watching them at any one time.

Various signs direct me to visitor parking, while informing me that my every move is being monitored by state-of-the-art infrared, ultraviolet, and motion-sensing technology.

This isn't the first time I've seen a client in prison, but this is the first max facility I have the pleasure of visiting. As I park the car, I can now make out the catwalks that encircle the tower, and the men on them carrying rifles, waiting for some desperate inmate to make a break. The guards on the wall wear glasses that seem to be torn from the same material as their tower windows, and I get a momentary feeling that I've stepped into *Cool Hand Luke*.

Unlike the Richmond courthouse, Sussex serves up only one entrance. Better to see and control who's going in and out. A guard at the automatic door asks my business. Since I'm a white man in a suit, he's probably got me pegged as an attorney and not someone visiting his brother.

The entranceway is stacked up with people waiting to get through. As I get closer, I see the door is actually two doors. Once you pass through the first, you're stuck in a small hallway, since the second door is locked. Then a guard, manning a metal detector or some X-ray device, gives the go-ahead, the light above signals green, and the door unlocks. Most of the people waiting are women, which makes sense, since ninety-five percent of everyone here is male. If I was going to be confined to a ten-by-six-foot cell for the next twenty-five years I wouldn't be that excited about seeing anybody but my wife (and the possibility of trying to get away with as much hanky panky as possible in the visitor area).

Directly in front of me, a black woman, wearing a muumuu and flip-flops, with a little boy in tow, hesitates at the door. She yells to the guard, asking if the boy can go through with her. Like bureaucrats everywhere, he doesn't answer the question, he just restates the rule. "One person at a time, Miss."

She hesitates for a moment, as if she's afraid that if she lets this one go for just a minute, this place'll get him, too.

"I can watch him while you step through," I offer.

She eyes me with a healthy skepticism I have to respect. If someone volunteered to watch my kid, I'd want references, ID, a cash deposit, and blood for DNA matching before I'd even consider it. But seeing as how we're entering a maximum-security prison, and there are probably a dozen men with guns just itching to use'm, I'm probably a safe bet.

Later, I'm surprised to find out that guards do not carry guns when they're on the prison floor. Guns are kept secured and locked down on each tier. That way, prisoners can't get a gun and start shooting their way out. The danger of this policy is that if you're a guard, and the prisoners decide to get uppity, the calvary's not coming over the hill for at least five minutes, which is a long time, especially if a prisoner's got a shiv and is attempting to create some new holes in your body.

The guard's calling for the lady to step forward on account of the line getting longer, and it's this fact more than my reassuring presence that moves her. To her credit, she goes, but with her neck craning backward to watch her little tyke.

A buzz, the green is lit, and now the boy goes through.

I follow.

The small hallway makes me feel like I'm in some quarantine film, or I'm John Travolta in that old TV movie, *The Boy in the Bubble*. The light goes green and I imagine my fumigation process is complete, or that I'm entering an undersea fortress through some hissing airlock. On the other side, however, there's no Disney underwater kingdom, but the same institutional off-white concrete and stucco, with long hallways that have bars and locks on each end.

One guard, a black man with a military bearing and crisp short hair, cut just above a long scar (like someone tried to scalp him), motions me over, while speaking into his walkie-talkie. "You inmate Preninger's new attorney?" I nod. "You're going to need an escort. Hey, Officer White, get over here." I'm gladdened by this, simply because I envisioned myself getting lost and ending up on the yard. Or worse yet, the showers.

The man being signaled over is black, well over six feet, and probably 300 pounds, with wide shoulders and the kind of gait that's more a heel-toe saunter. As he's walking over, tapping a billy club that's as thick as my wrist, he's shouting, "Taking the keys to lockup A, and B, and Stanton. Taking the keys to lockups A, and B, and Stanton." Another thing I discover is that second to guns, keys are watched, counted, and put away with a military precision.

The guard's gesturing for me to fall in behind. For such a big man, or the kind of man who, as a boy, was called 'big boned' by his momma, he's a fast walker.

"Let's go, Mr. Attorney, let's go. Don't need you getting lost and ending up in the Tombs." That sounds marginally worse than the showers, so I pick up the pace.

After about five minutes, we're at the first gate. There are two guards sitting behind glass, which looks thick enough to act as a submarine hull. My guard gives them the high sign, the men behind the glass nod, and another light goes green as the guard turns his key in the lock.

The keys definitely make you think of prison. They're big metal contraptions, like those skeleton keys that were used in dungeons in medieval Europe.

"Could I see those," I say, motioning to his loop of keys.

"Nope," he says, without breaking stride.

"How far we walking?" I offer, in hopes of opening a conversation.

"That was Gate A, got a long stretch to Gate B, then a short stretch to Stanton. I'd say about ten minutes."

Our tunnel, a narrow pipe, opens up and reminds me of the time my father took me to an air show at Moffett Field near San Francisco. We walked into this gigantic blimp hangar, which was big enough inside to operate balloon rides. Of course, my father thought it was too expensive and spent most of his time talking to some Air Force guys he knew from a bar nearby.

Sussex's Block A is not nearly that big, but there are three tiers with walls stretching high above, and the light diffusing through the long, barred windows is strained and gray on account of the grime plastered to them. All the prisoners must be in lockup at this time of the day because the prison floor is empty, except for the weight-lifting equipment and the old color TV mounted on the wall.

We haven't gone three steps into the open area when the hooting starts. Prisoners begin yelling about how cute I am and how they'd treat me right. The taunting quickly escalates, either because the inmates are trying to outdo one another, they're bored, or some of these guys in the middle section tiers are hard-core loons.

Now my mother's being assailed, my kids, but overall it's my butt that's of greatest interest. On a whim, I cup my ears like I can't hear them and point to my ass, as if unsure what they're saying. My action's like throwing gasoline on a backdoor barbecue. The hollering gets louder, the cons more engaged, and the threats more violent. Odd bits of toilet paper, and what look to be soap shavings, come wafting down.

Now they're describing in detail how I better shine that thing up and get it ready. I shake my head at all of this and increase my pace, mainly because my guard hasn't slowed or looked back.

The next pit stop's at B's guardhouse—and another green light. I feel like I'm watching *Mr. Roger's Neighborhood* with the red light-green light thing. I hear the old man's tweedy voice, "Okay kids, can you say sodomy, because that's what Mr. Heyerdahl was threatened with about thirty-seven times. Can you count to thirty-seven? Want to do it with me? You're a great neighbor."

B block looks just like A's, and I'm about to ask my guard about the weights. They seem like pretty good weapons if an inmate decided to throw them after taking all that time to lift'm, when the shouting starts, again.

This time I keep my mouth shut and my eyes peeled forward. These guys are less imaginative than the first ones, and nothing's very new except for a man who's got a woman's set of pipes and keeps asking Officer White to ask Officer Donovan for his meds. Like a man following behind his wife at the mall as she scampers from one dress to another, I follow Officer White as he walks on heedless, seemingly tired, despite his quick pace.

More guards, clipboards in hand, looking serious. Another green light blinks us through. The hallway to the Stanton Block is instantly different. The great cement expansiveness is gone, replaced by low ceilings and the sterility of a hospital corridor.

After about twenty feet and to the right, there's a TV room, where several women are watching the soaps my wife probably watches. To the left, there's a lock-divided door with a sign announcing that it's the library and detailing when it's open.

Officer White stops at a smaller version of the same guard booth I've been seeing and instructs me to, "Stand here." I do, and he walks over to the guardroom and confers with the men in the shack. One of them, a short white guy (actually, he just looks short against Officer White) with a head that resembles someone not shaving for a week, grabs a tall stool and walks out to greet me. Or rather, like Officer White before him, he walks by me, instructing me as I follow. "This way, she's right down here. Are you familiar with the rules of attorney-client contact on the Row?"

I want to remind him that this isn't quite the Row, but he's as humorless as any picture of George Washington, so I say, "No, I uuhh, I'm not."

"There is no attorney-client contact on the Row. You are not to touch the inmate, the inmate is not to touch you; you are not to pass anything to the inmate; you are not to accept anything from the inmate. You will be monitored at all times to ensure that you comply with the aforementioned guidelines." He says all this in one long breath that he could've used to blow reveille.

I'm about to object to the monitoring of attorney-client communication and remind the guard about the confidentiality between a client and his attorney, but he's obviously been down this road a number of times.

"I, or any other correctional officer, will not be in the room. We sit outside, observing through the door's glass. I will not eyeball you at all times. I will keep you in my peripheral vision. None of Sussex's correctional officers have been instructed on how to read lips, and none can be called to testify to a conversation thus obtained."

Yes, I think, but who else might you talk to if you got a particularly incriminating piece of info from watchdogging me and my client? "Well, that was a mouthful."

Officer Huntner—I can read his name tag now—doesn't crack a smile.

He places the stool he's been carrying kitty-corner to the door. Its window is one of those steel-strengthened ones, with the metal threads running through the glass, making it nearly impossible to break and jump through. As I'm noticing this, I get my first look at Cheryl Preninger.

I walk into the room and see Preninger sitting, reading the Bible. My first impression is how young she looks. She was eighteen when she committed the crime and now, at thirty, she looks a young twenty-five. Getting her on TV, I'm thinking, may be a way to get her sentence commuted to life.

My second impression is much less flattering. The waifish, strung-out druggie that went into Virginia's State Penitentiary system has ballooned to where she's now carrying at least fifty extra pounds in her orange jumpsuit.

Her face lights up when she sees me, the kind of light that gives her an almost angelic bearing, a light that usually comes from the strongly converted. Added to this heavenly assessment is her jolly round face. She's holding her Bible to her chest and I'm over to shake her hand, but then I notice she's cuffed with her hands in front. The door cracks open and Officer Huntner is calling in a monotone, "Do not touch the inmate, do not let the inmate touch you. Do not accept anything from the inmate..." He continues regurgitating, I guess, the guardsmen's version of a Miranda warning.

"Okay, okay, I get it, I get it," I say. I hear the jingles of leg irons when Preninger fidgets in her seat. "Hello, Ms. Preninger, I'm Joe Heyerdahl."

"Well, hello, Joe. I know this kind of meeting can be uncomfortable."

"Pretty unique, too. Before we get started, I think you should know, Ms. Preninger..."

"Cheryl."

"Cheryl. That I've never tried a murder case."

"Well, Joe, you won't be trying one with me."

"Yeah, that's right, but..."

"The reason I picked you is that the Good Lord sent an angel down to me in a dream."

"A dream?" Here we go, I'm thinking. Unfortunately, the defense must've already used diminished capacity in its appeal.

"I dreamt there was a man who had raven-colored hair and dark eyes, like you, Joe."

My hair's probably the lightest black possible, but I'd hate to argue with an angel.

"The rest of his face was obscured by something, but he wore a cloak and used—I don't have the right word—like a banjo from a long time ago, and he entertained people, and then one day he was traveling, and he came upon an injured bear, and instead of killing the bear he cared for it and nursed it back to health. As the bear grew stronger, the man would sing and play his guitar, and the bear would sniffle and grunt and dance to the rhythm. Soon, the bear was well enough to leave, and the man said goodbye and moved on. Many years later the man had been imprisoned for something he did not do, and in an evil pagan festival he was set to be fed to the wild animals that had been caught for this purpose. Of course, the man's executioner was the bear he had saved so long ago. Anyway, the bear refused to eat the man, and somehow the man was given his instrument, and he played a wonderful tune that was full of the love of the Lord and all his creatures, and the villagers were so moved they opened the gates and the bear and the man walked out into freedom."

"This was a dream? Usually my dreams are pretty chaotic, filled with sharks and tricycles and bagpipes."

"Of course, Joe. That's what makes this so divine."

"The two spent several years together, experiencing the joys of friendship under the heaven of God's green Earth. Then one day, when the man was alone, he surprised a mother bear with cubs. The mother bear, fearing for the lives of her young, ripped out the man's throat before he could raise his voice to sing.

"Smelling blood, friend bear came whumping back only to find the man dead on the grass, the mother and her babies already chewing at the man's dead body. The bear saw all this and grew angry and was ready to set upon the female bear, when a light arose from the dead man's form and he became the Christ. And he said, 'This is my body, take of it.' The male bear's anger faded and he partook of the flesh, and he was filled with the love of the Lord, and the animals transformed into a human family, and they worshipped Christ and their children, and their children's children worshipped the Lord all the days of their life."

As Preninger recites this story, she's definitely experiencing something. Her eyes lift to heaven, her hands clasp, and by the end her eyes are misty with tears. I'm thinking it's a little like the lions with the Christians, and the thorn in the paw fable, with a good amount of St. Francis of Assisi thrown in. "But you said the man's face was obscured. How do you know it was me?"

Preninger reaches for me, but now it's her turn to pull back before Huntner can start berating us. She continues, "The very next day, I was in the rec room and I've completely forgotten the vision the Lord had passed on to me, and I'm looking at the newspaper, and there's a small article about a lawyer getting his client free on account of caring for his sick dog. Just like that, I felt the whole vision rise up in me, as my inner eye went roaming across the Lord's Message."

"So I'm kinda like St. Francis of Assisi?"

"Exactly, and just by your knowing that part of the Word, it tells me you're a man who's accepted Christ into his life."

Suddenly, I can see how tense she is. All this has been leading up to this question. She's facing death in six months, but she's more concerned about whether I'm a believer in Christ.

"Yes," I hear myself say, "I accepted the Word about five years ago now." I say this with a seriousness I don't feel, but what can I do, the woman's looking at me like I just told her I got the Governor to pardon her and she gets to go home tomorrow. "But Cheryl, what do you really think I can accomplish?"

"You can walk with me in my final months, Joe. You can be the man nursing the hurt bear." And then with a winning smile, "You can sing stories and play your guitar."

I'm smiling now. "No guitar playing, Cheryl. And as far as singing, I'm the guy in the car who sings along to the radio and who other passengers tell to shut up because he's ruining the song."

She laughs. "Pretty funny for a married guy, Joe."

"Ha, you got that from my ring. Her name's Sarah."

"Any children?"

"No. I guess there's no ring for that."

"Well, I've heard there is if you count the rings around parents' eyes after they've been up three nights in a row with a colicky baby. Do you want kids?"

"Very much, we've been trying seriously for about six months now."

"Well, that's nice to hear. Sometimes, even with the Lord by my side, these walls can close in on me, and I find it always helps me to remember that other peoples' lives are going on, moving, changing, and growing."

"Honestly, I'd think that'd be depressing."

"Nah, it gets me out of my head, makes me see things in a new way. Speaking of which,"—pointing to my briefcase—"is that new?"

"As a matter of fact, it is."

"When I'm not reading from the Good Book, I enjoy reading mysteries, especially Sherlock Holmes. Let me guess. You bought the briefcase because you wanted one, on account of your big new case."

"Almost. My wife bought it on account of my big new case."

"Darn, I should've remembered the wife."

"She got me this pen, too," I say, holding the pen towards her. "Hey, if you like mysteries, tell me what the green button does."

She's moving away, backing up in her seat. In a second I know why.

The door opens a crack. "Do not pass the prisoner anything; do not receive anything from the prisoner."

Cheryl smiles. "Joe, you gotta remember the rules."

"I'm really a lot better with legal rules than the ones in prison," I say apologetically.

"Joe, the mere fact that you're here, and you believe the Word, fills my heart with joy that I'm being led along the path of righteousness and rebirth, that I'm being forgiven for the terrible deeds I did, and that the Lord plans to welcome me into his Heavenly Kingdom." For just a moment she loses the religious zeal that's characterized most of her talk. "Joe, I killed two people. I was strung out on drugs, and I got worse on what I took that hellish night at the pharmacy, but I know what I did was wrong, horribly wrong, and I take responsibility for it. If seeing the families of the people I killed testify to how much love I took from their world and replaced with sorrow wasn't enough, this book," grasping the Bible, "opened my eyes fully to the enormity of my sinful ways."

"Cheryl, I don't know how I can be of service. I've never even worked with a person on death row."

"And Peter was a fisherman before he took up the Cross and began to preach God's Word."

I don't know if it's the environment or how her eyes give off an almost palpable heat when she's talking about God, but I don't have my usual practiced voice of cynicism that's always making wisecracks about people who are spouting about the Book, the Way, and the Lord.

"I don't know if you're here as my lawyer. Frank became ill, God bless him. I pray for his recovery and I need an attorney, but I've made it clear that I will not appeal anymore. I will not challenge the State's plan to execute me. I have killed and I should face the punishment, but I would be lying if I said I didn't want to continue on this earth, leading my fellow inmates into a better understanding of the Lord. But that may not be what He wants. You know, there's a Spanish proverb that I've always liked: God writes straight with crooked sticks." Now holding her arms out. "We are the crooked sticks." She finishes her speech, and brushes her dirty blonde hair from her face.

I can't think of anything to say. The practical part of me is thinking that this case is certainly not going to take up a lot of my time, especially if my client is dead set against my doing anything to save her. But then there's the guy in me who worked any job to get himself through law school, the guy who'd drive to work or school and fantasize about the big murder cases he'd try, the expert legal crosses that'd break down the guilty parties and which would be talked about and studied throughout Virginia. Hell, the entire East Coast. That guy, he wants to do something dramatic.

Cheryl's still talking about Jesus, St. Francis, and her visions, and even with all this I don't think she's crazy. I mean, she's as sane as you can be when you're locked up and sentenced to die. "So, once I get your file," I tell her, "we'll set up another meeting to go over what your next move should be." She rolls her eyes at this. "Cheryl, I wouldn't be living up to the oath I took if I didn't acquaint myself with your case. Bradshaw's office is supposed to be sending the files over any day."

"You read them, Joe, and maybe then you'll change your mind about whether I should appeal this or that technicality. I'll see you soon; go with God."

Cheryl's movement to stand gets the guard's attention. I've glanced over now and again. Like he said, he only watches from the corner of his eye. He tells me to wait in the hallway and then hustles her down the corridor, as fast as someone can go in leg irons, and they disappear.

As I'm escorted out of the prison, I keep seeing her eyes and the kindness in them, and then I remember the hardness of those chains, and imagine it was that same hardness that looked down on poor Mrs. Jeffords, tied up as the life was strangled from her.

I'm walking with Officer White, going back through B Block and into A. The blocks are still empty and it makes me feel like a queen whose route has been cleared for passage. Several hoots and hollers remind me that "queen" may not be the best analogy at the moment. I don't know if I'm still energized from my meeting with Preninger or if Guard White's quiet demeanor is some kind of challenge, but I start asking him questions. "You work here long?"

"Long enough," he responds, in his deep, smooth baritone.

"You like your job?"

"Like it enough."

"What'd you do before you were a guard?"

He still hasn't changed his easy rolling gait, but his voice gets a little deeper and louder. "We are not guards. Guards are guys that attend a weekend workshop and drive armored cars, or even worse, try to stop snot-nosed kids from stealing things at the mall while they use their uniform as a way to put the moves on any woman they see. I am a *correctional officer.* I attended Breckenridge Correctional School for three months, 24—7; I'm licensed to carry a badge and a gun by the State of Virginia."

Officer White, I mean *Correctional Officer White*, says all this with the barest hint of humor, like he's teasing a newbie, and with the deepest voice this side of "Old Man River."

We're up to the lock, entering Cellblock A, where all my fervent admirers are waiting to trade insults, so I try one more time to find out about Mr. White. "Do you have a family?"

For the first time, he looks at me. Not angrily, but in a way that says I should stop asking questions. "Never discuss your family inside these walls," he tells me. "Inmates will use anything they can to get leverage on you. Any inmate asks if you got a wife and kids, your mom and pop alive, just remember you were an only child, you're single, you're parents are dead of cancer, rest of the distant family moved to Europe."

White's speech is the first time I've felt the full force of his presence and it's like having a mountain growl at you, so I nod my head in understanding of what he said. "So that wedding ring on your finger is...?"

"A memory of my poor dead wife who was killed along with my son in childbirth."

"So you must have a daughter," I say. "Because anybody who's a parent couldn't even remotely come close to mentioning a real child's fictional death."

Officer White seems to take a moment to think that over. "You are not correct, Mr. Attorney." He's about to unlock Cellblock A when he adds softly, "Do not repeat that, or the thinking that got you to that, to any—repeat, any—of these cons."

"Gotcha, Officer White."

Then we're back in Cellblock A and the men are talking it up even before I come into view from beneath the cement overhang. I think there must be some kind of signaling system between the blocks that I'm not privy to.

The monologues are already getting stale—threats to me, to my family, desires to explore various orifices of my body with the men of different tiers, and a few calls for cigs and representation. I cup my ears and pretend to glance at my butt, trying to say, "Is this what all the fuss is about?"

I know that I'm really irritating men who, if I were alone with them, I'd be in more than a little danger. But they're locked away, and the floor is free of everything but the metal dumbbells, and all I've got to do is try to keep up with my escort, who's the fastest slow walker I've ever seen.

# TWELVE

It's two days later, and my idealistic lawyer voice has been smothered under the huge number of boxes Bradshaw's office has sent over. Wall to wall, boxes cover my outer and inner offices. All I've got is a narrow alleyway allowing me to enter and exit from behind my desk. I feel like the Judge in *Miracle on 34th Street*, who unknowingly demands that all the mail sent by the post office to the defendant, Kris Kringle, be placed on his desk. Consequently, bag after bag arrives, overflowing the bench, burying him beneath it.

I'd like to pretend I don't know where to start, but Bradshaw, showing one of a dozen reasons why he was such a good trial attorney, is absolutely meticulous. Every box is labeled chronologically with annotations referring the reader to additional documents supporting, refuting, or illuminating anything in the Trial Bible—the case history, so to speak.

I send Stella out to get Subway sandwiches; she always has to sneak back in because Jimmy and Achmed would scream bloody murder if we ate at a competitor's business. Stella returns with my turkey and cheese on white bread with mayo, lettuce, and bell peppers, and I lean back in my chair and start reading from the beginning, which is the bio Cheryl furnished of her early years in the hopes of being granted clemency from execution during the penalty phase of her trial.

Cheryl Racine Preninger was born in 1983 to Laura and Stanley Preninger, who got married two weeks before the baby arrived. Her first three years were relatively stable. Her father worked at the Rapphanok Shipyards and took extra work as a contractor, when he could find it. When Cheryl was three, her father found work as a merchant seaman, which would prove to be the beginning of the end for both Cheryl's and her mother's relationship with Stanley Preninger.

For the next three years, her father would be gone for months at a time, leaving Laura with little money. She took various jobs as a maid, bartender, and hostess. Cheryl's maternal grandparent, Kathleen, took care of the child until she started school and later when she came home from school.

By the end of first grade, Cheryl was demonstrating such gifts in math and language that she was skipped to third grade. At the same time that Cheryl began to excel at school, her father stopped returning from his time at sea. One day at the age of seven, as Cheryl tells it here, she and her mother waited for the Hans Breckerman, a Swedish cargo vessel, to unload her father. He was not on it. Her mother asked questions of the crew, but they simply said Stanley had never showed when they were ready to set sail.

The next two years must have been a painful odyssey for Cheryl. Her mother contacted U.S. embassies and state departments in an effort to locate her vanished husband. All that Laura could learn about Stanley's 'disappearance' was uncovered in the first week: he had not been found dead, drunk, or in jail. After that, there was a succession of correspondence with the U.S. and Swedish government, who eventually stopped responding to Mrs. Preninger's pleas for information. She spent two thousand dollars on a private investigator who, despite their agreement, never went to Sweden, but stayed in Arlington and called many of the same people Mrs. Preninger had previously called.

Cheryl related how, at nine, she was convinced her father had run off to live in Europe, while her mother remained resolute, insisting Stanley had come to a foul end, or perhaps was a victim of amnesia and was wandering through Sweden.

Despite the abandonment, Cheryl continued to excel in school. The annotations refer me to her report cards from fourth to seventh grade where, even though a grade ahead, she achieved straight A's—at least until her teens, when the grades began to slip. By her freshman year she dropped out to pursue a life of partying and drug use.

Nothing explains the shadow that rushed over Cheryl's life. She seems to have been a particularly headstrong and intelligent teen who rebelled. Like James Dean when asked, "What are you rebelling against?" he replied, "What have you got?" Cheryl Preninger seemed intent on casting aside traditional values in a wild burst of teen angst.

Those two years before committing the murders were marked with arrests for vagrancy, minor drug possession, several charges of pick pocketing (something she must not have excelled at, judging by the number of times she got caught), and an assault on a woman over a spilled beer.

Even if one were to see this pattern as an escalation of violence and mayhem, the incline on the graph was about to steepen sharply. Cheryl Preninger, now all of eighteen, walked into a mom and pop pharmacy at closing time, produced a .22 caliber pistol she had taken off a squatter a week before and proceeded to tie the proprietors, Mr. and Mrs. Jeffords, and their assistant, Basada Delhi, to office chairs with rope she had purchased the day before at Home Depot. The prosecution would later use the hardware store's ID as proof that she had planned her assault and was therefore guilty of murder one.

Intent on more than a grab and dash, Preninger demanded to know the whereabouts of the tranquilizers Percocet and Halcyon, and the opium-based narcotics like Dilaudid and morphine.

Then the torture began.

First, Mr. Jeffords, husband of two, grandfather of three, had his forearms slashed with scissors. Locating hydrochloric acid (always all kinds of interesting chemicals at the pharmacy, I note), she doused his wounds.

Why did she do this? Cheryl imagined in her strung-out mind that a truckload of drugs was being dropped off that night. She thought if she had the password, they'd let her sign for them.

It was pure fantasy, which was brought up at the trial in the hopes of showing temporary insanity. According to the law, there's insane and there's *insane*. The law finds people sane if it can be shown that they knew that what they were doing was wrong. As a result, taking steps to hide evidence is proof enough that someone is not legally insane. Preninger did get rid of the murder weapon and did flee the scene; she also showed forethought in her assault on the pharmacy and its very unlucky inhabitants.

Mr. Jeffords had faced much worse long before in the tunnels that dotted the Ho chi Minh trail, but he had a wife to come back to. Now his wife was by his side. Fearing for her life, he quickly told Preninger where to find every Percodan, Percocet, Valium, and Dilaudid. Unfortunately, the use of these drugs did not calm her. Instead, they put her into a deeply frenzied state. (I couldn't help but think that the old man should have directed her to something with a knockout punch but, in a life and death situation, hindsight is definitely 20/20. And who knows? Preninger might not have been fooled; she was a junkie and probably knew drugs like monkeys know trees.

Still convinced that FedEx was bringing a truckload of drugs, Cheryl began torturing Mrs. Jeffords, whose hands were tied behind the chair.

Preninger began to strangle the old woman, relenting only when Mr. Jeffords offered a new stash of drugs.

Now beyond control, Cheryl strangled the woman. With the old man in tears, Preninger walked over and shot him in the head. Remembering Delhi, the cashier, she walked over and shot her in the head as well.

Reading the police report—and I had read my share of them—I realized that I had never read any as detailed. The bullet glanced off the Indian woman's head, she lost consciousness and bled profusely, making her appear quite dead to the stoned assailant, who fled.

Six days later, the police found Cheryl in a stupor, holed up in a tin-roofed motel off the Robert E. Lee Parkway, only twenty miles from the scene of the crime. The remaining drugs were sprayed across the room, but the murder weapon was not to be found. This would later be admitted at trial as evidence that she had tried to cover up her crime.

At her arraignment, she pleaded not guilty. A straight-up guilty plea would have probably saved her from the needle. I glance at the trial bible glossary and I see Bradshaw had tried an inadequate counsel appeal. I had hoped to show Preninger's first attorney had been incompetent in not pursuing this line of defense, but the prosecution demonstrated they had never approached Preninger's public defender with a deal for life in prison. Thinking cynically, I note the fact that although the D.A. had never approached her P.D., it didn't mean they wouldn't have taken a deal had it been offered.

The D.A.'s reluctance to deal seemed somewhat strange in light of the fact that they didn't have a good case. The drugs from the crime were present, but Preninger hadn't given a statement after emerging from her stew of chemicals, and the D.A. had little else.

Little else, until Ms. Delhi started to remember the events of that night. After being wounded, she had suffered post-traumatic amnesia, but after giving several statements to the cops that she couldn't remember the night in question or identify Preninger, her memory started to return, and she was finally able to give the police a detailed statement of the events leading to the Jeffords' murders and her attempted murder. It was this testimony that sewed up the case for the prosecution. A prosecution, I notice, second chaired by a fierce young A.D.A., Warren Metcalfe.


Sarah and I are getting ready for church. She's still on a high that leaves me waiting for the *big news*. Instead, I'm just getting a lot of cheery good humor, back rubs, and sex on demand.

Our church, The Church of the Benevolent Savior, is into Sunday greetings of Jesus with the parishioners dressed as plain as can be (kind of Amish of us, I guess). However, my Catholic upbringing insists I wear a dress shirt and tie. Sarah needs no convincing on dressing up, probably because women are more competitive about these things.

She gets the idea to walk to church. Not wanting to rain on her Disneyland parade of good feelings, I agree. We spend the next fifteen minutes picking our way through the back streets of our neighborhood, noticing that the one cherry blossom tree has still not bloomed, avoiding the sidewalk cracks and upheavals caused by the elm and poplar roots pushing up from below. The boy in me notices several slabs of upthrusting concrete that'd make an excellent bicycle jump. I'm a little sad that my childhood is so far away, but I'm cheered by the fact that there's enough of the boy in me to notice. It's a marvel how different the neighborhood looks on foot than from my usual perspective in the car traveling at twenty-five miles an hour (okay, maybe thirty-five).

To my surprise, there's a park nestled behind some trees; I had always taken it for someone's large front yard. After the trees, there's a large expanse of grass, some sand, a slide, baby swings and a large plastic jungle gym that resembles something out of Dr. Seuss.

A mother, with another baby on the way, sits on the grass. She's trying to read while her overalls-dressed, red-headed child attempts to dig a large hole in the sand. I'm thinking this would be a nice place to come when we have kids and I notice Sarah looking admiringly at the little boy, who's seemingly trying to locate China with all his digging. I can't think of a more perfect time for Sarah to tell me we've got a bun in the oven. But if I'm wrong, and Sarah's good mood is not on account of her being pregnant, I'd rather be a ship in a typhoon than have to deal with her darkening skies.

"Wouldn't this be a nice place to take a child, Joe?"

"Yeah, park's nice, kinda secluded, can't even see it from the street," I say, trying to fill my side of the conversation. Sarah smiles, a smile so clean it reminds me of how lucky I am to be with her and how much I love her.

"I just know we're going to have a child, Joe. Even as hard as it's been, I've always known the Good Lord would answer my prayers."

So the good mood isn't because we're pregnant, but because my wife's found a new certainty that she will get pregnant. Not to be cynical, but I tell myself that I better enjoy the prevailing warm winds and tropical breezes while they last.

I kiss her, hoping that the fair weather will last until her renewed faith and prayers are answered.

We're still early when we arrive, hand-in-hand, at the church.

# THIRTEEN

It's a month later at the prison and I'm feeling especially good, even in this tomb of concrete and steel. It's because of the great morning Sarah and I had, first on the floor in the living room, and then out on the back porch, in the beautiful, soft morning light. For the first time she seemed uninhibited, free to just feel good without all the baggage she's always carrying in our intimate moments.

Quiet Officer White is walking me through the blocks and I try to strike up a conversation. I talk about baseball and what he thinks of A-Rod passing Willie Mayes as the third all-time homer hitter, but all he says is that he doesn't watch baseball. Other questions follow, like do the officers worry about riots or being taken prisoner, but they only elicit a "Nope" from White.

We're back in A Block and the regular offers for representation, sex, and cigarettes filter down like carelessly thrown bricks. Maybe because my escort limits himself to short sentences, I find myself talking back to the prisoners. I'm a smart ass, theatrically shaking my head and covering my eyes, or fluttering my hands like I'm scared of what's being said. Of course, this just increases the threats, but after a minute or two I'm passing through the gate into Block B and then on to Stanton.

Signing in, I note a Sister's been here three times since my last visit; I try to remind myself to ask Preninger about her. Maybe she can write a clemency letter to the Governor. Cheryl would probably remind me she doesn't want any more pleas, notoriety, etc., and honestly, after looking closely at her file, I'm at a loss to figure what we could do. Anything I could think of, and quite a bit more, has already been tried by Bradshaw. The only thing he couldn't do was ask for an extension based on new counsel. I'm thinking the time it takes me to get up to snuff on her case shouldn't be deducted from the time she has left on this earth. But I need to know if she even wants that delay.

This whole thing troubles me. First, I get the D.A. trying to bully me into taking the case, then I get a client who instructs me not to put up a defense. As her lawyer, when do I heed her wishes? She doesn't seem crazy enough for a judge to call her incompetent, and if I do anything she doesn't like, she can ask to have me removed. At this point, any judge who can smell the political wind is going to be loath to give her a new attorney, especially so late in the game. I guess I could probably bring motions in her defense, even if she didn't like them. Now if I just knew what those motions might be I'd have some way to help her.

I'm transferred like a baton in a relay to Officer Huntner, who proceeds to give me déjà vu, with his monotone recitation of the same prison rules I heard last time.

"Okay, okay. I'm going to need her to sign some things. Just so you know."

"That's fine. Just make sure I'm notified in advance." Spookily, the man's voice is the same flat piece of metal even when he's not spouting prison policy.

Cheryl's seated in the same seat as last time. By her smile, I'm thinking I wish I was on whatever she's on. I tell her, "I need you to sign these papers naming me as your attorney." I grab a sheaf of forms from my briefcase, look Huntner's way while holding the pen high, like I just won the Olympic Gold. It takes a moment for his head to turn my way, and then he pauses, nods, and I hand the pen to my client.

Huntner continues to watch in that sidelong way the Feds use when they've got a wiretap and can only listen thirty seconds at a time, determining if the call is about illegal things or just Jimmy the Mouth's wife telling him to pick up the ragula and lasagna on the way home. If the conversation's not illegal, the Feds have to switch off and wait a proscribed time before switching back on. That's Huntner, with his head on a slide, tracking back and forth, back and forth.

I see Cheryl looks good. Sure, she's got the beaming look of *I know Jesus*, I know the *Truth of Life*, but that flightiness is given gravity by the certainty with which she carries the knowledge that she's much closer than the rest of us to finding out those answers.

One thing that's different is the delicate golden crucifix she's wearing. The chain is also gold and it's as thin as a spider's line. They probably let her wear it because they know she can't hang herself with it. "That's a very nice necklace, Cheryl."

She self-consciously fingers it, saying, "It's a little gaudy, don't you think?"

"Naw, simple elegance." This is a line I used on my wife about her dresses and jewelry, before she got wise from hearing it too often. Cheryl's obviously pleased; she mouths it under her breath. For a moment, I see a woman more nervous about her jewelry than her date with a lethal injection.

It makes me sad. For some odd reason, even with her extra fifty pounds, it makes Cheryl seem very pretty. Must be the gallant knight in me.

"Thank you, Joe, but you're my lawyer, not my fashion consultant."

"Why? Is that position filled? I am well qualified for that as well." Now becoming more serious, "You're worried it's not plain enough for God. The whole *no worshipping of graven images, relics* thing."

"Joe, the way you say thing makes me think you've still got some way to go toward accepting the teaching of Our Lord Jesus Christ."

With a practiced ease, I deflect the question. "Who bought it for you?"

Cheryl actually blushes. "Just a friend."

"The way you say that makes me think it's more than a friend."

"People write to me."

"Men?"

"Mostly."

"I thought that was a female thing with serial killers, like that Satan lover in California." I abruptly shut my mouth, and then open it to add, "Sorry, that was rude of me."

"No, I killed two people, tried to kill a third. I can't pretend what I did never happened. And even if I could pretend, the State's gonna remind me in a big way in about six months." She chuckles at her joke and I'm amazed she can find humor in someone sticking a lethal needle in her arm.

Suddenly there are loud voices coming from outside the room. I glance over at Huntner, but he's gone. I walk to the glass and I can see two women in the TV room. They're tearing at each other's hair and screaming obscenities, while two guards, and then Huntner, try to pull them apart.

Cheryl, speaking from behind me, "Is it Kate and Emily?"

I glance her way and then back at the scene. "Umm, does Kate or Emily have long blonde hair?"

"Yeah, that's Kate. She knows long hair's not good in prison, but she's vain about her appearance."

As the other girl lands a raking slap across Kate's face, I'm thinking her appearance is not going to be so good for a while. I can tell that the guards are loath to use their billy clubs, meaning they're having a hard time breaking up the fight. "The other one's got black hair and a pug nose." A pug nose that gets more pug when the other woman smacks her forearm across it.

"Yep, that's Emily. They've been at it ever since each one thought the other stole her cigarettes."

I'm only partially listening to Cheryl tell this story of bad blood. I'm fixated, like all males, on the catfight in front of me. The guards finally get the two combatants separated and, after the obligatory swearing and spitting, the women are taken away. Huntner's walking back my way; Cheryl's now glancing through her Bible, and I'm collecting the forms she's filled out.

"There you go, Joe. Now that you're my attorney, I instruct you to do nothing."

"I have to do what's in your best interest." That's not really true, but I figure I can slip it by her.

"No, Joe, you need to make me aware of my options and their consequences as they relate to a legal course of action. As long as I'm of sound mind, I decide my legal strategy. Besides, you've read my file. You find anything to set me free?" She delivers this last line rhetorically, without a trace of hope hidden behind a well-practiced skepticism.

"No," I confess, "I haven't."

She just shrugs, like then isn't the point of this conversation moot. "Joe, in a couple of weeks they're going to set a date." And it's not going to be to the Prom, I think. "And then I'm going to be segregated from the rest of the prison population." She sees my confusion. "That's the procedure for death row inmates who've got a date. They're kept in locked down solitary. Since I'm the only woman on death row they've lumped me with the lifers and the long years. I'm even in charge of the women's library. What I'm saying is, I've been fortunate to get the chance to talk to these girls about life and about Jesus Christ."

I jump in, "So let me petition the court for more time." She's shaking her head, even before I finish.

"Joe, Joe, Joe, it's been two weeks and you're already acting like a lawyer. Why should I hold up God's judgment one day longer? Just so I can sit in my cell?"

"No, so you can do God's Will on Earth by trying to bring those people far from God's Word one small step closer to the Light."

She's thinking this over. No doubt those women who were out there fighting have helped my case a bit. "This isn't a content motion, Joe. Just a few weeks to get you feeling like you know my case, and you get to be a lawyer and feel like your fulfilling the Canons of being a good attorney."

Her intelligence and her years in the legal system are shining through. I smile, knowing I've won. "Something like that, Cheryl."

At least I think I've won, until the next day when I get a call from her. She's changed her mind. I have to drive all the way back there to lobby again. At the same time, my wife's become the amorous lady of the morning and requires my performance yet again for some dawn frolicking.

At the penitentiary, I have to listen to Cheryl cite scripture for thirty minutes. At the same time, she's marking up her Bible with my pen, like a college student with a highlighter on too much caffeine. After she's done with her underlining, she returns my pen and calmly announces that says she's changed her mind yet again. I can go forward with my motion.

It's been announced that I'm going to be Preninger's attorney. Even with Stella doing her regular bang-up job of grabbing a call once every monsoon season, I've got over fifty messages. Some from newspapers, two from local television stations, and one from the ACLU which, in the matter of three sentences, manages to denigrate my legal abilities to the point where they've decided the best thing for me to do is act as just a go-between them and Cheryl, and CAD (Citizens against Death), who I gotta admit has a snappy name. After all, who's not against death?

CAD's a non-profit that spearheads the right to life of just about everybody from the unborn and death rowers to the fight against the Kevorkians of the world. At least they're consistent. Like the ACLU, they seem to think this case is too much of a burden for little ole me and my degree from Laverne, so they're willing to take it off my hands. That is if I get them an interview with Ms. Preninger, who for some odd reason has stonewalled all their requests. So now they're pushing for a meeting so we can discuss strategies to bring this case to the national consciousness. Zealous people scare me. If I think about this, it makes my close ties with religion somewhat contradictory.

# FOURTEEN

*Six months until the execution*

I'm in the Superior Court of Justice Ronald Crandall, a prematurely balding barrister who seems cranky about the fact that my motion is taking him away from his golf game.

He sits behind his desk, bangs a gold-banded gavel, and I wonder is there a pecking order for gavels like there is for sports equipment. *You may have the newest titanium Big Bertha, Judge Caufield, but I have a pearl handled gavel the size of a mallet.*

Anyway, across from me is Tommy Dean, looking like a tanned and pompadoured lizard. Next to him, I'm surprised to see is A. Malcolm Shriner, poised with both feet on the floor, arm over the side of the desk, like that's all that's holding him back from taking his bull head and running smack into the tower of the Judge's bench. I say "surprised" because this is quite the minor motion for a Deputy D.A. to be sitting in on, even for such a high profile case.

I take the floor. "Your honor, I'm simply asking for an extension of the court-imposed date of my client's death. As the court is aware, I've only recently been made counsel for Ms. Preninger. To properly exercise my legal duties, I need to fully apprise myself of her case."

Dean's up, unbuttoning his coat, which he probably just buttoned so he could show a little flair. "Your honor, if it pleases the court, Mr. Heyerdahl has almost six months to make himself knowledgeable on the facts of this case."

"That's ludicrous, Your Honor," I respond. "The prosecutor would like me to be caught up on this case the day they strap my client down." Now, I know that's not what Tommy meant, but it's what he just said.

Shriner's rising, throwing Tommy a little sneer, "Deputy District Attorney A. Malcolm Shriner, if it pleases the Court."

"Malcolm, anything that'll speed these proceedings along will please the court."

I think, there's the golf game.

"Your honor, we do not contest that Mr. Heyerdahl will need time to acquaint himself with his client's file. However, even while working on his law practice, as it is, he should be up on the principles within a week or two." I try to get a word in, but Shriner never breaks stride. "Nowhere is it mandated that the attorney of record must have read every last document as it regards the most ancillary items of his case. If that were true, Your Honor, we'd all have inch-thick glasses and never have time to go to court."

My turn. "Your Honor, there is just as much case law that says I need adequate time to prepare and confer with my client."

The Judge addresses Malcolm like they're old friends. "Has the date of Ms. Preninger's execution been set?"

Shriner, seeing where this is going, answers like a good schoolboy. "No, it has not, Your Honor."

"Well, that settles it. Mr. Heyerdahl, since there is no exigent circumstance for an extension to be provided, you will have your two weeks to get yourself up to speed. And you can do it without the court's interference of granting any extension." I try to interrupt, but the Judge's cold-hearted glance tells me not to try it. "And furthermore, if I know Frank Bradshaw, the case will be collated, related, and hyphenated every which way to Sunday. I, for one, would never have gotten through law school without the aid of that man's notes. Your motion, Mr. Heyerdahl, is denied." The gavel bangs an exclamation point onto the proceedings.

I'm shaking my head, and Tommy, who's smiling like he just whupped me, and Malcolm, who's grabbed up his briefcase, are striding out the door like they've just won Brown v. Topeka Board of Education.

Shriner pauses on his way out. "That's 0-for-1, Sport. Let's get a meeting together for this week so we can make sure you're fully informed of the legal ramifications of Preninger's last six months."

I smile and nod. He's only doing this so he can cover his office's ass, now that I've made a motion on Preninger's case. If she were to chuck me out the cell door, a new attorney could be intent on proving I was incompetent. That wouldn't stop the execution, but it might delay it. And a delay, I realize, might bring her death a bit too close to his boss's election.

It's a week later, and I've got nothing but false hope to give Cheryl. I get a call from Daniel, the man I met at the Kannabis Club, wanting my help with a little estate work and seeing if I want to do a little hanging out with Peter Tosh. On an impulse, and because Daniel seemed too sick for this to be some gay come-on, I tell him I'll be by that night.

The inside of Daniel's apartment is how I envision a gay man's place, tastefully decorated with a hint of whimsy, from the odd way he's decorated the walls to the Popeye and Bluto pictures in the hallway.

Daniel pulls down an old cigar box from his bookcase and places it on the table. The box is wood, with a weathered map of Havana on its top. It's about a third filled with pot and a couple packets of rolling paper are tossed in for good measure. Daniel grabs one and uses its cardboard backing to separate a joint-sized amount of weed, which he moves back and forth, tilting the box so the seeds get separated.

I can see Daniel's an old pro and he does this with single-minded devotion. I remember watching interviews with junkies who said they missed the ritual of shooting up almost as much as getting high. Seeing Daniel, I'm sure he fits into that group.

The grass is seed free and Daniel's drawing two papers from the roll and joining them with a lick. A brief fear of AIDS passes through me, but then I realize how stupid that is. He slides the weed onto the papers, tamps it down by running his fingers over the joint's edges, like a safecracker, and begins rolling it straight and tight.

That tightness, I remember, is the sign of someone who can really roll a joint.

Daniel grabs a lighter and hands me the joint. "The first hit goes to the guest."

I sit back in the chair and I take a deep toke.

"So, when's the last time you smoked dope?"

"Don't call it dope, sounds awful," I say, as I release a huge rush of the pot I've been holding in.

"Oh please, let's not call drugs nice names and fool ourselves into therefore thinking it's all okay. In my case," Daniel adds, "I like to call it The Chronic."

"Like the rappers do," I add.

"Yes, but for me it's a little more apt. So you didn't say when was the last time you had a blunt." Daniel finishes by raising his eyebrows, like look how down I am.

Another hit, holding in burning smoke, a choked clearing of my lungs, and I say, "Girl I dated about five years ago, and I hadn't smoked before that for years," I grab the bottle of Glenfiddich and pour myself a tumbler. "Alcohol has always been my drug of choice. Anyway, she had this cool loft with a huge skylight. I must've smoked two fatties." Now it's my turn to look 'with it.' "I just lay on the carpet, staring up through that skylight at a colossal full moon, and I remember feeling like I was floating, and I had my eyes cracked open just a bit and the moon's light was making these delicate traces across my retina."

"Like going to the Planetarium in your head."

"Good analogy. And it was a good trip."

"So why'd you stop?"

"Like I said, it wasn't really my thing, and the only thing smoking weed did for me was leave me with the munchies and make me sleepy. But the food never tasted as good as it did when I wasn't high. And the sleep, well, the sleep wasn't that satisfying kind of nap you get in the middle of the day, where you're in this deep sleep, but you come out of it every so often, seemingly so you can relish the comfort and ease of those great deep breaths your body is taking. And then you wake up with a sheen of sweat, feeling totally relaxed."

"Don't talk to an AIDS sufferer about waking up sweaty. Night sweats that leave your sheets soaked go hand-in-hand with AIDS."

"That reminds me, Daniel," I tell him, "you look noticeably better than when I saw you at the *drug* store."

"My doc's tweaked my cocktail and added some kind of new, derived protease inhibitor. I've put on ten pounds from my low point; another date with the Grim Reaper postponed."

I pass the joint his way. "I'm sure he'll understand."

"After this long, I know Death pretty well. He knows we'll be dancing with him sooner or later, so he lets us pick our partners as long as we save the last dance for him."

While we've been talking, he's preparing his dinner—a pot pie.

"Sure I can't get you something?" he asks.

"Naw, my father made me eat pot pies as a kid—I hated them. Only thing that belongs in a pie is fruits or sweets. I mean what kind of madman thinks of putting meat in a pie?"

Half a joint smoked and I can just feel it kick in. The drug lulls my senses, gingerly separates me from the anxieties and frustrations of the Preninger case, and gives the brandy a smoky, pungent flavor. "Hey, what's with the Popeye and Bluto stuff?"

"Well, as a gay man, we like reminders of our closeted brethren that went before us. You know, Oscar Wilde, Walt Whitman, Rock Hudson, Tom Cruise..."

"Oh, he'd sue you for that. Wait, are you saying that Popeye and Bluto were gay?"

"Oh, most definitely."

"How d'ya figure that?"

"Oh, I don't know: two extremely masculine guys, well-muscled, Navy men even, and you know how lonely it gets at sea."

"That's highly circumstantial, Counselor."

"Okay, Joe, look who their beard is, Olive Oyl. Have you ever seen a more mannish woman in cartoons, or anywhere for that manner? And she's got her hair tied up in a bun, with no makeup. Those silly long dresses that show no figure, not that she's got any. Hey, put jeans on her and you'd call her a man."

The joints burned down, and Daniel tosses me a roach clip to get the last bit, which strangely reminds me of the dentist appointment I have in a few weeks. Probably because they use the clips to give you that little paper bib.

"Joe, the whole conflict with the cartoon wasn't over Olive Oyl. After all, Popeye and Bluto spent ninety-five percent of the show wrestling, and grabbing, and groping one another, and as soon as they get the girl, who you might notice is never forthcoming with her favor, the show's over. The real conflict, Joe," Daniel's winding up for the big finale, "was that Popeye and Bluto were both tops, manly men, and they constantly were battling each other for that position."

"I must admit, I'm impressed, Counselor. What's the whole spinach thing then?"

Daniel shrugs, "Shit, I don't know. It's a kid's cartoon for Chrissakes. They probably put it in there so kids would eat their spinach."

With that, Daniel passes me back the joint. "So, Joe, you planning on defending your murderer?"

"She's not my murderer. The media thinks I can't, and my showing today doesn't do a lot for my case in that respect, and the D.A. is hoping I'm just almost incompetent. So in short, Daniel, I don't know."


Three days later, I'm standing on the corner of Mallow and Dickens, watching Shriner swallow chunks of hot dog from a vendor's cart. The dog, covered in sauerkraut and mustard, goes down like short bursts of anti-aircraft fire. In between the rat-a-tat-tats, he's sending bursts of schmooze my way. "Really, Joe, you can feel good about that motion you made. If I hadn't been there, Tommy just might've let you win it, the way he has of stepping on his tongue."

"Don't kid yourself, Malcolm. The Judge wanted to get in nine holes before dusk. He wasn't listening to much of what either of us had to say."

Shriner shrugs like, yeah you may be right, while half a hot dog disappears down his throat. "Joe, I'm just saying you can feel good about yourself now. You've tossed a motion into the ring and did it in front of a Superior Court Judge." This man's patronizing attitude is even more irritating because he's so totally heedless of it.

"I've argued lots of cases in Superior Court."

"I'm sure you have. It's just that you showed up and stamped this case as your own. No one's going to say or think you can't handle the big leagues, regardless of what those media talking heads say."

At this point, I'm desperately hoping some mustard makes its way onto Shriner's John Stevens shirt, but the guy's too quick and too ravenous, and watching him eat, I almost think he could suck the mustard out of the air as it fell toward his $500 button-down.

He continues to lay it on, spreading the b.s. thicker than his condiments. "People know you're a top-notch attorney; after this case is through, you can figure that people will be seeking out your services."

There was the carrot, I think. The Old Boys'll remember you, and maybe when this is over they'll let you play a round of golf with them and their black caddies. "That's all very interesting, Malcolm, but I intend to do what's best for my client."

"I know you will, Joe. I wouldn't have it any other way." With that, he claps me on the back and is off, hurrying to the next thing he's set to devour.

I look back at the bull shark leaving the scene, moving with a fish-like back and forth through the lunchtime crowds, and I curse. The son of a bitch left a huge glop of mustard on my shoulder.

Another prison visit and Officer White is there to gather me in and lead me through the blocks. I'm trying to piece together what I'll say to Cheryl when I'm pulled out of my strategizing by the racket of voices that I know as Cellblock A. But it's not the voices that slow my step, but the clinking and scraping of weights as they're picked up and put down. For all my teasing of the inmates, I'm realizing I made a large error by assuming that an empty floor was the normal state of affairs for Cellblock A.

"So Officer White," I inquire cautiously, "the times I've been here before..." White knows where I'm going with this and is probably loving every minute of it. "First time you were here, they were on lockdown, 'cuz a con used a shiv he made from soap on a guy who wouldn't give him cigs."

"And last time?" I say, as we're approaching the gate of Cellblock A and my stride's become as short as a circus midget's.

"Some prisoners make little stoves, so they can have soup. We looked the other way in the past, but two cons got into it over some soup, and one ended up with the small grill burned into his face." White, who had continued to walk and talk over his shoulder, now stops. "Mr. Attorney, you're going to have to walk faster; otherwise, by the time you get to your client, she's already gonna be dead." This is the first time I see Officer White smile. I have just enough perspective to realize that, in different circumstances, his broad, pearly white grin might be a nice thing.

I start walking. We're at Cellblock A's gate and White's calling in his bass voice, "Opening A, opening A."

I can see ahead of me, beyond the wall's overhang, where there are men of all sizes. Since the weight area sits in the middle of the block's floor, however, I see mostly large men, very large-muscled men who seemed to have added pounds of marble to their arms and torsos and then gone about spending hours chiseling these pieces so their gigantic muscles have the appearance of steep mountains colliding. Right now, I'm really hoping it's none of these men that I've insulted.

The noises grow louder and I try to tell myself this could be any 24-hour Fitness, with just a slightly off-center clientele. The block opens above me and I get a quick feeling of how the inmates must feel when they're walking under a guard tower, exposed to the dangers above.

Suddenly, White starts calling, "Civilian walking through, civilian walking through!" At the first sound of his booming voice, I nearly leap into the air. Any chance I had of slipping by has vanished. I then remember that I wore this suit on one of the occasions when I bantered with the cons. So there's no way to say they got the wrong guy.

I tell myself that White's announcement is just procedure, but I keep my head straight ahead, eyes downcast, as I try to scan for members of the convict clan who might have something to say to the smart-ass attorney. I'm like the kid who blows raspberries at the gorillas and suddenly finds himself in the cage.

I'm halfway across the block's immense floor and most of the prisoner's aren't even making eye contact. I don't know if that's an ingrained habit or because, like a little tugboat, I've pulled myself into the wake of the H.M.S. Destroyer Officer White.

I've made it two-thirds of the way through the block when I hear someone from behind. "Yo, fancy pants, you ain't acting so cute now." The voice is getting closer and I tell myself he couldn't possibly be talking to me. At the same time, the blood pounds in my temples. No way White's gonna let me get accosted by a con. The voice in my head is hard to understand because it's shrill and talking real fast, like it's scared or something (imagine that). Also, the voice is hard to hear because of the screaming directed at moi.

The voice is right behind me and it announces, "What, not such a smart ass now, Mr. Fucking Shit-for-Brains Suit?" Okay, he's definitely talking to me.

I'm still walking, but I have to turn back because all the hairs on my neck have stood up, just like when I was a kid and I had to go into the basement, which I was sure held the buried remains of vampires waiting to be awakened by the smell of young blood.

Officer White is still moving forward, but now he booms out something slightly different. "Civilian walking. Do not block, obstruct, or touch the civilian. Repeat, do not block, touch or obstruct the civilian."

White's announcement takes the edge off my fear because I can see his words are code for, you may walk up and harass the scum-bag attorney as much as you want, but do anything else and a billy club that's as thick as your wrist will be upside your head in short order. At least that's what I hope he means.

Thinking all this helps, until I see who's been trying to get my attention. My gentleman caller is white and my size, which about ends our similarities. He's got hair that's become dreadlocks because of a lack of washing, and his teeth remind me of a picket fence torn apart by a kid, and then slapped back together, the slats going every which way. And this same kid's been really cheap with the whitewash, or maybe he just doesn't have Tom Sawyer's charm, because the man's teeth are brown from root to tip. His eyes are huge, blue watery things that look pretty crazy. The question of whether this loon understands the subtlety of White's warning blows through my mind like a hurricane and sends my rational voice running for cover.

"Not such a smart fuck now, huh? Not such a smart fuck now!" The emotionally detached part of my mind, the part I'll use to tell this story at dinner parties—if I still have a tongue in my head—notes that the cons have adopted the guards' way of repeating everything.

Several inmates are walking alongside me now, giving me the evil eye and pelting me with profanities, but it's the ocean-eyed kook with the bad dental hygiene that's the ringleader. Or maybe, the main attraction.

So the situation lays out like this: One crazy-ass convict (I won't even mention the tattoos) is following me, screaming obscenities, while walking lock step behind him are several other evil-looking cons who are staring daggers at me. Which means they strongly dislike me or, even more frightening, really like me. Over all of this, Officer White's voice periodically booms out the warning about not touching the civilian.

I know I've got no leverage with the guy on my heels and that he's impervious to anything I could say. One, he's probably crazy, and two, he's probably in prison for life. There's not much lower he can go. This guy's the embodiment of the maxim that when you've got nothing, there's nothing left to lose. I'm ready to invoke the Christ manner of turning the other cheek, when I realize I'm going to have to walk through here many more times.

The creep notices my wedding band and starts in on how he'd hurt my wife in a variety of ways. "I'd fuck your wife 'til she bled for a week. I'd carve her up and butt fuck you while I'm feeding you her pieces."

I'm not good at anger management. I reach a flash point, and then I remember something I watched on TV a few times and heard on the radio a while back. My rage makes me take the gamble. "Do you know who I am? I'm Terrence McCoy. I have one client in this stinking hole, a Mr. Raymond Carpachio, who was transferred here a month ago. How do you think he'd feel about his attorney getting ragged by the likes of a scumbag like you?"

The crazy pauses for a second, eyes losing their unfocused state, and I can see deliberateness in them. Another con, who's as tall as Officer White but much more muscular, offers, "You don't know Carpachio." I shoot back, "You mean Raymond V. Carpachio, in the pen for racketeering, loan sharking, book-making, indicted by the Feds on three counts of aggravated assault with a baseball bat and a broom handle, two counts of violating the Rico Act, one count murder in the second degree, and two counts murder in the first? Oh, and don't forget the arson charge. However, thanks to my boss, Alex Clairborne, and some work by yours truly, the Grand Jury failed to indict on the assault and Rico statutes, and the premeditated murder we got kicked because we proved the Feds illegally obtained the wiretaps. The two for second degree, it took a jury ninety minutes to acquit, but the arson charge stuck, so Mr. Carpachio's serving five, of which he's already served two at Lompoc and one at Delni. Now he's here, until we get him released on good behavior."

I've been walking all this time, and me and my merry band of psychopaths are almost at the gate separating Block A from B. By the time I've finished my little speech, only the initial kook who threatened Sarah is left. I see he's frustrated, and he keeps looking at Officer White, who's never been more than an arm's length from me throughout this episode. The con would like to get physical, but the fact he's checking White over my shoulder tells me that's not going to happen.

The gate swings open and I'm away, and I can't help but raise a silent prayer to Talk Radio and all those true crime shows that I can't help watching again and again.

I see White's smiling. "Terrence McCoy?"

"What d'ya tell me, Officer White? Never use a real name."

"How'd you know Carpachio's not in A or B Block?"

"I didn't. The fruitcake back there just pissed me off. Besides, I'd always have you to protect me."

That smile again. "You definitely lie with some big balls.'

"What d'ya expect, Officer White, I'm an attorney."

I walk in for my meeting with Preninger and I've got to make an effort to keep my hand from shaking, with all the adrenaline I'm feeling. From one battle to another, I think.

Cheryl looks the same—her Bible in hand and habitual grin.

"So all the kind souls been at you to do some lawyering for the great cause of commuting my sentence to life in prison."

"People have spoken rather forcefully and eloquently in defense of that position and in reminding me of the Canon of lawyerly ethics."

"They're truly the salt of God's Earth. But like momma ducks, they need to realize when their baby's gonna fly on its own."

I cut to it. "Cheryl, do you believe suicide is a sin?"

"The casting away of the Lord's most precious gift is one of the gravest."

"You've heard of suicide by cop, where a person deliberately draws down so he'll get shot. Well, you are engaging in suicide by the State, deliberately not drawing down so the State will have no problem in executing you. Yours is a transgression before God. Don't you believe that you owe it to God to fight for your life?"

Cheryl manages to say, "Yes, but..."

"If someone is lost in the wilderness, surrounded by bears, the situation hopeless, wouldn't God want that person not to give up?" I'm obviously alluding to the dream vision she had of me, just to see if I can pressure her.

"Of course, they should keep trying, Joe."

"If I am part of God's plan, an agent of His Will, shouldn't you at least take my thoughts seriously? Truly ask yourself is your decision to give up

God's Will or your own weakness. Is it your own, very understandable, fear of having to hope again because we both know it's much safer and pain free to have no hope than to have hope and see it crushed, and, Cheryl, I don't profess to know much about God's design, but I know that acting from fear is never in His plans."

Cheryl had started listening intently when I mentioned the bears, and I can tell she's troubled by what I've said. She grips her Bible with both hands and slowly draws it toward her face. She's like this, her face against the Bible, for several minutes. Even Huntner, I notice, is staring. I'm about to call her name when she raises her head; tears glisten in her eyes. "I think you may be right, Joe."

I breathe a sigh of relief.

"Could I use your pen? I want to write, well highlight, something in Luke." Huntner, who had glanced away at the sight of Preninger's tears, sees me trying to get his attention. I motion for his okay to hand Cheryl the pen. After a moment, he nods and I hand it to her like it could be a bomb. She takes the pen behind the Bible and begins to furiously underscore passages of the Gospel.

I sit back. Huntner's robotic back and forth checking has decreased from thirty to fifteen seconds. Now she's scribbling in the margins.

I remember some papers I need her to sign so I start leafing through the contents of my briefcase. A minute or two and Cheryl's calling my name, holding the pen for me to take. Huntner's nodding and she hands it back to me. I notice that the pen, usually cold to the touch because of its steel-like finish, is now warm, from the frenzied speed and tightened grip of Cheryl's frantic writing.

I tell Cheryl goodbye and Officer White is back escorting me through the pens of lawbreakers. I'm feeling good; I've faced down two opponents today and I feel slightly better about my loss in the courtroom. Better, that is, until I understand that the goal I was working for—Preninger's okay to actively defend her—demands a defense that I have no idea how to begin.

# FIFTEEN

*Five months until the execution*

Weeks are passing; after all my efforts to convince Cheryl to accept a defense, I've netted nada toward actually mounting one. I feel like a hypocrite or false prophet, and while Cheryl asks nothing about the progress I've made when I arrive at Sussex every few weeks, the question of what I have done, and what I can do, hangs between us, unspoken and growing larger, and I'm getting more and more frantic to find something, anything, that will help.

On the personal front, Sarah's upbeat disposition has seemed to settle in for the long haul, for which I'm thankful, especially since I've been pretty much a grouch.

I'm back in my office, it's late, and I'm searching and re-searching Preninger's file. I've started and thrown out three different motions, from the reliability of the store clerk's recovered memory, to the improper search of Cheryl's motel room. However, after writing as much as a week on one of them, I realized I had no exculpatory law on my side. All I had was a swishy legal argument that any first-year law school student would know was bunk.

Now, I'm leafing through the post-trial notes. These are better because it's when Bradshaw took over on appeal and he's got everything from the

166

post-trial interviews of lawyers to the media's editorials on the outcome, all accompanied by who were the big winners and losers. The young, handsome Warren Metcalfe, I note, was counted a big winner in his handling of Bhasad Delhi and her testimony. Presciently, the paper cited Metcalfe as a man to watch in Virginia.

I'm trying to slow myself down. I know I'm not going to find anything if I flip through all the material that my gut tells me is worthless—but what if there's nothing to find, a voice nags me. I'm going through some of what the jury said after the trial, looking for tampering, improper contact with attorneys, statements showing they heard information from Aunt Jessie or Cousin Earl that was never admitted as evidence. The problem with this strategy is that eight of the jurors decided against post-trial comments.

I'm watching a DVD of the jurors: two women and two men meeting reporters at a little post-trial summit. Rita Mizuno spends fifteen minutes detailing, with impressive exactitude, the merits of each side of the case, while pointing out how damning Delhi's testimony had been. I spend another two hours checking the trial transcript against everything Mizuno said just to be sure it could only have only been gotten from the trial itself. She must have a photographic memory because she repeats some phrases, and a few whole paragraphs, word for word from both attorney's closing.

The other woman, Julie Sturgis, and one of the men, Sam Erickson, spend more time talking with the reporters about the Redskin's Super Bowl chances than about the case. The last man, Fred Waters, makes statements that are even less helpful, if that's possible. Composed as they are of grunts and nods and simple comments like, "She had the drugs. She had clothes stuffed in the closet with the victims' blood type." This was all before DNA testing in Virginia, which I guess is something to be thankful for. This last guy bothers me though. It's like I've seen him somewhere, somewhere recently.

This kind of not remembering thing can really irritate me. Some people will almost tear their hair out trying to remember the correct word or somebody's name. With me, it's the face. Probably because I stubbornly stick to the notion that I have a superpower, and that it's recognizing people. It's letting my mind go on to other things, and the confidence I have that somewhere in my subconscious that my brain's still worrying about the darn thing that helps me the most. It's this subtle turning of my mind that lets me get it. I haven't seen this guy before, but I have seen *the look*—Daniel.

No, this guy doesn't look gay, but something sunken around his cheeks, pinched in his eyes, the way his head pops up almost too far when his name's called, it all makes me hit the rewind button and watch again. I note he's even got the thinness of fingers like Daniel's. All the signs make me think this guy has AIDS.

I'm back in the front office, knocking over boxes, and because it's so late I'm suddenly worried that Achmed and Jimmy will think I'm a burglar and call the cops.

It takes me a while to find the juriss' voir dires. Of course, Bradshaw had those questions and answers all collated, and I'm making a mess of his carefully referenced system.

Okay, Fred Waters answered 'no' when asked if he had any debilitating illness or injury that would preclude him from sitting the length of the trial. That's a lie, and for a moment I'm excited, and then I remind myself, superpower aside, I'm only guessing he had the disease, and relying on that one question isn't grounds for appeal. Realistically, Waters could just say with good faith that his doctors told him he had several years to live and the case wasn't going to take that long. Also, there are lots of reasons why someone would want to lie about having AIDS. But then again, AIDS is an easy way out of jury duty and Fred Waters gave me the distinct feeling that he wasn't that much into doing his civic duty.

This is all supposition, tenuous at best. I need to find out if he actually had the disease. My excitement now has nearly gone out as I realize my big fat break could only be called thin, as in thinner than a pencil. How 'bout thin as the graphite in the pencil?

The next day and I'm driving through Craphole, Virginia (not its real name). Bunch of squat three-room, tin-plated, fabricated houses with flaking paint and raggedy arm chairs used as outside lawn furniture and as anchors for leashes to keep the pit bulls near the house and away from attacking anything that moves in the neighborhood.

125 Quarterdeck's the address, even though it's about fifty miles to the nearest ship. I'm searching on the left and I see the house, faded yellow, no dog, but there is a sofa out front and a small tree. A mustached fellow, wearing a blue cut-off T-shirt and dirty jeans, sees me spying him as sits on the sofa having a cigarette. By the time I've parked my car across the street and down a ways, he's gone. Great, that wasn't Waters, just some guy who runs from any white guy who looks like he might be five-oh.

I'm up to the door. The small porch bears witness to someone who lacks a green thumb. Small plants, mostly brown twigs in jars with dust, stand like dried pottery soldiers. I knock on the screen door. I figure the occupant might need some assurances I haven't come to repossess his car or get those seven years of alimony and child support he owes. "I'm an attorney looking for a man I'm sure is not you. Fred Waters. It's about a case from twelve years ago. Waters was a juror."

The dirty white curtains beside the door flutter; the man who vacated the sofa stands behind his screen door that has enough big holes to let in a cat. His shirt says 'Everybody Loves a Big Johnson' and has a small man hiding what must be an enormous penis behind a water-ski, while several silicon enhanced cartoon girls watch appreciatively. "He don't live here," he says. "I've been here since he moved out."

"Do you know where he might have gone?"

"To hell, most likely."

My stomach sinks and rises in equal proportion. Waters is dead and I can't question him, but what did he die of?

"He was a mean cuss. Came back tearing up the backyard, demanding I give him the junk he piled in the back. Started accusing me of ripping off some copper wire he couldn't find." He goes on a while with this Sanford and Son problem, then "I told him he oughta pay me for the fumigating I had to do on this place."

"What for?" I ask, briefly hoping he's about to launch into some ill-informed homophobic tirade about Waters spreading his AIDS germs everywhere.

"Cockroaches. Big ones. Let's just say I ain't seen a cat in the neighborhood for a long time."

I'm thinking the absence of cats might have more to do with the dogs I'm sure that live around here. "So, he didn't leave a forwarding address?" Of course he did, I think, and this fine gentleman immediately filed it away in case of this eventuality.

"No, can't say as he did. He was stayin' at that motel up on Greensboro, and I only knew that 'cuz I was having a beer across the way and he seen me and come over and started bitchin' me out again 'bout his damn copper wire. You'd think the guy'd lost all the gold in Fort Knox. I mean, copper was running about twenty-seven cents a pound back then and a guy'd be lucky to get twenty bucks for the stash he had.

"What's the name of the motel where Waters was staying?"

The man giggles at the question. "The Alibi Motel. Always wanted to get picked up by the cops and tell'm, 'Officer, I couldn't have stolen that tractor engine, I was at the Alibi Motel."

I smile. "What was your name in case I have more questions?"

He smiles, showing me dingy yellow teeth and thinks a moment. "Scott Baio. B - A - I - O."

I ask, "You pick Baio 'cuz you didn't know Chachi's last name?" and he smiles like, you got me copper. "It was Arcola," I add.

He nods and seems to be filing that nugget away so he can win some future bar bet. "That's why you're a big time attorney and I'm a metal salvager."

I'm about to inform the guy that knowing Chachi's last name was not on the bar exam—though knowing Pinkie Tuscadero was Fonzie's only real love helped on the Contract section—when I figure it's probably best to keep the lawyer mystique alive. I'm back in my car, feeling lucky some other salvager didn't get an eye for it. I figure, the way these new cars are made, there's probably not enough metal to make a decent Tin Man.

Cell phones are great when they aren't sending you into oncoming traffic. In two minutes, I'm talking with the Alibi Motel. Fifteen minutes later, I'm pulling into its run-down parking lot.

The Alibi Motel needs one. It's decrepit, seems to sway in the wind, even though it's only two stories, and its inner rows of bungalows have the broken toy, rusted hibachi look of habitual life, rather than the breezy 'we're on our way to see Mt. Vernon' look of a Motel 6.

It takes me some time to find the front office. I go to the screen door and no one seems to be home, but a stereo that belches out some Speed Metal Death music. I dead-end down a walkway where I see a small child, standing alone, peeing into a crawl space.

I find the manger, Sam Cook, a small guy with permanent sweat stains and heavy black glasses that look like they've got one of the office organizer magnets, there's so many safety pins holding them together. He chain smokes unfiltered Camels, so he might as well just gulp down containment rods of nuclear power plants, but he's friendly enough and tells me he's only run the place for his mom since '96 when he was laid off. Since then there's been no Fred Waters, but a tenant, Ida Mae, who's been here forever, she might know.

I thank him and he throws me some advice. "She likes to drink beer. Malt Liquor—Schlitz, if you're feeling generous. Give her a few of those and she'll tell you about Stonewall Jackson or even Action Jackson."

I walk down to number 107, which is unique only in that it has a doormat and a Tweety Bird on the door saying, Pweeeze Knock.

I do as I'm told and Ida Mae's at the door. She's forty—no, she's fifty. Wait, she's sixty. She's that indeterminate, gnarly, leather-skinned woman who drinks too much Old English. Her hair's mostly white and she's got it pulled into a ponytail that's held with an evil-looking skull and crossbones barrette. Ida's a skinny woman, rubber bands on her wrist, capri pants around her waist, and a potbelly through her center. But when she shakes my hand, she's got a grip like a pipe fitter. "Sam rang me you were coming. Said you were interested in Fred Waters."

"Did you know him?"

"That depends."

I smirk, knowing this is going to take a trip to the liquor store. "What's your poison, Ida Mae?"

"Any of the malted beers'd be fine."

I'm walking away when I stop. "You did know him, didn't you?"

"Lanky feller, about six two, awful skinny, brown hair."

The way she says skinny with just a little twitch of her penciled-in eyebrows makes me quickstep it out the door.


It's one hour later and we're finishing off a six-pack of 32-ounce Schlitz Malt liquor. Kids are running back and forth and playing some fantastic game we all forget when we hit our teenage years and start worrying about what's cool. Ferdinand—he's a gardener—sits outside preparing his family's dinner on one of those rusted hibachis, while his wife, Juanita, hustles in and out preparing tortillas and shouting advice to her husband.

I'm sitting on the stoop next to Ida Mae, which is really just two steps and a cement banister. I've hung my suit coat on a garden hose rack and rolled up my sleeves. Ferdinand's just finished complaining about a power mower that's been causing him grief and Ida finishes the last gulp of a Schlitz, which puts her even with me. That fact's depressing, or impressive, depending on who you're thinking about or what's your view on drinking sixty-four ounces of beer in an hour.

In the course of imbibing, Ida Mae's given me everything she knows about Fred Waters. "He had the AIDS," she says, confirming my superpower. "Had it good, got as skinny as an anorexic vegetarian." She cackles at this and I think she's taking her role as drunken High Priestess of the Alibi Motel too seriously. "Then he got better, then got the pneumonia, then he got better again and damned near moved away. And then one day he was just gone."

I question her about where he went, who he knew.

"Prostitutes. He was a mean son-of- a-bitch; the only one's who'd stand'm were the ones he paid."

"But he had AIDS."

"Well, they didn't know that, did they? At least, not at first. And even after, there was always some girl desperate enough, who needed money for crack or who had AIDS herself, that'd give him a tumble."

"A real ladies man."

Ida Mae stops to inhale a third of her next Schlitz. "He thought so. Thing was, he hated women. Hated them like a man who can only get it up with hookers."

"Do you think this hatred would've translated over into the case I told you about?"

"He said to me once it was a whore who gave him the AIDS, and it was only fair that a whore'd take the needle. He got a real kick out of that, a real kick. Said it was divine justice."

I'm trying to run through Waters voir dire in my head. They're at least a few more inconsistencies with what he said, and now I know what was bugging me about his post-trial statement. He mentioned the drugs and the blood, not Bhasad Delhi's testimony, as reasons he voted to convict. In Waters' mind, why would you mention the testimony of just another woman? She's probably a whore, like all the rest.

This is all damning for Waters, but it's also hearsay, and it's hearsay from a woman who would probably drink turpentine if you threw it in a bottle and called it beer.

Juanita offers me a quesadilla. It smells delicious, but I'm not going to wolf down food that could go into the stomachs of her little kids: the Nina, the Pinta, and the Santa Maria. "So you don't know where he went, and you don't know where anyone is who knew him?"

"Naw, can't say as I do, Joe. All them types, like Waters, either up and left some late night so as not to pay their back rent, or they died selling themselves or od'ing."

I nod, but my mind tells me I'm at a dead end.

I say my goodbyes and leave the last unopened Schlitz for Ida. She politely thanks me and I turn back saying, "Ida Mae, just remember what my father used to say: You mess with the bull, you're gonna get the horns."

Ida starts laughing to raise the roof. "Your father was a wise man, Joe, a wise man."

No, I think, as I unlock my car. Not a wise man, just a man who knew when to give up the malt liquor for the less potent kick of Budweiser.

Back at my office, I see that Waters lied on other questions like, 'Did you have a communicable disease? And is there anything else we should know about you?' Yeah, how 'bout 'I'm a big time whore fancier who likes to shoot heroin'? I need notarized statements from some people, but mostly I need a way to find Fred Waters. I call a few motels near the Alibi that rent by the hour, but get nothing and quickly realize how futile this is.

My best idea comes later that night, when I'm slipping off to sleep. I'll call some AIDS organizations and hospices to see if they have a record of Waters.

The next day I'm trying to do just that, but all I'm getting is a lot of road-blocking bureaucrats who spout patient confidentiality rights. I'm suffering from chronic indigestion thanks to Achmed and Jimmy's pizza, when I realize I might know someone who can get around these rules.

I'm sitting in Daniel's apartment. "You think all gay people know each other. Is that it, Joe?" Daniel remarks kiddingly.

Well, you do have a secret code."

"What?"

"Are you a friend of Judy's?"

"Ah, good point."

"Know anyone who can get me records on a guy who's had the virus since the nineties?"

Daniel asks why and I explain about Fred Waters. "I don't think he was gay," I add.

"That's what they all say," says Daniel. "Early on, Gay Men's Health Crisis was the only place to go, gay or straight. I was also in on the ground floor work at ACTUP, kind of a George Wythe."

"Who?"

"Representative from Virginia, signer of the Declaration of Independence. He was the first law professor of the United States— something a lawyer like yourself might be expected to know. Wasn't as showy as John Hancock. Really, Joe, gay men don't sit around all day with their fag hags discussing clothes, shoes, and men, no matter what every gay show on Bravo wants you to think. I smile and he adds, "Okay, I've still got some highly-placed friends; I'll see what I can do."


Twenty-four hours later and Daniel's standing at my desk, slapping down a small file. "Here's all I could get on Fred Waters."

"Sheesh, you work fast."

"There's not a lot to occupy my time, Joe, and by the way, your receptionist could use a complete makeover."

"What was that you said about gay men not talking about clothes and makeup?" I'm thumbing through the pages while Daniel summarizes, hitting the high point right off.

"He's dead, Joe. Died last year from pneumocystis." He's shaking his head like he's a Chicago Cub's fan and they've just come up short of the world series again. "He was getting AZT and the cocktail from a local center. His old address is on the last page."

I'm grabbing my car keys from my desk. "Want to go for a ride?"

"Sure, but can we stop downstairs and grab a slice of pizza?"

"Okay, but don't say I didn't warn you."

Daniel's eating his second piece, the first consumed while he's chatting with Achmed and Jimmy. Ordering his second slice cemented his friendship with my Moslem pizza makers, who love everyone the Koran tells them, including anyone who orders seconds.


South of Market is mostly industrial, populated by businesses not looking for much foot traffic and those bars catering to suburbanites who imagine city life as a kind of cement wasteland of hulking metal buildings, liquor stores, and prostitutes. The Excelsior Hotel looks like it hasn't had much to celebrate since Gerald Ford was falling down the White House steps. I get lucky and find a parking spot; even luckier when Daniel has enough change to feed the meter.

Daniel goes to lock his passenger side door and I tell him to stop.

"Joe, in this neighborhood, you're crazy not to lock your car."

I tell him I keep it unlocked so thieves can browse a little first, and Daniel eyes me like I'm screwy. I explain, "That way, nobody breaks the window to discover my stereo's worth five bucks, and my air freshener's not even fresh." Daniel shrugs at my reasoning and we go inside.

The Excelsior's lobby is spacious and empty. It holds a few ratty couches, one of them holding a person who's passed out with his back to us. The reception desk is a 2 x 2-length piece of polished wood sticking out from behind a thick metal screen so big it'd keep out bugs big enough to guard Shaquille O'Neal.

The attendant, a guy wearing a nametag that says Ed, has a gimpy curled up hand and fading greasy hair. He gives me a knowing smile. In a second I know why.

"Rooms are twenty five by the hour with a five dollar laundry fee," Ed says.

I'm feeling like Sam Spade, though Spade probably never went anywhere with a gay, terminally ill sidekick. "Maybe I don't rent a room and I just give you the thirty dollars." I slide Waters' picture toward him. "You know this guy?"

"Ah, that faggot's dead." Now looking at Daniel and me, "Nothing personal, you understand."

I give him a cold stare, like I'd imagine Bogie'd do. "The picture."

"Waters, Fred Waters. We called him oil and Waters 'cuz on account of he didn't mix with nobody."

Okay, the guy's a bigoted idiot, but at least he's playing along with the hard-boiled detective persona. "Go on," I say.

"Where's the cash for your room, Sir?" He says the last word with a pause, like it's a joke.

"Here's ten, keep talking. What'd you know about Waters?"

"He had AIDS," the attendant says, eyes flickering toward Daniel. "He liked whores, and he wasn't particular about which way they pissed, as long as they looked like a girl."

Daniel knocks me on the shoulder, maybe to remind me that the closet's still hiding a lot of gay men and hard enough to make me thankful he still doesn't weigh all that much.

"Did you talk to him a lot?" I ask.

He nods and I toss him another ten. "Did he ever talk about anything important?'

"He talked about hating fags and whores and how he'd read that the faggots had started this AIDS thing with the bathhouses and how they had two-and-a-half partners a night and we know what half they was interested in."

"Anything else? Anything he'd been involved with several years ago?"

Greasy Ed's smiling. "I knew you guys was here for that." I'd like to remind Ed that a few moments ago he thought we were here to spend a romantic hour doing the wild thing. "He stuck that Christian bitch with the needle just like he got the AIDS."

Waters was obviously pretty fickle over deciding just how he got the bug. After the trial, it was probably a better story to say he got AIDS from the needle. Ed goes on talking and I start taking notes. I also run out of money, so he almost doesn't direct us to the tenants who knew Waters. Daniel grumbles and reluctantly fishes two tens from his pocket, holding them next to the window. No question he's pissed at paying off this homophobe.

"The names for the tens," Daniel says. The guy's already got thirty, so he probably figures what's the risk. He rattles off four names and room numbers, and Daniel slides the money through the slot, but not before he gives the Alexander Hamilton's big licks. The man's face screws up in anger at getting what he figures are AIDS germs all over his cash, while I can't help but think this is definitely not a Humphrey Bogart picture.

There's no elevator, so we're tramping around and ignoring the woman shooting up in the second floor hallway, the puddles of urine in the stairwell, and a pile of something that Daniel and I are afraid to get close to.

The four people are at home in the middle of the day, which says something about life around here. All four of our noble interviewees paint the same picture of Waters: a man terribly bitter over contracting AIDS from whores, faggots, or junkies. It seems that Waters played a kind of merry-go-round of 'Who do I blame today?' and was quite happy to be sending someone else to death other than the prostitutes he'd infected with the virus.

I assured the four I was not with the police; Daniel tossed them a twenty and they assured me they'd sign affidavits that Waters had a big axe to grind when he took up jury duty; however, it was the last one who added a twist to the episode. Alexander, named as he told us at least four times, after Alexander the French Sun King. Since I needed to hear what he had to say, I didn't bother to correct his history.

When I asked him if he'd swear out an affidavit, he told me that he'd been busted for selling dope and that he'd offered up this same info to the police, in hopes of getting a lighter sentence. Turned out the bust got tossed and the police never followed up on his information. If they had, they would have contacted the D.A., who would've notified Frank Bradshaw, Cheryl's appeals attorney, and there would've been some note in the file.

Alexander couldn't remember the officer's name on account of having a bad spell with the drugs, but he knew it was last February on account of it being his and the wife's twentieth anniversary (had they stayed together). When Daniel asked how long they'd been together before the breakup, Alexander told us three months, which left us shaking our heads in sadness while at the same time trying to cover our laughter.

We thank Alexander the Sun King and retreat out of the hotel's lobby. In the car, I write Daniel a check for the money I owe him, and he tells me what an interesting day he's had. On my way home now, I stop off at the liquor store, and remembering Ida Mae's favorite, on a whim I grab a couple of Schlitz Malt liquors, even as I hear my father's warning about messing with bull and getting the horns. Other great witticisms from my father were, 'You drive like old people screw,' and 'In a fight always watch your nose.' I always thought it would be better to watch the guy who was trying to hit you, oh and, 'Stop signs are for beginners.'

Thirsty now, I flout the open container law and crack one open before I get home. Hey, I figure, if you're going to break this law, you might as well do it in a big way—with a thirty two-ounce bottle of Schlitz.

Sarah's happy I'm home and tells me dinner'll be ready in about an hour because there's some problem with the potatoes. I hit the backyard to wait and land in a lounge chair, quaffing back some beer and thinking over what happened today.

Fred Waters' credibility is shot to hell, but what does that mean for Cheryl's case? Waters lied all over his voir dire, and I'll have signed statements from sources in different areas to prove that. Also, I'll have hearsay testimony that he got himself on the trial with a hidden agenda. The problem is that the Court could still find that a reasonable person would have found Cheryl guilty, so probably no new trial. Though I'll argue it and give the Justices something to toss aside, but the penalty phase of the trial is where I've got my best shot. Twelve jurors had to agree to death for the judge to impose that sentence. I've got to set up my brief to show that this same reasonable person could very well have felt death was not the correct punishment.

The other thing is Alexander's contention that he told the cops about Waters. The problems with this are several. He couldn't remember the cop's name, so I'd have to subpoena his arrest record. Since the arrest got kicked, who knew if it was there, and who knew what would show up if the cops were doing a sweep? Probably a lot of cops with a lot of bad guys with a lot of arrest jackets.

The other problem is that any snooping I do is bound to alert the D.A., and I'll end up tipping my play to that asshole, Shriner, before I'm ready to file. I'll have to come up with a convincing lie of why I'm interested in a junkie with a year-old shadow arrest. He did say his arrest was tainted, so maybe I can play the ambulance-chasing attorney who's looking to sue the men in blue for civil rights violations.

Sarah and I have just made love. As I sit back and enjoy sex's last fading glimmer, today's events give me something to churn over and something to tell Cheryl, but only when I know my exact play and all the case law that's fit to print. I'll remind myself tomorrow to jump online and see what I can dig up as regards voir dire.

I'm at the precinct with a subpoena for Alexander's police record, and I'm keeping their printer busy spitting out a long list of drug arrests and petty thefts. The Watch Commander—he of the sad eyes, shuffling step and droopy mustache—hasn't pawned me off to anyone and is personally assisting me. I'm sure it's out of the goodness of his heart and not because he doesn't trust me. All the while, the Sergeant's attempting to pump me for information on why I'm interested in this ancient non-case, and my paranoid side can't help but think he's a mole for Metcalfe and Shriner.

"So what's up with this skel?" he tries to ask innocently.

"Oh, nothing, he's clean now, and he wants me to look into an arrest your guys made on him about a year ago. He says your boys got rough with him, then dropped the charges to cover your ass." I say all this slow and nonchalant, trying to convey the impression that I really don't believe his story. "Anyway, the guy's got an inheritance or something, and you know, I'll check outhouses for shit for two hundred an hour."

The cop smiles, but he's a seasoned pro who's been lied to way too many times to be fooled by the likes of me. "Yeah, well, he could've filed with the civil authority back then. A failure to come forward promptly is usually seen as suspicious," he adds like the seminar law trainee he is.

He's handing me the printer pages. There are ten of them, and sure enough, the last entry has an Officer Briggs busting Alexander Small. That's a letdown from his Sun King handle on March 11th, when he bought drugs from said officer. I notice there are notes in the margin, mostly cop jargon, numbers, times of day, etc.

I thank the Watch Commander and he comes back with a faux friendly, "Did you find anything?"

"Oh yeah," I respond. "It says right here in the margin, 'beat the suspect senseless,' and then in parentheses, 'see attached video.'" The cop actually leans forward to look until I mention the video.

"Yeah, and you solved the JonBenét Ramsay case, counselor. You are so full of shit."

I'm back at the office assembling my very first State Supreme Court brief, checking that I've dotted the i's and crossed the t's. In death penalty cases, in their final phase after a date's been set, the appeals are automatically referred to Virginia's highest court. Not because you want the best lawmakers looking at it, but as a cost-saving feature, and so the lower courts don't get jammed up when these cases are going to end up at the Supreme Court anyway.

I had a quick talk with Officer Briggs over the phone yesterday. It was short and sweet. Even after he looked at the file, he didn't remember Alexander. He reminds me they were busting crack heads that month up and down Smithfield corridor, some hard-on the mayor had for making Richmond a crack-free city. The cop laughs then, probably because that same mayor got busted a few months later for trying to buy sex and cocaine off an undercover vice officer. The mayor's defense, "At least the cop wasn't a guy," almost got him re-elected.

I asked Briggs if he kicked the case or did he bounce it upstairs for a D.A. consult. I've already queried the D.A.'s office on this and received a terse *no*. Briggs gives me a few paragraphs that amount to *I can't recall any of the details*, which I think is too convenient, and which I think leaves me only to fuss with my first State Supreme Court brief.

I'll file it tomorrow, and I'll tell Cheryl about the whole deal. I've met with her several times since I first learned of this, and it's taken all my self-control not to blurt out this slim chance, especially in the face of whatever new hope I've stirred in her.

The next day is the first really hot and humid day of summer, and A. Malcolm Shriner is cursing the morning sun as he walks across the outdoor mezzanine connecting the parking garage with the D.A.'s office. Shriner is so miserably hot—he has a tendency to sweat in any temperature over an air-conditioned seventy-two—that he fails to notice several comely female office workers. Like him, they're scampering toward the office building and the icy freeze of its central air.

No wonder they fought a war all around here, Shriner thinks. Without air conditioning, I'd be willing to fight a bearcat for an ice chip.

His phone's beeping at him and he checks the number before answering. "Yes, Warren, I'm just outside the office. He did what? That piece of shit! Give me the gist. No wait, I'll be up in a minute." Shriner hangs up, only to notice a crowd gathering around the entrance.

Asking around, he finds out the electric doors are sealed due to a bogus security signal, and it will be at least ten minutes before they can be opened. Shriner sits outside and fumes—inside and out—sweating through his Gabbani French-cuffed shirt and through to the Armani V-cut blazer. As Shriner overheats, he begins to fixate on a certain low-grade attorney and a case that he's certain will continue to piss him off.

Shriner is in his office, changing into another shirt. D.A. Metcalfe sits on his desk, knowing better than to tease him.

"So what's the brief?" Shriner growls.

'I'm still looking at it, but I had Dean write me a précis." Shriner's making a face. "I'll have Warshaw go over it after," adds Metcalfe. "He had some free time. Besides, you're the one who put him on the case because he and Heyerdahl have a history that might rattle Heyerdahl."

"So the $64,000 question is, who's he got?" Shriner's slipping his gold cuff links into the fresh shirt.

"For one thing, lowlifes to say that this juror Waters was a misogynistic, drug-taking AIDS patient who blamed women for his getting the disease, and then decided to share his misery by taking another worthless, deserving female with him to an early grave."

Shriner, looking for his tie, "You sure could pick your juries back then, Warren."

"It was Anderson who handled all that. The Preninger case was my first murder trial and I had my uses, but as Anderson, the ole coot said, jury selection was not one of them." He shrugged. "Anyway, Waters is dead. Anderson, too, for that matter."

"So it's all hearsay and we impugn the witnesses on their records. Hell, they've got to have felony rap sheets." Metcalfe's holding up two fingers, "Okay, there's no way the Court gives Preninger a new case on this."

"True, Mal, but might it not be enough to set aside the death penalty?"

"A couple of years ago, maybe. But Sumner's appointed two justices in the last eighteen months. They're part of the Governor's big rallying cry on 'Get Tough on Crime.' None of these Justices are going to want to look soft on a big case like this."

Warren's leafing through the brief. "This last guy, Alexander, is more problematic. He's geographically isolated from the other witnesses, and he says he told the cops about Waters." Metcalfe continues to read. "But there's no evidence in the police file."

The two men share an indecipherable glance. "Besides," Shriner says, finishing, "He was trying to plead a drug charge."

"Remember to read the brief before you start saying that around the office."

"Heyerdahl's throwing shit against the wall," Shriner adds dismissively.

Metcalfe, still thumbing pages, smiling, "Well, my friend, this is a pretty big turd, and if we don't duck we're going to have crap all over our faces."

Re-knotting his tie, Shriner frowns, as if to say *get serious*.

Metcalfe tosses the brief on his deputy's desk. "Damn good for a guy from Laverne, Mal. And stop making that face. I tell you, you're underestimating this guy."

"I beat him on the extension; I'll trounce his ass on this."

"Fine, fine, you do that, Mal. Just one question: Who didn't we want handling this case? Who were we afraid of? The royal shit disturber..."

"Frank Bradshaw."

"Right, so ask yourself this. Did Bradshaw come up with anything this good?" Metcalfe's shakes his head, wagging a peremptory finger. "No, he did not, my-oh-so-fierce Deputy D.A. So keep in mind that this thing may not be over, not by a long shot."

There are half a dozen reporters waiting for my return to the office. I answer as blandly as I can, expressing Cheryl's fervent desire to have her death sentence commuted, and explaining that I believe this motion is the logical step in effecting that commutation.

I keep moving up past the Pizzeria—where I catch befuddled glances from Achmed and Jimmy—to my office, where a woman reporter looks like she's ready to follow me in. I have to box her out, like I'm setting up to grab a rebound, before I can get into the office without her following me.

I'm back in my office in the early afternoon, after driving to Sussex and explaining to Cheryl what I'd been doing the last few weeks and what the appeal was. I downplayed our chances to where I'd favor Charles Manson getting out before us, but still I couldn't help but feel I was giving her some hope.

I ask myself if it's my fear of not giving her something to look forward to, then I realize that I'm simply afraid of failing. Even with someone's life on the line, there's a part of me that's more afraid of what the failure will say about me than of her dying as a result. I mean, it's one thing to play high school baseball, sit on the bench and watch your team lose. It's quite another to Bill Buckner the final out and cause your team's loss. And it's an entirely different ballpark when they're going to take the loser and push cyanide through her veins.

Stella is out, like usual, but she's left a pile of messages from media and other groups, which I have no intention of returning. I'm beginning to feel like a hostage and starting to understand that this case involves more than me, a woman who's going to be executed, and an asshole Deputy D.A. I'm thinking that this case is news, big news, that the U.S. of A. doesn't kill women that often, and that's when the blinds give a shake and in pops that pushy woman reporter's head with a mic in her hand, asking me if she can have just a minute.

# SIXTEEN

*Four months until the execution*

The State Supreme court of Virginia consists of seven justices: four white, one black, two Latino. They're all men, which I'm hoping plays to my advantage, as all men on some level envision themselves as the knight rescuing the fair maiden.

In the last two years, Governor Sumner has appointed two members to this court: Troy, one of the whites, and Rivera, a Latino. Since their elevation, they've voted one hundred percent against death penalty appeals. I tell myself most of these appeals were frivolous and their record has little relevance to my cogent, forceful, and well-thought-out arguments. (Yeah, right).

Three of the others are also pro death penalty, but with mixed voting records. Brankowski and Oshen—a black man—have sat the longest. As the realization sunk in that they never had to worry about getting re-elected, they gradually diverged from standard rightist positions. Most notably in Hendersohn V. Virginia, when they struck down a guilty verdict and ordered a new trial after the defense demonstrated that the appointed Psych. examiner had ties to the D.A.'s office. Most recently, Brankowski, Oshen, and the newest member, Shepherd, voted together with the oldest member,

Salomon, in writing the majority opinion that the death penalty had to be set aside. They found that the lower court judge violated the defendant's constitutional rights by disallowing several key defense statements made to the police that the lower court had ruled were self-serving and without probative value.

As for the last white judge, Lancaster, it's like that gopher game you play at the video arcade, where the gopher pops up and you get to smack it with the mallet. But he just pops up somewhere else, so you've got to smack him again. Lancaster started out as a dyed-in-the-wool liberal, but Reagan's America swamped liberalism and he moved to the center. He has swung from barring police testimony of a defendant's statement (when he may have been under the influence of drugs) to voting with Brankowski and Oshen on broadening police search and seizure capabilities. All in all, seven justices, seven opinions, seven egos, all deciding one woman's fate.

I rise as the Justices enter the court. I'm expecting some tough questions, but I'm more worried that I don't have good answers for some of them. To my right, Shriner and Dean also stand. Dean's out of his league; the only reason he's here is because Shriner thinks Dean bugs me. That's fine with me. Better Dean than someone who can actually help the Deputy D.A.

The bailiff's calling out the requisite oh yeahs, and Brankowski, as Senior Justice, begins asking questions. "Mr. Heyerdahl, I've read your brief and I need help understanding how any of this rises to the level of impeachable evidence."

There's one I can answer. "Your Honor, I would think that Mr. Waters' state of mind and the corroborating witnesses' lack of geographical proximity would certainly rise to that level. Second, the respondents' lack of motive to fabricate would further strengthen the petitioner's case." I'm starting out soft. I want to feel my way around, figure out who stands where and, in the process, not insult any members of the Court.

"Your Honors, if it pleases the Court," Shriner talking, knowing it will. "What we have here is a prima facie case of Mr. Heyerdahl assembling a group of felons to perjure themselves, in the hope of postponing his client's appointment with a lethal injection."

I'm ready for this. "Your Honors, Mr. Shriner's office has had ample time to depose my witnesses. Yet, I am unaware of any evidence he intends to present to you that supports this assertion."

Shriner comes right back. "Several of these statements were given by alcoholics, drug abusers, and two-time felons. Their proclivity for falsehoods is documented by their histories."

I'm checking some papers, but I know the citing, "Mr. Shriner's office used Stanton Delay, one of the felons in question, to testify against a drug smuggler in a recent case. Is the State now saying they've used testimony of persons they believed to be lying in service of their cases? I have a partial list of informants that the D.A.'s office has used to prosecute their cases. They have far worse records than my witnesses. I wonder if the District Attorney is ready to repudiate those cases as well?"

Lancaster seems to like this. "What of it, Mr. Shriner?"

"No, Your Honor, we are not prepared to repudiate cases where a jury has decided on a conviction. However, if I could point the Court's attention to the real issue at hand? Regardless of the veracity of statements Mr. Heyerdahl has managed to procure, the court still must ask itself if any reasonable person could have arrived at a different verdict, especially given the overwhelming evidence. I direct the court's attention to Broderick v. Virginia."

As the Justice's scan their notes, I try not to flinch. This is the State's strongest argument. Essentially, Shriner's saying, "Let's assume that everything the duplicitous snake, Mr. Heyerdahl, is saying is true. Is the Court prepared to say that, with all the evidence presented, another neutral juror would have arrived at a different verdict?"

Shriner's finishing, and I'm—hopefully—just getting started. "Your Honors, we've all been lawyers, and there is no need to belabor the point that juries can be fickle. Brankowski and Lancaster nod at this, which encourages me. "Trying to ascertain what a jury would have done is at least as difficult as determining what they will do. Example: I cite a highly publicized trial of a former NFL star, where I think many of us differed significantly from what my colleague calls "reasonable people." Again, a nod from Brankowski and Lancaster. "I'm simply putting forth that if the Court were to find that a juror committed perjury on his voir dire and in his deliberations, that to assume anyone could know the mind of another juror in that situation would be tenuous at best. I'd like to suggest to the Court that *tenuous* is not a word that should ever go hand-in-hand with the application of the death penalty."

I think I just slid my argument in without annoying the Court, making them think that my first motion was just for show—an offering to appease their desire to look tough, yet fair. What I'm really advocating is *keep the verdict, throw out the death sentence.* I can then bring in all of Cheryl's good works, including the statement by the Jeffords' daughter asking for the sentence to be commuted to life imprisonment.

For all his arrogance and bravado, Shriner is sharp, and he's on to my strategy as soon as my mouth shuts. "I would like to add that whatever the predilections of certain errant juries, the State has every confidence that the Justices here, steeped as they are in the law, will render a decision that determines what was, and would be, a reasonable verdict, most specifically in a case where the State has an eyewitness, blood evidence and..."

I'm shouting over Shriner, "Is it Mr. Shriner's intention to retry the case here? If so, I'm sure the Court could save us all some time and redirect a new trial now."

Rivera hits his gavel to shut me up. "Mr. Heyerdahl, do not interrupt. There are no objections here; it is our prerogative to determine what is essential to our findings, not yours." I'm figuring I've managed to piss off at least one judge, and then he says, "That having been said, in the interests of brevity, Mr. Heyerdahl is absolutely correct. We are not seeking to retry the case, but examining a specific point of law. Unless, Mr. Shriner, you'd like us to re-open the case?"

Shriner puts on his best look of repentance. For a guy as pompous as he is, it's pretty good. "No, Your Honor, the State does not."

The wind out of our sails, we do a little jockeying for position, but the race is pretty much run. The Court has our papers and dismisses us with its thanks.

The media contingent swallows us as we exit the courtroom. Shriner and his big head are like some powerhouse steamroller. The media simply bounces off him. Me, I'm like some cast-off piece of highway trash, lucky to not get caught in camera cables and hanging boom mics. I don't end up as media road-kill, but just barely.

The next few days pass slowly. Sarah seems to have come down from the happiness pills and keeps prodding me to tell her what the delay in the Justices' decision might mean. I think she's projecting onto my trial her fear of not being pregnant. This gets me wondering why she hasn't been on me this month to have sex. Maybe her refound faith has her falling back on the natural way of good ole straight sex for pregnancy.

Regardless, it's nice to make love without it seeming like an Olympic Sport, and without her pushing me off so she can tilt her pelvis to some optimum angle, parallel to the solar ecliptic.


I even go to the dentist. I've been missing these appointments every six months for the last three years, so I know I'm in trouble, and I shudder to think of the last time I flossed.

It's an early appointment and I was out late, so I kind of stumble in. The attendant, a Spanish guy with way too much good humor for this time of the morning, sits me down, slaps a lead blanket over me (so I guess Superman can't see the ray gun I'm hiding under my shirt), and stuffs that terrible cardboard X-ray paper into my mouth. He points the tube thing at my jaw and walks out of the room. For a second, I get the crazy notion to flip the tube the bird. I can just see the photographs coming back: my teeth superimposed over a skeletal hand giving the finger.

Of course, I don't do this and the Mozart playing sweetly in my headphones slips me into a cozy, relaxed state.

The dentist comes over and she's prodding my gums. I'm curious to see what the damage is and she takes a few more pokes to tell me I need a deep cleaning. I'm nodding, slapping the headphones back on while she continues to babble. She's an Iranian lady with finger-thick glasses that almost hypnotize me with their reflective power. She gives me a little gas, tranquilizing the small hangover I've been feeling, and sticks a cotton swab in my mouth to start the numbing process. All this relaxes me even more, so it's not surprising that the pinches I feel don't even register as needle pricks.

Even if they did, I probably wouldn't have had the foresight to see what happens next.

In my pocket, my phone starts playing a very tinny version of Wagner's 'Flight of the Valkyries.' My Arab mesmerist slash dentist pulls away so I can click on the phone. The number on the readout tells me it's the Court; my motion's been decided.

I'm telling my dentist we'll have to continue another day and I notice the left side of my face is numb. I'm trying to ask the dentist when cleanings started entailing novocaine, and she's repeating something about me needing a deep cleaning.

I'm shaking my head, asking her when the numbness will fade, when I accidentally bite down on my tongue, which lights up my eyes like I just hit three cherries in Vegas. My problem grows exponentially when I get in the car and realize I'm going to have to talk to the press like this.

It's an hour later and I'm being handed the Judges' written opinion authored by Brankowski: a 7-0 defeat. The Judges cite the hearsay nature of my testimony, the unreliability of all my witnesses, and the belief that a reasonable person would have arrived at the same verdict and the same punishment. To make things worse, Shriner's grabbing the ruling at the same time.

"Jesus," he says, "What happened to your face? One of your slip-and-fall clients get pissed and whack you?"

"Dentist appointment," I lisp.

"Well, that's 0 for two, Joe. But hey, when you're down, just remember your college cheer: five, six, seven, eight, schlemiel, schmazel, Hausen Pepper Incorporated," Shriner finishes his song and nearly skips down the hall, stopping to point to the pack of press waiting outside the judicial cordon, "Oh, have fun talking to the press."

I look past him and I see the same mob that spit me out earlier. I'm about to go on statewide TV to discuss losing the biggest case of my life with a face that looks palsied. I'm so tied up in my own wounded vanity I forget for a moment the trial I have to endure is nothing to me telling Cheryl that the hope I lit and nurtured inside her is now dead. The thought of the drive out to Sussex later today in comparison to what I have to do next makes it that much easier to face the hordes of awful questions the press is sure to fling at me.


I'm on the road to Sussex, and the road and the summer are stretching out before me. If I cared, I'd notice the magnolias and pines coming into their richer summer colors, but all I notice is heat and humidity. I thank God that, at least on this bad day of bad days, my air conditioner works, but even with the AC blasting, my quick trip to the liquor store has still given me a sheen of sweat that chills me, making me feel damp and icy.

In my trunk, I've got one of those cheap Styrofoam coolers that lasted about a half day before breaking when my old man tried to lift one on some grimy beach he'd taken us to on one of his blue moon larks. My father'd always end up cussing the thing and grabbing duct tape to hold it together so his twelve pack of beer wouldn't get warm.

I don't have any duct tape, so I place the cooler, the six-pack of Schlitz Talls in the trunk and lug some ice over to pour on top.

My plan is simple: go in, tell Cheryl that her last chance is gone and she better get ready for the needle, then ask Officer White if he'd like to accompany me to the parking lot for a few beers. When he declines, I'll walk out alone and sit in my car, no AC, windows open to catch whatever breeze I can, and drink the wonderfully chilled Schlitz that's been sitting on ice in the trunk.

I'm standing, waiting for Officer White while he grabs something from a cubicle that might be his desk. I try to see if there's a family picture, but all I get is a glimpse of what might be a pigtail.

We're back through Block A, but it's empty, or so, I think. God's not piling it on today. "Why the lockdown?"

"Con was doing deep time—that's solitary—gets out, takes a shower, grabs some better food, then walks over to a guy who's short a few weeks and tries to bite off his ear."

"I'm shaking my head. "Bad luck, him getting bit that close to getting out."

"Ahh, not really, the doc says he's gonna keep his ear, and he gets to spend his last weeks kicking back in the infirmary. The way some of us figure, it's a carton bribe for sure."

"A carton bribe?"

"Lotta cons get close to release on parole and stuff starts turning up in their cells. Illegal stuff like needles and makeshift shivs. Other inmates are jealous so..."

"...so they plant stuff, so the inmate gets his parole canceled. And who says there's no honor among thieves?"

"Well, this one all ends happily ever after."

"The one I'm working looks like it's going to be ending the other way."

We go under the overhang separating tiers A and B and Officer White pulls a piece of paper from his pocket. Offering it to me he says, "Before I forget, this is for you."

Printed in all caps is a note from one Raymond V. Carpachio. It reads: To Mr. Heyerdahl: I took it with a great deal of discomfort that you felt obligated to use my name in such a pejorative manner. I ruminated over possible responses to this new villainy; however, upon having it brought to my attention that you represented that Good Christian woman, and were doing your damnedest to save her from the needle, I forswore reprisals, and instead give you my blessings. Your secret is safe with me, and may God grant you the good fortune he has denied myself. Yours Truly, Raymond Vicente Carpachio.

I'm stuffing the note in my pocket, trying to decide if my giant escort was Mr. Carpachio's consigliore on this one. "How'd he find out?" I ask White, as I think of how much the note could get me on eBay, signed as it is by a Mafia kingpin.

"I told him." Before I know how to take this, White adds, "Figure I should, before some con does and Ray starts swearing blood oaths against you."

Surprised, I offer my thanks.

"No problem, I got a laugh how you stood your ground and then came back with the biggest crazy-ass lie I've heard since my Mamma told my Daddy that my little brother was in her tummy eleven months, on account of my father being at sea for the last ten."

We laugh and then lapse into the uncomfortable silence that follows when men, especially men so different in so many ways, share any kind of intimacy.

I can tell the word's gotten around and we walk through Block B with no trouble. Alone again in the junction between B and Stanton, I offer, "You know, Officer White, I was reading in S.I. a few days ago how Charles Barkley has a daughter 'bout thirteen years old." This gets me a sharp dart of Officer White's eyes. "Anyway, some reporters asked him what he was gonna do when his daughter started having boyfriends coming over." A smaller flash of eyes. "And Sir Charles thought for a minute and said, very matter-of-factly, "I think I'll shoot the first one. That way, the word's sure to get around." I only have to pause for a moment and then White's breaking into huge gusts of laughter, slapping me on the back, which I pretend doesn't hurt and nodding his head like someone's pulling it with a hook. A very big hook.

All this male camaraderie and hands-across-the-boundaries of race almost make me forget why I'm here, which is to tell a woman she will surely die. I guess I'm feeling a lot like a doctor who stares at an X-ray and sees masses of inoperable cancer. Except in my case, the doctor—me— never told the patient that she could fight this thing. It occurs to me that I still don't know what I'm going to say, but then I'm getting the hand-off to Huntner. Officer White's still laughing, and I'm walking into the room to see Cheryl.

I notice she's letting her hair go natural brown. Even if she might be sporting a few gray hairs, because of tension of her situation, she hasn't let that cut into her food intake. I figure she's put on a solid ten pounds since I started representing her.

One look at my face and she knows. "How badly did we lose?"

"Seven to nothing." I've never been able to decide if it was better to lose big or lose close in overtime. Most people'd say overtime, because it always seems better to be close, but I don't know. If you lose in OT, you really can't say the other team was better. Just a little luckier, a little more clutch. So you're left with the notion that you could've won if you'd just wanted it more, had more determination, more heart. On the other hand, the conciliation from getting your ass completely whooped was well, heck, the other guys were just way better than us.

I meet Cheryl's eyes, eyes that are as cool as those beers in the back of my trunk. Beers I want so badly to have right now. "I'm sorry, Cheryl. The Justices just didn't go for our...my argument."

"No, I'm sorry, Joe. I know how much you worked on this."

"Jeez, you're the one who's in here. I'm the one who's supposed to be apologizing to you. After all, I'm the jerk who made you try again." That last sentence is hard to get out, hurts in fact, but I force it through gritted teeth, reminding myself of the cool brews I'll drink after I get out of this torture chamber.

"Joe, my hope is in the Lord, and whatever happens is His Will. How can I be sad about that?"

I don't have an answer for that, and I'm not about to question Cheryl's faith, so I nod and add, "I want to keep trying. There may be something I can still do." The last part of the sentence comes out haltingly, like a guy in denial about his alcoholism, battling over that last drink, realizing the battle is the proof of his problem.

I know I've got almost nothing to go on. Like some old porn star, I blew my wad and I'm done for the day. I finish my vow, my promise, but I can see in her eyes she knows I don't have anywhere to go, and for a moment, I wonder if she's always known that. I mean, less than two percent of those on death row actually win their appeals for a permanent stay. Was she doing all this just to placate me? The way she gave in, allowing me to go after the extension in the first place. I treat myself to a remembrance of Shriner, head back, skipping like Laverne & Shirley at the start of the show.

The rest of the conversation is surprisingly pleasant. Cheryl continues to remind me that my faith in God's Plan is even more important than the actions I take, and I nod. After all, I had lots of practice looking religiously earnest in grade school and catechism. But what I really think is this: the things we want the most, God makes us earn. As any of us stands, smashing our fists against the obstacles and hardships sent against us, God watches, and when we grow tired and desperate and without hope, and our fists are bloodied, and we look to Him in desperation, asking what else we can do. He answers simply, compassionately, "Try harder."

It's a shift in Cheryl's tone that brings me out of my philosophical mumblings and alerts me that she's about to say something important.

"I've spent some long nights considering this, and I want you to know I can't be challenged; I'm as firm as Mount Calvary on this decision." She's going to demand I stop my attempts at appeals; she's throwing in the towel. "You can tell the D.A. and the Governor that I've chosen my method of execution, and I choose to be hung."

I'm open-mouthed and dumbstruck. I can't think of anything to say. Actually, that's not true. I imagine my seventh grade English teacher saying to Cheryl, "No, my dear girl, you wish to be hanged—pictures are hung, people get hanged."

Cheryl starts explaining the Statute put in place in '02, and how since she was convicted prior to it she has a choice of the means of her execution. I'd like to tell her she's got it all wrong, but she knows her facts, and all this is starting to spook me because I think she may be right.

Even as Cheryl sketches out her reasoning that death by garroting would be some kind of perfect retribution for her strangling Mrs. Jeffords, I know down deep that her choice is a way to thumb her nose at the system, and that I'm to blame for that. So now, I've got not just her death on my conscience, but her horrible death as well.

I have to talk her out of it. I hope I can. Maybe when she's cooled off, had time to think, she'll realize that death by hanging is not the way to go. But there's another voice saying, "Great, you use this to sensationalize her case." A white woman converted to Jesus, a model prisoner, what's the State going to do with the spectacle of hanging?

I want to tell her it's ridiculous, that she can't do it, but the guard is tapping on the glass. The visit's over, which is fine with Cheryl. She does a quick duck-walk out of the room, obviously attempting to get away from my attempts to dissuade her from greeting the hangman's noose.

# SEVENTEEN

*Three months until the execution*

It's a few hours later and I'm nearly asleep in my car. I'm parked in one of those quaint southern rest stops right off the highway that invite people to pull over, take a walk through the low woodlands and exult in nature, or it's the place people get robbed and killed, like Michael Jordan's dad. Right now, with the six-pack of Schlitz Talls nearly gone, and a client who wants to twist in the wind, I'm partial to the second description.

I shake my head at what's to come. Of course, some national news organization will take Virginia to court to have the hanging televised, and they'll lose like they do every time. Not because of any real legal reason, but simply because it's been decided by those in power that televising executions is barbaric.

I bottom out another beer.

It all just seems hypocritical to me. The State kills people for the People, but the people can't see it. The pro-death penalty crowd argues that the use of capital punishment acts as a deterrent, but doesn't want to show it to anybody. My thinking is that, if you believe in something as a society, you should be able to watch it.

Now, the decision to have my picnic in the park was only arrived at after I had to chuck the plan to drink in the prison parking lot, which wasn't easy after Cheryl dropped the bomb. See, some reporters must've put on their thinking caps and arrived at the very correct notion that, after the losing decision, I'd want to talk to my client in person.

So as I'm leaving Sussex, I'm hit with maybe a dozen news gatherers, peppering me with questions on how Cheryl was taking the bad news, what was my next move, and as a result of my lopsided defeat, did I think I was qualified for a case where someone's life was on the line? I managed to beat my way through them with a few choice "She's disappointed," and "I'm reviewing our options," and "Yes, you little cocksuckers, I do think I can handle, and have handled, this case well." (Actually, I left out that last response).

So I'm leaving the rest stop, after spending the last thirty minutes of my picnic giving the beer bottles a proper burial, and I'm zipping along Route 2, going the speed limit, listening to Frank and Ken on the radio. I phone Sarah, telling her I'd lost the appeal and she starts mouthing some religious platitudes about how it will all work out for the best. But I'd already heard enough of that from Cheryl, so I cut her off pretty quick and tell her I'd probably be a little late getting home. I'd usually be more sensitive to her feelings, but her reaction was so naïve. I tell myself that, with her food banks and church charities, Sarah has no idea the pressure I'm under. A pressure that gets worse when I hear my name on the radio.

The car swerves as I try to turn up the volume, and I remind myself that I've had a few beers. I get the car situated in the middle of the lane, check that I'm cruising only five miles over the speed limit, and listen like some audio voyeur as Frank and Ken use my stumble-mouthed, novocaine-induced interview outside the prison as comic fodder.

"Listen here, listen here," Frank, always the harsher of the two, points out. "He sounds like he's got marbles in his mouth. No wonder his client's going to get the needle. Her attorney can't speak without drooling."

There's laughter, but Ken is counseling a little understanding. "Now, Frank, it's important to remember he didn't argue the case sounding this way. Didn't the ancient Greek guy, Demosthenes, give speeches with marbles in his mouth?"

"Yeah, but back then they didn't have audio tape." There's a brief excerpt of me expressing regret at the Justices' opinion. My voice sounds almost like a cartoon. The sound engineer must be tweaking it a bit because I definitely sound like Deputy Dawg or Yogi Bear's cousin.

They continue their razzing and I start to get angry, not because of how it makes me look (at least that's what I tell myself), but because they're making a joke out of someone facing certain death. I eye my cell phone, where I keep it in the open glove box, and I'm just about to grab it and call the radio station to give them some whys and wherefores, when a blaring horn rips my gaze forward. My car's side saddling the oncoming lane, so I slam the car over into the slow lane. Luckily, the overreaction doesn't cost me; there's no one to hit in the left-hand lane. So now my heart's beating like a bongo player's got hold of it, and I pull my car to the side to get a grip. Frank and Ken continue to belittle my performance at the courthouse, but now I'm too juiced by adrenaline to care. Funny how a near-death experience can focus your priorities. I sit, not driving, just listening, losing the deeper effects of the alcohol, while my anger simmers, rising again in rhythms to the laughs that Frank and Ken are getting at my expense.

I'm still some thirty minutes from home when a sign flashes by, telling me that Larry Brown's Burger King is off the next exit. Now, I'm not the biggest fan of the Washington Redskins' running back of the 70s, nor am I that interested to see what he's done to the oh-so-stylish decor of America's second biggest burger franchise, but my stomach's growling, reminding me I haven't eaten since Sarah's bacon and eggs. Also, after drinking all those beers, I made the mistake of using the picnic stop's port-a-potty. I say mistake because, with beer I can hold my bladder a long time, but once I go that first time I'm back in the bathroom every thirty minutes 'til it looks like I'm pissing water.

I'm pulling into the parking lot of Larry Brown's BK, noting I'll probably have to park in the underground garage on account of all the cars out front, when it looks like I'll catch a break: a car right near the front starts pulling out. I stop across from him to let him out, and with that a minivan comes swooping in from the backside and slides into my spot. The driver's totally heedless and before I can even wave my hand in protest, three little kids deploy out the passenger side of the van, running toward the BK playground Larry has so conscientiously installed.

Ten minutes later, and three levels below in the parking garage, I'm trudging up urine-scented stairs. For a second, I wonder where bums take craps, since I always smell the piss but not the shit. Another moment passes and I'm deciding I don't really want to know. I'm still smarting from the embarrassment in front of the penitentiary and my anger at the radio show when I walk by the spot-stealing minivan. A type of car, I might add, which seems to be designed to allow you to take the insanity of your family and export it to any place on the continent. But it's not really the minivan itself that sets me off, it's the two car seats and what's on the bumper.

Three women (I guess I'm a little sexist) shake their heads before I get to the man who owns the van. Normally, my doing anything this confrontational would have disappeared as fast as the first woman shook her head in answer to my question, but for some reason my quest to identify the van's owner has energized me, and I'm like a locomotive gathering steam. Denied my time in court, I'm determined to get at least a few of my own questions answered in this less than formal venue.

The gentleman who just nodded yes to, "Is that your sepia brown mini-van?" is 30ish, with a receding hairline, glasses with stylish two-tone frames. His brawny forearms are linked to muscular hands that hold a newspaper's sport's section in the same way he probably holds his van's steering wheel. Those forearms make me glad he's not some near-sighted wimp, and that I'm not about to pick on him because I can, but because I really do want the answers to these questions.

"Sir, I noticed you had the Darwin sign on your bumper, the fish with the little feet."

He's nodding yes, and I'm sitting down across from him, my briefcase landing on the table. I was going to go over more legal material, but at least my tie and the fancy leather case give me a legit look. "I'm taking a survey that'll take just a few moments. I understand that the Darwin sign seems to be a response to Christians who put the fish symbol on their cars as a sign of devotion to Christ. I was just trying to see... my organization was just trying to see how many people who support Darwin have a working knowledge of his beliefs."

I take a breath. "What was Darwin's first name?" Poised with pen in hand, I get Popeye with glasses' answer, probably because he can't think of anything better to do.

"Charles, right?"

"Yes, correct, good. What about his middle name?"

A pause. "Uhh, I don't know."

"Erasmus." I give a sympathetic chuckle. "Not a name you hear much these days. Okay, next question. Darwin went on a journey that substantially influenced his thinking. Where did he travel to?"

"New York? England?" he says offhandedly.

"Nah, the Galapagos Islands, to which he traveled to on a ship named the H.M.S...?"

"Monkey, look, Mr., I really..."

"No, but I see you're thinking, Sir, and in fact it was an animal. It was the Beagle." I'm starting to get to him now.

"How many more of these questions before you leave, Mr.?" Now he's gripping the paper the way he probably holds the bat in his Sunday night softball league right before he's readying to hit the ball over the fence— recreational softball, where men live by the credo, 'The Older I Get, The Better I Was.'

"Just three more. I'll give them to you quick so you can go back to reading your paper. What was the name of Darwin's book that put forth his revolutionary theory? What year was it published, and what were its two central tenets?"

I can see this guy's a competitor, whether it be on the diamond or in Larry Brown's Burger King, and he's thinking. Even though this Bible freak doesn't deserve it, he's gonna burst my bubble.

"Well, his book was called Evolution. The year I'm not sure about, but it was in the early 1900s, and Darwin proved that man came from monkeys, and that evolution worked by survival of the fittest." He smiled then like he'd just peeled of a three-run homer.

"Wrong on all three accounts. His paper was titled 'On the Origin of the Species,' dated 1854, not all the way into the next century. And finally, Darwin's theory was not that we were descended from apes, as you said, but that they were our cousins. We and monkeys had the same grandparents, so to speak. We, therefore, could not come from our cousins—but maybe I'm hitting a little too close to home for you, Sir. And lastly," my voice must be rising because I notice a few worried looks from the women in a nearby booth. I could close now, but in law school they told us never to stop our summations. "Darwin never said 'Survival of the Fittest'; he said those who adapt survive. Saber-tooth tigers—very fit, didn't survive—couldn't adapt."

I pause, take a breath and finish up. "Well, Sir, you were one for seven. You did know Darwin's first name, so an equally ignorant Christian would only need to know that Jesus' first name was...well, Jesus. I wish there was a word for people who are ignorant and arrogant about their stupidity, because that's what you and almost everyone who rides around with those Darwin symbols are. You got a life and kids, and in your mammoth arrogance you think it's all because of your own skill, but you're not satisfied, you've got to poke fun at other's beliefs, but the reality is you're just exposing your own stupidity as some kind of Darwinian imbecile."

A man with a paper hat that's supposed to look like a cartoon rat is asking me to leave. The rat's action might be saving me from the brawny man, who looks like he'd like to turn my neck into the grip of his aluminum bat and turn my head into the ball.

The rathead's escorting me out, and he places his hand on my elbow like he thinks he's Bill Clinton shaking hands, so I shrug him off like I'm a ball player who's just been tossed from the game and after being restrained by his teammates is disdainfully heading toward the showers. The Rat starts talking, but it's just some warning about not coming back again. If this was Larry Brown in full pads, I might be paying attention.

I'm on the sidewalk and my mind feels like the sharp, hot reflection the sun makes off the melted, baking concrete. I'm not bothering to look back.

Nevertheless, I take a risk as I stomp past the minivan that started it all. I kneel down at the back bumper and peel off the Darwin logo. The symbol comes off surprisingly easy. I pocket my trophy and walk back down the smelly staircase to my car. It's only then that I realize that I didn't get anything to eat, and that I still have to really whizz. Well, I think, the stairs can't smell any worse.

The time it takes my car to loop up from the underground garage is enough to convince me the police will be camped outside the Larry Brown BK, circling the marred minivan, taking reports, and as I drive by the guy with the rat hat (a real rat fink) will see me and point a finger at me, and everything will go into slo-o-w motion. The crowd that's gathered—because there's always a crowd—will mime, "That's him!" Their accusation as strong as the 'Guilty, Guilty, Guilty! verdict Jor-el got for Zod and his band of baddies in the first Superman movie.

Of course, none of this happens.

No one's outside the restaurant when I finally make it by, so I stick the Darwin fish around the arm of my rearview mirror, like the ears of the VC that GI's kept around their necks, and I go off down the road to get a drink before I head home.

Hours later, I'm at the Essex, alone. I could say my ole bar buddies, Stan or Floyd couldn't make it, but honestly I didn't even care to call them.

After I caught my appearance on the TV news, I segued into some Black and Tans and started downing tequila chasers. Naturally, the stations went with my impaired speech outside the courtroom and not the one outside the prison. I've heard that the television news motto is, 'If it bleeds, it leads.'

After my performance, I'm wondering if they'd like to add, 'If it drools, it's cool.'

It's the local news, and I'm on again.

A guy down the bar starts pointing at the TV and starts talking. "Hey, check this guy out. It's the male version of Mary Buttafuoco," now talking like he's got novocaine in one side of his mouth or he's been shot in the head by his husband's irate teenage girlfriend—"Amy Fisher shot me. It was Amy Fisher."

I've got a client I can't help, who seems dead set on getting herself executed in the most gruesome and painful way possible, and I feel responsible because I was the one who gave her the little pep talk that got her to this latest awful decision.

I'm just getting ready to go over and talk to the drunken impressionist when Sam, a regular, bursts in. "Everybody look out, we got a cop eyeballing the place. He's probably low on arrests and needs a few DWI's, so watch what you're drinking."

Like a homing missile that's just acquired a new target, I bounce and weave over to Sam and say, "Where the hell's this cop?" with some macho extravagance.

Sam moves me out the door. "Look over my shoulder, down about five cars and across the street, the light brown Plymouth."

What is it with cops and unmarked cruisers? Everyone knows what they drive. These days it'd be better if they just put a flashing neon sign over the hood reading Five–Oh.

"That's entrapment," I say. The legal scholar in me is too drunk to note the difference, while the guy in me who's felt pissed on all day is too drunk to care. Unfortunately, both of me aren't too drunk enough to not spot the Plymouth and the dark shape sitting in it, and I'm not drunk enough to be unable to cross the street, though I almost get nicked by one of those sprightly colored new VW's.

I'm walking up to the car. There's no sign that my presence has registered, as the man's face is obscured by the faint and distant streetlight. I'm at the car now, and I realize I'm still carrying my half-empty beer bottle. I lean into the open window like a hooker looking for an easy twenty.

"Take a hike, Buddy," says the dangerous voice inside.

"Why don't YOU take a hike, Buddy," is out of my mouth before I can stop and think. Thinking, I might add, which is getting harder and harder to do.

"You walk away now and I won't cite you for an open container," warns the voice.

A strange power grips me and I start watching my actions from outside myself. "Oh, well, I guess I better empty my container, Officer." Something tells me to really shake the beer, so I do, turning it lose all over his car's window.

The beer makes a nice spray, reminding me of the suds of a car wash when you're inside and the soapy water's cascading down around you. It's this absent mindedness, and the beers I've drunk, that make me heedless to the oncoming officer's response. That is, until he grabs me from behind and spins me around.

Unfortunately, I'm unprepared for his jostling and the beer, like a dwindling fire hose, sprays its remains all over him.

He's screaming '*shit*' and I'm trying to pull myself from his grasp, but I'm fuzzy all over, and I can't seem to manipulate my arms in anything more than wild jerks. We're stuck together like this when one of my flailing limbs cracks against something hard, like his head maybe. There's a grunt, and then a fist simply melts into my solar plexus, knocking me whistling and wheezing to the ground.

That feeling of being outside my body ended as soon as the pain begins in my gut. Now, he's lifting me up and I'm still gasping for air, and I'm tossed against a storefront, and this time he catches me with a right hand across the mouth.

Damn, I think, I wish the novocaine was still working. My legs refuse to hold me and I slide down the wall like water running from a barrel.

My hands are pulled behind my back and I hear the telltale click of handcuffs. I'm lifted to my feet and force-marched to the car. I look toward the Essex, but my vision's not working well on that side, or I'm still too drunk to see very far ahead.

I land on the back seat of a car that smells like old vomit and greasy stakeout food. I'm hot and sweaty now, and the left side of my face is starting to pound in time with my pulse. "Hey, roll down the window, so I can get some air back here."

No response.

"Hey, roll down the window so I don't throw up back here."

The window rolls down part way, probably set so I don't try to jump out. Then the pain's back, and now I'm noting that the back of my head is playing some crazy, funky beat with the left side of my face.

With my hands cuffed behind me, I scoot over to the window. The breeze makes me feel no better, and I can't rest my head on the window because it's that side of my face that's really beginning to hurt. And all this without a hangover. I hear the cop talking over his radio. He seems mad, but I can't make out the words. I wedge the top of my skull into the nook behind the window and slide into semi-consciousness.

There are the gleaming lights of the precinct, the door opening, and my carefully orchestrated harmony of sleep and pain comes crashing down.

Now stiff as well as bruised, I'm yanked from the car and led up the steps and through the station's doors. Cops barely glance my way, and when they do I know that all they see is just another drunk who got a little too aggressive. Come to think of it, that's pretty much what happened.

"Public Drunkenness and Assaulting a Police Officer," my cop says to the guy behind the window.

A uniformed cop takes my manacled hands, and like he's leading a horse, we go trotting off to get processed into jail.

I always told myself if I ever got booked I'd smile. I figured everybody always looks so sad and guilty in his mug shot, why not wear a grin?

Even though I'm afraid that smiling would entail moving my cheek (the left one feels like I've got a small, very hot fruit growing there) I'm about to do just that when the Sergeant yells, "Don't smile!"

So I don't.

I'm led to what must be the drunk tank, the bars rattling shut behind me. Well, I've got a story to tell Cheryl, I think. However, not exactly one that instills a great deal of confidence in your attorney.

The drunk tank's nearly empty, probably because it's a weekday, so you have to be a hardcore drunk to get tossed on a night like tonight.

There are three metal benches bolted to the wall, with two guys occupying two of the benches. One guy's sleeping with his back to the room; the other fellow is laying back against the wall and snoring loudly. At least, like serious drinkers, they haven't vomited on the floor, and right now, with my head and face feeling this bad, having to retch myself would be especially unappealing.

I slouch over to the one remaining bench. My brain tosses out the idea I should call Sarah to come get me, but snuffs it at the thought of waking her at this hour. And then I'm thinking that it's actually not that late. A look at my watch tells me it's only 9:00. She'd still be up, but I have lots of reasons for not to wanting my wife to come down to bail me out. I could call one of my bar buddies, but they're too drunk to drive. One thing's for sure, I can't simply saunter in at eight a.m. and expect Sarah to be up, cheerful, waiting patiently with a plate of bacon and eggs.

The thought of food makes my stomach bubble, and I quickly go back to thinking who I can call. It's with these thoughts that I slip into a shallow stupor.

"Well, well, well, if it isn't my great legal adversary. What happened, the big pep rally and bonfire at Laverne get out of hand?" A. Malcolm Shriner stands on the other side of the bars, his whole body gleaming at me. "That's a nice bruise you got there, Champ."

Even this late he's dressed impeccably, with Ferragamo loafers, dark Kenneth Cole slacks, and a light blue Polo shirt. Shriner's yelling off to his left, "Officer, why don't we remand this troublemaker to my custody. He looks like the fight's been plumb knocked out of him."

The cop who told me to smile earlier is over, smiling, "Okay, Rhonda Rousey, let's go, you heard the D.A."

I pull myself into a standing position; the stiffness I experienced getting out of the detective's car is a shadow of the creaky, rickety response my joints and muscles give now. As I walk the few steps to the cell door, I have to suppress the urge to look down and watch the rust flake off my bones. For some reason, the movie, *Top Gun* comes to mind, when Maverick is being told his ego's writing checks his body can't cash. For a second, I imagine a huge void stamp descending on me.

Shriner's been smiling the whole time. "I get called out on a murder and instead I get a murderer's attorney who looks less alive than the corpse I just saw."

"Right this way, Counselor," the smart-aleck Sergeant directs.

We walk over to get my wallet and keys from the lockbox. Shriner takes them from the Sergeant, and I know I'm going to have to listen to him before he coughs them up. We walk out of the station and he says, "I talked to the arresting officer and convinced him not to press charges. He only agreed when I explained the nature of your...our predicament."

Now he's talking about how I'm a free man, but all I can think is, I have almost no idea what the cop who arrested me looked like. I could walk by him on the street tomorrow and not have a clue. I'm not sure why, but this frightens me more than anything that's gone before.

"Heyerdahl, listen to me. I didn't do this out of some attorney-to-attorney courtesy. I got you out of jail for self-interest. You start diving into the bottle, start getting disorderly and assaulting someone, and maybe your client's date gets pushed back."

"Yeah, right into your boss's re-election."

"Don't give me any shit, unless you want to be back there sitting with the other drunks, Mutt and Jeff." We're at the precinct's door. "You get yourself together, and hold your client's hand, and none of this has to come out. Chrissakes, Heyerdahl," he finishes snidely, "AA, twelve steps. You should be used to putting yourself in God's hands."

"Well, Malcolm, unless God can call Triple A, I don't have a ride home. Perhaps you'd like to give me a ride."

If a shark could smile, Shriner could to, but he tries. "I called your wife and I think that's her parked over there."

Several things happen at this point: I see Sarah sitting in our car, looking at me and looking worried, and Shriner, grinning like a fool, and he and I share a look, and I know he did this to punish and embarrass me. This guy's all about effect, from his macho posturing and stupid sculpture to his $1000 casual duds.

I glance at my wife through the window. Her expression is pained.

Shriner's mouthing words, and if I had a beer, I'd probably spray him. "Since everything's about the gotcha with you," I tell him, "I figure you'll really appreciate this. My client will officially notify the State tomorrow that she has selected her form of execution. On October eighth she will be hanged from the neck until dead."

Without waiting for his incredulous response, I turn and walk toward the car and Sarah. A hand grips me and turns me around. It's the second time tonight someone's done that, and I'm still not liking it.

"What the hell are you talking about? Don't think you can turn this execution into a goddamn circus."

I smile back. "I've always wondered how many pinheaded Deputy D.A.'s could fit into one of those tiny cars." I shrug off his grip and resume my walk to the car.

Thankfully, Sarah doesn't get out to greet me but simply unlocks the passenger door. I don't look back at Shriner because I'm much more interested in seeing how Sarah's taking all this. Besides, I don't want to give the S.O.B the satisfaction.

"Let's go home," I say, before I'm even in my seat.

We're out of the parking lot, across some surface streets and onto the turnpike before Sarah speaks. "That man, the District Attorney."

"Deputy District Attorney," I correct.

"The Deputy District Attorney said you'd gotten drunk and been in a fist fight with a policeman."

"I don't want to talk about it now." The seat is wonderfully comfortable after the cold, steel benches of jail. "It's more complicated than that." For a moment, I wonder if it really is. "I lost the appeal."

"I know, you called and told me."

I don't remember that. "Can't we talk about this tomorrow? I'll explain it then, okay? I'm just beat right now." This is selfish of me, I know. Wife's awakened by the D.A., gets up at one a.m. to go down to the jail and pick up her husband who's assaulted a cop, and the best I can do is a 'we'll talk about it later.'

Sarah's a little soldier and lets me sleep, unquestioned, all the way home. By the time we're there, I'm so wasted I tell her I'll come in later. And she doesn't object when I pull the seat back and fall into a deep sleep.

Birds are chirping, the sun's coming up, and I'm pulling myself out of a dream where the caterpillar from Alice in Wonderland is bringing me a giant talking fish to eat. My mouth is dry, and opening my eyes feels like I've put sandpaper in them. I pretty much fall out of the car and make it up to the front porch. I've gained enough lucidity to know my wife's going to be irate, but what can I do but face the music? Or in this case, the screaming and yelling. With a start, however, I realize that it's all going to have to wait because my punishment has already begun: Sarah has locked me out of the house.

# EIGHTEEN

*Three months until the execution*

M etcalfe's reading the précis prepared by A.D.A. Thomas Dean on the state of capital punishment: *Prior to '02, a lot of states gave prisoners a choice between the needle, the noose, or the chair. In Utah, they had the firing squad, and Gary Gilmore decide a gun barrel was what was behind his door #3. Nevertheless, almost all the prisoners chose the needle for obvious reasons; however, the law couldn't be made retroactive, so prisoners who were remanded to state custody before that date still have a choice. Just no one's thought anybody would choose anything other than lethal injection, least of all a woman.*

"Son of a bitch!" Very atypically, it's D.A. Metcalfe who's swearing and not his trusted deputy, Shriner. Metcalfe slams down the brief. "Do you realize what a spectacle this'll be? The media's gonna be all over us."

"What about a motion based on the fact that the State lacks the equipment, or the experienced personnel, to handle the convict's request," Shriner opines.

"The Court'd just tell us to find the experience and equipment."

"What about the excuse that the convict has no rational reason...no that doesn't work."

219

"Warren, there's nothing we can do about Preninger's choice." After a moment he added, "Legally, that is."

"Don't beat around it, Malcolm."

"We can pressure Heyerdahl to change her mind, dangle the assault charge over his head."

"We can't use that! How does it look if we suddenly reinstate charges when his client does something we don't like?"

Shriner counters, "Of course, but Heyerdahl doesn't know that. It's just the thought of it, like a sword of Damocles hanging over his head. "

"Sure, let's try it. I've got to call the Governor; he's going to blow a gasket over this."


Governor Sumner was a man in his late fifties. He carried a graying slash of blonde hair above two eyebrows that grew so profusely they needed a weekly trim 'less the Governor start looking like Mephistopheles. His face was long, cut in the shape of a hoe with an out-thrusting jaw—a sad face with a mouth that always seemed to be turning down.

Bob Sumner was not the most telegenic face of the fifty governors, but there was something in his eyes, a remote look of disapproval or disappointment. For that reason, and for whatever went as some kind of force of personality, people found themselves trying to please him. They pleased him by moving his bills through the State Senate, pleased him by toeing the line in whatever right-wing causes he supported, and pleased him by setting up dummy companies and organizations for laundering illegal campaign contributions—and there were many vital to his ongoing quest for enough campaign money to saturate the market with TV ads.

It was this disapproving glance he was using now on his senior aide, Marlon Evans, but Evans was one of the few who could stand up to it.

Where the Governor had a look reminiscent of a hound dog, Marlon Evans had a vaguely feline face. He had marched his way through years of being a political foot soldier until he was tapped by a college classmate to provide State Representative Sumner with key precinct polling info. His relationship with Sumner had grown, and he ultimately found himself at the Governor's hip. He coveted that trust and expected a big payoff. So when Governor Sumner talked about the Heebs, Diegos, and the Blacks, Marlon kept his mouth shut.

The best that could be said about Bob Sumner was that he was a politician. He knew when to say things and when to shut up, who could be fooled and who could be played. As with his noted tendency to disparage minorities, Sumner knew when to turn that part of himself on or off, and Evans would look on in wonder as his boss went from belly achin' every group to come over to America after the Pilgrims, and in the next minute jovially receive the members of the Virginia Black Caucus.

At the moment though, the Governor's ire had a specific target. "That son of a bitch! That little son of a bitch!" he hollered, while taking a gold-embossed letter opener and using its dull point to pound a notch in his desk. Evans keeps a close eye on the proceedings, as the Governor has been known to let items fly on occasion. "Does he really think that this grandstanding shit's gonna get me to commute his client's sentence?"

Evans has been listing patiently, waiting for his boss's venom to dissipate. "That is one interpretation."

"One interpretation, my ass. He's trying to make me roll over, intimidate me. This is just like my father and the Cuban Missile Crisis."

Now, Evans did his best to look attentive. Sumner never tired of telling of his father's crucial role facing down the 'Russkies' during the tense standoff over Cuba. The guy talked about it so often, you would've thought he'd been advising Dean Acheson, who in turn was advising President Kennedy.

"Governor, D.A. Metcalfe says we've got no legal remedy."

"Metcalfe's a pretty boy who uses that squid Shriner to do his leg work."

"Governor, he knows the legal as well as anybody here."

"I don't care what he knows or doesn't know. You have Weinstein and Witz check it out. They're the best Jew lawyers we got on this Constitutional gobbledygook."

Jordan Stuart enters like a dust devil. Short brown hair, Ivy Leaguer responsible for polling and more importantly for getting the pollsters to ask the right questions. If he had one fault it was excessive ambition.

"Preliminary numbers still look good for the execution," said Stuart. "Most importantly, Republicans still favor you signing the order, two to one."

"Good. Good news," the Governor says, his head nodding, while turning to Evans. "I got elected by thumping McNeil's law enforcement record, and I'm not about to look soft here." It was a favorite tactic of Sumner's, fighting perceived liberalism rather than engaging in dialogue. It was the tactic that had won him the governor's job.

The Governor seemed to need new opponents to fight. Initially, his gubernatorial campaign had floundered, only to be saved by McNeil's own negative campaigning, which detailed the drugs, turpitude, and economic recession among the Representative's constituency.

But Sumner suddenly hit back, not only charging that McNeil's chief aide was involved in illegal contributions, but claiming that the Governor's staff was profiting from too many perks. None of these charges was especially true, but Sumner delivered them with such earnest passion that his own staff wondered if the old man really believed what he was selling.

Once again, the Governor had a fight on his hands. This time he just wasn't sure who the enemy was.

"We've got to pressure her to change her mind," the Governor says, hopefully.

Stuart interjects. "Just offer her life in prison. I'm sure she'd go for that instead of the noose."

The Governor's nostrils flare like a bull's. "You want me to cave to this piece of trash? I'm not letting some murderer dictate to me and the State of Virginia what sentence she should receive." After a moment, he adds, "How's that polling?"

"About as bad as you'd expect," said Stuart. "People see someone who's committed a double murder trying to blackmail her way out of her rightful punishment."

Evans turns to him and says with a smile, "That's our position, right?"

"Yeah, Marlon, that and we get her to change her mind. This thing's a time bomb. The media'll go crazy when it gets wind. We haven't heard officially, so I'm thinking her attorney is just bluffing, hoping to back channel the whole thing. I mean, Jesus Christ, when was the last time someone was hanged in Virginia? In the U.S., for that matter."

Evans agrees. "That's something we've got to look into. Who knows how to build a gallows? Are there government specs we need to follow? I checked and no one on the death row team has experience with anything except lethal injections. You can bet that if her attorney can show one thing's not right, he'll be charging misconduct."

The Governor's growing more agitated. "Evans, find out who knows about this stuff and get it built. I want this Preninger to see it on the news, imagine that rope around her neck. If she thinks she can intimidate me, she's got another think coming."

"The press is gonna want to interview her," says Stuart. "They'll cite the First Amendment, blah, blah, blah."

The Governor jumps back in. "No way, my polling numbers'll turn south if some weepy blonde, white woman gets on TV saying she's sorry and she's found God."

Evans rubs his chin, wondering if that's not a better strategy. What if Preninger went on TV, kicked up compassion and tipped the polls towards leniency? No one's the loser.

As if he's reading his aide's mind, the Governor insists, "No deals." Turning to his pollster, he adds, "Stuart, research how many other murderers on death row could pull this crap."

Evans and Stuart share a look of surprise.

"Right," the Governor responds, enjoying the fact that he's actually foreseen something his Ivy League lieutenants have not. "We let her pull this shit and we'll have other inmates asking for the same 'special rights,' and they won't be white, reformed Christian women. They'll be black men, and I'll get the super-liberals saying I'm a racist, while the right pillories me for letting no-good-black murderers get a lifetime of free cable, three hots and a cot.

"It's Metcalfe's fault. This was his case, damn it," continues the Governor, looking about the room like some would dare argue.

"So we wait it out," says Evans. "We build the gallows, preferably in full view of her cell, then we watch her resolve crumble."

The Governor nods. "Call the warden, what's her name, Cullen? Preninger'll give in. I don't care what her sleaze ball attorney says; nobody can talk anybody else into hanging themselves."

Evans nods as he checks his phoNET for the warden's number.

It's the weekend. I've stayed in bed for two days, nursing a hangover and my bruises. Sarah has church work, so I manage to pull myself onto my feet, stumble into the bathroom and survey the damage. My left eye has a thick black dash under it that makes me look like I'm getting ready to play center field for the Orioles. The rest of that side of my face is the color of an overripe plum. I touch my bruised face like I'm picking up a snake for the first time. I'm not going to win any beauty contests.

I shamble outside. It's late summer and the humidity almost chokes me. With what reserves I have, I make a huge pitcher of alcohol-free lemonade and drag a lawn chair under the umbrella.

It's like ninety in the shade and the air is heavy enough to cut a pillow for my head, but I sit there for hours, thinking and sweating, drifting in and out of semi-sleep, awakening long enough to pour myself another lemonade before falling back into sweaty dreams.

As a boy, I was small, never got out of the first row of my grammar school class picture, but I used to love to play football— and not the organized helmet and pads kind—the Saturday morning football, kids in ratty shoes and shirts, wet grass field kind of football. It seemed like half the time we wouldn't even play football, but a game called 'smear the queer.' (Yes, at eight, I was not very politically correct.) The game consisted of tossing the ball in the air and the one who caught it would be chased around the field, zigzagging any which way, until he was caught, tackled, and dog-piled by everyone on the field. Then, that person would throw the ball in the air, and the game would start all over again.

The kid on the bottom of the pile is how I feel now.

I've got judges so hidebound they won't risk doing anything unpopular, even though they've got jobs for life. My client, who I always knew was hell-bent on dying, is now hell-bent on dying in the most sensationalistic and painful way possible. All under the rationale of an eye for an eye, when it's really just her vindictive way of trying to feel empowered.

On top of this, there's an angry prosecutor, the media, and a cop who doesn't like his car washed with beer. (Hey, people use it on their hair.)

At the office the next day and I'm surprised there are only a few messages from clients and none from the media. Then I realize Shriner's either not taking me seriously, or he figures I'm bluffing, looking for better—how 'bout *any*—terms for Cheryl. Shriner figures if he stays quiet, maybe I'll change my mind. Because once the press gets hold of the hanging angle, it's going to break nationwide, and like a tiger let loose from its cage, getting it back in is going to prove very difficult.

Stella's running down the few active clients and I'm listening to my answering machine. I have a call from an animal organization that wants me to speak at a charity function, and then there's an old man's voice, smooth with the tenor of the South, that reminds me of good sipping whiskey, bracing and deep. "Mr. Heyerdahl, this is Frank Bradshaw, Ms. Preninger's former attorney." Yeah, I'm thinking, like I wouldn't know that name even if I hadn't taken over this case. "I've been medically indisposed, but I'm feeling better now." *He wants the case back, and I'm surprised that I don't want to return it.* "And I thought you might want to give me a little interview, just to make sure you haven't missed anything."

I'm writing down his number and unplugging the answering machine, anything to silence the damn beeping noise.

# NINETEEN

*Two months until the execution*

T he next day I'm driving into the HighSmith section of Richmond: great old houses with gabled roofs and columned door fronts. I always figured I'd have made it financially if I had a house with columns to greet my visitors.

Bradshaw's home, like many around here, have front yards that make me think of lime daiquiris and horse racing. There's a cute cobblestone path that meanders up to a porch that runs the length of the house.

I hate walking on cobblestones in dress shoes. Besides, I've never found the value of walking a longer path when the grass is shorter and more fun. I guess that's what's left of the kid in me.

Long wood-worked steps usher me between those columns and I'm at the door about to ring the bell when there's a voice to my right. "Joe Heyerdahl, or is that someone come to sell me pamphlets from the Jehovah Witnesses?"

Frank Bradshaw sits in a lounge chair on the porch. Even with the heat, his lower half is covered by a woolen blanket, his upper half clothed in a crisp blue, short-sleeved dress shirt and a white T-shirt peeking out from underneath. Except for the extra wrinkles on his face, he's what I've seen on TV and in the papers so many times. While the hair I remember has been

227

sacrificed to the cancer beast, he wears his baldness well. Note to self: add Frank Bradshaw to the short list of white man who look good bald.

I must be looking at his head because he says, "You've noticed my gleaming pate," running his hands over his head with long strokes, like he's grooming a horse. "I've always thought it would be a singular pleasure to be out in the rain as the water strikes your clean, bald scalp. Unfortunately, the Good Lord has not been very forthcoming with the aforementioned storm, nor with many of my wishes lately, truth be told."

We shake hands and he motions for me to take a seat. I notice the small table next to him holding some kind of dark green drink. Leaning against the table is a wooden cane with a bear head that looks like it was worked by hand. Incongruously sitting on the table is a walkie-talkie, like the kind busy parents use to keep track of their kids at amusement parks.

Bradshaw asks, "Can I get you a drink, Joe? The Misses makes a positively swell julep. She uses a hint of tabasco with the bourbon and an extra touch of...I better not say or otherwise, she'll brain me with this cane." He lifts the glass with a shaky dignity and takes a long draught. "Ahh, so much better than drinking plastic hospital water from a straw."

"Plastic water?"

"Anything drinkable should be in nothing but glass." I must look dubious because he fires back. "Look at Coke. Coke in green glass bottles— much superior than its canned counterpart."

He might be right. There was always something better about Coke that way. "I remember reading—I think it was a poem in college: 'I was offered Swedish Love and French Love, but not American Love. American Love, like Coke in green glass bottles, they don't make it any more.'" I feel a little pleased with myself that I remembered some obscure poem, but Bradshaw's frowning.

"Don't know 'bout that. Seems a little airy to me." I would later come to understand that what Frank really meant was that it was metaphorically abstract. In general, Frank found abstract-anything distasteful. I think years of trying to locate compelling, concrete legal evidence probably left him hardheaded about things he couldn't prove.

"Millie, Millie, come in, this is the Bald Eagle." Frank's talking into the walkie-talkie, grinning at me over his apropos appellation.

"Yes, Franklin, what is it?" Says the woman on the other end, her voice tired in that way women have when indulging their menfolk.

"We've got a guest, woman. Bring us another julep." Now glancing at his drink. "Make that two."

I settle easily into the seat; just as easily, the conversation flows between us. Mostly, this is due to Frank's relentless quizzing me on various aspects of my career. He's surprisingly well informed. Something I comment on, which he responds to indignantly, reminding me that just because he's old doesn't mean he can't use the Internet.

Millie arrives with the juleps. She's got white hair tied up in a bun and kindly blue eyes. Except for her thinness, she looks like everybody's TV grandma.

I stand to greet her and she's motioning me down. We pass introductions and she's handing out the drinks. The julep is very good, a kind of bold minty flavor with enough sweetness to mask the liquor's kick. After I compliment her on her bartending skill, she retreats back into the house, letting Frank and me continue our talk.

"So, Joe, how d'ya unearth all that info on juror number five?"

Frank's still got quite the sharp mind, and by telling me he remembers Fred Waters' juror number, he wants me to know it as well.

"I've got a knack for faces and a friend with AIDS. Something just struck me as similar between the two."

He nods like this all makes sense and adds, "A hunch is a hunch, and in this case a damn fine one. So, what's your next move?"

This is one of the moments I've dreaded. The first was having to confess I went to a less than stellar law school, but Frank hasn't mentioned word one about that. I think of B.S'ing this answer, but Bradshaw's way too smart for me. Besides, there's something grandfatherly about the guy, something wise and seasoned that makes me want to like him and him like me. I guess I've kinda been feeling like the little kid who gets a chance to chat with a major league ball player. "I don't have a go-to strategy. That was it, the whole shebang."

"Nonsense, this new avenue you developed, didn't it elicit any new leads?"

I think about the D.A. possibly not coming forward with evidence and then lying about it. I explain this to Frank, who nods, and after a moment says, "You'll need to prove that, of course."

"But even if I do," I interrupt, "what does it get me?"

"You win points with the media and it pressures the D.A."

I'm nodding at this.

"But, what it really does is raise the question of why they suppressed it."

"Because they don't want anything derailing the execution."

Slam! His cane hits the table, causing me to nearly spill my drink.

"Wrong, Joe, nothing so mundane. This obfuscation of evidence, this foot-dragging, is purposely ignored because something is hidden there." I'm about to interrupt, but his cane hovers between us. "This thing they're hiding may not even be related, but it's the guilt, the paranoia, that fuels these things."

"So, what do I do if what they're hiding isn't even related?"

"It probably is. Just probably in an extremely tenuous way. Can you bring me the file to look at?"

This is the only time during this visit that Frank seems vulnerable, which is impressive for a man who looks tired just lounging and who's body has a martini-like shake to it. I realize he wants in on the case. His chemo's wound down, and he's looking for—probably needs—something to do.

He must interpret my pause as indecision because he's quick to add, "Just as an advisor, not acting counsel."

"That'd be great! Heck, come back as co-counsel if you like."

He stares off somewhere behind me for a second or two. "No, no need for that; this old body's filed its last motion."

I'm about to argue when the screen door suddenly closes and I hear steps going away. He hadn't been looking into space for his answer; he'd been looking at his wife.


Days later. "One thing that hasn't come out yet, but tomorrow I'll be filing a notice to the State," I say. Frank had been getting a little fuzzy, and maybe because I don't want to leave just yet I want to toss a bomb to wake him up. It works. He's asking me to repeat what I just said. By the time I do, I know that he knows what's coming next.

We say it almost together, "She wants to be hanged."

We both take a long drink.

"Why haven't you notified anyone yet?"

"Oh, but I did. I told Deputy Shriner when he was getting me out of jail."

Now Frank's fully awake and I'm enjoying the fact that I've got the esteemed Frank Bradshaw hooked like a fish, with a mouth that's gaping to show me where to put the hook.

"I got into a little scrape with an officer outside a bar. He was hanging out, waiting to bust some hapless fellow for a DWI."

"And Shriner bailed you out?"

"He got the charges dropped, but he called my wife to pick me up." Millie's already shown me what hold she has over her husband, so I figure he'll understand what I'm saying.

He nods, and then with a mix of pleasure and reproof, "But a fight."

"I'd had a few too many, and the officer wasn't particularly happy when I decided to empty my beer on his car."

Frank's incredulous now. "You poured a beer all over a police cruiser?"

"Well, it was unmarked."

Frank, who seemed entertained as all get-out by my little anecdote, suddenly turns serious. "An unmarked car, the officer was plain-clothes?"

He's smiling now, definitely hiding something, and I'm a little lost, so I say so.

"Joe, you need to know a little bit about police work. No detective is looking to bust some DWI. What he's doing is looking to radio some cruiser so when the drunk comes out and gets picked up by the uniform, no one's the wiser."

"I guess I just cut out the middle man."

Frank's smiling, and I'm feeling like a rookie who doesn't know the infield fly rule. "What did Shriner tell you he was doing, a police ride-along?"

"Catching a murder case."

"Which one."

"I don't remember. I was still a little buzzed from the drinking, and well, let's just say the cop got the better of the encounter."

If Frank could get up from his chair and slap me on the back, I think he would. As it is, he just pounds his cane on the deck.

Millie answers this with a question over the walkie-talkie, but Frank chuckles and says it's nothing.

"Joe, my boy, you were the prize that night. You frequent this bar often?" I nod. "Shriner know this?" I think a moment and nod again, and now I look like the caught fish. "They were trolling for you, buddy. You gave them trouble with that motion of yours, and Shriner figures, 'Let's hobble this guy by catching him drunk and driving; he'll be stuck with the publicity of a DWI.' I don't know, maybe he planned it all along."

I'm not buying this and I say so. "Then why let me go with no charges?"

Frank's clicking his tongue. "Malcolm's a smart one. You threw their plan off by making the unmarked cop before he could say boo, then you're getting tossed into the back of the cop's car. Malcolm knows if they try to bring you up on charges, people are going to ask the detective what the hell was he doing there in the first place. So Malcolm lets you stew a while, then walks in like the White Knight, thinking you'll feel he's got something on you. It's not the best he could've hoped for, but hey, half a loaf is better than none."

Frank takes a quaff of his drink and self-satisfaction almost pours off him. It doesn't take a genius to figure out that here's an old man used to being a mover and a shaker, and now he's weak and marginalized. That is, until I come along and my ineptness gives him a shot in the arm. "So, if you're right, all I have to do is check if there were any murders that night."

"Oh, but Joe, you must've misheard Malcolm."

"No, I didn't." And then I get it. "Right, he's got some backup excuse ready in case I go snooping."

"And the officer will have some fabricated reason for being down there as well, but check the logs, just to show Malcolm you know."

"You think this tells us they're hiding something?"

"Why else go through all that?"

I'm agreeing now. "The tough part's finding out what that something is."

Frank looks at me like I'm the master of stating the obvious.


I've been to Frank's five times in the last two weeks. In that time, I found out there was no murder on the night I was arrested (gotcha, Shriner) and met with Preninger. After she assured me she wouldn't change her mind, I notified the press of her decision to be hanged. Now I'm sitting on Frank's back porch, drinking our favorite drinks and enjoying some good conversation.

"Joseph, you've got to go on TV."

Frank started calling me Joseph after our second meeting. The last time someone did that was when I was in grammar school. Unlike then, I like it. "I don't know, Frank—TV?"

"You're going to have to thump the statehouse with the bully pulpit of television." It's eerie how Frank's mouth moves, but the rest of him remains immobile. I've noticed he fluctuates like this from day to day. One day, he's high energy, cane thumping, the next, conserving energy to the point where blinking seems a luxury. Today is a quiet day.

"Joseph, you still don't have anything to go on."

This is true. Powering through the files hasn't netted Frank or me squat, though I wonder if he has the energy to read the copies I pass along.

"This case must be tried in the court of public opinion. You're Preninger's mouthpiece, so hit the news shows, they'll be glad to have you. Just be soft spoken, low key, focus on Preninger's transformation in prison and her reasoning for the execution. Don't let the Governor's political hacks frame it their way. Remember, the reporters'll feed you the right lines; it's in their interest. 'Is there anything that can be done to persuade your client from her radical course of action?' Your response: 'Only the Governor can block Cheryl's state-sponsored suicide.' And always use her first name to make it more personal."

I nod at all this and take our drinks into the kitchen for a refill. I had told him my ideas on Cheryl's mental state and he agreed that it's a good angle to follow.

Millie's in the kitchen washing some dishes and rolls her eyes at the empty glasses. "Maybe I should make a big tub of these and you two could swim in it."

I shrug and go to the fridge, taking out the pitcher of juleps I know she's got cooling there.

"When am I going to meet that wife of yours, Joe?"

"Sarah's been real busy with the church and I haven't seen that much of her," I confess sheepishly.

"Best not to let that go on too long."

"It's this case and all the work I've got to do. It's Cheryl's last chance, and her execution's in two months."

I expect some sympathy over Cheryl's plight, and I'm surprised by her tight-lipped "uh huh" as her hands continue to clean, rinse, and dry.

Two pours and I'm about to carry the glasses back outside. Millie's still staring at her dishes when she says, "I want to thank you, Joe. These last couple of weeks you've given him something to look forward to, a reason to get up in the morning."

Frank never discusses his condition, and I'm afraid to ask. "He's not well."

"He's dying." She says this in a flat tone, like she's a bad actress in a high school play, her eyes carrying a world of hurt.

"How long does he have?"

"A couple of months, at most. He'll outlive Ms. Preninger," she says, like it's a bitter vow, and I don't know why. "After the case was over for Frank I was glad to have him all to myself."

She's taking the dishes from the drying rack, putting them in the cupboard to the right of the sink board. "He didn't do so well with nothing to do but simply be. These visits with you, his chance to still be some kind of lawyer, it's invigorated him. I guess I should've known that. Being a lawyer is what he is. I almost feel ashamed I didn't realize it."

"Well, he's a fighter, especially after surviving that last round of chemo."

"Frank didn't have chemo, Joe. That woman fired him."

For a moment, those blue eyes that I'd seen as soft and nurturing take on a steely cast. "Then why the chemo story?" I ask.

"It was her idea. She thought he could save face that way. Here he is giving her his all, sick as he is." She looks away. "Well, it was just the cherry on the sundae. All these years as one of the finest attorneys anywhere and he's fired on his last case."

I want to say something in Cheryl's defense, and then I wonder why I feel the need to defend her.

Millie's shaking her head as she dries her hands clean on the dish towel. "You just keep him on the case, Joe. Give him something to live for."

She leaves me, going deeper into the house, and I'm left thinking that, as if everything else wasn't enough, I'm now responsible for keeping an old man feeling so vital that he doesn't keel over and die.

# TWENTY

*One month until the execution*

I'm walking through Stanton, the smaller, final block that houses the serious female offenders. Cheryl's kept in solitary now, since her execution is fast approaching, but our meetings still take place in the same room that abuts the women's library.

Her execution looms one month away and the certainty of her fate and her faith give her whole being a discernible glow.

Our meetings have become shorter. I have scant good news to report, so we spend our time in tepid discussions of the Scriptures. I think Cheryl has designs on making me a better Christian, and I ask myself who am I to deny a dying woman's last wish? So I've tried to be more upbeat about Jesus, the afterlife, and God's plan for us all.

I do, however, have one question for her. "Why'd you lie about firing Frank?" To her credit, Cheryl looks pained by my question.

"When you mentioned he was helping, I thought this might come up. You must've gotten pretty close to him for him to tell you that."

I am surprised by how close Frank and I have become, but I correct her anyway. "His wife told me, and she's still a little miffed."

Cheryl smiles, like of course she is. "One more thing that tells me that the world's the Lord's mystery. I thought I was doing her a favor. My case

238

was going nowhere, and Frank, God Bless him, is obviously not long for this world. He's spending his time defending me, but he's always talking about his wife. I knew he wouldn't quit. I guess I thought the firing might hurt, but that getting him home for his final days was a good trade-off. I even thought of the cover story, about him needing treatment." She shrugs. "I figured the end justified the means."

"Kind of like your 'God writes straight with crooked lines' saying."

"Yeah, but when we mortals do it, Joe, I think it's just crooked."

I understand her reasoning now, so I try to smooth things over. "It's fine, really. He gets to rest, be with Millie, and still feel like he's contributing."

Cheryl nods at this and changes the subject. "So, have you noticed the hangman's tree they're building?"

She says this lightly but there's definite fear behind those eyes. "No, I haven't," I answer.

"Take a look when you're leaving. They've been nice enough to build it just a ways down from my little window. It's not enough that I have to see it, but that they start working at seven every morning."

"I'd think it wouldn't take them more than a few days to put it up."

"Well, someone's always finding something to do there in the morning."

I'm getting pissed. Everything I've ever read about a prisoner's final days is about pacifying them, keeping them calm for their last walk, and here we have a prison doing the exact opposite. It must be on the Governor's orders, I decide. The prick's been making speeches lately, criticizing everything from the media's sensationalizing of the case, to the disreputable tactics of Ms. Preninger's attorney (who he's sure talked her into the abomination of hanging). I think, yeah, Guv, I wish I could talk you into something similar.

"I'll get'm to move it, Cheryl, I promise."

For a moment, Cheryl, the person who's hurting and scared, and not Cheryl, the Sainted, comes through. "Thanks, I really appreciate it." Then the eyes are shining and her peculiar humor is back on display. "I've got a physical in a few weeks, and I'd hate to fail my stress test." She's laughing again, and then is suddenly serious. "So, you'll see what you can do about the gallows' location?"

"Yeah, I'll get'm to move it." I might have failed to save you from death, I think, so the least I can do is make your last month a little easier.

I'm saying goodbye and a scruffy Officer Walchek is handing me off to Officer White. We're almost out of Stanton when I notice the gallows going up. It's a bare wood platform with naked beams. Thankfully, no one's ghoulish enough to hang the rope from the center beam. Otherwise, the whole thing gives me the same impression as most modern art—unfinished.

"Officer White, is it penitentiary policy to make a scaffolding at seven in the morning?"

His face clouds over and his eyes lose their characteristic spark. He thinks about this and his eyes clear a bit. "No, it's not, but nothing's been normal about this execution."

"Yeah, and the normal calming of inmates before execution has been traded for a policy of frightening inmates by building execution sites within their view."

White responds somewhat defensively, "We can't have it outside, and it's too big to have it inside—so."

"I just thought that this kind of terrorizing ran contrary to your schooling as a correctional officer." I say this without an inflection of sarcasm; Officer White is not someone I want to anger.

He's a smart guy, though, and he doesn't need to hear the sarcasm to know it's there. His next response surprises me. "Sometimes, the professionals have to take a back seat to the politicians." He says the last word like it has a particularly bad odor.

"We'll see about that," I respond as the door buzzes me out.

I've 'come out' to the press, or at least that's what Daniel's calling it. I've spent the day doing interviews, even with Frank and Ken. I wasn't going to. I was still in a snit over their making fun of my novocaine-inspired lisp, but I reminded myself that Cheryl's story was more important than my ego (and also, after getting some distance from the event, lisping 'Amy Fisher shot me' is pretty funny, though Mary Ann Buttafuoco might disagree).

We're inside Frank's home and the blanket that once covered Frank below the waist is tucked up under his arms. A side of his face seems swollen, his left hand now shakes of its own will, and his eyes have taken on a yellow cast. Only his voice and mind seem untouched by this advancing disease. He's looking over some of the documents I uncovered during my failed motion.

"Joe, you try to check out all these notes in the margin of Alexander's file?"

"Yeah, Officer Briggs had no recollection of the bust."

"What about this note, 007?"

"I asked about that but he couldn't remember. Said he used to write prison intake in the margins, until some directive from upstairs cracked down on it."

Frank frowns. "So, Officer Briggs had a system, but it's one he can no longer remember."

I hadn't thought of it that way.

"Cops are about as imaginative as a TV sitcom. Hand me the phone." I do, and he stares at the keypad for a moment. I'm thinking he's trying to remember a number when he says, "You better dial," and I realize he's shaking too much to hit the buttons.

"Get me the number of the Richmond Police Press and Movie Liaison."

I'm on with information, quickly the number's being dialed, and I'm handing him the phone. "This is Fred Banks over in L.A., at Vista Pictures. We're thinking of using your fair city for some filming of a big-budget action flick." Frank's voice has lost its slow southern spark; he speaks as if he's biting off the words. "I've talked to City Permits and just want to touch base with law enforcement. I know we're going to need a lot of overtime officers for security...Great, great. Oh, and could I get a precinct sergeant? We've got a script that needs a little jazzing and we thought we might get a pro to help us out...Thanks. So you'll give Sergeant Carlson a quick call and have him phone me? We're just setting up here...No, at the Stark Building near that statue of Lee on the horse. Oh, sorry, Washington. Gotta get my presidents straight. Yeah, it's nice, but hey, when you're making a blockbuster you're gonna spend the dollars, right? Thanks again." He gives a phone number and hangs up.

"What was that?"

"You've got to know cops, Joseph. The police love overtime more than donuts."

"Uh huh, but, you're not producing a movie. So why do you want them to think you are?"

Millie's bringing our drinks and she's harassing me about meeting my wife. By the time we got back and settled I've forgotten my earlier question.

The phone starts ringing and Frank's motioning for me to pick it up. "Say you're Vista Pictures."

It occurs to me that Frank's illness may have brought on a little dementia, but I go along anyway. In my best office voice, I say, "Hello, Vista Pictures. How may I direct your call? ...And what is this pertaining to? ...I'll see if he's in." I place my hand over the receiver, waiting. "Sergeant Carlson, he'll be right with you."

I try to give the phone to Frank, but his hand's trembling so bad, bobbing and weaving like a prizefighter, that finally I get up, grab his hand in mine, plant the phone in his palm, and wrap his fingers around the receiver.

He nods a 'thank you.' "Sergeant Carlson? Fred Banks, line producer for Vista Pictures, 'Darkness at Dawn.'" Frank shrugs like it's as good a title as any. "Sergeant, we're going to need a dozen of your fellow officers for crowd control, permit enforcement, corralling shakedown hot dog vendors who suddenly appear and demand five grand to leave 'their' corner. Double time is not a problem." He listens, then "I'd leave it up to you as far as selecting the officers. Great." His grip on the phone is slipping. "Another thing is, we got a writer here doing a polish on the script. And we want to give it a ring of authenticity. What would be good lingo or code for a druggie?"

I help with the phone and step back. "I don't know, like on a police report. 747, 'cuz he's flying. Good, good, and what about an informant? Call him 411, 'cuz he's got the information."

Now, like Frank's talking to someone in the room with us, "Yeah, I'm getting great stuff." Then continuing, "What's the last one? Okay, last one, Sergeant, and it's going in the movie as we speak. What about like a back channel to the D.A.'s office, a cop to lawyer kind of thing? Uh huh, I see.

No, 007's a winner." Frank shoots me a look. "Because it's like James Bond. Got it... maybe we'll even use that as a line of dialogue. Thanks again, Sergeant. I'll be in touch by the end of the week and we can set up the OT schedules. Looking forward to it, take it easy."

Franks shaking, pointing toward the pile of files. "Check that Alexander's arrest report." I do. In the margin, 007 jumps out.

Frank nods. "Cops aren't very imaginative, that's probably why many of them are so brave."

I'm thinking of angles. "So, the D.A. did know about the tip and didn't report it to me, actually didn't report it to you."

"It's nothing unless it gets us grounds, and Shriner'll say he felt the lowlife's testimony didn't rise to the level of pertinent information. The court's already ruled on the voir dire matter."

"Yeah, but the State lied when they said they weren't aware of Waters' perjury."

"So they get a slap on the wrist months after our client is dead. And don't forget, you've got to work in this town, my boy."

The conversation goes back and forth like this for some time. When Millie walks in, we're both well into our second brandy and she's quick to chastise us. "Depleting the cupboard of booze, I see."

"Woman, my love, we have reason to rejoice. Yours truly just solved the Lindbergh kidnapping."

Unimpressed, Millie's asking about dinner and whether I'd like to stay. Previously, Millie had expressed surprise that Sarah was quite a few years younger than me. "I've got a business dinner with a friend. Need him to sign some paperwork."

Millie's waving an invitation before I even finish, "If he's a friend, invite him too. Heaven knows, Frank did enough business at the dinner table."

On the phone, I relay this to Sarah and Daniel and they seem happy to attend. I hang up and realize that Frank needs to move. Every time I've visited he's always been seated, ready to receive me like a king.

Millie's already out with Frank's wheelchair, fussing with him over the blanket he keeps perpetually wrapped around himself. "Here, Joe, give me a hand lifting the Bald Eagle to his perch."

It's all business, and like with my father, men touching men was never something we did. This, coupled with Frank's fragile nature makes me tentative.

Frank's trying to help, and I'm trying not to make eye contact with him and not touch him, which is not so effective when you're trying to lift someone into a wheelchair.

"Just grab him, Joe. He still eats enough to make this hard on an old woman's back."

Prodded by Millie, I make a support of my arms and lift him carefully into his chair. He's frighteningly light, and it's like he's a giant cricket, weightless, but bony and full of angles. In some kind of unspoken male accord, Frank keeps his gaze everywhere but on me.

Now seated in the wheelchair, Frank proceeds to grumble about someone pushing him into the living room. Millie's about to do it, when he stops her, and says, "Joseph, can push me, you get the dinner going." Something passes between them that I'm not quick enough to catch.

"You know, Frank, I used to be a whiz in a wheelchair," I say, just to fill the air.

"When were you stuck in one of these?" he asks suspiciously.

"I wasn't. My father got hurt at work, and after they operated on his foot they gave him a chair. He never used it, but I spent a few summer days learning how to do wheelies." I grab the chair's handles and pop Frank up and into the house.

"Your parents must've been quite proud, Joseph."

"I think they were a little embarrassed when I started showing off my new skill to the neighborhood kids. By the next week, I had four of my friends in the backyard doing wheelchair wheelie races through an obstacle course we made of brooms, benches, and garden hoses."

I finish rolling Frank into the living room and he's assuring me he won't be learning how to do wheelies over benches any time soon.

The living room adjoins the dining room and both are traced with a dark honey wood, from the dining room table to the hearth of the fireplace. A bookshelf, littered with novels of every stripe, stands against the wall underneath the stairway that leads to the second floor.

The one incongruous piece is the piano, a big black creation with the top held up at an angle that always reminds me of a European sports car with its hood up, looking like it's in need of repair. Above the piano are pictures of Judy Garland, mostly as an adult, and playbills for numerous Garland flicks, mostly done in an exaggerated cartoon burlesque fashion.

I roll Frank next to the coffee table and I'm about to walk over to the mantle to peruse the pictures of him and Millie—which I can see were taken when they were much younger, standing in places throughout Europe—when Frank tells me to get our glasses and refill them from the brandy decanter.

A little later he asks, "So how'd your old man hurt himself?"

"Drunk at work. Didn't see a forklift coming and it ran over the heel of his foot."

I spend the next few minutes relating stories about my father and his drinking episodes. As I tell the stories, I realize I only tell the humorous ones, or the ones that seem humorous in retrospect. It's like I've sanded off the worst aspects of my father, turning him into a living Homer Simpson—grumpy, a little addle-minded, but good natured.

Of course, this is far from the truth, but I wonder if that's not the way of things. Once a person dies, the good gets remembered and retold, while the rest is tossed in the ashbin.

By the time I'm through telling Frank about the episode with the Christmas tree and my Father drinking way too much eggnog, the doorbell's ringing. Sarah, and on her heels, Daniel, are arriving.

I only have time to put down my glass, when Millie's at the door greeting her guests. They've brought a nice bottle of wine and I briefly consider switching my poison, until good sense reminds me that brandy and wine don't mix.

I tell Sarah how beautiful she looks and give her a smooch, and I notice Daniel's still gaining weight. He's at the point now where someone might not even know he's sick.

The dinner's a lively affair, or as lively as you can get when two of the diners have terminal illnesses and another one is feeling no pain.

Sarah's warm and upbeat, and she seems to charm Frank with her love of all things Virginian, while Daniel spends loads of time in the kitchen comparing recipes with Millie. This leaves me with my jug of brandy and time to think over my case and Cheryl's impending fate. Nothing comes of these thoughts, possibly because of the brandy, also possibly because there's no place for these thoughts to go. I'm like the football team down 42-0 at the end of the third quarter. The game's over, but everyone has to stand on the field and pretend it isn't until time runs out.

It's while Millie's cleaning up dessert that Daniel remembers he left the *Enquirer* in the car. He hurries back with the paper and a long article detailing the life and times of Cheryl Preninger and her case before the State of Virginia. The article's surprisingly thorough, and seeing a photo of Cheryl at eighteen reminds me how much she's changed in body and mind. Daniel comments on how thin she appears in the photo, and I inform him of her love of prison food and her weight gain. Sarah notes how pretty Bhasad Delhi, the cashier was, and Millie throws in her two cents about how, in Frank's other cases, they never get the story straight.

Frank shoots me a glance that seems to say, "You see? These are the things that regular people are concerned with."

Daniel gestures over to the piano. "May I?"

Frank nods. "Of course, be my guest."

Daniel sits down, and without even a theatrical cracking of knuckles, bursts into a complicated, moody little piece filled with flourishes and sudden changes of tempo.

I have time to recognize that sitting with a brandy after a good meal, hearing the classical strains of the piano is quite a fine business. Frank seems to think so too because after Daniel finishes a particularly somber opus, he's exclaiming, "Damn you, Daniel, I'd give every one of my legal wins to play like that."

I can't help but feel the same. Not that my legal victories would be much to give up, I tell myself. It reminds me of a college friend I had who played in a band. One night, when I was over at his house doing something unmusical, he had an idea for a song, so he had the drummer sit, and they realize they need a bassist. Two minutes of lessons, and I'm picking away— da dum, da dum—while the other two riff out some raucous song.

It was sublime.

Well, the real bassist shows, and like Adam, I'm cast out of Eden. But in this case it was for plucking a bass, not an apple. So there I was, doing nothing more than keeping the beat, but it's like I was pulled into this swelling wave, and I found myself smiling like a loon because I was making music. Looking back, I probably had this same expression on my face when I had sex for the first time.

Now in the present, Daniel's music is far from the Led Zeppelin-like score I played then, but it's still thrilling, simply because, with my age and the amount of brandy I've had, slower is definitely better. Also, for the egotistical?—delusional?—reason that I always imagine myself playing whatever's being performed.

Daniel finishes, and Frank and I give a few hearty claps. The ladies decide to leave the dishes for later and Frank is shouting, "Bravo, bravo," and then to his wife, "Join him in something, Hon." Now, to all of us, "You know, Millie sang for the WAC's during the war."

Millie receives the requisite euhhs and ahhs for this bit of info.

"C'mon, Hon, sing a little."

Millie looks put upon, but Daniel strikes up a jazzy little show tune. "I noticed the Judy Garland posters," our fine pianist remarks.

I know nothing about Judy Garland except The Wizard of Oz, Mickey Rooney, and that she died addicted to a lot of pills. I guess I didn't really pay attention to her *A&E Biography*.

Millie's still not over to the piano, so Frank says, "Ahh, give me a song, Nip." There's a light that springs into Millie's eyes when Frank uses that nickname, and suddenly I feel that if I were standing directly between them, I'd experience a fast-forward photo shuttering of their life together. As it is, all I see is Millie agreeing to sit on the edge of the piano bench.

She whispers something to Daniel. I gesture for Sarah to come sit with me in Frank's deep leather chair. Sarah's over, cozying up to me, and Daniel and Millie are exchanging muted talk in the secret jargon of those who know that notes aren't just for passing in school when the teacher's not looking.

The first song's a quiet number. Daniel plays a lot of single notes, which fits Millie because she sings tentatively, sparingly, in a reserved and husky tone. In an odd way it seems to fit the same old woman who just a few moments ago was in an apron.

The number finishes and we're clapping, and Millie probably would've slipped away but Daniel starts playing an up-tempo number, and she gives him the, 'Oh you're a devil' look, which I know must mean this is a Judy fave.

Millie starts to sing and all I can figure is it's definitely not 'Over the Rainbow.' She's looser now, or maybe the song's more in her range because she sings louder, stronger, and the words of loss and broken promises resonate and her husband, who's very ill, is sitting wide-eyed, like a kid who's just stepped into Disneyland or a ballpark for the first time.

I hug Sarah, and I think even if we never have children, if I can look at my wife the way Frank's doing now, we'll have achieved something.

Daniel segues right into another number, and Millie keeps on going. I listen, while staring at Frank, watching him take in his wife, lapping up her image. There are more songs and they're good, but after that, it's all echoes of the first.


A little later, Sarah helps Millie with the dishes, and Daniel, Frank, and I sit on the front porch. The streetlights are dim and far off, and the distance between us and those burning lamps seems like a dark and alien landscape across which small glowing red wires flit, reminding any who cares to see that summer is not yet over and the fireflies have not packed it in for the year.

All three of us have stogies in our hands. Fine Cuban cigars, Frank assures us. Not that I'd know the difference, seeing as my only experience with cigars consisted of a few college parties where, feeling anti-social, I'd spark up a crappy grocery store bought smoke.

I puff the one I've got now, and maybe there is a difference, or maybe the brandy I've drunk is taking the cigar's harsher elements away.

The stars, I notice, are bright white pinpricks in sackcloth, or like diamonds on a jeweler's black velvet backing. I look at these two and I have a sudden urge to start singing Devo's 'It's a Dead Man's Party,' but Frank probably wouldn't get it.

Daniel takes a powerful toke on his cigar, which leads me to think he wishes it was something else, something from the land of Thai. "It's unreal how big the universe is," he says, "or even our own galaxy. It all seems like a colossal waste to think there's a God up there brewing all these things up."

"God writes straight with crooked sticks," I interject. Both men look bemused through the haze of their Havana's. "It was something Cheryl said," I finish lamely.

Later, we're saying our goodbyes, and Daniel's arms are flexing under the amount of leftover's Millie's given him. Sarah gets into my car. Looking at my cute wife makes me get nostalgic for the ole make-out seats.

Back at home, I lead Sarah to the bedroom and we make love slowly, both of us still in the spell of Frank and Millie's enduring love.

We take our time, exploring each other's bodies like they're brand new, or like we're rediscovering one another after a long absence. Maybe, we are.

This case has consumed much of my time and I realize that Sarah hasn't hassled me to get on board the ovulation train for a few months. Maybe being free of the pressure, nature'll take her course. Sarah's young, and we've got lots of time.

# TWENTY-ONE

Sarah had been caught in a deepening mix of confusing emotions ever since she'd picked Joe up from jail. If she hadn't been sure what the case was doing to him, seeing him ragged, face black and blue, and smelling of liquor made it clear. She knew it was for a good cause, the best cause, but she wondered if Joe would be the same after it was over.

The dinner at the Bradshaw's had gone nicely, and she enjoyed Millie's company as a welcome change from her confining circle of church friends. If Sarah had not known she would soon have a child, Millie's confidence and grace after being childless herself would have offered some solace.

After they'd made love, Sarah left Joe asleep, returning to grab her pajamas. Nestled securely on the sofa, she turned on the television and flashed through the religious stations she had programmed into the remote.

In the last few months, Sarah had turned increasingly to Christian televangelists to get her through the rough spells, times when she was assailed with doubt and uncertainty about her course of action. Now, like some ancient diviner of prophecy, she searched the channels that rhapsodized on Jesus for a sign that her baby would be born healthy.

She pulled her purse from under the coffee table and with practiced care, she undid its secret pocket. The picture was there. Sometimes, she feared she would not find it and all her hard work would have been for nothing.

The terror would cause her to awake screaming, her mind momentarily lost in some dark and awful place.

The picture was there.

This was the picture she had saved on that terrible day before she'd known she was going to have a child. Ironically, the fact that the photo was a remembrance of the day with her doctor was lost on Sarah's increasingly addled mind. Now, it was a symbol of hope, of promise in the Lord, and His vision for Sarah.

Sarah looks down at the black and white photo and the hazy gray of her uterus. Like the seers of old who looked to the intestines of goats to see the future, she sees shape and meaning in the picture's random tracing of shadows. The baby's head was there, Sarah thought, sketching imaginary lines into the resemblance of a fetal skull. She cradled the picture like an infant, though it was nothing more than a slim page of photo paper. If she could have, she would have hugged it to her breast in dizzying anticipation of its miraculous birth.

It was late and Sarah had a full day tomorrow. She turned off the TV and slipped off to sleep, comforted by the thoughts of holding her baby, feeding her baby. However, these visions soon turned dark and she was running down twisting and jagged corridors, afraid that some nameless creature would catch her. When someone did, it was Millie, who took her roughly by the shoulders and pushed her through a house that alternated between the Bradshaw's stately home, and her own childhood home, one that glowed red from an unseen sun.

Looking for her little sister, Ruth, Sarah heard the crumbling of her feet across the snow of their backyard, remembered how the winter had been so cold. Cold enough for the rest of the family to stay inside on a Saturday that had barely seen the sun's rays. She was at the door of the backyard tool shed, a structure some seven feet high and fifteen feet long. To Sarah, a child of eight, it was a huge black monolith, and a familiar dread rose in the child, like every child's fear of deep water—or the old, or the dark under the basement steps. Yet, she still pushed the door open.

In her dream, there is the sound of the rusting latch as Sarah pushes it. But it wasn't the sound of the latch hasp giving a crack, it was the other sound, the sound of a full bottle being turned over, water glugging as it hurries to run out, slamming itself against the bottle's narrow throat. A sound like that was coming from deep inside the shed and young Sarah, more curious than afraid, stepped into the dimly lit interior. Maybe Ruth was playing some game, or maybe, Sarah thought, as her eyes adjusted to the gloom, maybe Ruth was hoping to scare her.

Ruth did scare her.

Sarah was so used to the scene that she did not shrink from it. Instead, she examined it, dissected it, noticed things she had not when, as a little girl, she had run screaming to the house and her father.

The strain she had suffered over this phantom pregnancy, the effort it was taking to push reality into a ragged little package in the corner of her mind, these had seriously overtaxed her psyche. Like a child's toy bobbing to the top of the bath, so came her childhood tragedy and the guilt she held buried so close to her heart.

The memories that the fragile, young Sarah had kept buried. Memories of sadness and loss, and most painfully, of abiding guilt, guilt over what she had done years before, guilt, like a swelling, festering wound over what she had never done in all the years since.

# TWENTY-TWO

*Seven days to execution*

Warren Metcalfe sat at his desk. The call had left him stunned. For a political animal, he was, for once, anchorless. He kept going over what he'd just heard, his mind churning out the possible repercussions, but there were too many factors, too many unknowables in the equation. Metcalfe thought of the Governor, stridently pro-death penalty, anti-lawyer, and hostile to the media. According to Metcalfe, the same media that was about to enter a feeding frenzy that would have them eating their young to get at this story.

Assistant D.A. Shriner's knocks on the outer door, bringing Metcalfe out of his anticipatory reveries.

Shriner picks up a bad vibe in his boss's hunched shoulders and the way Metcalf fidgets with his Mont-Blanc pen.

"What is it, Warren?"

Metcalfe's attention is drawn back to the e-mail just received confirming what the doctor told him thirty minutes ago. He leafs through the pages as he speaks. "We now know what Preninger's having for her last meal."

"What's that?" Shriner says, studying his boss for a sign of where this is going.

"Ice cream and sardines." Metcalfe's a showman, so even now he can't resist drawing this out.

"Ugh. Does she think the Governor, who wouldn't stop her from being hanged, will commute her just to spare her the disgust of eating that crap?"

"Isn't that what Lucy made Ricky get when she was pregnant?"

"I never liked that sho..." Shriner's just catches up.

"She's pregnant, Malcolm."

Shriner is staring at his boss like he said Preninger had just spouted wings and escaped Sussex.

"About four months."

Shriner stutters. "How did this happen?"

Metcalfe meets the question with a raised eyebrow. "Some guard hard-up for a little action. Does it matter? This, my friend, is the screw-up of all screw-ups."

Shriner's still stuttering. "Have you told the Governor?"

"That's my next call."

"What're you going to advise?"

"I've been thinking about that. I guess he can stay the execution, wait for her to have the baby."

"And execute her?" Shriner finishes dubiously.

"I'm assuming that's what he'll want. He doesn't like to be fucked with and he's gonna see this as just another stratagem by her lawyer."

"Are we sure it's not?"

"Well, if it is, it's a damn successful one."

"The press is going to go nuts. I mean, this case has everything, from the death penalty to abortion." Shriner paused. "She's gonna have it, isn't she?"

"You do the math. Legally, she could end it, but she's a religious nut. Besides, this buys her another half-year on Earth."

The enormity of this is just starting to sink in with Shriner. "The Governor's gonna be a brick wall, especially if it looks like she did this on purpose. He's gonna think he's being made to look the fool—big time."

"Umm, just catching up. Didn't I just say that?"

Shriner's not listening, "You think Heyerdahl had something to do with it? I mean, he's been her attorney for five months so..."

"You think this is a legal strategy he cooked up? I can hear him now. 'Hey, Cheryl, get pregnant so you can go through all the wonderful pleasures of childbirth, then give the child up and be executed.' You really don't like this guy, do you, Mal?"

"You're assuming he knows where the Governor will stand on this. A stand, I might add, that could change if the public starts feeling sorry for the woman. You said it yourself, he's put together a hell of a good motion, and there's the hanging thing. Oh, God, can you hear the talk shows? The government wants to hang a pregnant woman!" Shriner shakes his head, "You need to get the hell away from this, and fast."

"I've been thinking just that. The media's going to nail us." Sounding like a reporter, he says, "In light of recent events, will you change your recommendation?"

Both men simply shake their heads in bemusement over the course of events.

Governor Sumner has been staring at his speakerphone for the past thirty seconds. His eyebrows are making a half moon 'O' of surprise. Like an old steam train, the Governor is sputtering, struggling to get some mental traction over the news he just received.

His aide, Evans, watches in surprise as the fury subsides. In its place is a cool monotone. From experience, Evans knows this is much more dangerous.

"Get Stuart and his guys in the bull pen and have them start spitballing ideas. I want all the options, no matter how crazy."

Evans nods and says, "How about this? You issue an emergency stay and then commute her to life after she has the baby."

The Governor cradled his head in his hands. For a moment he appears saddened, moved. But his next question dissolves that illusion. "Where are the polls gonna be on this thing?"

"I'll talk to Stuart," said Evans. "Thumbnail, I'd guess sympathy for the woman, lessened if we can deny her media access. But the story's big, and where the media can't find human drama, they'll do the next best thing: create it by interviewing those who knew her—high school friends, her attorney." Evans shudders saying that last one.

"That scumbag! Can't we put a gag on him?"

"I'm assuming you don't mean physically, Bob. But no, gag orders keep attorneys from discussing a pending case, but there's no case here, no reason to infringe on someone's civil rights."

"Civil rights, my ass. He's going to be pimping sentimental shit about his client to every station that'll listen. And Marlon, I don't need a schoolhouse lecture. What I'm saying is, look into this guy; find out what he had to do with this. Maybe paid a guard for a little roll with his client? Check his bank account; look for large cash withdrawals."

Evans nods, accustomed to the Governor's brainstorming. Usually his ideas were implausible or unconstitutional, indicating to Evans how unread and ego-driven his boss was. Now here was the old man saying, I've got a problem, make it go away. "I'll see what I can do, Governor, but right now we've got to work on the press release that's going to accompany your stay." He saw the Governor's expression. Even this retreat from a get-tough-on crime stance was distasteful. It was definitely going to be a long day.

I'm hearing that my client got knocked up in the joint less than a week before she's scheduled to be executed—well, actually, she was knocked up months ago, but anyway, as I'm hearing that little bombshell, Millie calls to tell me Frank's in the hospital. After our little dinner party, he'd gone to bed and she couldn't awaken him in the morning. He's awake now, she tells me, but somewhat disoriented. The doctors think he had a small stroke. I know Millie is hoping I'll come by and, for about thirty seconds, while she's detailing Frank's condition, I war with myself over going immediately to a meeting with Cheryl or going to visit Frank. I figure Cheryl's still going to be pregnant whether I see her or not, while Frank might not be here at all.

Sarah insists on coming with me to the hospital and she passes the time on the way over asking me questions about Cheryl. I know my wife's strongly anti-death penalty, like any good Christian, but I find that her questions actually help me focus on some of the legal issues.

"The Governor'll grant her a stay," I say. "Then we'll negotiate and get him to commute to life in prison, once she has the baby." The unreality of that statement leaves me shaking my head.

Sarah comes right back at me. "What if he won't commute?"

I patronize Sarah a bit. "He's got to. Who wants to execute a mother, for God's sake?"

"But she's not going to be able to keep it, Joe."

She's right, and suddenly I'm thinking, what would stop Sumner from giving her the noose? The Governor can keep denying her press access, let her have her baby, and, after a while, the whole thing'll go by the boards. I mean with time, I think, everything fades.

We're going up to Frank's room, the smell of hospital ammonia putting me on edge. It reminds me of when I was five, visiting my grandmother's convalescent home and fearing this one old woman who walked the halls, her lips puckered as she looked for people, especially young boys, to kiss. It was laughable how perfectly this old wrinkled woman could scare a small boy, but I spent every moment reconning the halls, waiting for that kissing old lady to make her appearance, dreading the kissing smack of empty air.

We're at Frank's room and Millie's giving Sarah and me a kiss and a hug and thanking us for coming.

Frank's eyes are closed, and he reminds of Hemingway—'How the old sleep with the look of death about them.' Frank sleeps that way, with closed lips and sunken cheeks. It's easy to imagine his hospital bed as his casket. I ask Millie how he is and she tells me the doctors think he'll recover.

"It was a small stroke," she says, and then adds, "I saw the television. Your client's pregnant?" And she gives me a look that says, 'Think before you speak.' There's nothing to think over. "She's definitely pregnant."

"Does she say who the father is?"

The way she stresses *say* makes me think that she believes there are lies at work, lies I'm supposed to be privy to. "Haven't spoken to her yet, came here first. I'll drop Sarah off and get over there."

Millie realizes I showed up here first and something inside of her softens. Her shoulders, which I hadn't noticed had been standing at attention, fall. She suddenly seems much smaller, tired and old. I give her a hug and move over to check on Frank.

"So he's going to make a full recovery," I say hopefully.

"Yes, he is," but it's Frank who answers weakly. "Hello, Joseph, I was just getting out of this fog when I heard something that made me think I had lost it completely. Cheryl Preninger is pregnant."

It's not a question as much as a statement of a problem. "Figure the Governor stays her, then commutes later?" I'm smiling, thinking I already know the answer, hoping in a sort of backwards way that I've solved Cheryl's execution problem.

"Stay the execution, you bet," Frank answers, his voice picking up strength. "Let her out of her date with Ole Sparky, I'm not sure."

I'd remind Frank that he means the hangman's noose, but he's just had a stroke, so I cut him a little slack.

"Joseph, you've got to start thinking about what to do if he doesn't." I must look confused because he says, "He commutes, no problem; he doesn't, you're back to square one."

Part of me thinks Frank's a little loopy, so I ask Millie what she thinks.

Surprised, she asks, "About whether Sumner will commute after your client has her baby? I don't know. It would seem to be humane, but I've always thought of him as a bad-tempered man. Remember, Frank, how he tried to get into a tangle with you a few years back at that ball? It was over your handling of some civil rights cases in the sixties."

"Sumner's a fighter all right, Joseph." Frank's looking about. "Hey, Joseph, where'd you go?"

I've walked to the foot of the bed and Frank's head is swiveling back and forth, zooming by me, my presence unseen. Millie gently pushes me to

Frank's right. "He can't see directly in front, but the doctor's say it should fade in the next twenty-four hours."

Frank catches sight of me and relaxes. "I told the Doc that not being able to see in front of me was no problem. Women have been driving that way for years." That gets a smile out of me and a frown from the ladies.

"Yes, dear," says Millie. "That joke went over very well with your doctor, who I might add is a woman."

Frank's always ready to argue a point, even from a hospital bed. "Just because she's some big shot M.D. doesn't mean she can drive."

I can see that Sarah feels uncomfortable here, the way she's been hovering around the fringes of the room arranging and rearranging the flowers. Maybe because she's younger, she's not sure what to do in hospitals. Experience taught me not to act any differently than I normally would, that the world does not stop, and being grim is not something a sufferer wants to see. Sarah brings the conversation back to Cheryl, asking Millie if she thinks they'll still execute. I realize that I've got a stroked-out old man, his anxious wife, and a young woman expressing distrust over the idea that this case will go sweetly into that good night.

Hours later, Sarah's hiding out at Frank's house because the press is swarming around ours. Though she told me she still plans to sneak through the Murray's house behind ours so she can do some housework.

I'm pulling into the prison parking lot, and like hornets on the warpath, reporters come zooming up to the car to give me my first real taste of life *vis a vis* the media in the P.C. (Pregnant Cheryl) era. I try to get out of the car, but the cameras and those behind them make it impossible for everyone to back up and let me open the door. Like a headless creature with many limbs, none of the reporters can take charge. I sit in my car for about ten minutes, long enough for reporters to get the hint that I'm not being difficult and camera shy, but that I simply can't get out of the car.

Finally free, my feet barely touch the ground as I'm nearly carried like a mosh pit diver through the crowd of reporters yelling questions, microphones, booms, and video cameras.

Closer to the prison and I notice the satellite trucks from CNN and Fox News, and I realize the story's definitely become national in scope. Unfortunately, the shouted questions reflect the tenor of the media's spin: Who's the father? Is her pregnancy a political statement? Is this some legal maneuver? Do you expect the Governor to commute her sentence?

That last one I answer. "Yes, yes, I do, and I would think the Governor would have the compassion to allow my client not to be hanged after she brings an innocent life into the world."

My comment chums the water and the sharks start clamoring for more blood, but I 'no comment' myself all the way to the prison gates and disappear inside.

# TWENTY-THREE

*Six days until the execution*

Striding with Officer White through A block, which is on lockdown because some convict used a weight to make an impression on an inmate's skull. The funny thing is, all the shouted questions I'm getting from the inmates make me feel like I'm outside with the press. "Hey, if you fucked her, why not me?" "Will you be my attorney? I need to get laid."

Okay, so the convicts' questions are a little more risqué.

We're onto Block B and I'm trying to extract information from Officer White. This is proving highly unsuccessful, as my questions about the guards who might be involved, and why are met with "I don't knows."

At Stanton now, and the guys in the cage eye me warily, and then one's leading me down to meet with Cheryl. Seeing her puts my thoughts into the proper context. The extra weight I'd noticed was not her way of dealing with the stress of an upcoming execution, nor was that healthy glow a sign that she had been transfigured by her faith in Jesus. Just goes to show what happens when you make assumptions from the wrong basis of fact.

Cheryl sits like always, quietly in her chair, Bible in hand.

She sees me and smiles, saying, "The Lord moves in mysterious ways, Joe."

"I don't think He's the father, Cheryl," I respond smartly.

She continues to smile, and I notice her eyes have gone past their normally wide-eyed appearance to a place that's a little scary. "Cheryl, are you saying that God is the father of this baby?" She nods, and I say, "That's not possible."

"It's a miracle, Joe."

Okay, I'm thinking, she's gone off the deep end. "Cheryl, who did this to you? Was it a guard? Are you afraid to talk because of what might happen?"

"Joe," Cheryl responds serenely. "The body is unimportant; it's what the Lord does with the body."

"So who was the body that created the baby with you?" Cheryl doesn't answer, just keeps that beatific smile plastered across her face. "Cheryl, on the way over here, I heard on the radio that the Governor granted you a stay. Even if he commutes you to life in prison, you won't be able to keep the baby."

"Oh, I know that. I've known I was with child for some time, and I'm planning to give the baby to a childless Christian couple that I've been exchanging letters with."

I'm surprised Cheryl knew she was pregnant, which shows me how wrong I was to think her so naive.

"I'm your attorney; you need to tell me these things."

"That might be true if you were my doctor, but my attorney... I don't think so."

Part of me is cataloging what great PR we could get with 'Inmate brings life to child when she's in danger of losing hers,' but I couldn't even be sure that Child Services wouldn't just take the child away and place the baby where it wanted. And what about the father? He'd have to agree to Cheryl's adoption plan. "What if the earthly father objects? He might not be as enlightened about God's plan as you."

"Well, that's true, but he will."

"So, he hasn't yet."

"No, but he will."

"How can you be so sure?"

"It's the Will of God, Joe." She lifts her hands in an abbreviated 'what ya gonna do' gesture that's hindered by her manacles.

The conversation cartwheels back and forth between who the physical father is, and what role God's playing in all this. Cheryl reminds me again how God writes straight with crooked sticks.

On the way out, the guards are still giving me hard looks and I realize it's because they think I'm the father. And why not? Other than them, I'm the only suspect.

Back in the car, my cell phone's telling me I've got eighty-two messages. I'm half expecting the little mechanical voice to shout 'I quit.' I drive and listen to a procession of reporters try to cajole, coerce, and guilt-trip me into giving their paper, network, e-mag an exclusive interview. The power of the media is brought home by a call from the *National Enquirer*, asking me to comment about Cheryl's Immaculate Conception. Figure them to have the first real lead. They go on, informing me that they plan to do an expose of the case, covering all aspects since the murders. Great, I think. At this point, anything they dig up is bound to help Cheryl.

Stella's also on my voice mail and she's warning me not to come to the office. There are several dozen reporters camped outside. This has made Jimmy and Achmed's business quite busy and they're so happy, she says, they're promising me a free pizza.

I'm curious, or maybe I don't fully believe Stella's warning, so I cruise by my office. The satellite vans are ranked around the tiny strip mall's parking lot and I'm suddenly worried I'll be descended on, so I hightail it out of there.

My phone's ringing the tune 'Home Sweet Home,' so I know it's Sarah. She doesn't sound too bothered, but she tells me she snuck in the back, and there must be a dozen reporters out front.

By the time I get there, that number's doubled.

The first thing that pisses me off is that the media's trucks are blocking my driveway. Second, my slowing down attracts notice, and quickly, I've got all kinds of press latching like lampreys onto the car, making it difficult to drive without fear of hitting someone. I think of going around the block and passing through the Murray's yard to get to my back door, but I figure I've got to at least establish a 'no comment' policy. Otherwise, they'll never leave my house alone.

I park a block away. A few reporters have managed to keep up and are running over to the car. Their cameramen are still quite a ways behind. I'm shouting, "No comment," and I'm hearing the same questions. "Who's the father?" "Is this a legal strategy?" Then a new one takes me back. "Does Ms. Preninger plan to abort the baby?"

I'm answering reflexively, "No, she does not. Cheryl is a devout Christian and the sanctity of life is of paramount importance to her. Especially the life of an innocent, like an unborn child."

"If she's so devout, why did she have illicit sex?" a reporter says, while trying to feed me his mic.

I fall into the trap of answering a follow-up question as clarification of what I probably shouldn't have said in the first place. "You're assuming this act was done of Cheryl's free will. She is quite naive and..."

"Are you saying that she was raped?"

Oh boy, I'm in trouble. "No, I'm saying the facts of the conception have not been made public and any speculation is irresponsible."

I've been walking to the house, and the reporters who don't train at Bally's 24-Hour Fitness every week are finally catching up to me. I've already said too much and so I bump my way to my own front door and into my home.

I'm inside and Sarah's just coming out of the second bedroom. It's the one I use to store anything that doesn't fit in the garage. She's positively cheerful.

"I'm thinking of fixing the room up, but you have to promise you won't look. Promise?"

"I promise. Uhh, Hon, have you noticed that the press is laying siege to our front door?"

She glances out the windows and with serious understatement says, "Oh, it's gotten bigger."

The phone starts ringing and Sarah notes, "It's been doing that all day."

The machine clicks on. "Mr. Heyerdahl, this is the *Enquirer*. We'd like to get your comments on the D.A.'s attempt to use DNA testing of your client's fetus to determine its father."

I'm grabbing the phone and talking with a Howard Mathis. Again, the *Enquirer* got the story first.

It's two days later.

The media horde around my house has grown worse, prompting both Sarah and me to make camp at the Bradshaw's. Frank's doing better, but he's still hospitalized. With Sarah there, she can help Millie with the household stuff and drive her to the hospital.

Malcolm Shriner and I are in the chambers of Superior Court Judge Simon Wright, a perpetually young-looking Justice and a legal scholar of some renown. I'm attempting to block the D.A.'s decision to test the DNA, and I'm getting the first word in. "My client has a right to privacy."

Shriner, who seems to be playing Joker to my Batman is quick to answer. "Ms. Preninger gave up her right to privacy when she was convicted of killing two people and became an inmate at Sussex Correctional. She has no expectation of privacy."

"No right to privacy of her possessions," I counter. "But some rights as regards her body."

"You Honor, Mr. Heyerdahl is mistaken. Ms. Preninger routinely submits to intrusive body cavity searches. Even in regards to her body, she enjoys no absolute right to privacy."

Judge Wright lifts a dark eyebrow in my direction, but I don't miss a beat. "These intrusions do not allow the State to abort Ms. Preninger's fetus," I insist. "So there are limitations to the State's power in this regard."

Shriner seems to puff himself up as these arguments go on. I'm hoping this one time to take him the whole fifteen rounds, just to see if he'll explode (like the guy who ate too much in that Monty Python movie). "Your Honor," he argues. "This is not an abortion, but the collection of a microscopically small sample of tissue to determine the father of the child and whether there has been a possible crime. Which, I may point out, Mr. Heyerdahl implied while talking with reporters."

I jump in with, "In effect, Your Honor, this is amniocentesis, which is only mandated primarily for women over thirty-five because of possible danger to the unborn child. My client is not thirty-five, meaning this procedure is medically contraindicated for both her and her child. Your order would be placing her unborn child in imminent danger."

Shriner's about to respond, when Wright shuts us both down. Wright looks so much like a professor that, if he had a pipe, I'd be expecting a lecture on the archaeological digs around the Palace of King Minos at ancient Crete. "I've read the medical literature, Mr. Heyerdahl. The danger to Ms. Preninger and the fetus is no greater than restraining a struggling inmate."

"But in this case, she's done nothing wrong," I ill-advisedly interject.

The Judge screws up his eyebrows in a detached scholarly fashion. "Hasn't she, Mr. Heyerdahl, hasn't she?"

"We don't know, Your Honor," I respond.

"Exactly, and unless you're ready to bring some proof, I'm granting Mr. Shriner's motion to extract blood for the purpose of DNA identification."

Shriner's smoothing his tie as he tries to appear inoffensive. "Your Honor, at this time, we'd also wish to have Mr. Heyerdahl submit to a similar blood test."

It's never enough for Shriner to just win; he's got to push my nose in it. "Your Honor, I resent Mr. Shriner's insinuation. Unless he has evidence, which I know he doesn't, this is nothing more than a fishing trip, and he's using your ruling as bait."

The Judge casts a stern glance Shriner's way. "I don't appreciate histrionics, Mr. Shriner, or using my chambers to blindside another attorney."

Shriner goes all apologetic. "I'm sorry, Your Honor. I just hoped to save the Court some time. But if Mr. Heyerdahl needs time to put together a legal argument..."

Now I'm the one who's puffing up. Shriner's plan, I'm sure, was to get me mad, but I don't care. "I do not need time, Your Honor. The D.A. has no evidence of my culpability in this affair. In fact, an officer always surveils my time with Ms. Preninger."

Shriner's presenting papers saying that fights and other distractions have been reported and sworn to by the officers, and that, I was left unobserved for appreciable amounts of time.

I let him finish because I know what's coming next.

"The District Attorney's office is just trying to be thorough. We're testing all the guards, so Mr. Heyerdahl..."

I counter. "They're not guards; they're trained officers who've signed employment agreements giving the State the right to use these intrusive methods. I remind the Court, as an attorney, that I've signed no such waivers."

Judge Wright's nodding like I just answered 'Mycenae' to his question on the geographic origins of the Trojan War. "What of it, Mr. Shriner?"

"As an attorney of the State of Virginia, Mr. Heyerdahl is bound by ethics that—"

I interrupt. "Ethics that say nothing about forfeiting my civil rights, so as to possibly implicate myself in a disbarrable offense."

Shriner should get a flea collar, he's such a pit bull, and he's about to attack again when Wright waves him quiet. "Don't bother, Mr. Shriner, you've got your test on Preninger. Without evidence, you're not getting your test on Mr. Heyerdahl."

Shriner's quick to try a new tack. "Perhaps Mr. Heyerdahl would like to volunteer for a blood draw, so we don't confuse him with the actual perpetrator?"

The response is out of my mouth before I can stop it. "Perhaps, Mr. Shriner would volunteer to wear a hat, so I don't confuse him with a giant penis."

I'm not as good as Shriner at phony apologizing, so the judge admonishes me strenuously for my less than proper comment. I must look sufficiently chastened because Judge Wright excuses us both.

Shriner follows me down the hall, threatening me with sanctions, insinuating several reasons why I won't take the test. I'm tempted to tell him my motive is a simple one.

I'm in my car and Shriner's still shrieking in my ear. As I get in I say, "Hell, Malcolm, put it in a memo. And, oh yeah, remember, the Nationals are still in the playoff hunt."

That last comment befuddles him a bit. "Yeah, so?"

"It's never too late to show your support by buying a hat." With that, my windows up, and I'm pulling away.

# TWENTY-FOUR

The Governor is watching Joe Heyerdahl's comments outside Sussex. "So the little cocksucker thinks he can pressure me into letting that murderer sit on her ass for the next forty years at the taxpayer's expense."

Evans did not respond. What he saw was a lawyer trying to set the stage for negotiations. In typical Sumner fashion, the Governor was circling the wagons and drawing battle lines.

"No deals, Marlon, he can sit and spin. We'll let her have her baby, feel the pulse of the people." Take twenty-seven polls, Evans nearly added. "And then we will, or will not, give her the needle."

"You mean the noose," Evans corrected. "She chose to be hanged."

"Whatever, just you remember, we cut this bottom-feeding lawyer of hers out of the process."

Evans was taking notes (*action memos*, the Governor liked to call them) while his boss talked and postured. Cutting Heyerdahl out, Evans thought, was unwise. Better to make nice, using the prestige of the Governor's office. That way, the Governor wouldn't have to worry about the Preninger's attorney going on TV and being so anti-administration. But his boss had his back up already, something he was more prone to do as his term continued and the criticisms piled up. So now they'd antagonize Heyerdahl and he'd start making more inflammatory remarks, just to get the Governor's attention.

A month later, the stay's in place, Cheryl's beginning her third trimester, and Frank's still in the hospital. I had fallen into the habit of visiting him and then stopping at some nearby bar for a drink or two. I was careful not to be followed after the incident at the Essex, and so I made sure never to use the same bar twice. As a result, I was drinking alone, not generally an agreed-on medically healthy thing. But the damn Deputy D.A. had forced this on me, so what was I to do?

It was at one bar, Chuy's, pronounced like the big furry guy in the Star Wars movies, that I caught the Governor's act on the news. He was talking with reporters, bad-mouthing my client, accusing her of manipulating this whole event to her benefit, threatening that this would be factored into any decision on her fate. Going further, he pooh-poohed the idea of talking to Preninger's counsel—me—making it clear that her fate rested solely in his hands, that he would not countenance allowing some ambulance chaser to stain his office.

I'd been letting a lot of this stuff go, figuring the Governor was just posturing for the cameras so he could look tough across the state, and when it came down to it, he'd decide to keep Cheryl locked up forever. But now, I don't know. It'll be hard for him to commute if he continues to paint my client in such a critical fashion. Or maybe it was how he seemed to go out of his way to deprecate me, or maybe it was his fuzzy white eyebrows and how they reminded me of a satanic figure I'd once seen in a painting by Seurat. Regardless, I started to hear my wife, Millie, and Frank's earlier questions about what the Governor would do, and I start to get anxious, real anxious, and that's not easy to do with half a dozen Courvoisiers in you, believe me.

Knowing I wasn't going to get any thinking done tonight, I drove home. The press was long gone after they realized that my 'no comment' responses weren't me playing the role of some hard-to-get media flirt who'd spread her legs as soon as she got dinner and a movie.

The next day I'm back at the hospital, blaming Frank for getting me hooked on good brandy, while I now have to suffer through the next day's mind shrieks of drinking the really bad stuff.

It's in the hospital where I hit on what I have to do. It's audacious, it's original, and it may even be dangerous for my client. The fact that Frank doesn't even raise his head as I detail my new legal strategy tells me I've either seriously overrated its revolutionary qualities, or Frank's beginning to lose his battle to stay around to figure out how it's all gonna end.

A few days later, I've filed the necessary paperwork, and I'm sitting back waiting for the fireworks to start.

My motion gets read across town and my source would later relate to me its volcanic response.

Shriner's storming around Metcalfe's office in disbelief, and Metcalfe has now completely lost the amusement factor he had for the scrappy attorney taking it to the big boys.

Shriner's huffing and puffing so much it looks like he's getting ready to play the big bad wolf. "He cannot challenge the Governor's stay! He just can't."

"Well, Mal, I'm staring at his filing, and he is." Metcalfe's leafing through the paperwork, pausing here and there. "Damn, I hadn't thought of that."

Shriner's still ranting, "The Governor has absolute power to issue stays, just as he has absolute power to commute sentences. Unlike some states, Virginia's Clemency Board opinion is non-binding. They're just a bunch of liberals who advise the Governor not to execute almost everyone who comes before them. Of course, Sumner never listens, because he doesn't have to. Heyerdahl is not fucking this thing up again! This is black letter law, for Christ sakes."

"Well, Mal, get the white-out because we need to get on-point in a couple of these areas post haste."

The phone's ringing and the Governor's calling. "Dammit, Metcalfe, can't you rein this guy in? I thought you had something on him."

"We did, Governor, but it was mostly a bluff. It seems Mr. Heyerdahl has called that bluff or simply doesn't care."

"Listen, Warren, if my star rises, so does yours. If you're looking to be a resident of the Governor's mansion in the future get this thing tossed or I'll be sending poison pen letters to every fund raiser you put on for the next twenty years." Metcalfe notes the Governor's always the height of tact. "This was your case, Warren, way back when, right?"

Metcalfe gets gruff. "Don't threaten me, Bob. You've got enough skeletons in your closet to work part-time at the Pirates of the Caribbean, so don't go there, Buddy."

❧ ———————— ❦

Sarah and I are staying at Frank's place because the press has continued to make our house unlivable. I'm shuttling between the hospital, the law library, and the office. The Governor won't lower himself to meet with me, and why should he since he's declared he's not worried about my motion? I'd go through Shriner, but I don't know how closely connected to the Governor he is. Besides, Shriner hates my guts, so he might not be the most helpful of messengers.

I'm stuck on how to get to the Governor and parlay this, because even though my challenge to the stay is legit, I'm hoping to cut a backdoor deal. My phone calls to the Governor's office are not returned. I'm at my wits end when Frank and Millie, of all people, come through.

I'm at the hospital, whining about the case, while the man who's become some kind of father figure lies dying. Half the time, while I'm going on about the case, he's asleep. This time, he raises a finger for me to come close.

"Joe, ask Millie to call Evan's father. He was a judge back in the sixties and he owes me a favor or two."

Later, I tell Millie what Frank says. She frowns but starts going through their old phone book that's held together with a rubber band. She finds the number and she's out in the hallway using my cell phone. I'm still inside the door, but the walls seem like paper and I hear Millie's half of the conversation.

She says, "Hello, Gerald, how are you? ...Me, hanging in there... It won't be long now I'm afraid... Gerald, I've called for a favor. The case of the pregnant woman on death row ...Yes, I know, Frank's case 'til he got sick again. Well, the young man who took over is trying to get a message through to the Governor but he's been unsuccessful so far ...Yes, I remember, Marlon sunk our boat that summer in Kennesaw ...Gerald, Frank thinks the world of this young man ... like a son to him these last months ...

Marlon deserves to hear him out. Thank you, I appreciate it ...I'll expect you at the Wake, wearing that top hat of yours ...Yes, I know the story behind it."

I barely notice my message is getting passed on because my head's still echoing with 'thinks the world of this young man' and 'like a son to him.'

Thankfully, the drapes are drawn, so the only light in the room is coming from the TV. That way, Millie can't see me blushing as she reenters the room and tells me the message will be passed on. I thank her, and though I need to do more research, I agree when she asks me to stay a while longer so she can get a bite to eat. She leaves and I'm left with Frank, who's sleeping, feeling no pain, almost gone from the world.

I hear the tip, tap on the ledge outside the window as an early fall rain starts to belt the glass. I remember a conversation I had with Frank when we first met. He wanted to feel what it was like to be a bald man in the rain. For a few moments I entertain the notion of waking Frank up, bundling him in a wheelchair, and rolling him through the hospital, while narrowly avoiding the orderlies and the irritated hospital personnel who most certainly wouldn't approve of a patient as sick as Frank venturing outside into a cold rain.

We would sit outside as the rain trickled down his scalp, painting moist squiggles across his deeply lined skin, and we would smile and laugh, a baptism sealing whatever special relationship our time together has become. I play this fantasy from different angles, savoring the slapstick moments of eluding the hospital personnel, and the more sublime moments of Frank laughing through this sprinkling of the heavens.

But Frank is far too sick to be tossed into a chair, and removing him from his bed, and thereby disconnecting the machine-like sentries that monitor his body would set off a dozen alarms that'd have an entire fleet of hospital staff on their horses, charging to aid the supposedly crashing Mr. Bradshaw...and I don't even know where a wheelchair is.

So, I just sit with him, and I hold his hand, and a new rain falls on the city.

I slip into the Essex Bar a little later, Millie's words still reverberating through my mind.

I drink several brandies and think of my father, and how little regret I have about his death. Frank's will be different, and I'm startled by the loss I already feel. Is it because of the situation we found ourselves in, or did the ole lawyer with the courtly demeanor fill a void in me I'd never acknowledged? So I sit there, thinking about Frank, honoring him in a way only my own father would approve, and I get shit-faced drunk.

A call from Evans tells me to meet him at, of all places, a Chipotle Restaurant. I'm there five minutes early and I'm trying to decide on the chicken quesadilla or the bean burrito when he arrives. There's nothing showy about Marlon Evans. His taste in suits is restrained fiscally and stylistically, and he exudes a quiet aura of unhurried command. We've never met, but we recognize one another from all the media attention. Oh, the burdens of fame.

He slides into the booth. "First, I don't like getting phone calls from my father, of all people, trying to broker some communication."

I'm about to say it wasn't my idea, but that'd be a cop-out, so I say the truth. "I apologize. My client's facing death by strangulation. I can't be bothered by niceties."

He seems to consider that for a moment. "So, what's your deal?"

"I'll withdraw the challenge to the stay, if you guarantee me a commuted sentence."

"Your challenge is bullshit."

"That's not what the legal pundits are saying on cable news."

He grimaces, showing me he watches that show, too. "Regardless of what people around the Governor may or may not want, the Governor is hell bent on exacting the State's pound of flesh."

"So the answer's no?"

"The answer is that I'll float it by him."

I'm getting an idea, so I just toss it out. "Listen, if the Governor's worried about the political fallout, let him pass the decision on to the Clemency Board." This was the body—four-person—in Virginia that gave recommendations to the Governor on commutations and pardons. In most states the Board's findings were merely advisory and therefore non-binding, and most Governor's made a point of ignoring them, coming as they did from previous Governor's appointees. Right now, Virginia's Death Row Quartet was composed of three liberal bureaucrats and one crotchety right-wing holdout from the seventies.

Evans is shaking his head. "You want the Governor to sign off on a Letter of Delegation, giving the Board the right to call this one? It'd look like he's passing the buck."

The Letter of Delegation. I hadn't known what to call it, but it seemed like a good idea. I'm trying to be helpful now. "Give some reason, like the polarizing nature of the case."

"He'll never do it, but I'll take it to him and give it the best spin I can."

As a rule, Evans must keep his meetings in strip-mall, fast-food outlets short, because he's getting up to leave. "It was nice meeting you, Mr. Heyerdahl. You're not quite what I thought."

"Just take him the message," I respond. "We can exchange addresses and Christmas cards later."

He smiles. "Now, I can see why you're such an irritant to Deputy D.A. Shriner."

He goes the way he came, leaving me with my original dilemma: Should I have the chicken quesadilla or the bean burrito?

# TWENTY-FIVE

The stateliness of Virginia's Supreme Court, with its brocade tapestries, and its illustrious wall hangings of the country's great forefathers, is in sharp contrast to the gang-like initiation Shriner and I just went through to get here.

In gangs, in order to become a member, you must walk, not run, between two tight lines of your would-be friends, as they try to beat the crap out of you. If you make it out the other side, you get to go one-on-one with the gang's toughest member. That's kind of what Shriner and I go through to get past the media gauntlet, with booms smacking you in the face, elbows knocking you in the sides, and cameras belting you everywhere else. The only true difference is that there's no one at the end of the line waiting to kick the shit out of you, but the way Shriner looks at me, I'm sure he'd volunteer for that duty.

The usual Justices are all there and Brankowski even greets me with, "Nice to see you, Mr. Heyerdahl."

It's later, and Shriner and I have just finished our statements, laying out our respective cases. Shriner's got the more orthodox view—that the Governor has the power to issue a stay for whatever reason he deems credible. In this case in particular, there's an incipient life to consider. My argument is that the Governor cannot arbitrarily issue a stay if it can be shown to infringe on my client's constitutional right to be protected from cruel and unusual punishment.

"Your Honors," I argue. "If you decide with the State's position, you are, in effect, giving governors absolute power to issue stays as they see fit. A governor with such power could delay a prisoner's execution, restart it, let it get to a few hours before the execution, then issue another stay."

Justice Troy interrupts me. "No governor would act in such a cavalier and sadistic manner as you outline here, Mr. Heyerdahl."

"Possibly, Your Honor, but the fact is, under your ruling he could. And if you say he would not because those actions would constitute a cruel and unusual punishment under the law, then I say look to my client and ask yourself how much cruel and unusual punishment is now being visited upon her as she readies to give birth, only to know the Governor plans to hang her at his earliest convenience."

Now it's Oshen, the black juror. "Didn't she put herself into a situation resulting in her pain and hardship, Mr. Heyerdahl?"

"That's doubtful, Your Honor. I believe my client was raped."

Shriner slams himself into the conversation. "He has no proof of that!"

"Then why," I respond, "has the State tested over twenty members of its personnel at Sussex Prison? In which, most damningly, not one has come forward to confess to this. All of this gives off the stench of wrongdoing by agents of the State. Also, I would ask the Court to remind Mr. Shriner that my colloquy is with Your Honors, not him.

Judge Brankowski now, "So noted. Mr. Shriner, refrain for issuing opinions unless the Court directs a question to you. Mr. Heyerdahl, is it, or is it not, your client's position that she was raped?"

"My client has retreated into a fantasy state where she believes she's carrying God's child, Your Honor." A few of the Justices lean back in their chair at that news. "I would add that this psychological retreat is a typical response to a sex crime."

Judge Oshen is asking me a question, and I make like I can't hear him. "I'm sorry, Your Honor, could you repeat your question? Mr. Shriner was grumbling in my ear and I was distracted."

Brankowski gets mad. "Mr. Shriner, you will desist from offering commentary, or you will face sanctions. Is that clear?"

Even Shriner, with his impeccable fake contrition, is hard pressed not to show some agitation, but he squeaks out, "I understand, and I'm sorry, Your Honors." He follows his statement with a big-toothed grin directed toward me. It makes me think he'd enjoy eating me, piece by piece. Of course, he's pissed because he hadn't been grumbling, but hey, just a little gamesmanship.

Now, Justice Troy is quizzing me. "Mr. Heyerdahl, isn't your attempt to free the stay imposed on your client a political ploy designed to pressure the Governor into commuting Ms. Preninger's sentence to life imprisonment?"

"No, Your Honor. I have informed my client of her options in regard to this matter. After keeping her own counsel, she has decided that if she is to die she wishes to die with her unborn baby. I cannot know what the Governor will do. In fact, I've been surprised he pledged to carry out the death sentence at all. Regardless, what Ms. Preninger's or the Governor's actions might be should not inform the Court's decision today."

Judge Oshen now chides me. "We will decide what should inform the Court's decision, Mr. Heyerdahl." I nod in agreement. "Mr. Shriner, what is the government's response to Mr. Heyerdahl's outlandish suppositions?"

Well, Justice Oshen's gone, I think.

Shriner, taking in air, readying for the fight, says, "We believe our State Constitution is clear on the Governor's power to grant stays, and that in granting the stay the State is in no way rising to the level of cruel and unusual punishment. All the stay demands is that the incarcerated felon carry her child to term." I'd like to interject, but I've already set myself up as the poster boy for good behavior. "Additionally, the State believes all of the defendant's actions surrounding this case have been a carefully orchestrated deception perpetrated on the Court by Mr. Heyerdahl, and possibly his co-counsel, Mr. Bradshaw."

I can tell that I'm getting to him, and I make this quite clear by jumping to my feet and dancing a little jig, like I'd like to say something but my good manners preclude me.

Judge Brankowski is cutting Shriner off, calling on me, seemingly curious about what I might say.

"Mr. Shriner's charges are utterly false of course, but they are not the reason I jumped to my feet a moment ago. I did so in defense of a good friend who is terminally ill. Mr. Shriner knows he cannot be here to defend himself. Just so there can be no misunderstanding, Frank Bradshaw has been an attorney of the finest standing, a man who has upheld the principles of the Constitution far longer than Mr. Shriner, or even some of Your Honors, if I might be a bit impertinent. In this case, as in all his cases, he has handled himself with dignity and acumen."

Shriner's still not aware of any error, but I've done some homework on a few of the Justices. As he goes to speak, Brankowski is cutting him off. "That's quite enough from you for the moment, Mr. Shriner. Frank Bradshaw set up my first clerk position, and I know that he and Justice Troy argued a civil rights case before the U.S. Supreme Court in the sixties. I don't think I'm overstepping my bounds to say that I speak for the Court when I say that your impugning of a man of Frank Bradshaw's stature, and at a time when he cannot defend himself, does not sit well with this court. Does not sit well at all, Mr. Shriner."

The other Justices are nodding at Brankowski's comments, and I glance to my right as Shriner seems to get smaller and smaller.

It's two days later when I get the news that Frank's dead. And, oh yeah, I lost the challenge to the stay. This time five to two, Troy and Salomon going my way.

So I'm taking the drive out to Sussex. I'd like to believe it's easier, since I've had to apologize for losing before, but the real reason it's easier is that Cheryl seems to have fallen deeper and deeper into a fantasy world of virginal births and Godly visions.

Even her orange prison garb can't conceal the fact that she's pregnant, and it's an odd sight to see her manacled hands placed lovingly across her full belly. Cheryl, in her blithe way, assures me she's following the Lord's Path, and that I am as well, and that I should try to do my 'lawyering thing,' but that I should have faith that it will all turn out okay. This is one of her more lucid moments. Several times in our hour together, her recitation of scriptures—in answer to my questions—leaves me at a loss. Or maybe I'm just having trouble focusing on what she's saying. Instead, it's her hand on her belly I find myself staring at her, fearing any way I act will put an innocent life at risk.

A week later and a few old folks are standing aboard a boat with Sarah and me. We're out past the surf of Virginia Beach and Millie's scattering Frank's ashes. There's to be a memorial service later this week, yet I'm surprised by the sparseness of those close to Frank. Or is it the simple fact that, if you live long enough, everyone you truly knew will leave the scene before you?

The next few days are a fog. Sarah seems depressed and spends her time at the Bradshaw's watching the Christian cable channels. Not that I'm so sober I really notice. I start off drinking six-packs of malt liquor and worrying about my only client, wondering how I can save her, or at least, so she can know her baby's happy and safe in the world.

The malt liquor quickly segues to Frank's remaining stores of brandy. By the night before the memorial service, my strategic withdrawal into the anesthetic of alcohol has become a full route. I have to get up and say something meaningful about Frank and his life. I've given lots of speeches as an attorney, but this one, in my alcohol-induced maudlin state, has me scared.

I can't think of much to say, and I scratch out some platitudes about duty and kindness. But none of it captures who Frank was. This self-doubt spirals me into greater recriminations over whether I really knew him at all. And who am I to be saying words on his behalf? I'm to be one speaker of seven, but in my overly sentimental mindset I forget the reality, that I am one small speech amongst many others, and focus on my lack of credentials, breeding, and respectability. The fact that Metcalfe, Shriner, and the rest of the legal establishment of Richmond will be there critiquing my performance doesn't help.

It's two in the morning, the memorial service is at ten and I'm still drinking, wondering if I can get to Kinko's to look up eulogies on the Net and steal one. I think it's emblematic of my personality, and my eccentric legal strategies, that after much searching for my car keys (I find them on the dining room table, of all places), I actually get behind the wheel, intent on driving to an all-night Kinko's. I'm not used to steering out of Frank's driveway and the car gets sideways and takes out a neighbor's sapling. So my quest to get to Kinko's is put on hold until I can learn how to back the car out of the driveway.

I spend the morning explaining to the neighbor how the car slipped out of gear when my wife was unpacking her groceries. I promise to pay for a new tree. The conversation makes me late getting ready for the service, so I tell Sarah to drive Millie to the church and I'll meet her there.

A shower and a shave, and I'm starting to feel slightly human. However, once in the car, I notice my left hand is shaking a bit. I immediately think I've got Parkinson's, since I remember that was the symptom Michael J. Fox first noticed. Then it hits me and I laugh, and it's a rough, hoarse thing without humor. I'm almost relieved to discover I don't have Parkinson's; I've got the shakes from needing a drink.

I quickly decide that driving to give a eulogy attended by several hundred important Virginians is not the time to tough things out, so I get off the turnpike and find a liquor store. Once there, I feel like I'm buying for an airline as I grab a half dozen or so miniature whisky bottles off the counter next to the cashier. The Korean guy behind the register looks at me funny, and I explain it saves me money over buying them in hotel mini-bars. What I'm really figuring is that I can keep some hidden away in various jacket pockets, making sure to put just one in each so the bottles won't click together.

I'm late, so I don't get a chance to see if the D.A.'s are here or where they might be sitting. I'm shuttled up to the front row to be next to Millie and Sarah, and even though I've already consumed some of my new provisions, I'm still fearful the bottles will start clinking together.

Metcalfe takes the dais and delivers a bland pronouncement about Frank's exemplary history of legal activism, and then, it's my turn to speak and my stomach's in a giant's grip because I didn't eat breakfast, I'm hung over, and I still don't know what I'm going to say. As I walk over to the altar and mount the few stairs, I notice my steps are a little too careful.

My speech starts out well, with me thanking the guests for attending and expressing the great loss that I feel so personally. I'm essentially cribbing what the other eulogists have said before me when I see Shriner in the audience and start to lose whatever slim train of thought I had. "And we can only hope that the same mercy that is afforded Frank in heaven will be granted to those less fortunate, who also have suffered here on Earth." I direct my gaze at where a blurry Shriner sits. "We must also remember, fellow parishioners, that there are those who seek to prosecute, ah, persecute people who are victims in their own right, victims of a state that only cares to execute the law regardless of the consequences. In effect, intent more on reading the public mood than ensuring the public trust."

My voice rises and I'm feeling quite clever in the way I used the word 'execute,' when I realize I'm pretty far off the point. I bring in the relief pitcher to end it. "And it's against forces like these that Frank so ably battled. Thank you." I do a little two-step down the stairs that might appear unplanned, and I'm back, sitting next to Sarah, who takes my hand in hers, patting it, almost like she's trying to soothe herself.

There are a few more speakers and then a blonde priest of about thirty ends the service with a nice reading from John.

People are milling about in the pews, waiting for their turn to file out. I figure while everyone's busy this would be a good time to excuse myself. I mention the bathroom to Sarah and I'm off through a side door and through the vestibule in search of a little down time with my disappearing cache of liquid refreshment.

I'm tossing back my last miniature bottle of Jack Daniels when I hear, "That's a real nice picture, Heyerdahl. What'd you do, roll a stewardess?"

It's Shriner. "What do you want, Malcolm?"

"That was a nice speech you gave up there, and an even better stumble you took. Of course, now we know why, don't we?" He's in full gloat mode, like when he called Sarah to come pick me up from jail. "But I guess you've got a reason to drink; alchies always do. Or, hey, is it a guilty conscience?"

I start to walk by him. "I'm going outside, Malcolm. You forget that the only time I have to listen to you is in court. Otherwise, you're just a short, bald headed guy who tries to hide his unattractive qualities behind expensive suits."

It's when I'm right next to him that he almost hisses in my ear. "We know it was you, so you can stop worrying about your client getting the rope. We're gonna hang you, too."

Shriner's threat makes no sense, but I stop and pretend to examine the wall-mounted shelf enshrining those whose charitable donations deserve getting their pictures in a crappy two-tone shelf in a back alley hallway of the church.

"We tested the guards, Joe. None of them could be the father. You did it. You fucked her, and fucked yourself in the process."

"Fuck you, Shriner. There's no way you could've got some lab to do that many tests so quickly."

Shriner's smirking. "Thinking pretty quick for a drunk there, Joe, unless you'd already thought of this situation. We had the goods on the guards, tested them right after we found out she was pregnant."

Now, I'm confused. "Then what was the deal with the judge?" Then I get it. "You wanted mine! It was all a bait and switch to get my blood."

"Yeah, leave it to you; the one you win is the one motion that deals with you and not Preninger."

"You've got no proof. You might've just missed somebody that's quit since Cheryl got pregnant, or some guard that sneaked someone else's shift and hasn't come forward."

"Yeah, Joe, get those press-ready lies up and running. I notice you didn't accuse of us of lying, but now that wouldn't occur to somebody who knows the truth, would it?" I'm walking back and forth now, like a caged bear at the zoo. "I don't know if I should be impressed by your legal strategy or repulsed because you were that hard up. What's the matter, Joey? The little wife a little too straitlaced for a guy who's into doing women murderers while they're shackled. Poor little Sarah too innocent for that?"

Many men are under the impression that the world they live in is a highly civilized place. They've attended the finest, most prestigious schools, have had heated disagreements over this and that, thinking that the physical remedies to confrontation have gone the way of the rotary phone. Many of these men consciously or unconsciously use this fact to become complete and total assholes, relying on this no-hitting rule the way a woman will, who's screaming obscenities at a man, safe in the knowledge that she won't get hit. Shriner had been too long in the legal byways and had forgotten there were other ways to answer words. My fist slams into his face, dislocating my knuckle and breaking his nose. A left catches him in the gut almost as quickly as the blood starts running from his face and staining his $500 shirt. But I give Malcolm credit, he adapts to this new/old world quickly and his right hand catches me across the temple, sending me off balance, stumbling, striking my head on the edge of that damn hanging shelf, creasing my forehead, making it look like someone took an exacto to my scalp. The pain would have put me down for the count, but the drinks keep it at arm's length long enough for me to rush Shriner, who's hesitated from following up his attack. My first shot catches him lightly across the body, then the second connects brutally across his already savaged nose.

Shriner flees, mouthing obscenities as he goes, and my attempts to chase after him are cut short when I slip on blood. His or mine, I don't know, but I fall badly, my head striking the hard linoleum floor. Maybe things go black, but voices coming from the outside get me up and to my feet, and I'm walking back through the naves, looking for a place to hide. Admittedly, my reasons for doing this are a bit unclear. Thoughts like Shriner's flagged down a cop and I'm going to be arrested for assault whisk through the mush that presently passes for thought in my barely coherent state.

The row of confessionals catches my eye and I make a quick dash, more like a lurch, really, into one of the boxes. Once inside this three-by-seven-foot standing coffin, the Catholic schoolboy inside of me reminds me of the spring-loaded latch that tells anyone outside that the box is occupied. This is not too good if I'm trying to hide.

I search my pockets, managing to cut up my hands from the broken glass, all that's left of my liquor stash, but I do manage to find my expensive pen and I stab it into the mechanism so the lock can't go all the way down. As I do this, I finally find out what the black button does when the pen's contents spill out onto the box's floor. I stare at the pen, noticing when the clip and the black button are pushed together the top springs open and what must be a spy capsule for sending secret messages flies out.

I'm bending over in the cramped confines of the confessional, trying to gather up the innards of the pen, when things suddenly get extra dizzy.

I'm awake.

My body's folded down in the box like groceries in the bottom of the bag. I sit on the small bench and my head feels like a barometer measuring the change in several thousand feet of pressure. My hands are slashed and I can feel dried blood along my forehead and pooled in my ear from my scalp laceration. One of the cuts on my hand is pretty deep and that's when I remember my pockets. This time, after some careful investigation, I catalogue broken glass in all pockets but the right front trouser. From it, I pull a pristine mini-bottle of Jack Daniels. Without hesitating, I've got the top off and I'm swigging my tiny sample of the finest Tennessee sipping whiskey ever made. The liquor feels good and hot as it hits the back of my throat and races into my gut. My hands are shaking, and the cap drops to the floor.

Remembering the trouble with my head the last time I tried this, I peer cautiously down and see the bottle's top, some broken glass, and my pen and its innards. Carefully, like an aqua dancer sliding into the depths of the pool, I bend my knees, making sure to keep my head upright. Almost blindly, fearing what will happen if I lower my head, I feel my way and grab the pen. Seated once again, I push the secret capsule back into place. As I do, I notice a small piece of paper coiled inside. I unwind it and written in Sarah's small precise script is, 'I Love You, Joe Heyerdahl.' I'm staring at this wrinkled piece of paper and I have to remind myself to breathe, while I think how beat up my body and soul have become.

I start to cry and I can't seem to stop. My wife's writing me cute little notes, but she's given up on us having a baby. I wanted to think it was because she just decided to go back to trusting God, but maybe she's just fed up with me. After all, I spend my time either at a bar, trying a loser case, or getting in fights with the law. I've become pretty much a drunk, and I see with an awful clarity how it's all that much worse because I've failed the woman I love, the woman who loves me. Or, at least, did before I started this case.

Another deep breath and a moment to wipe the tears from my eyes. I feel a prick and I notice a nice gash along my ribs, probably from a broken liquor bottle.

My head's still throbbing and my body's just a flashing railroad crossing sign of aches and pains, but it's the pain over what I've done to Sarah—her eyes at the police station when she came to pick me up; the pat of her hand after my foggy speech, the look I'll see again when I get home. That one hurts the most.

For a second, I wonder why Sarah hasn't come looking for me, then I remember she came with Millie. She's probably back there at the wake, waiting and worried over why I haven't shown up. Another wonderful thought cruises by, which is what's going to happen when Shriner starts telling the media I'm the father of Cheryl's child? What's that gonna do to Sarah? A fresh wave of guilt washes over me and I start searching my pockets. I've drunk everything.

"Maybe, you should just stop drinking, Joe."

In my shaky condition a thought flits through my mind that I've just joined up with Cheryl in hearing the voice of God, but the voice is coming from the other side of the confessional screen, where the priest sits, and this voice has a baritone quality that makes me think the guy on the other side is black. Not that God isn't, couldn't, or wouldn't be black when he chose; I just don't know why he'd be black when talking to me.

"Uhh, Father, have I been talking aloud?"

"For some time, Joe."

"I see, well, thank you. I really should be going."

"Do you want absolution for your sins, Joe?"

There are several voices in my head now: no, I do not need the rigid doctrinaire church to tell me I'm okay. Yes, I'm screwed up and getting worse all the time. And sadly, no, Joe, you don't deserve it, and you're just not worth it.

"Yes," I say. "That'd be fine, Father."

The Father recites the liturgy and instructs me to repent my ways and perform ten Hail Marys. I've always thought this was the silly part. I can see giving vent to your fears and evil thoughts, but don't give me a child's prayer to repeat.

I thank him and pull myself up and out the door. The church is empty and, except for the dais still in place, there's no evidence of what happened here an hour ago.

As I walk out, I notice the Stations of the Cross, and there's my favorite, Station number five, with Simon of Cyrene lifting Christ's burden. I realize in my arrogance I thought I could do that for Cheryl, when I can't even help myself, and I know now that, in this scene, I'm not the pious Simon who aids Christ in His most dire time, but just another sinner like everyone else. Those are my sins on the Cross weighing Jesus down.

I'm the splinters working their way into the flesh of His shoulders, the sharp angle of the T biting into His collarbone, and mostly, I'm the great weight driving Him down, tearing Christ's sinews as He rises once, twice, three times.

"I've always enjoyed the Stations, bit like a mini-pilgrimage," I hear coming from a familiar bass voice. I turn about and get my first glimpse of how I look when the Father's dark face get a little pale. "Are you all right, my son?" he asks.

I note he's a big man, somewhat reminds me of Officer White, but he's got darker black freckles on his cheeks, and he's bald.

"Yeah, I'm okay. They're just flesh wounds, Father...?"

"Father Greene."

"Well, thanks, Father. I mean, for back there. I'll remember what you said."

"No, Joe," he replies, "remember what you said."

I'm nodding, walking backward, and with a wave I'm gone.

# TWENTY-SIX

It's later that day. I've taken a shower, cleaned my clothes of glass and closed my cuts using that surgical super glue stuff. Now I'm sitting on Frank's porch, trying to think of a way to tell Sarah that tomorrow the D.A. is going to be accusing me of sleeping with Cheryl Preninger. I sit this way for some time, until Sarah comes out to be with me. We lay on the lounge together, feeling the warmth drain from the sky. It feels good, and I wonder why I'd ever think of leaving this spot.

"Oh, I got your message in the pen," I say.

Sarah's still looking worriedly at the cut across my forehead. "You finally figured out how to open it. Aren't you the clever one."

"Hardly," I mutter, as we both drift back into a meditative silence. I trace my fingers along her arm just to touch her. Something I haven't done in months; something I used to do simply to feel her. Something that became a prelude to sex, and finally something that was left behind like so many of the small intimate gestures that get forgotten in the rushing haze of married life.

Darkness falls and Sarah leaves to check on Millie. My body still grumbles when I unfold it from the lounge chair, but I get up anyway and amble into the study, for the comforts of Frank's big leather Barcalounger. I pour myself a drink and sit down. Millie's been cleaning, obviously as a way to keep herself busy, and she hustles by, pausing for a moment between flourishes of her feather duster. Her eyes catch mine. "He drank because he was dying," she says. "What's your excuse?"

Those kindly warm eyes are suddenly ice picks and I'm caught speechless, glass in hand, feeling like a little boy who's just discovered razor blades in his teddy bear. And then she's gone. Off to kill dust mites, I suppose.

I put the drink down.

I see Millie's eyes reach for me, filled with despair and anger, real unalloyed anger. I hear the Father's words saying, "Just don't drink, Joe," and I truly wonder for the first time if I can stop, which right there tells me there's a problem. Like a wall breaking down, I even hear Shriner, his alcoholic comments not as legal maneuvering to throw me off—like bringing in Tommy Dean to sit as his pet dog at trial—but because he thinks it's true. Just like I really think he does need a hat so he doesn't look like a giant penis.

My thoughts go round and round, as do I, circling the glass of brandy in a kind of wildly eccentric orbit. Several times I'm ready to fall into the drink's gravitational pull, as the liquor's mass seems to fluctuate from simple glass filled with liquid to the density of a small black hole. Each time, however, I pull away before my butt can hit the seat and I can reach for it.

Finally, tired from my pacing, I go upstairs and get into bed with Sarah. About three hours later my body awakens me. It starts to shake, like it's in the grip of its own internal earthquake, and for a moment I think I'm having a delayed concussion from my bout with Shriner. Then I think I've got a sudden raging case of the flu. Either way, I leave Sarah to her dreams and slip downstairs to have a drink. As my feet hit the first step, I reverse my field nearly as quickly, coming to the blinding realization that I'm experiencing some minor form of the DT's, that my body's clamoring for alcohol and figures that torturing itself will get it its way. Disdainfully, I go into an unused bedroom and try to get back to sleep.

That is one of the last purely rational thoughts I have. After a brief nap and some tossing and turning, I feel decidedly worse. For no apparent reason, my body flushes with sweat and I have to push the sheets off the bed, they've become so wet with perspiration. Soon, I'm too weak to do even this and I simply huddle on my side, back to the room. Then my head starts; I have experienced a migraine twice before, and this skull pounding, feeling your pulse in the side of your nose was similarly incapacitating. Now, I'm wracked by bouts of nausea that produce nothing to allay the dizzying sickness, leaving me taking air in tiny breaths through my nose, so as not to further disturb my psychotic stomach.

This is my lot for what I later learn was over a day. A day in which, though I was severely infirm, I had one burning thought. A drink would quiet all this. It would turn off the faucet that had become my sweat glands, calm my spinning stomach, and still the Cuban bongo player beating out time in my head. I didn't know how I knew this, but I did, and though I could've stumbled downstairs and poured myself an oh-so-satisfying amber brandy, I didn't. So whoopee for me.

My drinking problem could no longer be ignored or talked away. Jokey comments and references to my father's much wilder drinking days would not work. Nor would telling myself that I'm not as bad as he was, so I don't have a problem.

These are my thoughts through the night that turns to day. As the first light starts pouring through the window, my mind jumps its tracks and starts throwing out weird pictures of shapes that seem to dance around the corners of my eyes. After a time, the shapes change into strange half-animal/half-human figures. They talk to me and I talk back, in a baffling *speaking in tongues* sort of way. I see Sarah and Cheryl with the lower halves of snakes, and they're dancing together to music I can't hear. They can't seem to hear me either, so I have to raise my voice louder, all to no effect. Frank and Daniel, covered in neon green hair, enter and start wrestling each other on the bedroom floor. I'm thinking that the noise is sure to wake up Sarah, but then my mind remembers she's dancing with Cheryl. Millie appears, except that her body's that of a horse, and she's trying to tap a message with her hooves, kind of like the way circus people train their horses to answer questions—one tap for no, two for yes.

Now, I'm staring at Millie's hooves as they knock out a little mambo, when I see her face start to morph into what looks to be a younger version of herself. I start yelling for Frank to come see his wife, but then I remember Frank's wrestling with Daniel, and oh my God, what will Millie think about Frank's glowing green fur now that she's young and beautiful? This possible calamity throws me into a tizzy of high anxiety over the future of their marriage.

There's a break in my thoughts as I see Millie's face is no longer hers, but is now the Virgin Mary's, her belly full with life, while tiny, little people scamper all over the floor at her feet, which surprises me, but I remember I don't usually sleep in this room, so maybe this is a regular occurrence.

The little men all look like they've just stepped off the top of a wedding cake, and they're arguing, and all the little men start to cry, and it gets really loud with their voices melding together, and suddenly their voices start to sound like the cries of a baby.

I'm awake, and the room's lost its surreal glow, its strange inhabitants, and has gone back to being a rarely used guest room.

My body's feeling pounded on, like all those little men have been at me with hammers, and the all-over pain seems to have gotten worse, which I guess is the reason the visions have disappeared. I stay boxed in the corner of the bed, trying to draw some minuscule comfort from the coolness of the wall, the rocking motions of my body, and the groans that emanate from my throat.

I'd take a drink of anything now, to end this. My senses have been battered down and disintegrated against the fury of my body's rebellion, but I'm simply too weak, and I drift in and out of awareness. My groans turn into the Lord's Prayer and then the Hail Mary, which I recite like a mantra, getting lost in its pauses and phrases just enough to separate my consciousness from the wounded, desperate animal I've become.

I'm only aware of time passing because the pain finally decreases, allowing me to slip into actual sleep. I'm like that for some time, sleeping, awakening, too frightened to move, lest I disturb the small island of peace my body enjoys.

My eyes open to the sun coming through the window, some birds chirping, and my gay friend, Daniel, sitting on the edge of my bed, a pizza box in hand.

"Gawd, you look like shit, Joe."

"Well, I'd hate for my outside not to match my insides."

I'm tempted to go back to sleep, but the first whiff of pizza gets my stomach to growling. Sleep can wait, I decide. Besides, I need to go to the bathroom.

"Hungry?" Daniel asks as I make my way back from the bathroom, plopping down on the bed.

"Maybe in a minute." I feel my head. My hair is matted, but I get a wave of pleasure just by feeling my skull, wondrous that it hasn't changed shape under the skull-blasting pounding it took. "What time is it?"

"Eleven o'clock, Wednesday, Mr. Rip Van Winkle." Daniel produces bottled water from somewhere below the bed and opens the pizza box, placing a paper plate on the lid. I take a piece and it's quite possible that food has never tasted this good.

As I eat, Daniel relates how Sarah found me here the next morning, moaning and covered in sweat. She'd wanted to do something, but Millie told her I'd be fine. I smirk at that. He tells me that Sarah sat outside the door, heard me shouting the weirdest things about animals, Cheryl, and the Virgin Mary.

I've inhaled two pieces of pizza before I notice the box. "Ahh, Jimmy and Achmed's pizza."

"Their compliments. They told me to tell you this one's on the house that they've been making a fortune selling pizza to the press camped outside your office."

I grab a water bottle and stare at its clarity for a moment. "Daniel, I seem to have...sorry, wiggle words, too used to being an attorney. I have a problem. I'm an alcoholic...I think. Regardless of the title, I've decided never to drink again. My gawd," I say. "I'm just like Ex-President Bush."

Daniel simply nods at my last bit of silliness. "I agree with the plan, Mr. President."

"What happened while I was away?"

"The D.A. is holding a press conference today and the media thinks it's something major."

I suddenly remember my fight with Shriner and what started it. A new and loud voice in my head says, *Joe, your drinking started the fight.* Shriner was simply being his normal asshole self. "Ahh, Jesus, Daniel, Shriner's going to announce that his office thinks I'm the father of Cheryl's baby."

Daniel looks stunned and I use this opportunity to steal two more pieces of pizza. As I eat, I tell him of my tête-à-tête with Shriner in the church.

"There's no policeman at your door, so I guess he's not pressing charges."

"His word against mine. Besides, not good for his image. I kinda got the better of him."

"Didn't you say you sucker punched him?"

I shrug, like 'what's your point.' "I've got to go down and talk to Sarah. Tell her what's going to be announced." I stand. "My first day without a drink's turning out to be a very merry one."

I walk downstairs. Even with my fill of pizza, I'm still feeling pretty fragile.

Millie's in the kitchen doing dishes.

"Millie, where's Sarah?"

Millie looks me up and down without a trace of emotion. "She's in the garden trying to save my hepaticas."

I walk to the screen door and then pause. "Thanks for the wakeup call. I needed that talking to."

"You needed a kick in the ass, but I figured if it worked on Frank thirty years ago, it'd work on you."

She goes back to her washing. I just shake my head and step outside into the light. I find my wife, as Millie said, trying to save some flowers. "Hi, Hon, they gonna make it?"

She's on her knees, blinking up into the light. "You've got to free up the roots. Weeds get down in there and make a mess of things." She goes back to the pulling and clearing.

"I'm sorry for how I've been. I can't drink anymore, I know that now."

She's still focused on her work. "Woulda thought someone might've figured that out when his wife had to pick him up from jail."

I remember a conversation from maybe a year ago where Sarah was pointing out how all the beer bottles were pushed to the bottom of the garbage, like I'd been trying to hide how many there were. My retort sprang back to mind. "Don't worry, Hon, you're right. A sign of a drinking problem is hiding your drinking." Although, now I'm almost embarrassed to remember. "Honey," I told her, I didn't hide those bottles; I was way too lit last night to think of something as sneaky as that."

Sarah's gotten up, and with dirt on her knees, and still wearing her gardening gloves we hug, and I'm telling her I'm so sorry, knowing I'm going to be a lot sorrier in a minute.

"Sarah, this isn't easy to tell you after all I've put you through, but the D.A.'s going to give a press conference today, and in it they're going to say they think I'm the father of Cheryl's child." Before she can even say anything, I'm trying to reassure her the whole thing's groundless. "They have no proof. There's no DNA showing I'm the kid's dad. They've just done some Swiss cheese testing of the prison guards and haven't come up with the real father. Sarah, I didn't have sex with Cheryl Preninger."

Surprisingly, she's patting my hand like she did after my drunken memorial speech. "I know you'd never have sex with her, Joe. You are a moral man; you wouldn't destroy our marriage just so you could win a case."

I'm nodding, holding her close, but a voice inside me is wondering what I would do, what I already have done, and what I may still have to do to win this case.

# TWENTY-SEVEN

As soon as Joe left Sarah to pruning, she lapsed back into the altered state of mind that she had been falling deeper and deeper into over the last few months. However, as a testament to the untapped reservoirs of her cunning, she continued her bright and sunny veneer, ever stronger, like shiny Easter paint covering a rotten egg.

As she perfectly weeded and tilled this small patch of soil, her mind bubbled with delusions. Unknowingly, when Sarah was a little girl, her mother had planted hepaticas in their own backyard, and it was the flower's scent that finally burst the dam of Sarah's repressed memory.

Sarah kept digging while her mind flashed back to that day when she had gone searching for her sister, drawn to the tool shed and its strange noises. Back then, eight year-old Sarah stood high above the ground on that toolshed, peering down at her little sister, Ruth, five, dressed in Scooby Doo pj's, her hair in tiny braids.

"Sarah, you're not supposed to be up there," Ruth lisped cutely.

"I climbed up here yesterday and Daddy said what a big girl I was."

Ruth seemed to think this over a bit, absently pulling at her braids in that way she did when in deep thought.

"Look at me, I'm a princess. I'm Princess of all Virginia. I can stand up here, I can jump up here," Sarah finishes, jumping again, and again. The last jump ending with a crack that was lost over Ruth's cries, "Stop it, Sarah, Daddy said."

"Daddy also said I was a big girl and looked mighty pretty standing up here," Sarah shouts the last comment into the sky, daring the spirits of the air to disagree.

Sarah weeds more furiously, whole plants hacked away by her gardening fork. She's sweating and grunting with exertion as she sits on her knees, slamming both fists into the rich, dark brown soil, assaulting the earth as memories pour forth, soldiers pooling together for their final assault on a psyche's faltering resistance.

The next day. The past. There's a light mist hanging in the air that Sarah never remembered, but now she sees her wet jeans as she trods through the backyard snow-covered grass. She's wondering where Ruth's gone. She might be hiding, waiting to jump out and surprise, so she can be the center of attention. The tool shed door creaks open and there's that sound, the sound of water running too fast through a narrow opening.

Sarah now, digging in the ground, the tool forgotten, dirt flying everywhere, the few hepaticas that haven't been rooted out getting battered by fountains of dirt.

There was light in the tool shed, too much light. Sarah stepped into the shed and moved beyond the shadow of the door. It was coming through the roof. Light, slanted like beams of wood, cutting down through the hole, revealing in an eerie glow what lay beneath: little Ruth, impaled by a pitchfork, a farmer's tool, with a stout wood handle and a frame of iron. Its curved blades always frightened Sarah, made her think of the devil when her father cleared the dead underbrush from their land. And now one of these blades was protruding from her sister's chest. Ruth had been jumping, like her older sister the day before, the older sister she adored, wanted to be like even though it was Ruth who was always been better at capturing their father's attention with her soft brown eyes and performing ways.

The child's Sesame Street overalls were staining with blood and the wound in her neck bled, gurgled, like slowly subsiding water from a fountain. Her eyes were so vacant that Sarah thought her surely dead, but the little girl's fingers twitched, her eyes blinked, and her mouth tried to form words. Sarah leaned forward. "Don't tell Mommy and Daddy," her sister sighed.

Sarah had failed her sister throughout her short life, and her last betrayal was to run screaming from the toolshed, calling for her father again and again.

Sarah never told anyone about her own time atop the tool shed. She always suspected that her father remembered pulling her down and chastising her. She could see it in his disapproval, his cold stares, the shake of his head, each exasperated look whenever she failed to live up to his high expectations.

But of course, Sarah couldn't expect more. She was their only surviving child, the child who buried her guilt beneath the good-girl themes of excellent grades, a cheery disposition, and the church. Always the church, the only part of Sarah's life that wasn't a lie. How could it be a lie? Sarah went to church and God knew her heart. He had seen what she had done and Jesus bled for her sins. While the other girls confessed getting felt up by boys in the back of cars, Sarah never told. Twisting her sister's dying request to suit her own weak, pathetic ends, in time Sarah even forgot what sin she wasn't supposed to share with the priests, burying it in her heart, away from even Jesus's understanding gaze.

Sarah was covered in dirt, having lain waste to Millie's hepaticas. You poisoned your soul with the death of your sister, she thought. And now God has poisoned your womb as punishment. But why should a murderer feel God's touch growing inside her?

Part of Sarah's mind set down these cold stones of logic and another part still held to the delusion there was life in her belly, that she should be preparing for her child's birth. A life that was growing day by day, Sarah's addled mind offered. With that, her mind wandered away from the pain of Ruth, the reality of death and barrenness, toward the fantasy of childbirth, lapping these visions like a thirsty dog at a water bowl. Her mind encircled this happy future with Joe and their baby, and she left the past in the dust, like skin sloughed off by a snake.

I'm driving my car, which means I'm not drinking, though driving certainly hasn't deterred me from doing both in the past. Doing something while not drinking has become a refrain of mine: I'm mowing the lawn and not drinking; I'm replacing the neighbor's tree that I ran over and not drinking; I'm seeing a movie with Sarah and not drinking. This mantra has diminished slightly over the last two weeks. There is progress when the idea of taking a drink does not intrude in every offhand moment; it gives me hope that I'll be able to quiet my drinking voice until it becomes the barest whisper.

My thoughts run back to the night and day I spent rolled in a sweaty ball, rocking and moaning to the prayer of the Virgin Mary. The pain has faded, but the wacky vividness of my dream has stayed with me. I run through the half-animal versions of the people I know, wondering if they're a key to unlocking my mind, or if they were just a slice of my cerebral cortex vomiting up a kind of static as it collected and filed the day's events.

A car cuts me off and I hit the horn. My mind flutters back to those dreams, the Virgin Mary so pregnant, so obviously a stand-in for Cheryl. Though hardly a saint, her punishment of death by hanging is far more severe than having to sleep in the barn. If Mary were alive today, she'd get maternity leave and have Joseph around for...

I don't swerve the car, but if some animal had darted onto the road, I'd have plowed right through it, spreading its brains all over my front windscreen, and I probably would've just kept going like nothing had happened, so quickly and mesmerizingly were my thoughts spinning.

I take the nearest off ramp and spend twenty minutes reviewing my wild insight, or epiphany—mad hunch or bogus legal strategy—deciding that it actually holds together. I call Sarah. She's at home, the press having retreated from their vigil, and I tell her I have to go to Sussex and that I'll be late for lunch. She says to send Cheryl her regards, but I don't bother to explain that I'm not going to see Cheryl.

# TWENTY-EIGHT

The file—tome might be a better word if the gathered pages weren't fresh out of the printer—lands with a thud on Shriner's desk.

Metcalfe in his Prada suit, soft blue Italian silk shirt with an all-the-style matching colored tie, looks at Shriner, whose black eyes and broken nose are finally fading. "It's not over, Mal."

That Shriner instantly knows who and what Metcalfe's talking about is testament to Joe Heyerdahl's tenacity and ingenuity, not to mention the abiding hatred Shriner feels whenever his thoughts drift toward the pain in his face, or Joe, *the pain in his ass.* "What now, Warren?"

"It's...it's original. I don't want to say anything. You read it over and give me your opinion, okay? Whatever it is, be ready. I'm calling the Governor because I think we're going to need his feedback on what he wants to do."

Forty-eight hours later, the Governor, looking like he was ready to carve the Thanksgiving turkey and just found out it's filled with salmonella, sits at his desk, which is the size of an aircraft carrier. Evans rises and falls in time to whatever point he needs to make. Metcalfe and Shriner sit across the desk, looking relaxed, though Metcalfe appears put out by the whole deal, and Shriner's expression fluctuates between white-hot anger and a grudging respect for Heyerdahl's cleverness.

They're making small talk, which the Governor monopolizes by describing in painstaking detail his father's role as an aide to Kennedy during the Cuban Missile Crisis. Evans knows that the others have heard the story, but he dare not attempt to head his boss off when he gets going on his favorite subject.

The small talk is a ruse to cover the collective tension and anticipation. They're waiting for the arrival of Ted Clark, a noted legal expert. The mere fact that the Governor is waiting patiently for someone who is twenty minutes late is evidence of the esteem he holds for Clark.

Ted Clark, the man famous for his encyclopedic memory of the law, and the man who gave it all up to pilot a boat in the America's Cup, which he won in brilliant fashion by belaying a topsail during high wind and overtaking the leader who had foundered during the storm. That ESPN II caught it all made him stratospherically more famous in the prestigious blue-blood clubs and drawing rooms that have existed for moneyed ages up and down the eastern seaboard.

Later, he became one of only a handful of men to ever turn down an appointment to the US Appellate Court. Ambitious attorneys from San Francisco to Washington were shocked and then offended that one of theirs would turn his back on such a prestigious appointment. They were not appeased to discover the man planned to sail around the Cape of Good Hope in a year that promised the greatest swells of the past century.

Clark accomplished this...and more. The documentary made about his journey around the tip of South Africa made him an even greater legend in a world where the law and yachting were often one and the same.

Clark finally arrives thirty minutes late. He's wearing jeans, a white 2 x 2 pinpoint shirt with buttons at the collar and boat shoes without socks. The man is tanned, with ghostly green eyes and a thatch of white hair that guys wish for and women dream about. He's smiling, as if all this legal shit is just a hobby and there's not one person in the world he has to be nice to unless they deserve it. Governor Sumner is definitely someone who does not.

"Bob, good to see you," he says, and the Governor walks over to greet him. Introductions move quickly around the room. Before they can all be seated, the Governor gets to the point. "So, Ted, what's your take on this Equal Protection nonsense?"

Ted appears to be enjoying this, the power to cast his opinion with no worries about who he'll hook, or who'll be pissed because he caught the hook in someone's eye. "I think you've got a royal cluster-fuck here, Bob."

The Governor is known to hate foul language, except when he uses it himself. It is a reflection of his regard for Clark that he listens intently, lips slightly parted.

"This guy, Heyerdahl's good," says Clark. "Creative as hell."

Shriner scowls, as if unwilling to be cowed by anyone wearing worn topsiders, no matter what his reputation. "He's one slimy bastard, knocking up his client so he can pressure the Governor to commute her sentence."

Clark smiles. "As I said, creative as hell. It's his job to see that she doesn't get the needle. Sorry, the rope." He shakes his head at that one. "Like I said, fucking creative."

The Governor clears his throat, but it's Evans who speaks. "Let's get back on point, gentlemen. We can argue about Mr. Heyerdahl's disbarment proceedings later. The question is, does Heyerdahl have a winning case?"

Clark pauses, as if loving the drama, the acting. "Winnable, maybe. Can he litigate it? Let me lay it out for you. He has fourteen male respondents on your death row, all claiming that the State of Virginia is denying them their constitutional right of Equal Protection under the law. Why? Because by granting an emergency stay to a woman, based solely on her pregnancy, means that the State is giving her greater de facto protection under the law."

The Governor responds. "But she's a woman."

Clark stands and walks about the room. "That's what makes it brilliant. I ask you, why is it always the attorneys with the worst morals that are the best?"

The Governor shakes his head. "I looked at those other murderers and none of them has similar standing. They're not fathers-in-waiting."

"Irrelevant, Bob. I can't give Malcolm extra rights because he wears nice suits, while not giving them to you because you can't afford the suits yourself."

The others stare at this courtroom legend that could chat amiably, rattle off insight like he was pulling the leaves off trees, dominate a room so effortlessly—even with men who had such a high opinion of themselves. "I bet you've already got calls from a few governors," he says, and the Governor nods. "Mr. Grant in Texas, for sure." Another nod. "Anything that cuts into that son of a bitch's kill rate will raise his hackles."

Shriner's still scowling. "Texas figures that any ruling here can be used to gum up their judiciary."

"And they're right," says Clark. "On top of this, Heyerdahl's got the Americans with Disabilities Act, giving express rights to not only women, but to men whose wives are pregnant."

"But these are prisoners," says Metcalfe.

Before he can finish, Clark jumps in. "And they have strictly limited rights. But," he adds with unconscious aplomb, "death row inmates also have greater rights to contest the actions of the State because the cost of the

State's actions are so high." He sighs and adds, "If you just locked'm up forever, you'd save so much hassle. Anyway, you're opening a Pandora's Box, win or lose, and you might just lose."

Shriner harrumphs, "I've beaten this so-called creative attorney every time I've faced him."

Clark shakes his head. "I read your last head-to-head. He out-argued you and got Salomon and Troy to flip his way. A five-two decision is almost unheard of in those circumstances."

"So, say we fight this," says Evans, like he's been waiting for this moment. "It's just like a stay; it could take the Court a year to decide."

The lines around Metcalfe's eyes deepen. "That could tie up a lot of our resources. Remember, it's fourteen cases that Heyerdahl will try to litigate separately."

Clark seats himself and folds his hands, but his joie de vivre is not so easily contained. "What if you give this guy what he wants?"

The Governor's face reddens. "I will not be shown to be some pushover to some screwball defense attorney."

Clark smiles. "No, what I mean, Bob, is this Heyerdahl is bright." A glance at Shriner saying, 'Are we gonna argue about this?' "He knew that if he let your stay continue, she'd have the baby and then you'd off her. What's in it for his client to go to the gallows without kicking up a fuss? He challenges the stay, and forces your hand. No stay, no way she hangs."

The Governor's rolling his eyes at what he sees as an offense to his power.

Clark continues. "Bob, release the stay. Put the ball in Heyerdahl's court. Then, he's got maybe a week or two before his client's set to be executed. Suddenly he's the one behind the eight-ball and he's got to do something fast."

Shriner rises in protest. "I still say we fight this. This motion is no bull's-eye."

Again, it's Clark with the apt reply. "Malcolm, in darts the bull's-eye gets you fifty, but the inside band on the twenty gets you sixty points. My *point* is that there's more than one way to win at darts. Just like there's more ways to win a case than actually winning the case."

Evans turns to his boss, who says, "Yeah, yeah, what Ted said about canceling the stay. Let's put the screws to this shyster; make him think he'll be responsible for this convict's death. We'll even tell the press that his litigiousness has forced our hand."

The Governor nods. "I like it. I still look tough on crime, and a few days before the execution we get a scared attorney begging for a stay. We let him twist in the wind a bit, then we give it to him with no assurances of what will happen to his client."

"Like your dad and the missile crisis, Bob." Clark's playing him, but the Governor's the only one not in on the joke.

"You're right. This all parallels the discussions my father had with Jack and Bobby before the Russians knew that we knew. Heyerdahl will be just like the Russkies steaming toward our warships, and he'll be the one who blinks. Good ole fashion brinksmanship."

That settled, Clark indulges his interest. "How come this Heyerdahl couldn't get all seventeen of the guys on death row to sign on? These type usually love to jam up the courts?"

Metcalfe turns to Shriner because his lieutenant always knows the dirt. Shriner pipes in helpfully. "Richie Samkins is incommunicado."

"From his attorney?" Clark questions.

"From the world. He barely eats, shits himself when the mood strikes him, and he hasn't showered in over a year. The other two are in deep solitary. One for attacking a guard, and the other for using a spork to try to dig a hole through his own stomach."

"A spork?" Even the ever-so-sharp Clark has to ask.

"A plastic spoon-fork. You know, spork with a beveled end."

That question satisfied, the conversation moves on to sports, sailing, and other masculine pursuits that men in suits read about but rarely participate in.

Going unsaid is everyone's unquestioned belief that Heyerdahl will break, but it's not the attorney's life on the line, and what if the Governor digs his heels in further? Those against the death penalty may protest, but who's going to make either of these two men budge so that a woman and a blameless child don't die.

# TWENTY-NINE

*Four days to execution*

At first I'd been pissed, then gratified, and then I was fearful. Pissed because, when the Governor removed the stay, my best chance to beat Shriner and actually win something in this whole fiasco was gone. Gratified because I'd forced them to do exactly what I wanted, release the stay on Cheryl. The resulting storm of protest would pressure the Governor into giving in. Faced saved, Cheryl saved, baby saved. And here's where the fear part kicks in. What if the Governor is not just an uncompromising, hardheaded, and hard-hearted political stooge, but a sadist?

After the stay was lifted, the Court ruled that the State had ten days to act on the execution order. I'd hoped the State wouldn't be able to get it together in time, so I could bring another motion on that point. But the gallows continued to be erected. Though I'd heard they were having trouble getting the five men necessary to pull the levers—you need five, one to pull that actual lever, and the other four to pull dummy handles so no one knows who the true executioner is, but so far, the trouble with volunteers is more a hint of a rumor than an actual rumor.

For the first four days of the countdown I shuttled between the prison and our home away from home, the Bradshaw's. The media had again descended on my house when it looked like Cheryl was going to be executed.

As for Cheryl, she remains mind-numbingly upbeat, just as she remains increasingly pregnant. She talks about God and the awe she feels at being witness to His power, but I'm more in awe at how out of hand this case had become. Governor Sumner has to give in. If he doesn't, I can throw myself on his mercy and ask for the stay I so effectively got repealed.

I realize now that he knows I'll do just that, so it's all up to me. I'm the one with a client about to be executed. Unless something happens in the next five days, he's got me, I'll eat humble pie and they'll reissue the stay, wait for Cheryl to pop the kid out, and then kill her.

Damn, my brilliant maneuvering has only resulted in getting me out maneuvered.

It's eleven o'clock at night and I'm parking a block away from my office and walking down a back alley and hammering on the pizzeria's back door. Achmed's at the door in a flash to usher me in. The only reason I know it's Achmed is that he favors Jay-Z caps, while Jimmy sticks to Eminem and Oriole headgear.

"How are you, Joe?"

"I'm fine, Achmed, and you don't have to whisper."

"Right," he nods.

Jimmy comes around a corner carrying a bag of frozen pizza dough. He lowers his head when he sees me.

I caught the whole deal last night when some reporter, trolling for info, got Jimmy talking and he blurts out how they'd given me a special milkshake to increase my fertility. Well, now poor Jimmy's surrounded by reporters, all of whom are shouting questions about what else he knows about my fathering Preninger's child. As if some Arabic folk magic is conclusive proof I'm the baby's father.

Achmed, who's older by ten minutes, and is always assumed the controlling aspect of a big brother says, "Get over here and apologize to Joe."

Looking chastened, Jimmy puts down the dough and walks over. "I am sorry, Joe. Please accept my apologies."

"No problem, Jimmy. I know it can be fun to be on TV."

Jimmy's eyes light up. "Yes, exactly, the cameras are on me, and the pretty woman has her arm on my back so I stay in the picture, and she's asking me about you. The next thing I know other reporters are shouting questions to me, and there is a big craziness."

Achmed snaps a towel in Jimmy's direction. "My brother, the TV star."

I'm shrugging it off. "Again, no problem, Jimmy. You didn't say anything that wasn't true."

"But we know you, Joe, and Achmed and I know you would not do this thing to your wife."

Achmed still chides his brother. "I tell him, Joe, America great place, but media full of lies, and still he watches *True Hollywood Stories* and buys newspapers like these," gesturing to piles of newsprint on the cutting board. "I tell him the *Washington Post,* you read, good; the *National Enquirer...*," Achmed grabs the copy. "Bad."

I take the paper from Achmed and read the sensationalized headline, 'Eyewitness To Death In Love With D.A.?'

On the magazine's front page is Bhasad Delhi, looking older, but well kept, sitting with a man I first take to be Warren Metcalfe. But the photos new and, besides why would he visit her?

Achmed's getting me a slice of pizza and praising me to Allah over their 500% increase in business. They're doing so well, they're thinking of opening a second pizzeria.

I'm uh-huhing and flipping to the article. Like all these tabloid stories, they're high on innuendo and low on attributable fact, but they've broken some big stories in the past because they're willing to pay cash money. Reading further, a background source claims he signed Bhasad and Metcalfe into the Rocker Motel (nice inset of quaint little bungalow motel) on several occasions before and during the trial. The couple stopped coming right after the trial, when the informant said he heard them having a fight. The paper ratchets up the romance angle another notch by showing Bhasad's husband, older and gray-haired. There are some similarities between this guy and Warren Metcalfe.

The paper goes on to opine that Delhi was broken-hearted by Metcalfe's betrayal and could only find comfort in the arms of a man who looked like her lost love. A photostat copy of her marriage license issued three months after Cheryl's trial gives it a shadow of legitimacy, masking what is a very hypothetical tale of a jilted heart.

I sit with my pizza and coke, my trip to the office forgotten, and I realize that this may be useful. I can't win in a fair fight with the law so, as my dad always said, "If you're losing at something, change the rules 'til you can beat the sumbitch." I realize that's just what I'm going to have to do.

*Three days until Cheryl dies by hanging.*

It's the next afternoon. I'm outside on the courthouse steps and the Richmond PD has had to call out the mounted police to keep the throngs of media from swamping me. My phone calls to the networks about a big announcement have made it even worse.

Interestingly, I find that reporters are much better behaved when armed policeman atop large animals are present. I'm at the makeshift podium now, and after some jostling I express my indignation at the cavalier attitude of the Governor's office, but I steer clear of antagonizing the man directly. And then I segue to the good stuff. "It has come to my attention that the D.A. engaged in a clandestine affair with the State's key witness in my client's trial, a witness, I might add, who was the State's only witness against my client. Without her, they would have only circumstantial evidence—some drugs and bloody clothes that were not even typed for DNA. Additionally, I've recently discovered that the police have lost this evidence."

"Are you saying your client's innocent?" someone shouts.

I don't answer because I don't want to lose my momentum, also I want to let that question hang there and simmer.

"My client's very life, and the life of her unborn child, are at stake. There is mounting evidence (yeah, right) that the then A.D.A, hungry for his first murder conviction, enticed an impressionable young woman into an affair in the hopes of influencing her testimony." Good, I had their full attention.

"If you read her police interviews," I went on, "she couldn't remember anything of the crime. However, as the trial approached, her memory suddenly came back. And now it's reported that she again does not remember the events. How utterly convenient for the State."

Some shouts of, "But Preninger confessed," which I also ignore.

"I have also been a target of the D.A.'s mysterious overzealousness in regards this case. I have right here," I say. I go on, holding up a microcassette (it pays to be technologically illiterate and unable to erase messages from your answering machine) a time-stamped tape that has the D.A.'s office calling me to inform me of my selection as Cheryl Preninger's attorney. It's dated the day before the P.D.'s office notified me. Additionally, I was asked to an urgent meeting with Deputy D.A. Shriner, who demanded to know my intentions vis-a-vis the Preninger matter. At the time, I took this as a desire to insure that an untested attorney, like myself, was up to the challenge of a capital murder case on appeal. Now, I see it was because they had something to hide. The Deputy wanted to make sure his boss's secret wasn't revealed."

"Furthermore, a few months ago, I was arrested after coming out of a local tavern. This policeman was not a uniformed officer, yet he arrested me, going as far as getting into fisticuffs with me. I was jailed, fingerprinted, mug-shotted, and allowed to sit in a cell for several hours until Deputy Shriner dropped all the charges. I should note that the Deputy arrived at the jail at almost two o'clock in the morning. He stated that the reason for this was because he had caught a murder case that night. But I've checked Mr. Shriner's alibi (love using the word alibi when talking about Shriner), and it does not hold up. There were no murders in the Richmond area that night. I have here," holding up some papers, "a copy of my booking sheet, and the police logs from that night showing no homicides." I can see by all the scribbling that the press is eating this up, and I figure my use of props makes for good TV.

"Upon reflection, and in light of these new events, it is clear to me that Shriner was there to be certain I would be stopped and charged with DWI, thus diminishing my reputation and my ability to work effectively for my client. That this happened shortly after my first appeal lends heightened credence to the story. As it is, the D.A.'s office clearly believed I would be a legal pushover, and when it was proved that this was not the case, they took steps to discredit me. The only reason their plan was unsuccessful was that I happened to 'make' the plain clothes officer while he sat in his car."

I thank them for coming and walk away, ignoring their shouted questions, thinking I've given the press a small amount of fact covered with a whole lot of nothing, kind of like a McDonald's hamburger. Now, I've got less than three days to sit back and see what happens, or four days before I have to beg the Governor for Cheryl's life.

The Governor and his aide are sitting in the Governor's office. "Can you believe this shit," says the Governor, breaking his no swearing policy. "The press is eating this up: a love struck dot-head, an ambitious lothario of a D.A., and his sneaky deputy. What the hell is Warren saying about all this?"

"He says it's crap, that he never told Mrs. Delhi to remember things that didn't happen."

"Sounds like legal horse shit to me, Marlon. He didn't say he didn't sleep with her or that he coached her to remember. This doesn't look good, and what about Shriner's cockamamie scheme to make this *attorney* look bad?" The Governor says the word attorney like it's the disgusting habit of some primitive Guinea tribesmen.

"He denies he told Heyerdahl it was a murder. Says he was there because a detective Randall called him on a murder case they'd been working. Says Heyerdahl was drunk as a skunk and couldn't remember his last name if you taped it to his hand."

"Do we know if that's true?" asks the Governor.

"This is political now, Bob. It's not about the truth, it's about the impression the public's forming about the entire process. And right now, it's not good."

The Governor rockets from his seat. "I don't give a rat's ass," he barked. "I didn't come this far to be beaten by some bottom-feeding shyster. We've got three days. We hold the fort, he'll come calling. His boats are getting close to our blockade. He's scared, so he's shooting his mouth off. But just you wait a few days and he'll be making a deal on our terms."

***Two days until Cheryl dies by hanging.***

Like a bloodhound with a good scent, the media is ferreting out everything it can. I'm not sure if it's this pressure, or that somebody in the Governor's office gets a conscience. Probably it's the former.

Twenty-four hours after my speech on the courthouse steps, CNN gets hold of a memo developed by the Governor's office. It outlines how best to deal with a pregnant Preninger. The memo is ten pages, single-spaced, and buried in a paragraph is the suggestion that Preninger be encouraged to allow herself to be executed by hanging. The report goes on to mention that death by hanging can take as little as three or four minutes, that with the mother's body shunting its last reserves to the fetus, it might be possible to harvest the child through an immediate C-section after the death of its mother. The report notes that these are the 'positive merits' of hanging, unlike electrocution or lethal injection, which would immediately kill both mother and infant.

This piece of ghoulish cleverness looks bad for the State and quickly snowballs into an allegation that it coerced Preninger into making the decision to be hanged. This is completely unsupportable from the timeline evidence, but the public mind has been excited and where there's a lack of facts, facts will be quickly created.

None of this would matter, except for one Morris Huntner, Sussex correctional officer.

Marlon Evans runs into Sumner's office, opening the television cabinet. "Quick, Madeline Scherr over at CNN just told me they're going with an exclusive that we're going to want to see!"

Sumner, his feet on the desk, is reading the financial section. "An exclusive what, Marlon?"

"On the Preninger matter, and she says it's huge."

This pulls the Governor's attention away from his stock portfolio. "Huge, how?"

Evans shrugs and grabs the remote to click to CNN.

After a few minutes of reporting on civil war in Malaysia, the camera switches to Madeline Scherr, and with her, a short haired, purposeful looking fellow in his twenties. "Good evening, I'm Madeline Scherr. There is an execution scheduled to take place in less than three days. The gentleman to my left is Morris Huntner, a six-year veteran officer at the Sussex State Correctional Facility. Mr. Huntner has come forward because he believes he has vital information relating to this execution." Turning toward the guard, she asks, "Officer Huntner, why have you come forward?"

"I don't care why he came forward," the Governor growls. "If I wanted to know this squarehead's motivation, I'd hire an actor."

Scherr takes Huntner through his exemplary record as a prison officer, citing his numerous commendations, mentioning the injuries he's sustained at the hands of violent offenders. Completing her litany, she pauses for Huntner to speak. "When I seen that letter from the Governor, I just knew I had to say something. I felt like it's my duty as an American. So I was working a few months back when the Deputy D.A. came through."

"That's Deputy D.A. Shriner, correct?"

"Yeah, he talked to inmate Preninger for about ten minutes. I didn't hear what they talked about, but he left quick. I was escorting the prisoner back to her cell and she looked real shook up. Usually, she's got a good word for everyone, you know? Then she says, 'They mean to hang me, Morris.' She just kept mumbling, getting whiter and whiter."

"And what did you do?"

"Well, nothing. I just thought she was talking all heated as all. She does that quite a bit. You know, with all her Bible reading."

Scherr begins to wrap up the interview; Evans turns the TV off.

"Well, that wasn't good," the Governor states mildly.

"That is a serious understatement," replies Evans, as if fed up with the whole thing. His voice changes to that of a tough cop. "Governor, you cannot execute this woman and you cannot continue to play hard ball with her life."

"I'm not, her attorney is."

"This office and the D.A.'s office, we're all tainted now."

"That guard's probably lying."

"We don't have time to find out."

The Governor's shakes his head before Evans finishes. "This is just..."

"Governor, remember the Cuban Missile Crisis? Well, that little press conference just made us the Russians. We're the ones who look dirty, who knew things before the public."

The Governor is wavering. Evans is making sense, even for a political hack like Sumner. Evans goes for the one-two punch. "We still don't have the requisite number of executioners. We're stuck at three, and we've already got people in the streets calling on the guards not to participate. This thing with the D.A.'s office, maybe there's something there. You've got to commute her sentence."

"I don't know what this'll do to my credibility."

The expression on his face says, 'I'm stuck. I want to back out and I don't know how.'

"The Clemency Board," Evans says, offering a solution. "It's non-binding in Virginia..."

"It sure as hell is," said the Governor. "If not, most of those who went to the chair would still be sitting on death row."

"Precisely, you make a speech declaring that you've been astonished and angered at the D.A.'s handling of the case. As of yet, you don't know if there has been any illegality on their part, but you fear that there is the possibility of impropriety. You are therefore sending a Letter of Delegation to the Clemency Board, forfeiting your decision-making powers on this case and charging them to reach an equitable solution."

"So we're laying all this on the D.A.'s office?"

"Sir, Shriner met with Preninger, called Heyerdahl and got him arrested, and Metcalfe banged the State's eyewitness."

The Governor does a poor job of suppressing a smile. "What was the Clemency Board's earlier recommendation?"

Evans has it ready. "Three-to-one to commute, with Fitzimmons dissenting."

"Hah, he's the one hardcore conservative in the group. All the rest are dyed-in-the-wool liberals. What do they care what the public thinks. Unlike me, they're appointed for life."

Under his breath, Evans hums 'Oh Cry Me A River.' "I'll draft the Letter Delegate, sir," says Evans. "You give that press conference and kick this whole mess into their lap."

"I don't want to go with their three-to-one ruling; it'll look like I'm gift wrapping this commutation."

"Sure, there's new evidence, right? Allegations that the Clemency Board needs to review before making a determination."

The Governor nods, rubbing his hands together. "As for the letter, make it clear this is a one-time thing. I'm not ceding any power to a bunch of super-liberal bureaucrats."

"No problem, even in normal situations it takes a majority to make a recommendation. A two-two split and they can't even draft a memo. The letter will state that because of the unique nature of the case, you are exercising a singular and unique abdication of your commutation power to the Clemency Board."

"You know, I think we just turned vinegar into wine." The Governor goes searching for a Cuban cigar to celebrate and misses the scowl that crosses his aide's face.

The Governor's Office doesn't even bother to call me about the Clemency Board, so I end up hearing it second hand from Stella. She reaches me at Frank's, and I spend twenty minutes flipping through channels before I hear the Governor give us the win. Legal talking heads are weighing in, describing the Governor's office's ability to do almost anything regarding clemency. Most pundits are buoyant in their praise of Sumner, citing his politically savvy solution to what had seemed a terrible impasse.

I don't take it badly that the Governor is getting credit for my idea. I'd only mentioned it to Evans as an afterthought. What mattered was that Cheryl was not going to die, and I was going to be able to tell her.

The one loose end was Metcalfe and Shriner. Had Metcalfe really had a relationship with Delhi? And if so, had he cajoled her into remembering? And what about Shriner? What was he covering up? Or was he just acting on the belief that his boss needed the Preninger case to go away? Like so many bad conspiracists, if Shriner had left things alone, nothing much would have happened.

Now that Cheryl's got the life sentence, I can push for a new trial. Digging into the Metcalfe and Delhi connection may give me the ammo I need. Without the eyeball witness, all the D.A. has are drugs from the robbery and some bloody sheets. With a new case, I could just argue that someone was there with Cheryl and that he was the murderer. She was a hapless junkie looking to score some drugs. The only sticking point of my new defense theory is the question of why she confessed. She didn't have a list of life-long friends she'd be willing to take the rap for. Even her middle-aged mother never came to visit her when she was in prison. Also, her mother doesn't seem the type to torture and execute two people, and her father seemingly disappeared with King Arthur aboard those white ships, so no likely suspects in the area of blood relations.

Whatever we do, we've got time. And what matters is that Cheryl's not being fitted for the hangman's noose.

# THIRTY

*48 hours until the execution*

I'm driving to Sussex and as I speed through Virginia's northernmost spine, for the first time since this case landed on my lap, I'm noticing the trees and woodlands. Part of me wants to have a drink of celebration after I tell Cheryl the good news, which would be okay if I were normal in that regard. But I know I'm not, because the greatest part of me wants to pull off at the next junction, hunt down an ABC liquor outlet, and swig a jug of almost anything they've got.

I arrive at Sussex and Officer White's not there, so I get this German guard who looks like he was one of the original sackers of Rome. I head to Stanton Block, where I'm handed off to a guard who's not Huntner, and I wonder if he's off duty or if he's been given a leave of absence.

Cheryl's where she always is, but she's smiling, and for this one moment I'm feeling awfully glad I took this case. It's a moment I know I'll never forget.

She's got her Bible out and the first thing she says is, "Let's pray, Joe."

Her hands are still manacled, but she puts them out to hold mine. I glance at the door and then at the guard. Either this guy's new or the rules have lightened, now that Cheryl's got commutation, because he's not even registering the question in my eyes.

331

So I hold Cheryl's hands. This is the first time we've ever really touched and she looks quite lovely, with her happiness shining from every pore and her belly big enough that I have to lean a little over the table to reach her out-stretched hands.

"Dear God," Cheryl begins. "I thank you for this boon. I thank you for the chance to continue my ministries in whatever form you deem. I thank you for the breath in my lungs, the taste on my lips, and the sounds in my ears. I vow to educate myself to Your Word and renew my faith in Your Everlasting Benevolence. And lastly, thank you for Joe Heyerdahl and for touching him with your insight and determination in order to effect and deliver Your Will. In the name of the Father, the Son, and the Holy Spirit, Amen."

I'm touched and a little wet in the eyes, and then I'm embarrassed, and then I'm embarrassed I'm embarrassed.

On the other hand, Cheryl's beaming. "So the Clemency Board will rule soon?"

"They've got to rule within forty-eight hours."

She's nodding. "They all seemed like caring people."

"You've met them?"

She tells me that she's met them several times, when they were gathering information to make their first finding to send to the Governor. The women, Thompson, and the short fellow, Dutton came twice more. They told her it was for fact gathering, but she thought they felt sorry for her, especially seeing since they, and a few religious workers, were among the few people allowed to see her. I told her that I'd call her when I heard, but that it was really just a formality.

"Thank you again, Joe," she said. "Bless you, and bless your wife."

Cheryl still hasn't taken her hands from mine, and we sit this way, and I let her talk about her plans. Plans that she's quietly sealed for years. Plans for a Bible reading group; plans for a better prison library; plans to make plans. Plans for some kind of life.

I'm in no hurry to leave, but the new guard knows when the visit is supposed to be up, probably because he gets his lunch break or something. I'm saying goodbye and Cheryl's thanking me, to the point where I need to leave just so I don't get all embarrassed again.

I get back to Frank's and Millie and Sarah have made dinner. Afterward, we go out on the back porch to enjoy the last warm summer night. We talk about Frank, and the case, and the only ache I feel is from the alcohol-free lemonade I sip. It would seem, I muse, that my drinking is not predicated on happiness, or even depression, for that matter. Like the North Star, it is a fixed point, hovering on the edge of my consciousness, pulling my attention to its glow. A glow I must grit my teeth and forget; a glow I pray will dim with time.

The next day Sarah's at church with Daniel to do some flower project and I'm watching C-Span's coverage of the Clemency Board handing down its ruling. Thompson votes Yes to commute, Fitzimmons a No, Falchetti a Yeah, and Dutton a No.

I'm staring at the TV and the decision, or non-decision, is not computing. Dutton voted No, which means a two-to-two tie. As my brain tries to figure out what the hell this means, the TV reporter is throwing it back to the Studio and TV commentators to answer that exact question.

A tie is not a recommendation to commute. The absence of a positive vote stops a change in the order to discontinue Cheryl's hanging. This isn't hockey, I think, and a tie here is a lot less attractive than kissing your sister.

What to do? What to do? My hands are starting to shake. Without the commutation, Cheryl's set to die in forty-eight hours. I can't get a fucking appointment at the DMV in forty-eight hours, much less formulate some kind of appeal. Reflexively, I'm over to Frank's liquor cabinet to pour myself a drink. I'm so caught up in my cascading fear for Cheryl, the cruelty of a life, two lives, so narrowly denied, and the prospect of having to tell her, that I've suddenly got a full glass of brandy sitting on the table in front of me.

I stare at it. My drinking problem seems quite small compared to what Cheryl's now facing. Ironically, this makes it easier for me to take a drink. What's a little alcoholism in the face of an execution of a woman and her unborn baby? An execution that I failed to stop.

The soft amber-red brandy still stares at me, luring me toward an attractive oblivion. While I fumble over whether I should pick it up, my brain buzzes, bouncing through possibilities to help Cheryl. The State's still got a problem getting the requisite number of executioners. I can bring a motion charging improper methods of execution, or maybe I'll make Cheryl change her mind and say she doesn't want to be hanged. She can't change her mind, I know, but at this point I'm ready to hijack a spaceship and break her out of prison.

I stop and take a breath. Calm down, Joe, and look at things carefully. I've got forty-eight hours. Give me an hour to organize my thoughts and I'll go from there.

"If you're going to drink it, just suck it down." Unnoticed, Millie's walked up and spied the tall glass on the bar. "Don't be a coward about it and sip your way back into the bottle, Joe. Jump in with both feet. That way, you'll hit the bottom that much quicker."

"I was just thinking about drinking it," I say lamely.

"Well, do it or don't, but either way don't just leave it there. I don't want a ring on Frank's oak bar."

I give her flippancy a smirk. "The Clemency Board didn't okay the commutation. I've blocked the Governor from the stay, and now he can't commute her."

"Well, boohoo for you. What? Since Cheryl didn't pick the poison, you figure you'll take it for her?"

"And I thought you were a nice old lady."

She smacks me with the dishtowel she's holding. "I am a nice lady." With that, she turns and walks out.

Now I'm left with only one friend.

I turn to it.

In my heart of hearts, I'm an obstinate cuss, and I resent the hold alcohol has on me.

I walk out.

Then I remember Millie and that damned ring on the bar, so I go back and pick it up. I go to pour the glass in the sink, but I stop. I don't want Millie to think I drank it. It's stupid and silly, and I can hear Millie telling me not to worry about my pride. Just worry about not drinking the damn brandy, Joe. But I care about what she thinks, so I grab a coaster and leave the full glass sitting there, untouched.

I walk back to the study.

I don't know what I'll say to Cheryl, but I've got to call her to at least tell her I'm on it and that I'll think of something.

I'm on the phone now, dialing the prison and getting patched through quick enough so that I don't have time to chicken out. If I don't call her now, I'll be thinking of making the call, dreading it, and my head won't be clear enough to figure out how to get her out of this.

Cheryl's voice comes on the line.

"Cheryl, I want you to know I am on this. This thing is not going to happen."

Cheryl's voice is back to its holy, emotionless state, but I detect a hint of nervousness beneath the calm glow of religious certainty.

More soothing words by me and Cheryl keeps repeating, "It's God's plan, and remember, Joe, God writes straight with crooked sticks."

The smart-ass in me died when I heard the Clemency Board's decision. Otherwise, I'd tell Cheryl where God could shove those pointy little sticks. Besides, I can hear the fear and the lost hope threatening to overtake her, so we talk until her time runs out, which I'm afraid is now just a day away.

In the Governor's office, Sumner and Evans are having a nearly identical reaction to Joe Heyerdahl's. The difference is they have scotches in their hands.

"This thing's like an albatross around my neck," the Governor complains.

"More like a damn boomerang," Evans says with a shake of his head.

"I can't commute her? Shit! Marlon, did you get a hold of Clark?"

Evans takes a long drink as he says, "He's out at sea off Nova Scotia, doing some layout for some yacht fancier magazine."

"This is all such bullshit. Leave it to the damn bureaucrats to screw everything up."

"Some in the media are hypothesizing that Dutton cast a No vote to give you the finger over your many snubs of the Boards' previous findings."

"This is no pissing contest," the Governor replies, even though they both know it has been. "Dutton was a pinko in the sixties, but I never thought he'd go this far. Nova Scotia, huh?"

Evans nods and the two men go back to their scotch.

⸎ ⸎

I hang up with Cheryl and start wracking my brains for options of any kind. The Governor can't commute because he signed the power over to the Clemency Board. When they did not affirm the stay, the execution just moved forward—like a steamroller. We're out of options, trapped like rats in a maze that we both worked to make. It's while thinking of that maze, and then the Gordian Knot that Alexander the Great simply cut (showing what historians later called a great ability to think out of the box) that gets me thinking about my Alexander, The Sun King, the druggie slash informant, and his small piece of the story and how he was lucky to get his case kicked. When a thought flickers by, I almost dismiss the notion before I really have time to consider it. Given a few more moments to reflect, I realize it's so outlandish it might just work for both Cheryl and the Governor.

I'm pacing in circles, the idea and the plan now brimming over, as my mind tries twenty different ways to pull it apart, but each time it holds together and seems to work a little better. I call out for Millie and tell her to get her beaten-up old phonebook because I need to make a call. Everything depends on convincing Marlon Evans that my plan will work.

After a little flattery on my part, and a stern word or two from Millie, (damn, she's good at that), Marlon's father gives us his son's cell number.

"Evans here, who's this?"

"Joe Heyerdahl, I just wanted to talk…"

"Mr. Heyerdahl, the Governor's not looking to talk to you right now."

"Actually, it's you I want to talk to. I've got a way out of this that'll make everybody happy."

After my first sentence, Evans laughs and almost hangs up. To his credit, however he doesn't, and after a few more minutes he's adding to it, embroidering the whole thing, and that's when I know we've got a chance.

"Just tell the Governor that I'll…"

"Okay, okay, Joe, but just let me pitch it. Not to put too fine a point on it, but the Governor hates your guts."

"Marlon, he can hate me 'til the cows come home. Just sell him this, and then we all get to go home, cows or not."

Evans knows the best way to put a bow on this whole thing, so he sits down and writes the speech Sumner's going to give. He spends two hours on it, stopping only to field calls from Joe Heyerdahl, who's demanding to know what the hell is going on. Evans tells him he's setting the table and to have patience, but Heyerdahl can only groan and make threats about Evans not screwing this up.

Evans enjoys hearing the man squirm. After all, how much shit has he had to shovel because of Joe Heyerdahl?

With the speech completed, he walks into Sumner's office. The Governor is again perusing the *Financial Times.*

"Governor, I've got something for you to read, but I want your word you will not say a thing until you've read it in its entirety."

Sumner looks a little confused, but nods. He takes the pages from Evans and begins to read.

Evans is watching. When the Governor reads about two thirds of the way through, he exhales and starts to speak. Evans is quick to shut him down. "You gave your word, Governor."

Sumner nearly coughs up a lung, but he swallows it and goes back to reading. By the end, his face has lost its redness. He places the papers down on his desk, not wadding it up and throwing it into the trash, as Evans feared he might.

"Okay, he says. "Let's talk the angles."


By late afternoon Evans has notified the major media players that the Governor will be giving an address in one hour, which kicks off a flurry of activity. In no time the office looks like a film set, with wardrobe and make-up people working on the Governor, while an assemblage of technical folk cable in, tie down, and mic up the State's oval office.

A hush, the camera's green light goes on, and Sumner, sitting at his desk, looking earnest and steadfast, begins to speak. "I've asked the media here because of the incredible events surrounding the Preninger execution. I am not here to discuss the details of the case or defend the decisions I've made along the torturous path we've moved these past few months. What I do know is simply this: through the immoral actions of Ms. Preninger's attorney, and his misuse of the rules of law, my office finds itself in a difficult—very difficult—situation. One that was made that much harder by some strongly alleged improprieties on the part of the D.A. and his Deputy, right here in Richmond.

"In the interest of fairness, I decided to turn the question of commutation over to the Board that has been designated by the State to handle these very serious matters. My actions were met with equivocations and base politics.

"At all times, my office has found itself blocked by those who would use the law for their own narrow interests, and from those bureaucrats whose liberal sensibilities are more concerned with a cause than with the life of a woman. And more importantly, the life of a blameless child. After long and difficult reflection, I came to the realization that the child should be my paramount concern."

The Governor pauses here, his bearing becoming more of a teacher than the effective lecturer of a moment before. "There is a simple rule that stands as the basis of our Constitution. That rule states, 'Better a hundred guilty men go free than one innocent man be imprisoned.'" The Governor looks into the camera and gives a reluctant smile. "We have here a little of both." His face converts back to grave seriousness. "I know my decision is right and just: I will not let one innocent person be punished for the guilt of the hundred. Or in this case, the one. That is why, effective tomorrow, I am officially pardoning Cheryl Preninger."

There's a gasp from the camera crew.

"Know that in some ways I do this with a heavy heart. Nevertheless, I stand by my decision and ask for you, my fellow Virginians, to pray to Almighty God that the second chance I'm giving Ms. Preninger, the first chance I'm giving her innocent child, will be used to magnify God's goodness here on Earth. Thank you."

The green light flicks off and Evans is smiling. The Governor will be seen as a man standing for principles, a man blocked by unscrupulous lawyers, tainted by state attorneys, and stymied by liberal bureaucrats. A Trifecta, a hat trick of everybody the Right likes to hate. He'll be seen as a champion for all, particularly for the rights of the unborn. Evans is so happy he talks to himself. "And the cherry, the fucking cherry on the sundae is that in spite of these left-wing hindrances, the Governor's—'the People's Governor's' final act was one of compassion."

Evans readies these thoughts, and more like them, as he hustles to meet the press and leak to them the painful agonizing their Governor had to go through in order to come to this decision.

There's a lesson here, which he won't discuss. And that is, when life hands you a giant piece of coal, just make like Superman and squeeze the fucker into a diamond.

# THIRTY-ONE

The sun is falling and Daniel has been helping Sarah again at the church. They had been pulling weeds and re-fertilizing the flowerbeds for an hour when a group of congregants comes out of the church. Daniel sees them coming his way, and for some reason, perhaps the way they walk, mincing little steps, not really looking forward, he knows they're bringing bad news.

Only the man in the lead has purpose to his stride.

Daniel tries to get Sarah's attention, but she's involved in digging and clearing the soil. More than involved, consumed, like she is losing herself in some kind of void.

The group's almost upon them and Sarah finally looks up.

"Hi, I'm Phil," says the guy with the too small slacks, offering his hand uncomfortably to Daniel who's sitting in the dirt.

"Nice to meet you. I'm Daniel."

This brief hello gives Daniel and Sarah time to rise, time for Daniel to dust the dirt from his shirt and pants. Sarah stands but pays no heed to the dirt that covers her jeans and cotton blouse.

Phil is talking. "Sarah, there's no easy way to say this. With all that's happened with Joe being involved in this case, and umm, his marital infidelities, we—the Board and myself—are here to inform you that you and

342

Joe are no longer welcomed as members of the Church of the Benevolent Savior."

Sarah seems not to have heard Phil's excommunication. Daniel keeps looking back and forth, between her and this balding tub of a man.

Daniel finally says, "Excuse me, but Joe's made it clear that those charges are false and that the D.A. is trying to discredit him. They've already moved to have him disbarred, for God sakes!"

Phil adjusts his poly-blend tie. "Exactly, and it's things like this disbarment that stain the church. On top of that, you have reporters calling our members trying to find out anything they can. It's just too much, and we've decided that they should leave."

Daniel's not giving up. "But where are they supposed to go? Isn't the church supposed to be a haven from this kind of persecution? The same kind of persecution Jesus knew so well." Now, he's done it, Daniel realizes. Never mention Jesus to a holier-than-thou type.

Phil starts to fume. "Satan will cite the Word to suit his purposes."

"So, let me hear some," Daniel adds snidely.

The intercession of Reverend Tolliver stops the situation from getting worse. "This has nothing to do with Sarah, but the decision of the Council is final. We are simply asking you to leave."

Daniel can't believe that Sarah hasn't said anything. Instead, she's nodding, as if it all makes sense, and then she's back on her knees collecting the gardening tools. Daniel glances her way, seemingly flabbergasted and put out by her simple abdication of the fight.

"The DNA shows no one else could be the father," Phil announces.

"Oh, give me a break," Daniel says, his voice dripping with scorn. "You don't even believe in evolution, and you're going to start citing science?"

Sarah starts to walk away and Daniel follows, his brow creased with confusion. They reach the car and Daniel offers to drive. Sarah acquiesces.

"Aren't you upset at all this?" he demands. "I mean, you've done more work in that church's name than all the rest of them put together."

Sarah pats his hand. "It's really all right, Daniel. God will provide, and what He's taking away from me is a tiny sliver compared to the bounty I'm about to receive."

Daniel appears mystified, perhaps a little frightened. Sarah had seemed withdrawn lately, showing almost no emotion, and her speech had taken on almost canned church-like quality.

"I can see you don't believe, Daniel. I haven't shown anyone yet, so I guess this is as good a time as any. Take me home, and I'll show you."

Daniel drives to the neighborhood and follows Sarah's instructions to go around the block, avoiding the media camped on the lawn.

Daniel parks the car and Sarah's quickly out, showing the first verve he's seen in a while. "The Murray's are nice enough to let me go through their backyard," she says, pushing open the gate, and then she's over to the short back fence, headed to the house. Daniel is transfixed, his mounting unease made even worse by the simple robot-like way she just jumped a fence.

They're up the steps and Sarah's opening the back door. Sarah giggles and says, "Why lock your house, when you've got four cameras tuned to your front door twenty-four hours a day?"

Inside, the drawn shades and growing twilight make it difficult to see. Garbage stands in small piles on the coffee and kitchen tables, in the sink and on the sofa. Daniel loiters around the mess, only entering the hall in answer to Sarah's call.

The passageway is further cluttered with paint, two-by-fours, rags and easels, the latter covered with rough drafts of cartoon characters.

"I'm kind of nervous to show this to anybody, but you're so good at decorating I figure you'd be my best choice," Sarah says, beckoning him inside the room.

Daniel is rounding the corner and the room opens up before him. The colors, the figures, the imagination, they almost take his breath away. Sarah is speaking, leading Daniel over to a small black and white photo at the heart of the far wall. The picture stands in contrast to the vivid Crayola look of the rest of the room.

Sarah's still talking, and what she says and what he sees, scares the hell out of him.

I'm sitting with Millie watching in disbelief as Sumner lays it all out. I realize my client's gone from death to life in prison to freedom all in the space of twenty-four hours. Of course, Sumner called me immoral and unscrupulous, and I know the Governor's about as compassionate as mailmen are for dogs, but Cheryl's going free! The thought's too big and it keeps bouncing around my head. *Free.*

I must be walking around the room because I nearly trip over Frank's chair, then the phone's ringing and Millie's over to get it.

It's for me. "It's Daniel," Millie says.

Probably calling to congratulate me, I think.

I'm so full of oblivious good cheer that it takes a few moments to catch the dry despair in his voice and the fact that he's telling me to come home right away.

I'm driving through my neighborhood, careful to avoid being seen by the omnipresent media. I'm around the corner at the Murray's house, sliding by their back gate and jumping the small fence that separates our two backyards (one of which, I note, is in desperate need of a mowing).

I'm in my back door and Daniel's at the kitchen table. "She's in the guest room." The way he says this makes me think he just said she's in the grave.

I'm confused. In our brief discussion, I got from Daniel that Sarah hasn't been hurt, but that I needed to get home immediately. I'm home now, and I'm hoping for a little more explanation.

Daniel must sense this, or he's got the brains to figure out the questions behind my puzzled expressions. Nevertheless, he seems unable to articulate anything.

"The guest room. Just go and see, Joe."

I leave him and walk down the hall. I can hear Sarah humming. I'm wondering why there's so much garbage and paint stuff all around. When I walk into the room, Barney, the big purple dinosaur, is playing on an old tape cassette, "I love you. You love me. We're a happy family." It's on some kind of loop that goes on and on throughout the next few minutes.

This was the room that contained a broken desk from my office, dusty files kept because there was probably a thin sheaf of papers buried there that was actually important and that I had been too lazy to go through. I also had a weight set in a corner that I hadn't used since I was in my twenties.

Now, the room is transformed. Maybe transmogrified is more apt because it was now the ultimate children's bedroom, or on its way to becoming that. The walls, the ceilings, the floors, even the back of the door have all been painted with spaceships, dolphins, and a long rainbow that swirls and dives through all six sides of the room. Riding this rainbow and floating everywhere are literally hundreds of familiar cartoon characters: Bugs Bunny, Marvin the Martian, Daffy Duck, Donald Duck, Mickey Mouse, the Road Runner and the Coyote, Pooh Bear and Piglet, Barney, the Cowardly Lion, Tin Man, and Scarecrow. Also, things I vaguely recognize as the Pokémon creatures, and then there's Sylvester and Tweety, Big Bird, Oscar, Bert and Ernie, Kermit. They're all in action, a huge tableau of what Ren and Stimpy, who I see on the floor next to my left foot, would call, "Happy, happy. Joy, joy."

I've been standing, unnoticed, staring at all of this, while Sarah's back's been to me. She turns now and her face is cutely marked with white paint, but it's her eyes that grab my attention. Even with the vivid scene painted all around, her eyes seem eerie and glassy. I can't think of what to say, or know what the hell this all means, so I state the obvious. "You paint?"

"Oh, Joe, it's not done yet. Daniel must have told you—that Poop. Well, surprise! What do you think?"

What do I think? I think my wife is the Michelangelo of kiddy rooms. Jesus, I think, the ceiling's alive with characters running and jumping. There's the Flintstones, and Scooby Doo, and Yogi Bear and Boo-boo (he was always my favorite).

I also think I'm scared. Sarah's expression is fixed, like any one of the hundreds of cartoon characters she's painted. Unblinking, she's stares at me, waiting for a response.

"It's wonderful, Hon," and then I fall back on "I didn't know you could paint."

She makes a dismissive motion with her hand, like don't be silly. "This really isn't painting, but come here, I want to show you some real artistry."

She goes to grab my hand and suddenly I have to fight the urge to pull away. It's the same feeling I had when I was five and that old lady was wandering the halls of the convalescent home trying to kiss me. But I'm not five and this is my wife, not some ancient, wrinkled kook, so I let Sarah take me by the hand and lead me to the far wall.

It takes only a few moments, but it seems much longer as I stare at all the various scenes, almost like I'm walking through the dense and fantastic forest of my childhood all over again. That's when I see the one non-regular of the Cartoon Network, Jesus. He's coming out of a spaceship, throwing what looks to be candy to some of the animated animal characters surrounding him.

Sarah's still pulling on my arm, gesturing to the out-of-place little black and white photo tacked onto the wall with a happy-face pin, right below Jesus and His spaceship. Sarah's pointing to the photo and I'm just noticing the characters all across the room seem to be faced, or moving toward, this spot on the wall. And then I recognize the photo, or ones like it. It's someone's uterus, rendered on slick photo paper in grays, whites, and blacks. I'm no doctor, but I can see there's nothing in the photo but a lot of meaningless gray slashes of shadow. As I'm just figuring this out, Sarah tells me we're going to have a baby, and that Cheryl is going to give us her child. My first thought is, why would Cheryl do that? My second is, when did Sarah talk to Cheryl?

Sarah's still talking, but I'm having trouble understanding anything she's saying. It's all mixed up with the Bible. I listen to her incoherent ramblings, and I begin to be very afraid.

I'm running to my little home office nook, off the kitchen where I keep my computer and the printer. I'm on the phone calling information. All those visits and I don't know the number to Sussex prison. I get connected and I'm asking to speak with an Officer White. I'm transferred and spend an interminable three minutes listening to some soft rock crap, while my brain tries to deny what my wife has just told me. I realize that even if I'm right, Sarah's in need of some serious counseling.

White's on the phone.

"Officer White, I need you to do me a favor."

There's a pause of about five seconds and then an "Uh huh" from the other end of the phone line. "I need you to e-mail me the visitor register for Cheryl Preninger, from October to March, those six months before I became her attorney."

"You need a court subpoena for those records, Counselor."

"Dammit, I don't have time! Besides, you heard the Governor—it's over. She gets out tomorrow."

"Regardless, these are Correctional Facility records. You cannot be privy to them without a court order."

I take a deep breath so I don't scream. "Officer White, you know me...somewhat. I give you my word this does not have to do with the case. But it is very important to my family," I finish, stressing that last word.

This time, the pause lasts ten seconds. "Well, Joe, factually, this is a question for our legal eagles. You know eagles see and hear everything that comes in and out: phone records, e-mails." I'm desperate to see the records, and then I notice a dust-covered device shoved in the corner on the floor.

"Officer White, do you still happen to have an old fax machine laying around? A device that's gone off the tech grid so to speak?"

A pause, and then he says, "Do you have a number that someone from Correction could reach you at, Counselor?"

"Yeah, and I'd appreciate anything you could do, Officer." I dust off the fax, give him the number and start connecting the machine, hoping I've just read his message correctly.

Fifteen minutes later, just when I'm thinking I didn't read him right, the fax light goes green. I'm checking the sending number and it's got Sussex's area code. The pages start coming through, but White has sent me dates in reverse order, starting with this month and working back. I hope. September and August, and there I am, and a Sister Genevieve, and Board members Thompson and Dutton. The machine halts at March and I get this mental picture of White being called away to stop a fight and forgetting. Worse yet, I'm thinking he misunderstood and sent the visitor's log, not up 'til I took the case, but after.

The green light starts flashing and the fax kicks back to life, and I make damn sure the machine's got enough paper.

Here comes February, and there's no one I don't know. January's the same, then December rolls through, and I'm just starting to be relieved that my wife is merely a little crazy, and not devious. And then my heart misses a beat and my stomach goes south: Sarah appears on the sign-in sheet. My apprehension turns to relief and back to apprehension, all in the span of an instant, because it's not Sarah Heyerdahl I see, but Sarah McClure. Of course, that Sarah's maiden name, a name she would've had to sign in with because that's what her driver's license still says. The same driver's license she says she was unable to replace because of a DMV screw-up. Conveniently then, when Joe Heyerdahl shows up a few months later, no one knows to mention that there was a Sarah Heyerdahl that used to visit Cheryl. I now remember Sarah mentioning something about Jesus in the prisons. It seems Jesus wasn't the only one visiting Cheryl.

Still not completely convinced, I run into the kitchen and find the drawer where Sarah keeps the canceled checks. I compare the first name on the checks with the signature on the faxed visitor logs. The upper loop crossing over itself and the end of the H shooting up and then curling back.

Even if they weren't, that would just mean Sarah was thinking ahead and altered her John Hancock when visiting Cheryl at the prison.

Daniel's been poking around the back yard, probably figuring how he would garden the place if he had the chance. I explain to him where I need to go, and now he's the one giving me a 'what the hell is going on' look as I leave him to watch over Sarah.

# THIRTY-TWO

I drive like a demon, breaking speed limits left and right.

I'm at the prison and Officer White's walking me through. He keeps glancing my way, either because I'm glaring at the air in front of me, or because even the reserved Officer White can sense something, and he's curious to know what it's all about.

I owe him big-time for helping with the logs, and I tell him so. Frankly, I wouldn't know what to say or where to start with anything else.

We're onto Cellblock A and I'm not paying attention, and suddenly Officer White's saying, "Well, that's a first."

The prisoners have started applauding, and I realize after a moment they're applauding for me. I'm so completely lost in a fog that it takes me several moments to figure out why: I got one of their own pardoned and she'll be free tomorrow. I start nodding and raise my hand in acknowledgment of their applause, but my victory, if you want to call it that, is not looking quite as clear as I once thought it was.

Preninger's seated, chained, as always, smiling as I enter. I'm staring at that smile and I know it must be what I know now, but there seems something hollow and deceitful in that grin. Something I had previously taken as the natural effect of religious fervor combined with a fear of death.

Cheryl's jubilant. "Joe, isn't this the most amazing news!"

"What did you tell my wife?"

Her brow furrows and she doesn't bother to waste my time by lying. "What'd she tell you I said?"

"She said that you said that you'd give us your child. She said you had a vision of Jesus and He told you Sarah was infertile." I started out angry, but by the time I end the sentence I'm just more confused. "What did you do, Cheryl?"

Cheryl leans back in her chair like she's a CEO. "A lot more than I set out to do, Joe. Just imagine sitting on death row with nothing more to do than think about when you're going to die. Well, I get to do a lot of that thinking, and I research, and I find out about this hanging loophole, and I get to thinking on how can I use this."

Cheryl's lost her gee-whiz attitude and now talks smarter, more matter-of-fact. "Well, I know my case is going to be watched because I'm a woman, so I figure I'll play the redeemed Christian girl, decide to get hanged, and the case'll be such a cause celebre that the Governor'll have to commute me to life."

I nod. "And Huntner's coming forward, was he part of it?"

"No, no, he likes things so straight I'm surprised he ties his shoes. Huntner was just doing his duty."

"Like you knew he would."

Cheryl shrugs like 'I had a hunch.' "I did have a meeting with Shriner, but it was about removing Frank as my attorney. Shriner goes hustling out, leading with that bald head of his, and when Huntner comes to get me, I put on my act about what they're trying to do to me.

"So you just thought the hanging, the guard coming forward to say you were coerced, these would create such a political stink that the Governor would be pressured and have to commute."

"Precisely. I didn't know jack about politics, or what a right-wing asshole Sumner would be. But you, you wonderful man! I mean, who knew you'd turn out to be such a great lawyer."

I hate to admit it, but I'm actually pleased by that comment.

"Finding out about that juror, getting the stay removed with that legal sleight of hand, and giving the Governor's aide the idea for the Clemency Board."

As Cheryl continues to talk, it's like she's de-thawing an older persona, a persona she's kept under wraps which is finally breaking free.

"However, at the time, all of your antagonizing was making it much harder for the Governor to commute. But like they say, luck happens to those who prepare for it. I knew I had the commutation all locked up when the Governor sent it to the Clemency Board, but then I figured, hey, why not roll the dice? If the Clemency Board doesn't commute, no way they're going to kill me now, and what if now the Governor can't commute? Might he be forced to pardon me? Dutton's a total activist liberal, so I give him the chance to tweak the Governor by cutting off his easy political out. I mean, how often does a nobody wannabe like Dutton get to do that? And after all the shit he's taken from Governor Sumner. All Dutton had to do was go along with Fitzimmons. If the Governor hadn't folded, Dutton would've done a quick reverse and recanted his vote, citing some emerging mental health problem which, believe me, he's got lots of."

I nod my head, and if I had a hat I'd likely tip it. "You're very smart, Cheryl. So what're you going to do when you get out?"

"Joe," gesturing to the Bible, "this wasn't all a pose. I really do believe in being a good Christian."

"But your lies, your manipulations?"

"Joe, I was a strung-out, piece of white trash junkie. You think those three terms are redundant? Anyway, I did something terrible that night; something I know I'll never get over, nor should I, and something I'm sure I'll pay for in the next life. But in this life, maybe I should've been executed. But you know, if I had money, I would've gotten a good attorney. Maybe you, Joe, who would probably have gotten the charges knocked down to voluntary manslaughter because of my state of mind."

"Cheryl, there was a time a while ago when I thought you might not have done it, that you were covering for someone else."

That gets a laugh. "Who, Joe, the boyfriend I didn't have? Oh wait, how 'bout my missing father come back for some nights of heavy partying with his grown daughter?" She starts laughing again, and even though she's not really the person I thought she was, I can't deny that her laugh's not a pretty thing, the way it bubbles out of her like trapped water held in by the seismic pressures and tectonic plates of a looming death sentence.

"Joe, I'm not denying that the State has a right, maybe even a duty, to execute me, but where is it written that I have to help them do it?"

All of this has been a revelation, but I'm still not understanding a few things. "The fortune telling, how'd you know Sarah was infertile?"

"I didn't, but ask yourself, what did I have to lose? She meets with me as one of those Christian missions to spread the Word of Christ to inmates, and we get to talking, and she starts telling me about herself and you, and how much she wants kids, and I can just tell she thinks something's wrong with her, so what do I have to lose if I'm wrong telling her she can't conceive? If she can, she doesn't need me anyway. But if I'm right, well, with Sarah's ironclad belief in Jesus Christ, I just got myself some powerful leverage. And you know what Archimedes said: "Give me a big enough lever and I'll move the world." Well, all I had to do was move one scared young woman who seemed to be holding onto a lot of guilt."

Still, I think, things aren't quite making sense. "I see how the whole subterfuge over who the phony father was probably wouldn't have worked with a dying Frank as the father. But I'm still not getting one thing: Why do you need me? You could've just requested a healthy young public defender to represent you."

Cheryl's eyes alight on mine, and for a moment she reminds me of Shriner, the time he watched Sarah pick me up from jail, relishing my embarrassment with an almost malicious glee. With Cheryl, it's not malicious, but it's not real nice, either.

"But, Joe, it's not phony. You are the father."

She says this with an unbreachable certainty and I want to think she's crazy, and I say, "You're crazy," but her eyes are clear, almost merry. I think, what do you do when impossibility meets absolute certainty?

"Joe, I'm not the prettiest gal on the Block. At least when I was on drugs I was a skinny thing." Cheryl chuckles at this. "And these guards are pretty professional. I wasn't going to get one of them for a roll in the hay, and do you think they'd have done it without a condom?"

The reality of the whole situation moves up a notch when the supposedly reformed Christian girl talks about condoms.

"Every time a woman ovulates she's got a forty percent chance to conceive—if she's got a willing partner."

"You need a test to know when you're ovulating." That's at least something I know, I think.

"Some women can feel it. I can, and anyway, it doesn't take a rocket scientist to know it's going to happen about fourteen days after your period."

"But how..." I can't even frame the question. I feel like I'm Alice in Wonderland—I am the Egg Man, I am the Walrus, I am the Father, Koo-koo-kachoo. These thoughts might have spun me dangerously out of control, but Cheryl brings me back.

"You're pen, Joe. Can I see it?"

I take out my titanium secret agent pen from my jacket pocket and hand it over. The guard's definitely new because he doesn't even bat an eye. I watch as Cheryl hits the black button and the clip and the end opens, delivering whatever was there secretly into the palm of her hand.

"I told Sarah after she found out she was infertile that she should buy a diaphragm, and after you were intimate to pour the contents in a capsule. You know, like pharmacies have." She raises one eyebrow like Mr. Spock, something else I didn't know she could do, like implying there's some kind of irony in her statement. "Of course, to Sarah, I cloaked all this in the heavenly visions I had received from Christ himself. And remember, I had been the one who foresaw her barrenness."

She pauses now like a General thinking back over some great victory. "Remember, Joe, when I'd borrow your pen to scribble furiously in the Good Book. All I'd do is simply palm the pen and out would come the capsule. My days as a pickpocket came in quite handy."

She shows me.

I'm staring at her hands, and it's still impossible to see she's done anything.

"I tore out a little seam in the crotch of one of my horrid orange jumpsuits—gawd, I can't wait to own a pair of jeans again—and I'd insert the capsules. They rarely do body cavity searches, and the pills dissolve almost immediately."

I think I'm okay, that this isn't fucking with my head, but then I hear my voice emerge all shaky and high. I clear my throat and make an effort to give it some steady bass, and ask, "And this worked?"

"Give a girl some sperm, baking powder and distilled water for a non-acidic culture, mix, and keep near freezing and the sperm'll be viable for hours. And we didn't need nearly that long. But still, it didn't work in the first month. Remember that call you got after we had just met? I could tell you were put out to come all the way back here the next day, and on top of that I sat here and spouted the Word the whole time. Well, that was our second try that second month, so I guess what they say is true, the third time's the charm. Forty percent, three shots—you do the math."

I'm stunned to say the least. "You're having my child," I giggle and then start to laugh.

After a moment, Cheryl joins in. "Remember what I said, Joe. God writes straight with crooked sticks."

"And you, Cheryl, are as crooked as they come."

"Is that a way to talk to the mother of your child, Joe?"

"So when you said you had a childless Christian couple who you'd been in contact with...

Cheryl through smiling white teeth, "It was you, Joe. Devious, isn't it?"

I'm afraid my laughter might turn a bit hysterical, so like a shark I keep moving forward. "So, what're your plans?"

"Retire, take long walks. I think I'll get a dog."

"Uhh, Cheryl, unless you robbed banks along with pharmacies and stashed the loot somewhere, you're going to need to get a job."

"No, Joe, my working days are done. I'm planning on a quiet life."

"Then how?"

"My story. Think a publisher will shell out some big bucks for it?"

Now, it's my turn to be one step ahead. "No way, Cheryl, the Son of Sam law. You can't in any way profit from your crime." Okay, I thought I was one step ahead.

"That dear Joseph, is why you are going to write it."

"I can't. You have attorney-client privilege. Even if you waived it, in this case it'd be a transparent attempt to dodge the law. It wouldn't fly."

"But I won't have to worry about waiving immunity because you're going to be disbarred, Joe. You had immoral congress with an inmate and a client. Even if this wasn't a huge case, there's no way the Bar Review lets you walk, especially with so much public scrutiny."

I'm about to argue, but she's right of course, though she forgot to mention that we didn't have immoral congress. When I finally do get one step ahead, or really just catch up to her. "But I can't tell anybody that because, if I do, you won't give us the baby."

"Yep, and what's more, adoptions take a year. That way I guarantee you hand over the profits from the book and movie deals you're going to make."

"And you retire."

"I retire."

"And I'm out of a job."

"And you're out of a job. But don't worry, I'll give you some startup cash to tide you over. Maybe get you going on your next venture."

"What if I just say screw it, Cheryl?" But I know I can't, even as I say it. My wife's sanity is a fragile thing that's going to take a lot of love, care, and therapy, and taking care of a child that's mine can only help. While denying her that child—God, I just think of the hours she spent painting that room, and I think of what the press would do to her over her role in all this, and I know I can't even bluff.

Of course, Cheryl knows this too. It's just taking me a while to figure it all out. Cheryl's reading me even now.

"I'm not some evil genius, Joe. Hell, I wasn't even the smartest girl in junior high. I was just motivated, very motivated. A woman who had enough time, and enough smarts to play the angles and get the dice to roll her way. Cheer up, you lose a career, you gain a little girl."

Cheryl's like the fucking mechanical jackrabbit that the greyhounds chase at the dog races. She's always ahead of me...the DNA test.

"You and Sarah are going to have a little girl, Joe."

# EPILOGUE

It all ended that way. Cheryl was released the next day, and two months later gave birth to a healthy baby girl, who Sarah and I named Ruth, after Sarah's little sister. Cheryl did exactly what she said she would. She bought a little house in semi-rural Connecticut, but she did deviate from her plan a bit: she got two dogs. I asked her why no cats, and she said she wasn't a cat person. I told her she was the most cat person I'd ever met. After a moment, she seemed pleased with my analysis.

Warren Metcalfe lost his bid for a second term as D.A. and retreated nicely to the offices of a highly prestigious Virginia corporate law firm. A. Malcolm Shriner did not follow his boss to such a tony address. After much of the malfeasance fell on his shoulders, he started his own practice, where he's now building an enviable reputation as a master slash-and-burn defense attorney. Oh, how the worm has turned.

Governor Sumner has decided to run for the U.S. Senate, with Mr. Evans still standing by his side. After his compassionate Gordian Knot-like cutting of the Preninger debacle, the Governor was seen by the right as its champion against the forces of legal liberalism and government bureaucracy, and by some on the left as a principled soul who showed heart at the most crucial of times (yeah, right). Political pundits are already talking about a try for the White House.

And me? I did get disbarred. Considering the circumstances, I didn't even fight it. Sarah had a couple of hard months, but she was on her feet mentally by the time Cheryl had the baby, and she's been going to therapy and doing better, little by little. And the small, dimpled, brown-eyed girl she takes care of probably helps a lot.

Oh, and I wrote this, (with the help of certain highly placed secretaries) and again, Cheryl was right. I got, and promptly handed over to her, a check from a publisher for $1.7 million with an additional $1.1 million for the movie rights (ouch and double ouch!). However, Cheryl was a woman of her word. She let me keep two-hundred grand, so in her words, "My daughter won't grow up like I did," and I coaxed her into a six-figure donation to a victims' rights organization. Oh, and there was that $100,000 she had to give to Dutton. It seemed political activism and the chance to give the Governor the bird wasn't quite enough motivation for a certain State bureaucrat after all.

After wondering what to do, and spending a lot of time hanging around the house staring at my daughter, I visited Daniel. Okay, I went to smoke pot. What can I say? I can only handle quitting one vice at a time. Anyway, I got an idea, or remembered an old one I had right before I met him. I told him about it, and he agreed to go in with me with just a few minor changes here and there.

Daniel and I are now partners in a Krispy Kreme Donut franchise-slash-coffeebar-slash-artsy-nightly-poetry-folk-music-show-tune/performance house. We're doing quite well, thank you. I think where the store is located might have something to do with it—right next to the Cannabis Distribution Center. Like they say in real estate, it's all about location, location, location. It must be true because Achmed and Jimmy are planning to open their second pizzeria across the street.

It's a few months later and I'm busy helping Daniel run the shop and trying to write this book. I want to get it all down. That way, maybe I'll understand it better. When it's done, I'll go back and whitewash Sarah's part of it. I got a funny phone call from Cheryl the other day, wanting me to paint our 'prison love child' as momentary passion on our parts and not the devious legal strategy I planned to say it was. I told Cheryl she'd gotten over two million dollars, but asking me to write that it was an act of passion was just too much.

We both had a good laugh.

I would've talked longer, but I told her that Sarah and the baby had been sick, and while the baby was feeling a lot better, Sarah was not, losing weight, feeling awful, and we were scheduled to see her Doc, so I had to go. Cheryl wished Sarah the best and we said good-bye.

We're at the Doc's office and I'm there because Sarah's still shaky around doctors. The woman's examining her, asking questions, and the next thing I know she's up in the stirrups, jelly on the belly, and I'm looking into the dragon's cave again, just barely registering what's going on. Suddenly, I'm terribly fearful we're going to see another thin, web-encrusted, spider-like, a chrysalis without a pulse. The monitor goes black and white, expanding and contracting like those sixties film projectors that kaleidoscoped while people did LSD, and there it is, a butterfly encased in gossamer. But this time there's a beeping, and a pixel on the screen pulses like the You Are Here sign at the mall.

Sarah's grabbing my hand and crying. The doctor, not to be overcome by emotion, is prattling on about changes in Sarah's PH because of her altered mental status, but she'll have to review the literature, and the word doctors dream about, *publish*, enters the conversation.

The doctor puts her dreams of the *New England Journal of Medicine* aside for a moment and gets down to business. She measures the little person, pointing out the healthy placenta, sac, and mesentery.

It's when she's detailing the placenta, which looks like a white snaky coil (the dragon's tail perhaps), that she finds it. Off to the side, slipped in behind a bend in the uterine wall, some motion. She performs something akin to an ice skater doing a double salchow with the sonogram device, and now we can see two little bundles of gold in the dragon's cave. Heartbeats, running in near perfect rhythm, like two metronomes keeping the beat to a song only they know.

Seven months later, Sarah gives birth to two healthy fraternal twin boys. Achmed and Jimmy demand credit for what they say was the secret Persian fertility herbs they sprinkled on my pizza. I'm not buying it and I name the boys Frank and Daniel. Daniel's actually a little put off about being paired with a dead man. Even though he continues to do well, he can be a little superstitious about that stuff. I have to add he's put off only until I explain that our real reason for the name is to ensure we have a baby sitter well into the 21st century. Daniel was pleased, to say the least.

It's now Tuesday night at the shop and I've just called Sarah to check on the kids. I'm standing at the edge of about a dozen people who sit on couches and comfortable chairs, some eating donuts, some drinking coffee, while smoke of various kinds wafts through the room. Millie's on the small stage in front, and she's just launched into a smooth, sad number, probably something from Judy's triumphant Carnegie Hall comeback (see, I'm learning things here), and she's good and getting better, her voice clear and deep. The depth you only get from living life, and I guess for a minute I feel like Bogie in Casablanca, with a cloudy haze of smoke catching the last few bars of soft outside light, while an old broad croons a song of melancholy, and I wonder at it all. Was that my life? Is this my life? And of its strangeness, and of its familiarity, and I think: crooked sticks indeed.

Made in the USA
Columbia, SC
29 March 2019